The Fall of a Sparrow

A Novel

Robert Hellenga

VIKING

VIKING

Published by the Penguin Group
Penguin Books Ltd, 27 Wrights Lane, London w8 5TZ, England
Penguin Putnam Inc., 375 Hudson Street, New York, New York 10014, USA
Penguin Books Australia Ltd, Ringwood, Victoria, Australia
Penguin Books Canada Ltd, 10 Alcorn Avenue, Toronto, Ontario, Canada M4V 3B2
Penguin Books (NZ) Ltd, Private Bag 102902, NSMC, Auckland, New Zealand

Penguin Books Ltd, Registered Offices: Harmondsworth, Middlesex, England

First published in the United States of America by Scribner 1998
First published in Great Britain by Viking 1999
1 3 5 7 9 10 8 6 4 2

Copyright © Robert Hellenga, 1998
The moral right of the author has been asserted

The acknowledgments on page 463 constitute an extension of this copyright page

Printed in Great Britain by Clays Ltd, St Ives plc

A CIP catalogue record for this book is available from the British Library

ISBN 0-670-88189-9

To my wife, Virginia, and our three daughters—
Rachel, Heather, Caitrine

Acknowledgments

I would like to acknowledge my indebtedness to the following people: to my first two readers—my agent, Henry Dunow, and my editor, Maria Guarnaschelli—for their enthusiasm and for their practical suggestions; to Katya Rice, my copy editor; to Janet Smith and Paola Polselli for help with Italian and for answering dozens of questions about Italy; to Sandra Batmangelich and to the entire Soomekh family (David, G. Ahou, Jamshid, and Jacqueline) for help with Persian words; to Jon Wellerdieck for help with Dutch; to Jeff Clark for help with farm language; to Steve Fineberg for his translation of Hesiod's *Theogony* 176–82; to my wife for her unstinting moral support and for her translation of Ovid's *Amores* II.4; to Alireza Djalali for information about the life of an Iranian rug merchant in Italy; to our neighbor in Florence, Sig. Giovanni Lodovici, for help with *Errori della Tavola*; to Bernard Gitton and Mike Kantor for help with the chaos waterwheel; to Emily Lynch for answering questions about Harvard; to my Greek teacher, W. Robert Connor, for his classical wisdom; to Peter Burian for reading the bound galleys at the last minute and keeping me from making *brutta figura*; to Roberto and Irma Bottazzi, Angela del Monte, Umberto and Pia Broccoli, and Stefano and Giulia Liporesi, for their hospitality in Bologna; to Franco and Vincensina Cipriani for their continued hospitality in Florence and for letting me plunder the stories of their lives; and above all to the Association of the Families of the Victims of the Strage of 2 August 1980: Torquato Secci (now deceased) gave me one of the three remaining copies of the book he'd written about his son's death and about the activities of the Association; Paolo Bolognese, Sig. Secci's successor as president of the Association, took me to the morgue and to the Ospedale Maggiore, introduced me to the public prosecutor, and invited me to march with the families of the victims in the demonstration on

2 August 1996; Paola Sola, the secretary of the Association, and her assistants, Chiara and Andrea, provided me with information about the *strage* and about the trial.

I would also like to acknowledge my debts to the following organizations: to Knox College and to the Illinois Arts Council for their continued support of my writing career over the years; to the National Endowment for the Arts; to the National Council on US-Arab Relations for making it possible for me to visit the Middle East when I first began writing *The Fall of a Sparrow*; and to the John and Elaine Fellowes Fund of Knox College for making it possible for me to spend three months in Bologna in the winter of 1995 and to return to Bologna in the summer of 1996.

And finally, the "life notice" on page 340 was originally addressed to the father of my friend Umberto Broccoli; and the epitaph on Cookie's tombstone, page 458, was taken from the death notice of Alexander Lenard, the man who translated *Winnie the Pooh* into Latin.

Author's Note

The events that shape *The Fall of a Sparrow* were inspired by the bombing of the train station in Bologna, Italy, on 2 August 1980. I have drawn upon published accounts of the bombing and of the trial of the suspected terrorists, but the characters in the novel are the work of my imagination and are not intended to represent real people.

Contents

Part One

The Mountain of Lights	17
In Memoriam	28
Halloween	60
Sunday Morning	90
Christmas 1986	114
Power Suit	138
The Ring of Gyges	167
Commencement	201
House for Sale	247

Part Two

Christmas 1987	263
Testimony	296
Mr. Jelly Roll Baker	312
La Vita Nuova	335
Children of the Sun	357
Ergastolo	376
A Dark Cimmerian Land	388
My Love Is Carpet	420
In Another Country	441

Are not two sparrows sold for a farthing? And yet one of them
shall not fall to the ground without your Father knowing.

—MATTHEW 10:29

"Such," he said, "O King, seems to me the present life of men
on earth, in comparison with that time which to us is uncertain,
as if when on a winter's night you sit feasting with your ealdor-
men and thegns, a single sparrow should fly swiftly into the
hall, and coming in at one door, instantly fly out through
another. In that time in which it is indoors it is indeed not
touched by the fury of the winter, but yet, this smallest space of
calmness being passed almost in a flash, from winter going into
winter again, it is lost to your eyes. Somewhat like this appears
the life of man; but of what follows or what went before, we are
utterly ignorant."

—BEDE, *Ecclesiastical History*,
BK. II, CH. 13

There's a special providence in the fall of a sparrow.

—*Hamlet* V.II

Part One

The Mountain of Lights

On Friday, August 15, 1980—Assumption Day, the middle of the August holidays—a bomb exploded in the train station in Bologna, Italy, killing eighty-six people, including my sister Cookie, who was sitting in the second-class waiting room, about two meters from where the bomb went off, waiting for a train back to Rome.

The station has been repaired, of course, but part of it—part of the waiting room—was left the way it had been after the bombing. You can see the bomb crater, which is about the size of a bowling ball. I didn't see it myself till years later, but I often imagined it. Daddy had a picture, a poster, rolled up in a cardboard mailing tube at the back of his closet. On the wall above the crater a marble stone, a *lapide*, lists the names and ages of all the people who were killed. Cookie was twenty-two. She was on her way to study international law at the University of Bologna. We thought she was in Rome, staying with friends, but she'd gone up to Bologna for a couple of days to look for a place to live.

I was sixteen years old at the time, and Ludi was twelve.

The bomb went off at 10:25 in the morning. That's 4:25 in the morning in Illinois. We were all asleep.

Before breakfast that morning Ludi and I took our books and walked up to the cemetery to wait for trains, not knowing that Cookie was already dead, or close to it. Pretty soon the Illinois Zephyr came by from Quincy—it ran an hour later on Saturdays—and about half an hour after that we saw four freight trains coming

17

together on the two sets of tracks that cross about halfway between our house and New Cameron. The Burlington tracks go over, of course, and the Santa Fe tracks go under, but it was exciting anyway, because for a while it looked as if all the trains were going to collide.

Our house was a quarter of a mile from the crossing, and at night, lying in bed, you could feel the house tremble when a train went by, and when the windows were open you could make out the different sounds of the different cars, boxcars and gondolas and flatbeds; and you could hear the whistles blowing as far away as Cass City, on the Spoon River, where Daddy used to go duck hunting with Peter Abbott from the Biology Department; and you could hear the engines switching in the hump yard in St. Clair, three miles away, and the loudspeakers blurting out instructions to the engineers. Overnight guests sometimes said they couldn't sleep; but the sounds had become such a part of our lives, like the sound of Daddy playing his guitar at night, that we didn't hear them till we went away, and then *we* couldn't get to sleep.

I don't remember what book I was reading, but Ludi was reading Italo Calvino's *Italian Folktales*. She couldn't get enough of those folktales, every one of which began with a king and three daughters. The two older daughters were always mean and ugly, but guess what?—the youngest was always beautiful and smart and wonderful. We read for about an hour and saw a few more trains, and when we went back down Mama and Daddy were up and around, but we still didn't know about Cookie. After supper Daddy was reading *The Lord of the Rings* out loud to Ludi and me. He used to say that he'd read *The Lord of the Rings* aloud three times, once for each of his three daughters; but that wasn't quite true, because he didn't finish it the third time, which was for Ludi. We were getting close to the end, though. Frodo and Sam had climbed up Mount Doom, followed by Gollum, and Frodo and Gollum were teetering on the edge of the crater when the phone rang. Ludi had been upset by the death of Thorin Oakenshield in *The Hobbit* and Daddy'd promised her that no one really important dies in *The Lord of the Rings*. But things were not looking good for Frodo, and Ludi was nervous, and when the phone rang she started to cry "You promised."

It was Allison Mirsadiqi, an old friend of Daddy's, calling from Rome to tell Daddy about the *strage*, which is Italian for massacre or slaughter. She was worried because Cookie had called on Friday morning to say she'd found an apartment and would be back that afternoon. Allison had spoken to an official at the city hall in Bologna. Cookie's name hadn't been on the list of dead or injured, but a lot of bodies hadn't been identified, and over two hundred people had been injured. Everything was in chaos.

Daddy was saying uh-huh, uh-huh on the phone in the upstairs hallway and shouting for Mama to get on the phone down in the kitchen, and Ludi was still crying "You promised." I'd heard the story before, of course, and I knew that Frodo wasn't going to fall into Mount Doom, and I kept telling Ludi that everything was going to be all right.

Daddy spent the rest of the evening on the phone, and the next morning, Saturday morning, he and Mama flew to Milan and didn't come back till the beginning of September—classes had already started at St. Clair College, where my grandmother had gone to school and where Daddy taught Latin and Greek—because Mama had some kind of breakdown and had to stay in the hospital in Italy.

I couldn't remember a time when the house hadn't been full of students and faculty on Friday nights, reading naughty poems aloud in Latin, or putting on Greek plays, or just singing and making lots of noise to celebrate the end of the week; I couldn't remember a time when Daddy hadn't made pizza on Saturday nights; I couldn't remember a time when Mama and Daddy hadn't made love on Sunday mornings, staying in bed till ten or eleven o'clock; I couldn't remember a time when Daddy hadn't told us a story and played his guitar for us every night, or a time when he hadn't been working on his book on the early Greek philosophers, which he was going to call *The Cosmological Fragments*.

But when they came back from Italy Mama needed to rest a lot, so we didn't have anyone over. In the evenings she stayed in her study and read her Bible and religious books that Father Davis from Corpus Christi gave her. She tried to get us to read them too: C. S. Lewis, G. K. Chesterton, Father Ronald Knox. On Sunday mornings we started going to mass at Corpus Christi. Mama sang in the choir and went to see Father Davis two or three times a week, and helped him organize a novena, a series of prayer meetings at our house every Friday night for nine weeks in a row. Ludi and I didn't have to get down on our knees and say our prayers out loud, though Mama said it would make our grandparents happy in heaven, and Cookie too; but we had to come into the living room and let Father Davis put his hands on our heads and bless us; and then we had to pass around the plates of cookies that the women took turns bringing. And Mama ordered a tombstone for Cookie that said *La sua voluntade è nostra pace* on it—His will is our peace. Daddy went to mass for a while, and he fixed supper for Father Davis once a week and drove him home if he'd had too much to drink; and he drank coffee with the people from Corpus and St. Pat's who came to the novena. But he wouldn't go along with the inscription for the tombstone. "It's a cliché, Hannah; it's the one line from the *Paradiso* that everybody knows because it's one of Matthew Arnold's touchstones."

"When something's a cliché there's usually a good reason for it."

Ludi and I, sitting at the top of the back stairway, could hear them in the kitchen, and I can remember how sick I felt, because I'd never heard them quarreling before, not like this.

"What kind of God would will a bomb to go off in a crowded railway station?"

"That's not what it says, Woody. Read the line. Please read it aloud to me."

But Daddy wouldn't read the line aloud, and pretty soon Mama stumbled up the back stairs, walking right past Ludi and me without seeing us.

In January Mama took a job at a Catholic girls' school run by an order of Ursuline nuns, in Oak Park, just outside of Chicago. The Latin teacher had resigned. Mama found a little studio apartment in River Forest—cheaper than Oak Park—and took the Illinois Zephyr home on weekends, which worked out OK, but to get back to Chicago she had to take the 8:00 train on Sunday morning, so she had to stop singing in the choir. She made us promise to keep going to mass, but by Thanksgiving the novelty had worn off. Ludi was the first to drop out. She simply refused to go. Then Daddy stopped. He said he liked the *idea*, but that his body started twitching when he thought about going. So he drove me in to Corpus on Sunday mornings. He'd go to his office at the college to do a little work and then pick me up afterwards. Maybe I lasted a little longer than the others because I'd gone to bed with Aaron Gridley, Cookie's old boyfriend, while Mama and Daddy were in Italy, and I was afraid . . . I'm not sure what I was afraid *of*, but when I finally went to confession and told Father Davis that I'd committed the sin of unchastity, he asked me if I was truly sorry, and I said no, not really, and that was that. I don't think he heard me, or else he was thinking of something else. I didn't say my ten Hail Marys; I just walked out of the church and sat on the steps till Daddy drove up in his truck with the dogs in the back and we drove back to the farm. That's what we called home— "the farm."

It wasn't so simple, though, because I *was* sorry too. Not sorry that I'd done *it*, but sorry that I'd done *it* right after Cookie died, done *it* while Mama was in a hospital in Italy, thinking she was Mary Magdalene, sorry that Daddy and I couldn't go up to his study and have one of our grown-up talks about *it*, and about everything else too. But by the time I was ready to talk it was too late. Mama was already gone, and Daddy had already told Mr. Steckley at the Steckley Monument Company that he wouldn't pay for the stone unless they sanded off the inscription, which they did, even though the sanding cost more than the stone itself.

For years I've tried to imagine that time in my parents' lives, that month in Italy. I was hungry for facts, for details. I looked through a guidebook of Bologna that Daddy brought back and got a sense of the city—a circle, described by the old medieval wall, with spokes radiating out from the center. If I close my eyes I can see my parents in front of the bombed-out station.

Allison Mirsadiqi—Cookie had been staying with Allison—has driven up from Rome to meet them. Allison, the first grown-up who ever asked me to call her by her first name, was Daddy's girlfriend when she was in graduate school at the University of Michigan, and later on she married an Iranian businessman she met on a train from Rome to Naples. She went to St. Clair as an undergraduate, and now she's an important trustee of the college.

I located everything on the map, which was sort of a cross between an aerial photo and a perspective drawing, as if you were looking down on the red roofs of the city. I located the Ospedale Maggiore, where Cookie died, and the morgue where they took her body for an autopsy, and the Policlinico Sant'Orsola, where Mama was hospitalized. I studied the map as if it held an explanation, but I never found what I was looking for.

DADDY ALWAYS said that at the heart of everything—religions, countries, families—you'd find not doctrines or philosophical propositions but stories, that stories took you as close as you could get to the heart of things. As far as he was concerned, the greatest storyteller of all was Homer, and he was always threatening to read the *Odyssey* and the *Iliad* to us, but as far as we were concerned the greatest storyteller of all was Daddy himself, and we always wanted him to *tell* us stories, not read them out of a book. It wasn't till I was in high school and began to read grown-up books on my own that I realized what had happened. Daddy hadn't made up his stories at all; he'd stolen them. From Dickens and Jane Austen and from Homer too. And he'd changed them. In Daddy's versions my sisters and I were always in the stories. Three little girls. Sometimes one of us would be the main character, and sometimes we'd just be minor characters going along for the ride: in Polyphemus's cave with Odysseus; swimming down with Beowulf to the bottom of the mere where Grendel's mother lived; going into Humbaba's sacred forest with Gilgamesh and Enkidu; packed off to Salem House with David Copperfield in Mr. Barkis's cart; a few extra sisters in a Jane Austen family; in the belly of the whale with Jonah; hiding in the bushes at the sacrifice of Isaac. But even as minor characters we would usually play a crucial role: one of us would suggest the "nobody" trick to Odysseus, or tell Abraham to look in the bushes for the ram, or warn Elizabeth Bennet about Lady Catherine de Bourgh. When I read *Pride and Prejudice* for the first time I didn't even recognize the name because I'd always heard Daddy pronounce it so that it rhymed with "crow." But when I read *Combray* in my French class at St. Clair I recognized Marcel, except that in Proust he was a little boy instead of a little girl, and he didn't have any sisters.

I reminded Daddy of Marcel as we were driving back from Grin-nell College on Interstate 80. We'd taken Ludi down—or sideways if you look at a map—for her freshman orientation. That was at the end of August 1986, six years after the bombing. Daddy'd wanted to take Ludi and me out to dinner in Grinnell, which is a town of about a thousand people, plus the college, but Ludi just wanted us to go so she could be on her own, so we left early. Daddy said that at the heart of *every* family there's a story like Marcel's, and I knew that he was thinking about Cookie, and about that month in Bologna. I asked him whatever happened to Marcel, or Marcelle, as she was called in Daddy's version; but he didn't know. He'd tried to read *Remembrance of Things Past* three or four times, but he never got past *Swann's Way*.

DADDY WAS a man who cried easily, even before it became fashionable. "Well," he'd say, when he'd pulled himself together, "Beowulf cried when he said good-bye to Hrothgar, and Achilles cried when Patroclus died, and Sir Launcelot . . ." He had a whole list. And he could make *us* cry by singing "Danny Boy" or "Just Before the Battle, Mother" or "The Poor Lonesome Cowboy." When we took Argos, our German shepherd, to the vet to have him put down, I was on the edge of tears, but Daddy was so far over the edge it was embarrassing. He'd just had a hernia operation so Mama had to carry poor old Argos downstairs—he couldn't even stand up the last day—and hold him on her lap in the truck. Ludi and I rode in the back. I thought Daddy wasn't going to be able to drive, and in the vet's office I tried to pretend I didn't know him. But I never saw him cry after Cookie's death. I thought about that when we read Wordsworth's "Immortality Ode" in my English Lit. class. Professor Arnold said that the last two lines were a blemish on an OK poem, a decline into sentimentality, and when she read them aloud they did sound a little silly. But Daddy said that the little bump in the rhythm at the beginning of the last line knocked out the sentimentality, and that anyone who read the lines aloud paying attention to the rhythm would *feel* their strength, and when *he* read it aloud, not really accenting any syllable between "thoughts" and "lie," I could hear what he meant:

> To me the meanest flower that blows
> Can give thoughts that do often lie too deep for tears.

When we got home from Grinnell after taking Ludi to school, I opened the pocket door that separates the living room from the dining room—Ludi had it closed to keep Laska, our other dog, out of the dining room, where she'd been working on one of her projects—and a bat fell out of the crack. There's a colony in the attic, and sometimes when it gets too hot they crawl back into the walls and get turned around. They follow the air currents to the opening in the pocket door. I can't stand them and got Daddy to nail a little strip of wood over the opening, but then you couldn't close the door. Ludi was an animal lover and didn't care one way or the other, though she wouldn't let Daddy kill them with his badminton racquet, so when she wanted to close the door she took down the strip of wood. The bat must have been taken by surprise when I pulled the door open, because it dropped straight down, almost to the floor, and then flew in a straight line right into the dining room closet, where it smashed into the wall. Daddy found it in a Waterford crystal tumbler. He dumped it in the sack of garbage under the sink and washed out the tumbler, but I never wanted to drink out of those tumblers again.

THAT WAS *my* last week at home too. I was going to Chicago to look for a job. Daddy and I had found an apartment for me in Hyde Park with three roommates, students at the University of Chicago, so I had a place to stay; but I was feeling like a failure. Scared of the future. After four years of college—I'd gone to St. Clair—I didn't know what to do. I didn't have a clue. No one had recruited me; I wasn't on a track that was leading anywhere; I didn't know what was going to happen to me. And I was thinking about Daddy living all alone for the first time in almost thirty years. And Mama all alone too in her little room in her little studio apartment where the bed— two mattresses, one on top of the other—doubled as the couch. Nothing could convince me that *she* could be happy. Ludi was gone, and I knew now that I'd never be able to understand Cookie's death; it didn't make any more sense than the death of the bat, smashing into the wall. I was starting to think of it as a test, a test that we had failed. I don't mean that I thought that God was testing us, the way he tested Job. Just that it was a challenge, and that instead of rallying, or pulling together, or loving each other more, we'd allowed ourselves to be pulled apart. We hadn't been strong enough. We'd had all the love in the world, and it hadn't been strong enough to hold us together. But that night after I'd gone to bed, Daddy came into my room and sat down on the edge of the bed the way he used to and told me a story the way he used to.

I closed my eyes and let the words wash over me, like the waves on the beach up in Grand Mere, Michigan, where we rented a cottage one summer.

"Once upon a time," Daddy began, "there were three little girls named Cordelia and Seremonda and Duva."

All our stories began this way, with three little girls in a village with a schoolhouse, and a churchyard, and the baker's great stone oven, and of course the great highways that bound together east and west, north and south. On our adventures we always set out on the north-south highway, north to the mountains or south to the sea. The east-west highway was more mysterious, more metaphysical, I suppose. If you went west you came to rolling meadows and fertile valleys that led to the ancient city where the king held his court. The road was kept in good repair, and every now and then some of the villagers—either to seek their fortunes or to escape from sickness and trouble—would pack up their belongings and set out for the city, never to be seen again. But the highway that led to the east disappeared into a dense forest and was impassable.

I turned over and Daddy tickled my arm the way he used to do when I was a little girl. He used to say he needed an extra hand for the three of us. But now he needed only one hand, and soon he wouldn't need any.

There was a river on the eastern border, and the remains of the bridge that once spanned it. The villagers were afraid to go that far into the forest, and no one went any farther, not even the three little girls. There was a mountain in the east, too. You couldn't see it from the village itself, because of the forest, but you could see it from the churchyard, which was on a high hill. It was cold and white even in summer, and on holy days at night you could see little lights, like fireflies, where the top of the mountain should have been, just like the mysterious lights we could see up in the cemetery at night, except those turned out to be car headlights, high school kids parking along the edge of the moraine.

Daddy said he wasn't sure what they were. The schoolmaster

said they were only shooting stars in the sky beyond the mountain, but the priest said they were fairy lights dancing on the mountain itself. The villagers were divided, but there was no way of settling the question because there was no longer any traffic on the eastern highway.

"No one ever ventured eastwards," Daddy said; "they never even thought of it." He paused. "*Except*," he went on, "no one ever ventured eastwards *except* the wandering minstrels and *jongleurs* who came out of the forest in the fall, dressed like wild animals, bound for the west."

When we were little we always used to interrupt with questions, but that night I was too tired and sad, so I just lay quiet.

Years ago, when Ludi was only a baby, we all took the train into Chicago to see Maurice Jenkins' popular one-man enactment of the Pied Piper of Hamelin at the Old Town School of Folk Music. Mr. Jenkins, who was a friend of Daddy's, hopped and skipped around like Danny Kaye and played a pear-shaped German lute. Cookie was the first to join in, even though she was almost fourteen, and then I couldn't resist the strange medieval music. We danced three times around the rows of folding chairs, and when we disappeared through a narrow curtain at the rear of the hall, it was Cookie who went back into the main room to explain to the audience that the other children had gone to live under the mountain and would not be coming back. I knew at the time that this was what Daddy was remembering, but it wasn't till years later that I realized that this was the story he had told Mama when she was in the hospital in Bologna on the night that Cookie died. It's just a story, I tell myself now. But it's a story within a story, one of the stories within the story of Cookie's death, which is itself a story within the story of our family, just as the story of our family is a story within the larger stories of the Woodhull clan (Daddy's family) and the Clifford clan (my mother's family), and of St. Clair College, and of the town of St. Clair, of Harrison County, of the state of Illinois, of the United States, of the Northern Hemisphere, of Christendom, of the world, and so on. Concentric rings of stories till you get to the story of the universe itself. I used to think that the bigger stories explained the smaller ones, that the bigger rings gave meaning to the rings that they enclosed, but now I think it's the other way around, and that each story illuminates and gives meaning to the larger story of which it is a part, till you get to the farthest ring, the primum mobile, and even beyond, where the universe folds in upon itself and there's nothing left to illuminate, nothing left to give meaning *to*.

In
Memoriam

About twelve thousand years ago an advancing lobe of the Lauren-
tide Ice Sheet—the same ice sheet that scooped out the Great
Lakes—deposited a load of glacial till about a mile from Woody's
front door. Powdered rock and gravel and chunks of rock the size of
baseballs—a terminal moraine. The slope was so gentle that Woody,
walking through a field of seed corn that was eight feet tall, couldn't
tell exactly where it began. He kept talking to the dog, a husky who
didn't like the corn and kept threatening to turn back: "Come on,
Laska, it's all right. Don't leave me now." He crossed Kruger Road
and then walked through another field of corn, and when he came
out of the corn he was halfway up to the little cemetery where the
founding fathers of Harrison County—a coalition of Presbyterians
and Congregationalists from New York State—had buried their
dead before the county seat had been moved from New Cameron to
St. Clair. The cemetery was maintained by the county, but nobody'd
used it for fifty years, and Woody'd had to get a special permit from
the county clerk's office to have his daughter buried there. He'd
bought five plots while he was at it—one for everyone in the family.
He didn't figure that Sara and Ludi would stick around, but you
never knew.

Laska sniffed the grass around the edges of a tombstone and
peed on the trunk of one of the white pines lining the gravel drive
that circled the cemetery. The grass between the road and the edge
of the moraine was marked by tire tracks. The high school kids who

parked along the road on Saturday nights—Woody could see their lights from the kitchen window as they pulled in and out—tossed their used rubbers up into the branches of the trees, a row of white pines and a stunted white oak that hadn't done too well in the thin soil of the moraine. The rubbers dangled like damp socks with golf balls in the toes, milky white water balloons.

Woody picked up a couple of pinecones and tossed them down the slope. The cemetery was the highest point in Harrison County, and from Cookie's unmarked grave on the north side he had a view of the town, St. Clair, named after Arthur St. Clair, the first governor of the Northwest Territory, a Revolutionary War general who'd lost almost every battle he was in, like the St. Clair football team. From where he was standing, just outside the circle of the road, Woody could see the tower of Clair Hall, the original college building, and the steeples of two dozen churches. (According to the Chamber of Commerce sign at the edge of town, St. Clair was a "city of churches.") A slow-moving freight train, pulling out of the hump yard in St. Clair, was picking up speed on its way to the West Coast. On the far side of the Burlington tracks he could see the Warren Farms—corn, soybeans, and hogs. Dick Warren had been the secretary of agriculture for a while under Ike and again under Nixon. The farms, which had prospered, were occasionally visited by foreign dignitaries who wanted a glimpse of American agriculture: Khrushchev in 1962, Woody's first year at St. Clair; the Iranian minister of agriculture in 1978, just before the revolution; President Mitterrand of France, Benazir Bhutto, and others. The Warren family also owned the second largest ranch in Texas.

Below him Woody could see his own farm, though it wasn't really a farm, just an old farmhouse on two acres of land and an octagonal barn that served as a garage for the three-quarter-size John Deere tractor that he used for plowing out the drive, and a 1978 three-quarter-ton Ford pickup, and occasionally three or four hundred bales of hay when Curtis Hughes over at the Warren Farms needed some extra space. He could see his daughters come out of the house and then go back in and then come out again. Ludi jumped into the driver's seat of the pickup and raced the motor. Woody couldn't hear the whine of the engine, but he could see the exhaust fumes and the cloud of dust that the tires kicked up. He watched the truck turn onto Kruger Road and followed it till it circled around to the other side of the moraine.

AT THE beginning of the summer Woody had received two invitations to which he hadn't responded. The first was from the clerk of the *1ᵃ Corte di Assise di Bologna*, inviting him to testify on behalf of the *parti lese*, the injured parties, at the trial of the neo-fascist terrorists accused of blowing up Cookie and eighty-five other people. There were seven defendants, including two secret service agents and the woman, Angela Strappafelci, who had actually put the bomb in the station, and who had been arrested recently in Argentina, in a suburb of Buenos Aires, where she'd been living with Franco della Chiave, an international terrorist wanted by intelligence agencies in half a dozen countries: Interpol, the CIA, Mossad, the Quai d'Orsay, Sisde, the Bundesnachrichtendienst. Strappafelci's boyfriend, Niccolò Bosco, who'd been with her at the station, had been killed in prison. These two were the *esecutori*, the executors, the doers. The others, who'd been arrested on information provided by informants from a number of different neo-fascist organizations, were the *mandanti*—the senders, the instigators. At a still higher level, the shadowy figure of Bruno Conti, head of the secret fraternal order FL (Fraternità e Lavoro), had also been indicted; but Conti had fled to Switzerland and the Swiss government had refused to extradite him on the grounds that the charges against him were political.

Hannah had always thought of the *strage* as an act of God, as inexplicable (or explicable) as a tornado or a hurricane, a tidal wave, or an earthquake, or the eruption of a volcano; but the impending trial reminded Woody of what he'd known all along, that the *strage* had been planned and carried out by human beings. Human beings had built the bomb; human hands had placed it under a seat in the second-class waiting room in Italy's busiest train station, on a crowded summer holiday, as a message for the Communist government of Bologna and for all humankind.

The second invitation, from the secretary of Cookie's class at Harvard, came with Cookie's fifth-year class book, a soft crimson paperback about the size of a prayer book. The class of 1980 would be holding a memorial service, during Harvard's 350th anniversary celebration, for the four classmates who had died. The service would be held in Memorial Church on Sunday afternoon at two o'clock. Parents and friends were invited to speak, to send videos and cassettes, and to contribute to a memorial fund for the library.

Woody's fifty-second birthday had just passed without much notice, though Ludi and Sara had fixed a nice dinner: a risotto with the last of the dried *funghi porcini* that they'd given him for Christmas, an *arista* cooked on the grill with sprigs of rosemary, a simple salad, and a bottle of expensive Chianti, which he drank most of himself. Fifty-two years old and he thought that he was standing at the high point of his life, just as he was standing at the high point of Harrison County, and that he could look down on the rest of his life just as he could look down on the farms and fields, corn and soybeans, spread out in front of him and the train tracks disappearing over the horizon. Cookie was dead, and Woody and his wife, after almost thirty years of marriage in which they'd seen eye to eye on all the important things and had never fussed at each other over the unimportant ones, had gone their separate ways. Or rather Hannah had gone her separate way. After the years of anger at the terrorists and guilt for failing to protect his daughter, after the years of simple leaden despair, the years of reliving over and over and over again the moment of Allison Mirsadiqi's phone call and the visits to the hospital and to the morgue—the times when there was still a gram of hope and then the heavy certainty of death, weighing down on him, crushing him like a landslide—Woody didn't want any more pain, so he kept his head drawn in, like a turtle. By the end of the month both the girls would be gone, Ludi starting school at Grinnell College, in Iowa; Sara off to seek her fortune in the big city, Chicago. Ludi was eager to be on her own, but Sara, the middle child, who'd always been happy and peaceful, was apprehensive if not actually afraid. "I'm tired of being the one that nobody worries about," she told him. "*I'll* worry about you," he said; "I'll worry about you all the time."

He'd paid off the mortgage on the house and was putting a good chunk of money into TIAA-CREF every month. He was lying low, treading water, defending the Classics Department against the depredations of the new dean, doing his duty as a member of the Curriculum Committee, teaching his classes and doing a good job too. But he wasn't taking any risks; he wasn't venturing out into deep water; and the numerous women—the number was increasing every year—who had struck out on their own in academia instead of following husbands around had stopped inviting him to intimate little dinners. They had him pegged as a nonstarter, and they were right. He didn't want to start anything. He didn't need any more adventures. That's why he hadn't responded to the invitations from the *Corte di Assise di Bologna* and from the secretary of the Harvard class of 1980. He didn't want any more adventures. He thought that life had already taught him all the lessons he needed to learn.

HE COULD hear the tires of the truck squeal as Ludi pulled into the cemetery, taking the turn too fast, narrowly missing one of the crumbling stone posts that no longer supported the weight of wrought-iron gates. She let the clutch out too fast and the truck shuddered to a halt. She gave her head a shake, like a dog shaking off water, before getting out of the truck. Sara got out the other side and shaded her eyes as she looked up at a rubber dangling from one of the lower branches of the white oak. "Disgusting. Kids." The ground at the base of the tree was covered with owl pellets—indigestible bits of rat and mouse compressed into pellets and regurgitated by a pair of barred owls. Woody, who had learned to call owls from Peter Abbott, looked up into the tree and gave a four-note hoot, "Hoo hoo hoo hooauagh"; but there was no answer. The owls liked their sleep.

They had no plan, just an unspoken agreement not to let the day pass without notice. Three thousand miles away, in Bologna, thousands of people had already marched from Piazza Maggiore to the station. At ten twenty-five the crowd in Bologna had observed a minute of silence, and then there had been speeches. There would be no demonstration in St. Clair, no speeches, but Woody had brought a poem to read. He'd been rereading Horace's *Odes* in preparation for the fall semester and had stumbled upon the poem, which he hadn't read in years, quite by accident. The book was too big to fit into his pocket and he'd left it on the kitchen table, but he didn't need it.

"*Quid si prisca redit Venus,*" he said aloud.

Ludi rolled her eyes. "In English, Daddy."

What if the old love should return
and bring together under her bronze yoke
those who have been parted?

He looked from Ludi to Sara and back again. "Not a very accurate translation, but it suits my purposes."

They were silent for a while.

"What do you think?" he said. "*Quid si prisca redit Venus.* For Cookie's tombstone? Just the first line: *What if the old love should return?*"

"I don't know, Daddy. What's the rest of it about?" Sara reached out to scratch the dog.

"About his old girlfriend."

"Do you think it's appropriate?"

"I suppose not. But I like the first line: *Quid si prisca redit Venus.*"

"I like it too, Daddy, but . . ."

"Anybody else got any ideas?"

"Do you think Mama would have left," Ludi asked, "if she'd gotten what she wanted on the tombstone?"

Woody pretended not to hear.

On the way back down to the farm he rode in the back of the truck with the dog. Ludi drove too fast and bounced him around, but he didn't mind.

> *Quid si prisca redit Venus* [he shouted into the wind],
>   *diductosque iugo cogit aeneo,*
> *si flava excutitur Chloe,*
>   *reiectaeque patet ianua Lydiae?*

What if the old love should return
and bring together under her bronze yoke
those who have been parted?
If red-haired Chloe has been thrown out,
will the door lie open again to Lydia,
who has been rejected?

Sara was right. It wasn't appropriate. He'd deliberately mistranslated it, in fact, to make it fit. But he'd been thinking about his wife as well as about Cookie, and about the long years that lay ahead. Through the back window he could see that Ludi was driving with one hand and talking with the other, and that Sara, her feet tucked up under her, was laughing. He couldn't hold on to *them* any more than he'd been able to hold on to Cookie, or on to Hannah, who was planning to give up her studio apartment in River Forest and move into a room in the convent itself. To save money. *Quid si prisca redit Venus?* What if the old love between them *should* be rekindled? What if he asked Mr. Steckley to carve the tombstone anew, to let Hannah have her way? *La sua voluntade è nostra pace.* But he knew he couldn't do it. A man had to take a stand somewhere, and this was where he'd taken his.

IN MEMORIAM

CAROLYN CLIFFORD WOODHULL died on August 18, 1980, in Bologna, Italy. She was born on June 14, 1958. She prepared at St. Clair High School in Illinois. At Harvard she was a resident of Lowell House and received an A.B., *cum laude*, with our Class. Her field of concentration was government. At the time of her death she was planning to study international law at the University of Bologna. She was killed when a terrorist bomb exploded in the Bologna train station.

Woody'd put the invitation to the memorial service up on the refrigerator in a little magnetic clip, like a clothespin, and pretty soon it was buried under other invitations, clippings, *New Yorker* cartoons, notes to Sara and Ludi, notes to himself. He had no intention of going. He hadn't wanted to think about it. He'd suffered enough over Cookie's death. There was no point now in opening old wounds, old griefs. And he wasn't even remotely interested in the hoopla of Harvard's 350th anniversary celebration. Prince Charles would be there, and Senator Moynihan, and Tip O'Neill. Over a hundred seminars were being offered, and a helium-inflated tube would span the Charles, like a rainbow. Besides, there was no way he could get away from St. Clair at the beginning of the fall term. It was out of the question. He'd have to miss his first class and the first faculty meeting, at which he planned to speak out against a proposal by the dean to fold the Classics Department into a new World Literature concentration.

But on Friday afternoon—on his way to a junkyard in the Quad Cities to pick up a float chamber that he thought might work in the carburetor of his tractor—instead of following Highway 74 west, he turned right on Interstate 80 and just kept going. He stopped in Ottawa to get gas and buy some food for the dog, who sat on the seat beside him, her head out the window, and then again, five hours later, at the Angola Oasis on the Indiana Turnpike. By this time he was having second thoughts. He was tired, not sure of himself. He didn't have a change of clothes. He didn't have a razor or a toothbrush. He was too old for this sort of thing, not sure he could drive all night, not sure what he was driving *for*. What would he *do* when he got there? What would he say? What could he say that he hadn't said before? How could he make sense of Cookie's death in five minutes when he hadn't been able to make sense of it in five years?—six years in August. If he turned around, he'd be home in eight hours. He wasn't even halfway there. But he didn't turn around; he kept going, imagining himself standing before a small audience in Memorial Church, a small congregation of friends and of parents who, like him, have lost a child. In his imagination he clears his throat and leans forward on the podium, waiting, like his audience, for the sound of his own voice.

What he hears himself saying—what he's wanted to say all these years—is that Cookie had still been alive when he got to Bologna, not fully conscious, but alive. And suffering. Had she been waiting for him? Had she recognized him? Had she grasped what had happened? Had the little fluttering noises that came from deep inside her, as if her soul, like a bird, were beating its wings against the bars of a cage, been an attempt to communicate?

Three days of agony and pain, incomprehensible. Woody couldn't get his mind around it, couldn't say to himself, *At least she didn't suffer.* If she had died instantly he could, and would, have imagined her life as short and glorious; not what he would have cho-

35

sen for her, but not a bad shape. Like Achilles, she would have died before her prime, in the bloom of youth, her mature years—husband, career, children—still ahead of her. But she would have died happy. But trapped for three days, burned, maimed, semiconscious, not understanding what had happened, unable to speak, no way to get her mind around the terrible blow. Woody tried not to imagine it, tried to blot out the memory of the little fluttering noises, of the flesh that wouldn't support his touch, of the raw stumps, but sometimes he couldn't help himself, and a great rage surged through him, and he could understand why Achilles had dragged Hector's body around the city of Troy, from morning to night, twelve days in a row, for Hector had killed the one who was dearest to him, dearer than his old father, or his mother, the immortal goddess, and his hands trembled as they grasped the steering wheel of the pickup, as if he were dragging the body of Angela Strappafelci behind him down the Pennsylvania Turnpike.

AT THE next oasis he called his old friend Mac—the other half of the Classics Department—from a pay phone and asked him to cancel his classes and call the dean. Mac was amused.

"Call her yourself," he said. "You've got a calling card." His voice sounded hollow on his new cellular phone. Woody could hear him sipping his drink, could picture him with a big jelly glass full of bourbon, on his back on the couch, glasses on the tip of his nose, a book open on his lap, swirling the ice around in his glass. Bourbon and water. Not much water, just a few drops to release the flavor.

"I can never get it to work."

"You called me, didn't you?"

"Mac, give me a break."

"You want to talk to that woman, you call her." That's the way Mac thought of the dean: "that woman."

"Thanks, Mac."

"You going to make it back for the big meeting?"

"I'm going to try, but I may not make it. You'll have to hold the fort."

"I'll cover your classes for you. Beginning Greek and Advanced Latin Poetry, right?"

"Just get them started on the alphabet in Greek, and tell the Latin students to read Horace *Odes* III.9."

"Don't worry."

"Thanks, Mac."

The dog squatted and pooped on the pavement. Woody took a plastic bag out of his coat pocket; he put it over his hand, picked up the poop, turned the bag inside out, knotted it, and dropped it in a trash bin.

They drove all night and got to Cambridge about four o'clock the next afternoon. Five o'clock Cambridge time. Too late for Prince Charles, too late for Senator Moynihan and George Shultz and Caspar Weinberger, who had all returned to Washington. The Galbraiths were hosting a large garden party, but Woody hadn't been invited. He tried to get a room at the Holiday Inn in Somerville, where they'd stayed for Cookie's graduation, but it was full and he had to drive all the way back to Auburndale before he could find a motel with a vacancy. He bought a package of shorts and a package of T-shirts at a Kmart, and a plastic razor, and then he went back to the motel and slept for twelve hours. He would have slept longer, but Laska, whom he'd smuggled into the room, wanted to go out. It was seven o'clock in the morning. Sunday morning. They drove into Cambridge and found a parking place behind the Common. They walked down J. F. Kennedy Street to the river and then back to Harvard Square, where he bought a cup of coffee and a bagel, which he split with the dog, sitting at one of the outside tables at Au Bon Pain. And then they walked around the Yard for a while, past Canaday Hall, where he'd visited Cookie the fall of her freshman year, and sat on the steps of Widener Library, opposite Memorial Church, a white, colonial affair with Doric columns, rectangular windows, and a high steeple. He felt that he was in one of those central places of the American imagination—like Boston Common or Times Square or Greenwich Village or Telegraph Hill or North Michigan Avenue—but that he didn't belong.

The memorial service was not till two o'clock. The dog attracted a certain amount of attention on the church steps, but there were no signs in the vestibule saying NO DOGS ALLOWED, and no one seemed to mind. If it had been their old German shepherd, Argos, instead of

Laska, Woody could have put on his sunglasses and pretended to be blind.

About a hundred fifty people. Three names on the program. About fifty people per death. Not bad, though Woody thought there had been four names on the original invitation.

The young men and women handing out programs—all smiles, as if they were welcoming guests to a party—were all Cookie's age, which wasn't surprising, since they had been her classmates. Woody recognized Ayosha, Cookie's Korean roommate, who had spent Christmas with them two or three times. Woody had taught her how to make kimch'i.

"Mr. Woodhull." She was a big girl, and when she embraced him she wrapped her arms all the way around his shoulders. "I'm so glad you could come. I almost called you."

"To tell you the truth, I wasn't planning to come. I didn't think I could get away. Then at the last minute I just started driving . . ."

She bent down to kiss the dog. "I'll never forget the wonderful dinner you fixed for us when you came out here the first time. You wanted to take us out to an Italian restaurant in the North End, but Cookie wanted *you* to cook in the dorm."

"I enjoy cooking," he said, "even under adverse circumstances."

"And none of us had ever eaten artichokes before."

"I thought it was odd. But I was pleased, too. I was afraid you'd be too sophisticated for Cookie."

"And the Christmases in St. Clair." She laughed. "Do you still make kimch'i? My mother couldn't believe it when I went home. That I never learned to make kimch'i at home but that I learned in the United States."

"No, I haven't made kimch'i in years. Not since Cookie was killed."

She reached down and patted the dog. "You still miss her."

"I try not to think about it, her, too much."

"Ben and Alex are here too. And Frieda and Sue. Do you remember Sue? She wasn't at the dinner, but she went to the Din and Tonics with us that night."

"Yes, of course. I remember Sue. I remember all of you. I've always been glad that Cookie had such good friends."

Woody meant this sincerely. They'd been interested in everything. Informed. Friendly. Helpful. Not at all what he'd expected. Brilliant, too. Cookie was worried that she wouldn't be able to keep up. But what he remembered most was sitting on the edge of her bed that night, after the artichokes, after the Din and Tonics, after brandies for everyone in her room on the third floor of Canaday.

"*Babbo*," she said. "I'm so lonely. I'm so lonely I cry myself to sleep every night." She was crying then, and he didn't know what to do. What to say.

"It's too hard," she said. "Everyone else is so smart."

"You're smart too. You're a smart cookie."

"I've never had a real boyfriend," she said. "I'm nineteen years old and I've never . . . never had a real boyfriend." Silence. "Everybody just wants to be friends."

"That's not such a bad thing. You've got plenty of time for . . . the other."

He remembered sitting on the edge of her bed, telling her a string of lies, unable to acknowledge that her fears were real. It would have been too painful.

"Would you like to say something?" Ayosha asked. "I'll watch the dog."

"Yes," he said, "of course. It won't be very eloquent, I'm afraid."

"Why don't you sit up front with me?"

"What about the dog?"

"The dog too. No one's going to mind." She gave him a nudge with her elbow and they walked together down the red-carpeted center aisle of the church while a young man in jeans and a white shirt played a Mozart sonata on a grand piano, which shared the stage with a large-screen television.

"I thought there were four people on the invitation?" he said.

"One was a suicide," she said. "The family decided to pull out. It was a last-minute thing. They couldn't face it."

Woody nodded.

The chaplain—the same man Woody listened to on *Cambridge Forum* every Tuesday night, after *All Things Considered*—said the usual things. He said that they had come together to *celebrate* the lives of Christina and Stephen and Carolyn—that was Cookie. He was younger than Woody had pictured him from his radio voice, and every time he used the word "celebrate" he looked down at a piece of paper to see where he was. The man was waffling. He wanted to say that *it* was OK, but at the same time he wanted to tell the truth, and the truth was that *it* wasn't OK. His Christian convictions weren't strong enough to see him through. There was no talk of God, no confident hope in an afterlife. He was just trying to put the best face on *it*, and Woody couldn't blame him; but if he didn't believe, then why didn't he get out of the chaplain business, find a real job?

The first death to be *celebrated* was Christina's. Christina, a dancer, had died of leukemia after two bone-marrow transplants. She was survived by a husband and daughter as well as her birth family. Two friends spoke, about her bravery, about her dedication to her craft and to her family, about her conviction that everyone had the right to dance, that everyone *could* dance. Everyone could find a way, she believed, not just the talented. One of her brothers spoke too, and then her father announced a memorial fund for the dance program at Harvard.

Then another friend read part of a story, about the death of a nun. It seemed in poor taste to Woody, but maybe it was OK, and then the huge television screen flickered into life, without the usual technical glitches, and music poured out of the big speakers—something modern that Woody didn't recognize—and there was Christina, dancing on the screen. Woody, who didn't own a TV or a camcorder or a computer, cringed. "One year ago," said the young woman who was operating the remote control from her seat in the front row. It was a free-form dance, and yet regular at the same time. The young woman—Christina's sister—read a passage from Shakespeare in which a dancing woman is compared to a wave of the sea.

Christina had a wonderfully expressive face that mimed a lively commentary on the dance itself, like a Shakespearean clown ragging the romantic love of the principals. Woody tried to think of her as a wave, not of the sea exactly, but a part of the rhythmic principle that extends throughout the cosmos. He sometimes thought that if only he could find the right metaphor, the right analogy . . . Death fans the flames of metaphor, but all our analogies burn out in the end without consuming the awful reality. Dead is dead.

Laska began to worry a spider crawling up the back of the seat in front of them. Woody watched the spider scurry back and forth to avoid the dog's wet nose. When he looked up, a child was crawling into the picture on the TV screen. Someone darted in and pulled the child out. The dance continued, but the child crawled in again. A pair of hands retrieved the child a second time. The child appeared a third time, and this time without breaking stride the dancer picked up the child and incorporated it into the dance, holding it on her hip, tossing her hip out as she twirled around, tossing her hip out again. Woody searched the chapel for the child. He was never enthusiastic about technology, but what a wonderful memory. His heart ached; he was getting worked up.

The video came to an end. The big screen went blank. Christina's sister sat back down with her father and brother. It was someone else's turn.

Another series of friends began telling stories about Stephen. Friends from all over the country and from Cambridge too. A woman for whom he used to baby-sit told how he had played with her children. How he'd sung to them. How he'd picked them up and run at the wall with them, as if he were going to smash their heads. How he spent an entire evening in their room singing to them. They adored him.

A Cherokee Indian spoke, Stephen's voice coach from New York, where Stephen had been studying to be an opera singer. The Indian, the head of the entire Cherokee Nation, had already conducted a service for Stephen in Central Park, near the lake. During the ceremony seven crows had perched on a telephone wire on Fifth Avenue, and at the end one of them had flown away.

Another brother spoke; another fund was announced by Stephen's father, who looked like a college president: tall, squarish, white-haired. And there was another performance. "Danny Boy." Stephen singing "Danny Boy" at his own funeral. *Come on.* Woody was astonished. The whole place would break down. The song was corny, especially the later verses, but how could you not cry? Woody used to sing it to the girls to make them cry. They'd get furious, but they'd cry anyway. *And in my heart I'll keep you free from sorrow, Through time's long years, O Danny Boy, where e're you go.*

But Woody refused to cry for this young man whom he'd never heard of in his life. He was worried about Cookie. He remembered sitting on her bed. "What about Ben?" he'd asked.

"He just wants to be friends."

"Just-Friends Ben" Woody'd called him after that, trying to make a joke of it. But she'd been so lonely she cried herself to sleep every night. And what had he said to her? What had he come up with? Nothing but a string of lies, though now that he thought about it, the lies, the conventional wisdom, had all turned out to be true: Cookie had done well, she'd made friends, gone to bed with a man, several men in fact. She'd had a false alarm about syphilis that cost Woody and Hannah some sleep; she'd spent a summer on a Walden Two commune in Mexico, and she'd shared a platform with B. F. Skinner, discussing her experiences in Mexico in front of five hundred students in the introductory psychology class. That was before she decided to switch to a concentration in government.

Ayosha, at the podium, was telling one of Cookie's B. F. Skinner stories. Skinner had come to her psychology seminar—this was before the summer in Mexico. "He sat right next to me," she told Woody on the phone afterwards. "I could have touched him." Woody, who'd always despised Skinner for his deterministic view of human behavior, had reread *Walden Two* and this time found it compelling. If you want people to change their behavior, don't scold them; change the environment, the system of rewards and punishments . . . But what was the point of Ayosha's story? He'd missed it. People were laughing.

Just-Friends Ben spoke about Cookie's singing. During the January exam period their sophomore year—when everyone was "totally stressed out"—she'd gone out into the quad and sung about twenty verses of "Trouble in Mind" at the top of her voice. It was freezing cold and there was a foot of snow on the ground, but pretty soon everyone started opening their windows so they could hear. *I'm all alone, at midnight, And my lamp is burning low, Never had so much trouble, In all my life before.*

Just-Friends Ben's turtleneck was a little too tight and he kept pulling at the collar. "It became a tradition," he said. "When things got really tense people would start calling for Cookie, and she'd come out and sing 'Trouble in Mind,' and then we'd all get back to work." He gave a final tug at his turtleneck, and then he started to cry. "There are a lot of us," he said, pushing back the tears with the palms of his hands, "who wish we could still do that, just open our windows and start calling for Cookie to sing 'Trouble in Mind' so we could get back to work."

Ayosha whispered to Woody, "Alex and then you, OK?"

"Alex?"

"Alex Sakyfio. He was the head resident in Lowell House. He teaches in the Psych Department."

Alex Sakyfio, whom Woody had never met, told about Cookie starting an "Italian accent" table in the dining hall at Lowell House. He started speaking with an Italian accent to demonstrate: "'You smoke-a one-a cigarette, you shorten you life-a by five-an-a-half-a *minuti*.'" The problem, he said, was that Cookie really knew Italian. "Pretty soon she'd be speaking Italian and she couldn't figure out why no one could understand her."

Alex went on, but Woody wasn't listening. He was starting to worry about what he would say. "It takes too long to wait," Cookie had said as a child, and he'd been thinking that he might work that up into something. He could almost see it on her tombstone, in fact: *It takes too long to wait.*

One of the grief books that Woody had consulted in the St. Clair Public Library after Cookie's death had contained a map, sort of like the trail map you might pick up in a state park, that had stuck in his imagination. The major trails—Shock, Panic, Denial, Numbness—originated at a point (Death) on the lower-left-hand corner of the map, and each led to a fork in the road. If you chose the wrong turning you could wind up going in a circle. If you chose the right turning you'd follow the new trail into new territory where more trails—Anxiety, Loneliness, Helpless Yearning, Confusion, Fear of the Future, Hostility, Guilt—led not to forks in the road but to dangerous crossroads. If you weren't careful, if you didn't exert yourself, if you turned off the main trail, you could wind up in Hopelessness, Mental Illness, Chronic Anger, or Low Life Satisfaction; if you stayed on the main trail, however, you'd move on straight ahead to Readjustment, New Life Patterns, Building Self-Esteem, Renewing Dormant Interests, Renewed Sense of Well-Being. (Woody tried reading Schopenhauer and Plato instead, but he soon realized that they didn't know any more about death than the authors of the self-help books, and they didn't have any practical advice.)

Looking back, Woody could see that he had willy-nilly followed the main trail from the lower-left-hand corner of the map to the upper-right-hand corner. He'd had to. For the sake of the girls. He'd taken over the shopping and cooking; he'd helped the girls with their homework, and their college applications, though he encouraged them to stay close to home. A day's drive. He'd taught them to dance, and seen to it that they had piano lessons, that they got to the school dances, that they had dresses for the prom, that they had their friends over.

But dead is dead, he thought, and life goes on, and if you think about it seriously, if you consider the alternatives, you'll even see the value of death in the natural cycle of things, and you'll see that death gives shape to life. That's the great lesson of the *Iliad*. Compared to Hector and Andromache, to Achilles and Priam, the lives of the gods who live forever are meaningless. The lives of the gods, who confront no limitations, who make no important decisions. But the truth, of course, was more complicated; the truth that he'd never spoken. He'd never been able to locate it on the trail map of grief.

Ayosha nudged him. Alex Sakyfio had finished speaking. Woody hadn't brought a leash and wasn't sure the dog would stay put. "You'd better hold her collar," he said to Ayosha, and then he walked up to the stage. He could see the dog watching him, Ayosha's hand on her collar, as he leaned forward on the podium and cleared his throat. Like the chaplain he wanted to celebrate Cookie's death, to say that *it* was OK. And at the same time he wanted to speak the truth, the truth that he dragged around behind him like a gunnysack full of bricks. But he didn't see how he could do both, didn't see how he could ask anyone, not even a roomful of strangers, to help him carry this sack, this burden. He didn't know what he was going to say till he started to speak. What he knew was that he couldn't speak the truth here, not on this day, not in this place. He couldn't ask these people, who had all suffered in their own way, to help him carry the truth that he'd been dragging around behind him for six years.

"I'd like to tell you about saying good-bye to Cookie when she left for Harvard," he said. It wasn't *the* truth, but it was *a* truth, a truth that came to him like a gift, out of nowhere. "We drove up to the airport in the Quad Cities. None of us had been out to Cambridge; we hadn't wanted to spend the money for her to visit. I drove her to the airport in Moline. Someone else was going to Boston. A young man. He was leaving Moline on the same flight as Cookie, and I thought they might sit together, keep each other company, but he had a different flight from Chicago to Boston. I wondered if he was going to Harvard too, but it was hard to get any information out of him. He was there with his father and his girlfriend, but none of them were talking. They were joined by some high school pals in maroon and white jackets. They horsed around and made a lot of noise. The boy was nervous. I could tell. His father was trying to give him some last-minute advice.

"And Cookie? What last-minute advice could I muster up for her? My heart was full, but I didn't have much to say. I was trying to summon up some words of wisdom, trying to distill everything I'd learned over the years.

"The Midwest Airways plane taxied up. There was no feeder tube, just a set of stairs that they pushed up to the plane. Cookie walked across the tarmac—is that the word?—just like Ingrid Bergman in *Casablanca*. She didn't look back, and I knew it was too late now for any words of wisdom.

"The boy walked out with his father and girlfriend, even though there was a sign that said PASSENGERS ONLY BEYOND THIS POINT. He was walking slower and slower, so slow I thought he might miss the plane. He kissed his girlfriend, and then shook hands with his dad. His noisy friends were standing with me, looking through the glass.

"Cookie was already at the top of the stairs, but if she turned and waved just before entering the plane, I missed it, because I was watching the young man. He seemed to be struggling with his father, and it took me a minute to realize that he was trying to turn back. He'd panicked and didn't want to get on the plane. His father was threatening him; his girlfriend was yelling. His friends rushed out and surrounded him, like prison guards surrounding a trouble-some inmate. They hustled him out to the plane and the stewardess led him up the stairs.

"We waited around for the plane to taxi out to the runway. I tried to say something comforting to the boy's father, but he was too upset to listen. His son had embarrassed him. And I was embarrassed for him, but I was experiencing a kind of triumph. *His* son had dis-graced him, *he*'d made *brutta figura*, as they say in Italy; he'd cut a bad figure in front of his friends and girlfriend. But Cookie had done me proud. But as I was driving back to St. Clair, something came up from a deeper level, and my heart went out to the young man. He was the only one who really grasped the magnitude of the occasion. This wasn't summer camp or a visit to his grandparents; this was the end of a chapter, the end of his old life. And I wished that Cookie had been a little more reluctant to leave, to say good-bye. I wished she'd tried to hang on a little tighter, like that young man."

Woody was pleased with this little twist at the end of the story. He liked the way the meaning stepped out of the shadows and ambushed the listener, just the way it had ambushed him as he was on his way home from the airport. But today he wasn't satisfied. Still another meaning had stepped out, from deeper shadows, taking him by surprise, though he knew now that he'd known it all along.

"I've carried that wish with me over the years," he said, "like an old pocket watch that doesn't work anymore, or the key to an old padlock that's disappeared long ago, but I see now that I was wrong, and that Cookie was right. I've always tried to hold on to things, but Cookie was always ready to move on. She was never afraid to say good-bye."

Woody stepped down from the podium. He still wasn't quite satisfied. He'd thought, for a minute, that he had it just right: "Never afraid to say good-bye." But it was a little too inspirational. And she had been homesick, hadn't she?—calling every night, till he finally went out to see her, and then he'd sent Sara out for a week, taking her out of school. He was still trying to sort it out when he got back to his seat. The dog was waiting for him, but Ayosha had gone. When he looked around for her he saw that she was slipping a video into the VCR.

"This is Cookie at the talent show," Ayosha said. "Fall 1979, the beginning of her senior year."

Woody knew she'd been in the talent show, but he hadn't realized that the talent show was such a big deal. It was in Sanders Theater, no less, where they'd seen the Din and Tonics. The camera was focused on the stage, but you could hear a lot of crowd noise, and then a few guitar chords and a voice that reminded Woody of Ruby Green. It was Cookie.

The guitar player—Woody recognized Just-Friends Ben—was strumming the chords instead of picking the notes, but it was Woody's song, an old Otis Spann song that he'd arranged for guitar. He'd taught Cookie to sing the first verse in Italian and in French.

She should have been out in front of Ben, downstage right, but she was standing behind him, so the spot caught them both, glinting on her wire-rimmed granny glasses. She had her hands on his shoulders and was singing to him, something private and personal, but really belting it out at the same time, and Woody knew she'd been fucking him. They weren't just friends after all. And why not? he thought, but he was startled by the image that came to mind— Cookie's thighs loosening slowly like Leda's to admit a swollen, engorged cock. Perhaps we're as reluctant to imagine our children in the act of love as we are to imagine our parents, but Woody could see it as clearly as if it were right in front of his face, the smooth tip of the cock nestling for a moment between his daughter's lower lips and then disappearing slowly, like a snake going into its hole. Woody looked around, but he couldn't see Ben, who wasn't sitting up front with the other speakers.

The audience was with Cookie all the way, not clapping, because the rhythm was too subtle for clapping, but keeping time with their bodies. She got to the last verse and then sang the first verse again in Italian, and then she sang it in French, and then in German. "I didn't know she knew German," he whispered to Ayosha. "She didn't," Ayosha whispered back. "She didn't know Spanish either, but that didn't stop her." Woody was tickled. *Signor Pasticciere, Monsieur mon Patissier, Herr Biskuitrouladenbäcker, Señor Confitero.* All baking jelly. At the end she sang the verse in English:

> Mr. Jelly Roll Baker,
> Let me be your slave;
> When Gabriel blows his trumpet
> You know I'll rise from my grave,
> For some of your jelly,
> Some of your sweet jelly roll;
> You know it's doing me good
> Way down deep in my soul.

THERE WAS a reception afterwards at Lowell House where they drank white wine and ate hors d'oeuvres that had been left over from an earlier reception for Prince Charles. The wife of the master of Lowell House had made all the hors d'oeuvres herself, thousands of them. She made hors d'oeuvres all year long and froze them. There were seven large freezers in the house. Cookie had given them a tour at Commencement, and Sara had fallen in love with the room where Cookie'd slept on several occasions when she was baby-sitting for the master's kids and dogs. It had a canopy bed and sheer Austrian curtains and pictures of horses, and its own fireplace. The master and his wife had been very kind to Cookie. The master had even flown her to Moline in his private plane one time when she couldn't get a flight home for Christmas—when she'd waited too long to get her ticket, that is.

It was less crowded than it had been at Commencement, a hundred people instead of a thousand. There were student waiters now, as there had been at Commencement, but they didn't need radio headphones to keep in touch with the kitchen. One of them brought a piece of rope so Woody could tie the dog up outside. Inside there was lots of hugging and kissing and weeping, more than Woody cared for. He talked to Cookie's suitemates, who called him Mr. Woodhull and who apparently regarded the dinner he'd fixed for them on the two-burner electric stove in the small dorm kitchen as one of the high points of their gastronomic lives.

"I guess you never forget your first artichoke," he said. Surprisingly, he was enjoying himself, but all the time he was keeping his eye out for Just-Friends Ben. He'd have to think up a new name now. When he finally found him, in the kitchen, which was equipped with two of everything—two restaurant stoves, two refrigerators, two sinks—the hair stood up on the back of his neck. Just-Friends was tearing individual sheets off a roll of paper towels and folding them in half. Woody washed his hands at one of the sinks and then followed him into a small sitting room—Woody wasn't sure what to call it—where a fire was burning in a large fireplace, though the windows were open. Two children, identical twins, were sitting on one of the sofas with their mother, their feet sticking straight out in front of them. Ben passed out paper towels and the twins wiped their

48

faces. Woody wanted to know everything, but he didn't want to intrude, not in front of the man's wife and children.

Husband and wife looked up, not recognizing him, too preoccupied with their children to make the connection, though they must have seen him at the service.

"Excuse me," Woody said, "I was looking for someone."

He wanted to touch the man, to embrace him, wanted to hear Cookie's name one more time on his lips, wanted to hear him call her name out the open window, and to hear her answering voice: *Trouble in mind, I'm blue, But I won't be blue always; 'Cause that sun's gonna shine, In my back door some day.*

ON HIS way home, September in the trees—touches of rust, yellow, amber, Chinese red—the year winding down, Woody, who'd been following a shiny stainless steel Peterbilt rig down Interstate 90 out of the Adirondacks, was suddenly overcome by a craving for the blues. Old songs crowded his imagination, old voices, old memories. How to describe the sensation? A deep, piercing spiritual longing, or a Big Mac attack? Woody reached over to pat the dog, who had her head out the window, even though they were going sixty-five miles an hour. Woody had his window down too and the heater on full blast. More like the longing a man feels for a woman he used to love, a long time ago, how he wants to hold her in his arms, hear her voice. He wanted to hear the old words, the old songs. Not Eric Clapton and Bob Dylan, not Muddy Waters and Howlin' Wolf, but something older, something deeper down. He wanted to hear Blind Lemon Jefferson sing "One Dime Blues." He wanted to hear Son House sing "Pearline." He wanted to hear Bukka White's "Poor Boy, Long Way from Home" and Blind Blake's "Police Dog Blues." *All my life I been a traveling man, stayin' alone, doing the best I can.*

There was a cassette player in the pickup, but he hadn't brought any tapes with him because he hadn't been planning to go to Boston when he left the house on Friday afternoon. Maybe, subconsciously, he'd been planning all along to go, but if he had been, would he have taken the dog, who was letting out high keening sounds every now and then to remind Woody that it was eight o'clock, well past her supper time? Woody started to sing:

You're gonna quit me, Lasky,
Good as I been to you,
Good as I been to you,
Doggone.

They stopped at the next rest area, just outside of Syracuse, and
Woody let the tailgate down so Laska could jump into the back of
the truck. His knee was giving him a little trouble from all the driving, so he scooted up on the truck on his butt and poured out a pile
of food from a sack of Purina Dog Chow he'd bought on the trip out
and then went in and got a cup of coffee for himself from one vend-
ing machine and some peanut butter crackers from another. He
drank the coffee, but he didn't eat the peanut butter crackers. He
wasn't hungry. He lay down on the seat of the cab for a minute, and
when he woke up it was three o'clock in the morning.

When they got to Toledo Woody turned north on U.S. 23. It
was nine o'clock when he got to Ann Arbor, so he drove around
town for an hour, past the Michigan Union, where he'd taught Hannah to shoot pool; past Angell Hall, where they'd poured out liba-
tions of champagne on the steps after her midterm exams, and the
Co-op House on Maple Street where she'd been living when he met
her, and the apartment on the corner of Spring Street and Hiscock,
just past University Microfilms on Miller Avenue, on the way out of
town, where they'd begun their married life together. He stopped
and got out of the truck and let Laska run around and pee. The toilet had clogged up one spring. When you flushed it, everything, shit
and all, came up in the bathtub. The landlord, a Greek, lived two
houses down. "You can use my toilet," he said, "till I get it fixed." And
his wife used to bring them trays of Greek pastries—kourabiedes,
baklava, honey puffs, custard with filo. Every day until the toilet was
fixed. Cookie'd been in diapers. One of them had flushed a diaper
down the toilet; that's why it was clogged. Woody wouldn't believe
the landlord till he saw the diaper with his own eyes.

Crossroads Music, on Main Street, two blocks south of the station, was just the way he remembered it, except there were racks of
cassettes where the records used to be, and the vintage instruments
had been moved from the mezzanine to a glassed-in gallery that ran
the entire length of the store, from front to back. God's plenty, he

thought—Brazilian rosewood, pale Engelmann spruce, golden cedar, and, in a special display case behind the counter, a National Steel guitar, shiny as the silver semi he'd played tag with from Albany almost all the way to Cleveland.

It was ten o'clock in the morning and Woody was the first and only customer. He picked out a couple of tapes—a collection of old slide guitar pieces and a reissue of John Jackson's *Piedmont Blues*—and put them on the counter.

"I bought my first guitar here," he said to the black clerk, who was restringing a guitar on the padded countertop. "Back in fifty-three. I was an undergraduate here."

"Is that right?" The clerk—about twenty-five, maybe a little older—was clipping the strings as he went along.

"Yeah," Woody said, "that's right. It was a used Stella that had a crack in the soundboard. Mr. Cross sold it to me for twenty dollars."

"Is that right?"

"Yeah," Woody said. "I bought a Martin here too, when I got my first job. A Martin OM-45."

"Is that right?"

What the fuck. "That's right," Woody said. "First guitar Martin made with a fourteen-fret neck."

The man rang up the tapes and put them in a paper sack.

"I play a little," Woody said. "Used to. Used to play at the Ark in the Friends Student Center and at the University Club in the Union. It was mostly folk stuff then, Kingston Trio, Joan Baez. Then Mississippi John Hurt came to campus, and Tampa Red and Son House. That's when I started playing the blues."

"And now you fancy yourself a bluesman."

"That's right," Woody said.

"You can't *play* the blues unless you *live* the blues."

"That's one theory."

"That's the only theory."

Woody paid for the tapes with a ten-dollar bill.

"You don't *talk* like a bluesman," the man said, "but you sure look like one."

"Thanks."

Out on the sidewalk Woody took a look at his reflection in the store window. He hadn't shaved; he'd slept in his clothes; he looked like a bum. He knew he couldn't afford the National Steel guitar and he didn't want to waste the man's time, but he wanted to have a look at it, just try it out for a few minutes.

Reentering the store he heard a string snap.

"The bluesman returneth."

"You should be more careful," Woody said. "You could lose an eye."

"Eye me no eye." The clerk pulled out the bridge pin with the tip of a stringwinder and removed the broken string. Woody could see that the man was older than he'd thought at first. Maybe in his forties, even fifty.

The guitar on the counter was a huge Gibson Super-Jumbo with big round curves and big crown inlays on the fretboard.

"I never cared for the looks of these," Woody said. "Everything's too big, and I don't like the sunburst coloring. Look at the pick-guard; it's huge."

"This is a stage guitar," the man said. "You got to be able to see it from far, far away. It's a cowboy guitar. Look how the edges of the bridge curl up, like a cow's horns. Tex Ritter played a guitar like this. Gene Autry, Ray Whitley. They all played Super-Jumbos at one time or another. Emmylou Harris plays a Super-Jumbo." The man cranked up the string with his left hand and plucked it with his right. "But you," the man said, "you're no cowboy; you're a bluesman."

"How's that?"

"That's what you told me."

Woody shrugged.

"The blues," the man went on, "is a meditational site in which all antinomies are resolved, or dis/solved; a site in which you'll find inscribed the manifold interconnections of the Hegelian dialectic; a site on which is troped the experiencing of experience itself."

"What the hell is that supposed to mean?"

"It means that the blues started with a slave walking at the ass-end of a mule."

"Are you connected with the university?"

"The University of Michigan?"

"Is there another university in town?"

"You know," the man said, "I'd rather have this country run by the first hundred people in the phone book than by the U of M faculty."

"That's an old one." Woody paused. "You don't look like a faculty member," he said, "but you sure do talk like one."

"Well," the man said, "you might say I'm connected. But everywhere you go you'll find me connected, lying in wait, 'cause my name is legion."

"Well, Mr. Legion, would you mind if I tried that National Steel guitar in the case?"

"It's not for sale."

"What do you mean it's not for sale?"

"Not for sale to you."

"What's wrong with me?"

"Look at yourself. It'd be like selling a rifle to a kid, or a drunk, or someone who's crazy. You don't know what they going to do with it."

"It's a guitar, for Christ's sake, not a gun. You don't need a permit to play a guitar."

"Guitar like that you do."

"What kind of permit?"

"Visa Gold, MasterCard, American Express. That guitar belonged to Tampa Red."

"I thought Tampa Red had a gold-plated guitar?"

"A man can have more than one guitar."

"I interviewed him for the *Michigan Daily* when he came to Ann Arbor. He didn't have a gold-plated guitar then. He didn't have this guitar either."

"That's another reason not to sell you that guitar."

"Why's that?"

"'Cause you're shittin' me."

"How much is it?"

"Precisely eight thousand nine hundred and ninety-five dollah."

"Now you're shittin' *me*. That's more than I paid for my truck. That's half what I paid for my house."

"German silver," the man said, tapping his finger on the window of the display case. "An alloy of nickel and tin. This was a special display model for trade shows, just before the Dopyera brothers split with George Beauchamp and started their own company."

"Let me just try it. I haven't played in years. Not since my daughter died. I'm not going to run out the door with it."

"You don't have to make excuses." The man took a key ring from

53

a drawer under the counter and unlocked the case. "You know," he said, "with a guitar like this you don't *have* to play; just show it to people, let them look at it."

The guitar, in fact, was the most beautiful thing Woody had ever seen, except for a woman's body. It had a lily-of-the-valley pattern on the front coverplate with three fronds that circled the upper grilles, and on the back the engraver had engraved two spheres on which the continents were clearly visible, the Americas on the left as you looked at the guitar (and Australia and Hawaii); Europe, Africa, and Asia on the right. On the oceans the lines of longitude and latitude suggested the curvature of the earth. The hemispheres were supported by two naked Negro figures, male and female, kneeling on one knee, arms stretched to balance the hemispheres, taking the weight on their backs. Beneath the two figures waves curled towards each other, splashing upwards and outwards, following the shape of the guitar, coming together to suggest, at the center of the bottom, the cleft between a woman's buttocks.

Two other figures, also male and female, were seated on top of the two spheres. The man held a guitar on his raised left leg, and the woman sang. Her short skirt revealed long black legs and you could see that she was beautiful. Behind each figure rose a radio tower; and between the towers dangled a microphone into which the woman was singing. Above the towers the artist had depicted the sun and the moon and the stars so clearly that Woody could pick out the North Star and the Drinking Gourd; and on the sides a great city was linked—by a railroad that curved around behind one hemisphere and reappeared on the far side of the opposite hemisphere—to the countryside, to freshly planted fields, a man plowing behind a mule, a lonely crossroads, a railroad station, a prison. The city might have been Chicago; the prison might have been Parchman Farm; the railroad might have been the Illinois Central.

"Must have used an old map," Woody said. "Look at the political boundaries. No Poland. No Czechoslovakia."

The clerk took a look at the back of the guitar before handing it across the counter to Woody.

The guitar was heavy, even heavier than it looked. Woody pulled up a chair and sat down with the guitar and ran his thumb across the strings. It was tuned to an open D.

"You got a slide?" Woody dug his thumb under the low D string and snapped it, hard. "Funky."

The man rummaged in the drawer behind the counter. "You know, when cheese gets a little off, it's called 'sweet' or 'funky.'"

"I didn't know that," Woody said.

"It's a good word. Sort of like 'stunk' or 'stinky' or 'stunky' but, you know, funkier." He handed Woody a heavy bronze slide. Woody slipped it on his little finger and ran the slide up to the twelfth fret, where the neck joined the body. Three hand-spun resonator cones amplified the sound like the horn of an old Victrola so that the natural and artificial harmonics of the high notes rang out like bells, loud and clear, rich and warm, and kept ringing till Woody laid a finger across the strings. He hadn't picked up a guitar since Cookie's death, but he hadn't forgotten. He bent over the instrument, attentive, letting his fingers rest lightly on the strings, breathing deeply, before beginning to play: "'Twas in the spring," he sang, "one sunny day. My sweetheart left me, Lord, she went away. But now she's gone gone gone and I don't worry, 'Cause I'm sittin' on top of the world."

The guitar's response was sexual. The entire body resonated with a human sound, radiating warmth and light. This was a guitar designed to cut through the noise of traffic on a busy street corner, to cry out like a woman having a good time in a crowded juke joint, to break the heart like the whistle of an old freight train crossing the country in the middle of the night.

Hannah had never liked this song, but that was because she hadn't understood the irony. Woody wasn't sure he understood it either, but he could feel it in his bones. Woody sang all the verses he knew and then stood up abruptly and handed the guitar back to the clerk.

"Would you play something," he asked, "so I can hear how it sounds out front?"

The man took the guitar, and sat down in the chair, and began to play the same song. Woody heard it coming back at him, brighter, sharper, more intense than the reality of his own playing, but a reflection, nonetheless, of an inner reality. Bittersweet. Funky.

There was a time, I didn't know your name,
Why should I worry, cry in vain,

But now she's gone gone gone and I don't worry,
'Cause I'm sittin' on top of the world.

The guitar had tremendous power and volume, tremendous reso-
nance and sustain, more than Woody had been able to control; but
the man skillfully damped the strings, now with his left hand, now
with his right, so that the sound that came through was clean and
penetrating, free from the resonator rattling Woody'd been aware of
when he was playing. He didn't know what to say.

"Guitar like this can change your life," the clerk said when he'd
finished the song. "You don't *have* to play it; just show it to people,
let them look at it."

"You've already used that line," Woody said, sure now, for the
first time, that the man actually wanted him to have the guitar.

"Eight thousand five hundred dollars. For you, 'cause you're a
bluesman."

"I can't afford it."

"You don't *look* like you can afford it, but you never know; you
might be some kind of eccentric millionaire bluesman. I can't be too
careful."

"They stopped making Nationals after the start of the war,
didn't they?" Woody wanted to show off a little.

"No market for them. Everything went electric: Rickenbackers,
Fenders, Gibsons." The man leaned forward, resting his elbows on
the counter. "*You* can't be too careful either," he said. "Remember the
man who found a pearl of great price." It was an imperative, not a
question.

"Yeah," Woody said. "He had to sell everything he had to get the
pearl."

"That's what the kingdom of heaven *is*."

"Sounds more like forbidden fruit to me," Woody said.

"The knowledge of good and evil," the man said. "The world we
have chosen."

"Enough," Woody said. "My dog's waiting in the truck."

"What kind of instrument your dog play?"

"She doesn't play," Woody said, "but she likes to sing."

•   •   •

WOODY and Laska listened to the John Jackson tape as they drove down I-94, and then they listened to it again on I-80. *Come on in this old house, nobody here but me.* It was late afternoon when they got home. Woody read his mail sitting at the kitchen table drinking a beer. And then he went up in the attic and brought down his old guitars. The Martin OM-45, an Ovation acoustic-electric, the Stella with the crack in the soundboard that he'd put high strings on, and an old Gibson twelve-string. After he'd stopped playing Hannah'd gotten tired of having the guitars lined up under the piano, like horses standing in their stalls waiting to be fed, and had taken them up to the attic.

The damage wasn't as bad as it might have been. The bridge on the Stella would have to be glued, and the frets on the twelve-string would have to be refitted. But the Martin—he didn't really care about the Ovation acoustic-electric—had survived the cold and the heat without any apparent damage. It was one of the first OMs, nice balance, big sound but not too heavy on the bass. Woody sat on the back steps and played "Roll in My Sweet Baby's Arms" and "Mountain Dew" and "Alberta, Let Your Hair Hang Low."

That night he let Laska sleep on the bed with him, something Hannah had never allowed, and the next weekend they drove back to Ann Arbor and bought the National Steel guitar. He got three hundred dollars each for the Stella and for the acoustic-electric, a thousand for the twelve-string, and three thousand for the OM-45, but he still went over the credit limit on his Visa card, for the first time in his life. He hadn't even known there was a credit limit. But the clerk—who turned out to own the store—took a chance and let him have the guitar anyway. Woody was nervous about spending so much money. Almost four thousand dollars over what he got in trade. He wasn't broke, but he was trying to build up a little estate for the girls. Ludi was on a tuition-exchange program at Grinnell, but he still had to pay her room and board, and he had to pay Sara's rent in Chicago till she could get on her feet. As he signed the yellow credit card slip his hand trembled and he remembered signing the mortgage papers for the farm—$18,000—remembered sitting next to Hannah in the lawyer's office, his knees pushed up against the back of the lawyer's desk, running a high fever, signing papers next to the little *x*'s the lawyer had marked in red ink; and then afterwards the fever was gone and they walked down Main Street right past their car, forgetting where they were going. The farm was everything they had dreamed of. At the time it had seemed like the promise of a new life, and that was what the guitar seemed like now, the promise of a new life.

Woody left the store and drove straight to the EconoLodge on the edge of town. No man was ever more anxious to bed his new bride than Woody was to get his hands on that guitar. He knew he shouldn't have spent the money. He knew, moreover, that possessions don't bring happiness—knew it as certainly as he knew anything—but it had been so long since he wanted something, he was so unused to wanting *anything*, that it made him dizzy.

He poured a glass of water for the dog before taking the guitar out of its case and laying it on the double bed. He went into the bathroom and peed and washed his hands. There was a full-length mirror on the bathroom door, and he looked himself up and down. He thought he looked pretty good. He ran his fingers through his hair, which was still dark and thick. It hadn't really changed much in the last ten years, though he needed to shave twice a day if he was going out in the evening, which he never did, so it didn't matter. He sat on the edge of the bed and played every song he could remember in open D. When he ran out of songs he tuned the guitar all the way up to an open A, keeping his eyes closed in case a string snapped.

He ran the slide up to the twelfth fret. The guitar cried out. The tension was incredible.

> I went down to the crossroads,
> I fell down on my knees;
> I went to the crossroads,
> Fell down on my knees;
> Asked the Lord to have mercy,
> On poor Woody if you please.

Everyone knows what it's like to have a word right on the tip of your tongue. You need that word; no other word will do, but you can't find it, you can't find it, and then it comes to you, and you can finally say what you need to say. That's the way Woody felt. He'd found the words he needed. They wouldn't bring Cookie back, but they'd throw a little light on his path, help him see where he'd been, figure out where he was going.

He played till the fingers of his left hand began to bleed, and then in the middle of the night they drove home with the windows down and the heater on full blast, the guitar in the front seat between him and the dog. As he turned off Kruger Road into the long driveway he had the funny feeling he was in the wrong place, or at least in a new place. Nothing looked familiar in the early morning light. Not the house, not the barn, not the neglected apple trees behind what used to be a garden, not the tractor waiting in the open barn door for a new float chamber. It wasn't till he opened the mailbox at the end of the long driveway and saw his name on a letter from Sara that he knew for sure he was home.

Halloween

The first guests arrived at six o'clock, two Iranian students, Turan Mirsadiqi and Shahla Golestani, in Ms. Mirsadiqi's racing-green Alfa Romeo convertible. It was the end of October, but the weather was warm and the girls had the top down. "We came early to help," Ms. Mirsadiqi shouted. Woody waved them all the way back to the barn, to make room for other cars. The electric motor on the hog cooker, which he'd borrowed from Curtis Hughes, the manager of the Warren Farms, had shorted out and he'd been turning the spit by hand while he figured out what to do. He walked across the yard to greet his guests, wiping his hands on an old towel he'd tucked into his pants.

"I need someone to turn the spit for a few minutes," he said.

Turan Mirsadiqi—Turi—was the daughter of an important trustee, Woody's oldest friend, a St. Clair alum who'd gone on to graduate school in classics at the University of Michigan. Woody'd met her in Professor Müller's Persian class, which she had taken on a dare. She later married a wealthy Iranian businessman, Alireza Mirsadiqi, whom she met on a train from Rome to Naples. She sent two or three full-pay Iranian students to St. Clair every year, first from Iran and then from the expatriate Iranian community in Rome, where they had moved just before the revolution. The college was expecting a very substantial gift from her husband to kick off its capital fund drive.

Woody had studied Persian at the University of Michigan

because his advisor, Professor Müller, taught Persian and filled his classes with his own advisees; later he'd spent a year at the University of Esfahan on a fellowship sponsored by the now defunct Iranian-American Friendship Society. He spoke a sort of literary dialect, like someone reading poetry out of an old book, and could never figure out if the Iranian students found his attempts to speak their language charming or merely amusing.

Ms. Mirsadiqi greeted him in Persian: "Mr. Professor Woody, our distinguished teacher and gentle host, we are deeply indebted to you for your generous hospitality. As you see, we have worn our traditional chadors for your Festival of the Dead." She pulled her flowered chador up to cover her mouth and nose. It wasn't a chador at all, Woody saw, but an old sheet with paper flowers pinned to it. Under the sheet he could see the legs of her jeans.

Woody replied in kind: "Welcome, my dear guests. Words cannot begin to express . . ."

"I've brought a draft of the first chapter of my honors thesis," Ms. Mirsadiqi said in English, "and we've been practicing 'The Craft of Gourdmaking.'" She tucked the thesis chapter under her arm and twisted her hands into a shape that didn't look like anything except twisted hands but that would cast an interesting shadow on a sheet or screen, like bunny ears in a beam of light from a slide projector, only more complicated.

"I'm not so sure that's a good idea," Woody said. "They wouldn't let you do it at the International Fair."

"Yes," she said, "but that's because there were parents there. Tonight we're on private property, and I don't believe shadow plays are illegal in this state of Illinois."

"There are parents here too, with small children."

"Yes," she said, "but not parents of potential full-pay St. Clair students."

"Leave it on the kitchen table," Woody said, meaning the thesis. "No, better put it on the piano in the living room. Put it on the music rack on the piano."

The girls disappeared into the house. Woody went back to the hog cooker, giving the crank a turn every few minutes while he looked for the short.

• • •

61

At the end of August Woody and Sara had taken Ludi down to Grinnell for freshman orientation. A week later, on a Sunday morning, Sara had left for Chicago on the Illinois Zephyr. To seek her fortune. A day had come that Woody'd been dreading for years: he was alone now for the first time in thirty years, for the first time in his life, really, except for the year in Esfahan, but there he'd stayed with Ebrahim Agha and Ashraf Khanom. But he hardly noticed. He was too busy. A new life had already begun. He was occupied with his classes—there were nineteen students in his beginning Greek class and twelve in his advanced seminar on Ovid, and he was directing Ms. Mirsadiqi's honors thesis. He'd given a concert, sponsored by the prison-education department of the local community college, for the prisoners at the new minimum-security prison out on old Thirlwell Road, across from the Jewish cemetery; he'd finally located a new float chamber for the tractor; he'd begun revising the manuscript of a book he'd been working on when Cookie was killed—*The Cosmological Fragments of the Early Greek Philosophers*—and had discovered that his ideas were fresh and interesting, not just a mishmash, as he had feared, of old arguments drawn from Burnet and Guthrie and Diels. Parmenides—a more robust figure than Heraclitus in his search for a thread of permanence—now seemed to him to be the key, seemed to provide a clear point of departure. He was occupied in other ways too: he was taking Hebrew lessons from the dean, every Sunday morning at the temple; he'd resolved to write a letter every day and hadn't missed a day since the Sunday that Sara left; and he'd been practicing the guitar for an hour, sometimes two, every evening after supper, before getting down to work on *The Cosmological Fragments*. Really practicing—scales and arpeggios, finger-stretching exercises, improvisation, repertoire (learning new songs from old tapes and records—not just fooling around). He was too busy to feel sorry for himself, though on Saturday nights he sometimes gave way a little. He'd fix pizza, as he'd done every Saturday night for years; he'd listen to the first half of *A Prairie Home Companion* while he made the dough and drank two or three beers, and the old house would creak and make noises, and after the third beer he'd imagine that the girls were upstairs, getting ready to go out later on, and right after he put the pizza in the oven he'd open another beer and light up one of Hannah's Pall Malls—she'd left six cartons behind—and smoke it out on the back porch while the pizza was cooking. He wasn't used to smoking and the first drag would almost knock him over, especially on top of the beer, and he'd grab on to a shelf or lean up against the wall, like a man having a heart attack; and if a car drove by he'd imagine it was Hannah coming home from town with a jug of red wine, just in time to catch the "News from Lake Wobegon."

The first letter he'd written was to Hannah. *Quid si prisca redit Venus*, he wrote, *diductosque iugo cogit aeneo*—"What if the old love should return and bring together under her bronze yoke those who have been parted?" The students in his class hadn't liked the poem at first because it was too unsentimental, but Woody liked it so much that he wrote out the whole poem in his letter. He wrote slowly and carefully with his Parker Duofold fountain pen in the italic handwriting that he used to make out the place cards for the annual Phi Beta Kappa banquet and to write an occasional letter to be presented to a visiting dignitary, along with a college medallion. Then he wrote to his daughters, then to old teachers, old colleagues, old friends, former students, and finally to distant relatives—not too many of them left, apart from his cousin Peter in Ann Arbor, who wrote back reminding Woody of how they used to boil shrimp and eat them with the corn from the garden that Peter and his wife froze every year. They made their own catsup too, and mixed it with horseradish and lemon juice for the shrimp.

A letter a day is a lot of letters. If you write a letter a day, you ought to *get* a letter a day. But it didn't work that way. Woody received the letter from Peter, and one from another cousin, his mother's sister's daughter, in California, and a letter from Hannah's brother in Minneapolis, and a card from his old college roommate, who was the religion editor at *Time* magazine. That was it. Some letters had come back stamped ADDRESSEE UNKNOWN.

When Woody'd gone off to college his mother had put a letter in his suitcase. She must have stuck it in there after he'd already packed. He couldn't remember what was in the letter, but he could remember how he felt sitting on the edge of his bed in Adams House at the University of Michigan. When he opened it he felt embarrassed, as if he'd opened a jar of honey and spilled it in his lap. He was lonely and homesick in his little narrow single room, but he didn't want to admit it. He never answered the letter, never even said anything about it. But when Cookie went off to Harvard he stuck a letter in her suitcase, and he did the same for Sara and Ludi. And none of them ever mentioned those letters. Had they been embarrassed too? He didn't even know until he read Evan Connell's *Mrs. Bridge* that there was a name for these letters. They were called "train letters," and Woody figured from the way they were described in the novel that there was a time when all parents put train letters in their kids' suitcases when they went off to college. The Bridge girl—Carolyn? Ruth?—reads her train letter in bed with her lover. She's embarrassed too, but then she realizes that no one will ever offer her the kind of love she got from her parents. And, Woody thought, Mr. and Mrs. Bridge weren't even very *good* parents.

There were other letters too that Woody remembered. There were the three letters written by his mother that had turned up in the attic one day, in a strongbox they'd bought for important papers, but they'd never had any important papers to put in it. But here were these letters, written when his mother was a student at St. Clair. They were written to *her* mother, Woody's grandmother, in Chicago, and in them she talked about the classical mythology class that she was taking, which was the very same course that Woody had been teaching at the time. And then there was the letter he'd found in the street in Esfahan, just outside the bazaar on Chahar Bagh Square, an envelope lying facedown in the dirt. Woody'd picked it up, and it was addressed to him.

Whitman talks about finding letters from God in the street. Woody couldn't have been more surprised if it *had* been a letter from God, but it was from Hannah, in St. Joe, Michigan. That was before they were married. Hannah had pulled away from him in Ann Arbor—she'd thought things were moving too fast—and Woody thought he'd seen the last of her, till he found this letter. Lying facedown in the cobbled street. Normally he didn't believe in Destiny or Fate, but it took an effort *not* to believe that something had been intended, had been meant to be, and that was why his heart always quickened its pace a little when he pulled the pickup over to the side of the road, slid across the seat, rolled down the window on the passenger side, and pulled open the mailbox door.

• • •

WOODY WAS a little nervous. It had been years since he'd put on one of his Homeric banquets, and he wasn't sure now that the small hog he'd bought from Curtis was going to feed sixty people, even with the turkey he'd cooked for Muslims and Jews, and the corn he'd roasted on the grill, and all the dishes that people had brought. He was keeping an eye out for the dean's little red Corolla, wanting her to arrive, to see the *tableau vivant*, like something out of Breughel the Elder, some peasant festival, that he'd arranged: faculty children playing Frisbee and badminton, the hog cooker, the gallon jugs of cider in big tubs of ice, Frank Swanson tapping the keg of beer on the back of his pickup, the cornstalks and soybean stubble in the background, the grain trucks lined up on Kruger Road waiting to get into the elevator in New Cameron, the distant boom of the Burlington hump yard where they made up trains in the evening, the big bonfire where the kids would make s'mores after supper, the long tables—two-by-tens on pairs of sawhorses—piled with food. Stacks of pita bread, bowls of kalamata and Chalkidiki olives, plates of feta cheese and sliced tomatoes from the farmers' market, big two-liter bottles of pale golden retsina. Musical instruments lined up near the fire. Larry Taylor's twelve-string Martin, Jessica Lowden's battered old Gibson, Curtis's long-neck Stelling banjo, Dale Peterson's washtub bass, Blind Bob Martin's flatiron mandolin, Nora Stout's hammered dulcimer. The Midwest wasn't so bad. Woody'd put a hog roast up against a clambake any day. There were plenty of easterners at St. Clair with degrees from Ivy League schools. At first they planned to move on, and some of them did; but mostly they went native, like British consuls in Africa and the Middle East; others, like the dean, stayed but had trouble adjusting, never stopped complaining.

"Just stop it, Jane," Woody told her one day after the Hebrew lesson. They were in the kitchen at the temple; she was examining a store-bought bagel as if it were a piece of dried buffalo dung. "Jesus Christ, you'd think you couldn't eat a bagel if it didn't come from Zabar's. Stop complaining. You can get five kinds of good olives right downtown at Cornucopia; you can get good olive oil, and Parmigiano-Reggiano. You can get good bread at Uncle Willy's, better bread than you get in New York."

"And you can drop in to see the Krasners at MoMA."

"At least you can walk down the street at night in St. Clair, which is more than you can say for Central Park. You *chose* to come here, Jane. We invited you to be our leader, and you agreed to come. It's a small midwestern town. Some of us like it. Why com*plain* all the time?"

"There's a Lebanese place in Brooklyn," she said, "where you can get *twenty* different kinds of olives, *twenty*," but then she stopped herself. "I'm sorry," she said, and smiled. "I was a complaining Jew in New York; I'm a complaining Jew in St. Clair; I'll always be a complaining Jew." Somehow Woody liked her better after that. She smiled, as if a sudden breeze had dispersed the clouds of anger and frustration that concealed her true nature.

MANY OF the students wore togas, but some of the more imaginative ones had borrowed costumes from the Theater Department. A Greek warrior—Achilles, perhaps, or Odysseus—bearing a round shield was filling plastic glasses with beer from the keg and handing them out to a bearded Socrates, to a seventeenth-century musketeer, and to a girl from Woody's Latin poetry seminar in a Neapolitan fisher-girl outfit that Nora had worn when she danced the tarantella in last year's student production of *A Doll's House*. Ghosts and goblins mingled with civilians in jeans and sweatshirts around the hog cooker, watching the hog turn slowly over the bed of charcoal. Turi Mirsadiqi and Shahla Golestani were taking turns cranking the spit—Woody hadn't found the short—holding back the long sleeves of their flowery impromptu chadors, which covered them completely except for their faces; and Mac, a tumbler of gin in one hand, was using a pair of barbecue tongs to turn the vegetables on a long grill that Woody had borrowed from the college: zucchini, peppers, sweet onions, mushrooms, baby eggplants cut in half, ears of corn that had been soaking all afternoon in their husks.

The dean didn't arrive till after dark. Woody had almost given up hope. He'd already carved the turkey and was starting on the hog, cutting thin slices from the shoulder with a twelve-inch butcher knife and sliding them onto a platter. He wasn't sure that he'd really *wanted* her to come anyway. The dean, not a very social person to begin with, was not especially attractive; or rather, she made no effort to *make* herself attractive. Makeup might have softened her craggy—"craggy" was ungenerous, but it was the word people had

66

settled on—features, and if she'd fix her hair differently, instead of tying it in a bun, she'd look less like the picture of Elizabeth Cady Stanton that hung on the wall behind her desk. Woody had served on the committee that brought her to St. Clair and had an interest in her success. He thought she was a good person, a person of strong convictions, of integrity, and he was drawn to her in part because he wanted her approval. But they were on the opposite sides of too many issues—from the role of Classics in a liberal arts education to the Palestinian question—and had fallen into a kind of half-joking relationship unrelieved by moments of real seriousness or genuine humor. It was only on Sunday mornings, in the multipurpose room at the temple, sitting around a folding table with Mrs. Schubach and Mrs. Beckstein, and Mrs. Goldfarb and Mrs. Goldfarb's twelve-year-old daughter, who didn't want to be there, that they were able to put this habit aside and speak freely and unaffectedly to each other— perhaps because she was the teacher and he was the student. The other students—formidable as ocean liners, except for little Elena Goldfarb—had been reciting the responses from the Reform prayer book ever since they'd been bat mitzvahed and couldn't understand why Woody had trouble with the Hebrew letters. Of course, they couldn't understand a word of what they read, and they couldn't understand why verbs didn't take the same prepositions in Hebrew that they took in English, or why there were two infinitive forms in Hebrew instead of just one, or why you couldn't just say "have" in Hebrew instead of adding an inseparable preposition to a noun. Woody didn't understand either, but at least he didn't challenge the dean at every step of the way, as if she were deliberately inventing arbitrary grammatical rules just to make life difficult. He submitted himself to the mysteries of prepositions and infinitive absolutes. He liked being in the student role. Let someone else do the driving.

"There's lots of stuff on the table, Jane," he said when she brought her plate up to the cooker, "including grilled vegetables, and there's plenty of turkey right here."

"Turkey?" she asked, as if she didn't believe him. "I expected lamb at a Greek banquet."

"Yes," he said. "The oldest food of humankind, acceptable to Christians, Muslims, Jews, and Hindus. Well, some Hindus. But Eumaios serves pork to Odysseus in the fourteenth *Odyssey*, and he complains that the suitors are eating up all the young pigs." Woody turned up his palm and extended it towards the students and faculty around the bonfire. "Besides, Curtis doesn't have any lambs, so I decided to make do with a hog and a turkey. You're the first person to complain. Light or dark?"

"Light."

"I've been saving these pieces specially for you," he said, putting two thin slices of breast meat on her plate. "Not too done. Moist."

"Woody," she said, "you're the perfect host."

THE CHILDREN were still making s'mores—toasted marshmallows and Hershey bars sandwiched between graham crackers—when the musicians began to tune their instruments. Larry Taylor, from the Anthropology Department, had brought a new electronic tuner and the musicians were taking turns fastening the clip to their instruments and tuning them to concert pitch, and Woody was handing out songsheets that he'd Xeroxed that afternoon. Woody was looking forward to the singing. He'd been practicing the guitar regularly and felt that he'd arrived at a new level. An hour a day, he calculated, is three hundred sixty-five hours a year, over forty-five full working days. Songs that had once seemed beyond his reach—Leo Kottke's "Last Steam Engine Train," for example, or Reverend Gary Davis's "Death Don't Have No Mercy"—suddenly seemed to lie under his fingers, as easy and responsive as his wife's body when she was aroused. He'd forgotten how important music had once been in his life, a powerful magnet that had drawn him into an improbable circle of friends, inside the small world of the college and outside as well: a circle that included a dentist, a farm manager, a retired mechanic who'd lost his sight to glaucoma—all bound together by the premise that music was too important to be left to professionals.

Woody stepped up to join the musicians, who were still tweaking their instruments. (He had tuned his guitar earlier to his own electronic tuner.) He picked up a paperback copy of Yeats that he'd left on top of his guitar case and cried out in a loud voice, "The Fiddler of Dooney." He didn't need the book, but he thought it looked good, as if he were reading a lesson from the Bible. "'When I play on my fiddle in Dooney,'" he began loudly, and then he started over:

When I play on my fiddle in Dooney
Folk dance like a wave of the sea;
My cousin is priest in Kilvarnet,
My brother in Mocharabuiee.

I passed my brother and cousin:
They read in their books of prayer;
I read in my book of songs
I bought at the Sligo fair.

When we come to the end of time
To Peter sitting in state,
He will smile on the three old spirits,
But call me first through the gate;

For the good are always the merry,
Save by an evil chance,
And the merry love the fiddle,
And the merry love to dance:

And when the folk there spy me,
They will all come up to me,
With "Here is the fiddler of Dooney!"
And dance like a wave of the sea.

That's how Woody was thinking of himself, as the fiddler of Dooney, but before he could open his guitar case and take out his National Steel guitar in all its shining glory, like the shield of Achilles, there was a flurry of excitement. A group of students who'd been carrying dirty dishes into the kitchen came running out of the house. "Bats!" they screamed as they ran down the path to the bonfire. "There are bats in there."

"Oh, for crying out loud," Woody said. "You're running away from a little bat?"

"There's more than one," shouted Carol Nelson, a local girl who'd once translated αἰδοῖα, the Greek word for genitals, as "valuable possessions." She was standing right in front of him. "They're flying around. The dog was jumping way up into the air; you should have seen him." The line, Woody recalled, was from Xenophon: "They waded into the water up to their 'valuable possessions.'"

"Her," Woody said automatically. "The dog; it's a she." He walked up the path to the house, followed by several of the students, as if he were leading a Greek scouting party against the Trojans. Other students were waiting nervously on the porch. He went through the house, turning lights on in each room, followed by the students, who didn't want to miss the action. He kept a badminton racquet on a hook in the front-hall closet to kill bats, but sometimes the bats were hard to find. They'd hide in a closet or roost behind a curtain, and then you'd just have to wait. The first one surprised him as he was climbing the stairs. He lashed out with the racquet and missed, lashed out and missed again. The students were afraid of the bat and hunched over to keep their heads down while it circled the room, but they were laughing too. The bat continued to swoop in circles around the room. Woody slowed himself down, took the bat's measure, and struck it from behind with a sharp backhand. The bat shot across the room and landed inside the piano. The second bat he killed in the upstairs bathroom, with the door closed behind him.

"There's another one," Carol said. She was still out of breath from running. "There were three of them."

Woody searched for fifteen minutes but couldn't find it. He scooped the dead bat out of the piano with a piece of cardboard and dumped it in the garbage, along with the one from the bathroom, and then he took the paper sack outside and dumped it in a plastic garbage can. The singing had already started without him. A children's song. From the porch he could hear Curtis's tenor voice and then the children: "With a knick knack paddy-wack, give a dog a bone, This old man came rolling home." The musicians were standing on the other side of the bonfire, which was in a little hollow halfway between the barn and the house; Woody could see their faces in the firelight; and he could see their instruments, highlighted against their clothes, jeans and dark sweaters: the bright white face of Curtis's banjo, like a full moon; the pale golden Engelmann spruce of Larry's twelve-string Martin; the ugly sunburst of Jessica's old Gibson, the strings catching the light. As he walked down the path he could see their hands moving—Curtis frailing and Larry using a pick, Jessica strumming with her whole hand. When he got closer he could hear Blind Bob's mandolin—a tiny obbligato—and he could feel, rather than hear, the thump of Dale Peterson's wash-tub bass, right in the pocket. *Tump tump tump.*

Melinda Dirkson, another girl from Woody's beginning Greek class, scraped out a decisive rhythm on the washboard with a scrub brush; other students shook or pounded various rhythm instruments that Woody had collected over the years: an African talking drum, rattles, finger cymbals, a twelve-tone tong drum from Guatemala, half a dozen chickenshakes (plastic eggs filled with metal shot), and several sets of wooden bones. Woody had almost bought a small Italian accordion that he'd seen in the window of Jackson's Music Shop on Main Street, for under a hundred dollars. It was a beautiful instrument, and he *would* have bought it if someone hadn't beaten him to it.

This was the moment, but instead of getting out his guitar he sat down on a log—the farthest log from the fire and from the singing—next to the dean.

"*Shalom,*" he said.

She didn't say anything.

"You didn't bring your flute," he said. The dean played in the St. Clair Symphony.

"No, was I supposed to?"

"I hoped you would."

"Then you should have said so."

"It said on the invitation . . . Never mind."

"I don't think it would fit in."

"We're not particular."

"Maybe you're not, but I am."

"I see."

Curtis was singing another children's song with a lot of animal sounds in it. The children oinked and mooed and neighed and barked and meowed and squeaked.

"You don't make it easy," Woody said, shifting his position a lit-tle on the rough log. He picked up a stick and scratched in the dirt. The dean had her hands at her sides, fingers spread out on the log.

"Make what easy?"

"Conversation; small talk; being friendly."

"You mean I don't massage your ego? Tell you how wonderful you are for throwing this marvelous party . . . ?"

"It is marvelous, isn't it? Just listen. Seriously. Look . . . We used to do this all the time."

"Back in the good old days?"

"Yes, back in the good old days, back in the golden age, before Cookie was killed, yes." Pause. "Did you know," he went on, "that Franco della Chiave and Angela Strappafelci have been arrested in Buenos Aires?"

Woody felt that he was revealing something deeply personal, though it had been on the front page of the *Times*. He hadn't spoken of it to anyone. He had, in a way, tried to pretend to himself that it had nothing to do with him.

"I saw something about it in the paper," the dean said. "Red Brigades?"

"Red Brigades? Come on, Jane. The Red Brigades were not nice people, but they didn't put bombs in supermarkets or train stations. These people are neo-fascists, right-wingers."

"Della Chiave's a terrorist, isn't he?"

"He's wanted by everybody: Interpol, all the secret service agencies. But to tell you the truth I'm more interested in the woman who was arrested with him. Angela Strappafelci. She's the one who actually *put* the bomb in the station, she and her boyfriend. And Aldo Trimarchi, who built the bomb and delivered it to Angela and her boyfriend in Bologna."

"I thought the paper said seven or eight?"

"There are three *esecutori* and four *mandanti*, depending on how you count. Bruno Conti's been indicted too, but he's in Switzerland. And Angela and della Chiave are still in Argentina."

"What makes *her* so special?"

"Because she's a woman. Because she's just about Cookie's age."

"You can understand how a man would do such a thing, but not a *woman* . . . ?"

"Could you drop the ideology just for a minute, Jane."

"You can never drop ideology; you can pretend that it's not there, but you can't drop it."

"Forget it, Jane."

"Sorry, Woody; I just wanted to make the point that—"

"I know what point you wanted to make. I don't want to hear it."

"You've never gotten it, have you?"

"I think I *am* getting over it; that's why I decided to have a party."

"I didn't say 'gotten over it,' I said 'gotten it.'"

"I get it, Jane, I get it; but I'm getting over it too."

"That's why you're giving guitar lessons at the prison?"

"I'm not giving lessons," he said. "I gave a sort of concert for some of the prisoners."

"And you're going to work with the Black Student Union on a blues program for the spring term, is that right?"

"You seem to be keeping close tabs on me. Where do you get your information?"

"Word gets around. The new Professor Woodhull. You're a new person. Looks like a bona fide midlife crisis to me."

"I hadn't thought of it that way, but I suppose you're right."

"The next thing you know you'll buy a sports car and find a mistress."

"I'd like that," Woody said. Was this an opening? he wondered. The moment he'd been waiting for? Or was it genuine sarcasm? He wasn't quick in these situations. He needed to prepare himself. He'd been planning to proposition her, but later, after the singing. But how do you proposition a radical feminist?

"I'd like an Alfa Romeo Spider, like Ms. Mirsadiqi's, only I think I'd go for a red one. And I'd like a frisky young woman to— You know," he went on, as if he'd interrupted himself, "I haven't . . . been with a woman since Cookie was killed. I was starting to think that part of my life was over."

He waited to see what she'd say. But she didn't say anything. The musicians were starting "Roll in My Sweet Baby's Arms."

"Well," he said, "I think it's time I got my guitar out."

THERE WAS a certain rhythm to these parties. You started with a few children's songs, and then Michael would row the boat ashore and it would be as dark as a dungeon way down in the mine, and then you'd sing "Corinna, Corinna, where you been so long, Ain't had no lovin' since you been gone." Curtis understood the rhythm without Woody's songsheets.

Roll in my sweet baby's arms,
Roll in my sweet baby's arms,
Gonna lay 'round the shack till the mail train gets back,
And roll in my sweet baby's arms.

Everyone else Woody knew played that song in G, but for some reason Curtis played it in A. It was a terrific song with a hard-driving
rhythm. You couldn't really hear the whomping of the washtub bass,
but you could feel it, like a train going by in the distance; the washboard too—*ch*-ch-ch-ch, *ch*-ch-ch-ch, *ch*-ch-ch-ch—like another
train going by in the distance, only farther away. But it was the big
sound of Curtis's banjo that bound them all together, like a cooper's
hoop around the staves of a barrel.

Woody opened the case, got out the guitar, fumbled around in the
case for metal finger picks, which he needed to compete with the
banjo. He felt that everyone was looking at him. The guitar was so
spectacular that it raised expectations, and for a moment he felt that
he was not worthy of this instrument and that he should not have
bought it. And when he joined in he discovered that he was not quite
in tune with Curtis, though he'd tuned earlier to his own electronic
tuner. Curtis made a face. Woody sounded the harmonics softly, but
he couldn't hear what was wrong. He tried again. Curtis nodded his
head and mouthed a big "A." Woody tightened the A string just a hair.

Where was you last Saturday night,
When I was hanging 'round this old jail?
Walking the streets with another man,
And you wouldn't even go my bail.

The National Steel guitar was not really suited for bluegrass,
and when Curtis looked at him to see if he wanted to take a solo, he
shook his head. He wanted to climb right into the music, like a man
hopping a freight train, not knowing where it will take him, but he
didn't want to jump too soon and miss his footing.

When they ran out of verses they sang the chorus several times
in ten- or twelve-part harmony, some of it very close, and then Dick
Colwell from the English Department sang a song—his one and

only—full of double entendres. "Let me overhaul your car . . . A squirt of my oil would do your engine good." And then they took a break. Curtis and Larry were eager to examine the new guitar. Curtis, who had perfect pitch, strummed a chord and tweaked the strings before handing it back to Woody.

The younger children were starting to fall asleep. Their parents—junior faculty mostly, though Art Johnson from History, who was in his late fifties, had married one of his students and now had a four-year-old son—were either getting ready to take them home or carrying them into the house to put them down on one of the beds upstairs, or on the sofa in the living room, which Woody had opened up into a bed. What about bats? Nora Stout wanted to know. She was a new professor in Psychology whose husband had stayed home with their new baby and who was waiting for a chance to play "When Irish Eyes Are Smiling" on her hammered dulcimer. A few of the older children were running with the dog again, throwing the Frisbee in the dark. The dog leaped wildly into the air, as if the Frisbee were a bat. Woody coaxed a glass of beer out of the keg. Jessica Lowden, who taught philosophy, vamped a little blues in the background.

Curtis lit a cigarette, inhaled deeply, let the smoke out slowly. "Did you read that Bukka White died?" he said.

"No." There was general amazement among the three or four people who remembered Bukka White. Mike Brady from the English Department. Ed Wilson from History. Rob Griffith from Chemistry. And Mac, who preferred opera to blues.

"That man was eighty years old," Curtis said. "*Eighty* years old. You know he was here back in sixty-two or sixty-three, right before Kennedy was killed. He stayed at your place, didn't he, Woody? Isn't that when he took you into the bathroom and gave you a drink of 'soft' whisky?"

It wasn't much of a story, really, but the younger faculty hadn't heard it, and it meant something to Woody, just the way a chance encounter with a rock star would mean something to a teenager.

They played and sang for over an hour, and when they stopped at last Woody looked around him and saw a Roman soldier trying to pump another glass of beer out of the keg, and Turi Mirsadiqi and her friend Shahla coming down the path from the house with a sheet and the big nine-volt flashlight that he kept in a drawer in the pantry. She must have taken the sheet off one of the beds, he thought. Not the sort of thing *he* would have done when *he* was a student.

He'd forgotten for the moment about the arrest of Angela Strappafelci in Argentina, but he hadn't forgotten about the dean, who was still sitting in the shadows, where Woody had left her. Was she waiting for him, or was she just waiting? As he approached her Woody felt that he'd been gone a long time, like a man coming back from another country. He wasn't nervous anymore, in the darkness. He was curious, rather than anxious, about what he would find when he returned.

Two Iranian students did a stick dance in the firelight, accompanied by Nora Stout's hammered dulcimer, while Turi Mirsadiqi and Shahla Golestani were getting ready for their shadow play. Khosrow Baqirzadeh and Ahmad Zahed were holding up a sheet and Ms. Mirsadiqi was experimenting with the flashlight that she'd found in the pantry while Shahla Golestani made various figures using both her hands. Woody had seen shadow plays, which tended to be obscene, at the bazaar in Esfahan. "The Craft of Gourdmaking" had been listed on the program for the International Fair but had been canceled at the last minute, after the dean of students saw the dress rehearsal.

"This is a very moral story," Ms. Mirsadiqi said, once the flashlight had been properly positioned, "that I learned at my grandfather's summer home in Tabriz. I learned by watching the *darvish* who came every summer. My grandfather wasn't too happy when he found out I was learning shadow plays, and he sent poor Kazem away. The dean of students wasn't too happy either"—laughter— "but I don't think she will send me away.

"There once was a servant girl," Ms. Mirsadiqi went on, "who had taught a donkey how to make love to her."

She put her hands together and thrust them into the beam of light. A silhouette of the donkey appeared on the sheet.

"This servant girl was not at all stupid," she said. "She knew that a donkey is, well . . ." Ms. Golestani put one of her hands into the light and the donkey's huge penis appeared. Everyone laughed, but it was a little unnerving to see the huge penis waggling back and forth.

"She was so clever that she carved a gourd to fit over the donkey's *kir* so it wouldn't penetrate too far, a sort of *gardan band*—How do you say it in English, Professor Woodhull?—*flangia*?"

"Flange. Collar. Necklace."

"Yes, a flange or a collar. You can see it worked very well."

The two girls moved their hands and the donkey mounted the servant girl. The gourd/flange was not perfectly clear, but you could see that the huge penis had penetrated the girl only halfway.

"Well," said Ms. Mirsadiqi, "one day the mistress happened to be passing by the stable and looked in the window and saw what was going on. She was married to an old man, so of course she was eager to try what her servant girl was obviously enjoying so much, so she sent the girl away.

"The servant girl, who had had enough of the donkey for a while, was thinking, There's something you ought to know, and she tried to warn the mistress, but the mistress pretended not to understand. She was too greedy. She was dizzy with excitement, and her *kos* was glowing like a furnace."

The servant girl went away, and on the screen the mistress knelt before the donkey. You could see the silhouette of her raised buttocks jutting out just above her feet. Once again the donkey's huge penis emerged. The audience kept looking from the figures on the sheet to the hands of the two girls, trying to make the connection. This time there was no gourd; the penis disappeared entirely into the kneeling woman, penetrating her intestines and killing her instantly. The shadow woman fell to the floor; the donkey wagged his head from side to side. The penis drooped and then disappeared.

"I told you," Ms. Mirsadiqi explained, "that it was a very moral story. Now does anyone want to tell me what the moral is? I want to know if you have understood." She opened her arms, palms up, and then brought them back together and shook her clasped hands back and forth, as if she were shaking dice. Woody realized that she was imitating him. "No, no," she said, "don't look down at your feet. You are all good students here, I don't want to see you looking down at your feet. Your feet do not know the answer. You must think. Think think think," she said, and once again Woody recognized himself.

No answer.

"Well," she said, indignant. "I see that no one has understood.

Isn't it obvious? Haven't you read the Rumi? Haven't you read Hafiz?"

She waited a long time.

"Very well then, I'll have to explain. Now listen carefully. You don't want to be like that woman, do you? The mistress? Do you? Answer up!"

There was some mumbling and outbreaks of suppressed laughter.

"Then don't sacrifice your life to your animal-soul. Keep moderation in all things. Don't be too greedy for pleasure. There. Now you know."

"But what about the servant girl?" someone asked.

"Ah, now I see that at least one person is awake out there and has been paying attention." The two girls put their hands into the beam of light and once again the dark shapes appeared, first the donkey, then the penis, and then the flange. "You see, the servant girl set a limit on her pleasure. Her mistress was too eager, she wanted to take her pleasure before she had learned the craft of gourdmaking."

Another train went by as they were applauding. Woody followed the beam of the headlight till it disappeared behind the moraine.

"Isn't cultural diversity a wonderful thing," he said to the dean. "I think this would have been a great success at the International Fair. Maybe next year."

"I think it was disgusting. Did you put her up to this?"

Woody raised his hand: "Scout's honor."

"Did you?"

"No."

"That child has had too much to drink. Is she driving?"

"Khosrow will drive her home. She's not used to it."

"I suppose she's been eating pork too?"

"Yes, in fact, I believe she has."

"So this has been quite an enlightening evening for her. She's feeling emancipated. I hope her father doesn't get wind of this. I can't imagine he'd be too pleased."

"You're putting the touch on him for big bucks, right?"

"I'm not putting the 'touch' on anyone. I was thinking that that performance was disgusting. You shouldn't have encouraged her."

"It was a very moral tale. You weren't paying attention."

"Nonsense. It was titillating, that's what it was. The moral was fluff. You deal with these students by eroticizing them; you can't keep your eyes off them; you think you're mentoring them, but really . . . you're teaching them to flirt, to make sexy for you. It's the same old game."

"What about Marsha Connelly? She did honors with me last year."

"What about her?"

"She weighed in at three hundred pounds. She should have been in the beef trust."

"You see what I mean?"

"I didn't eroticize her."

"No, but you think about her as someone who weighs three hundred pounds. That's how you identify her. You were willing to work with her even though she wasn't up to your standards, and you want extra credit, a pat on the back."

"I was just saying that I didn't eroticize her."

"We both know what you were saying."

"What is it you want, Jane? Do you want me to pretend . . . Do you remember Book III of the *Iliad*—"

"No, Woody, I don't remember Book III of the *Iliad*."

"—where Helen comes down to sit on the wall with the Trojan elders? Homer says that the old men sound like cicadas, too weak for battle, but strong at gabbing:

> γήραϊ δὴ πολέμοιο πεπαυμένοι, ἀλλ᾽ ἀγορηταὶ
> ἐσθλοί, τεττίγεσσιν ἐοικότες, οἵ τε καθ᾽ ὕλην
> δενδρέῳ ἐφεζόμενοι ὄπα λειριόεσσαν ἱεῖσι.

And when the old men see Helen they say they can't be angry, they say it's no wonder that the Greeks and Trojans have gone to war over her, she's so beautiful."

"And you're asking me to applaud? A whole culture goes crazy over a beautiful woman and destroys itself?"

"I'm not asking you to applaud, Jane; I'm asking you not to deny the reality of experience, our experience of beauty. And I think that's what Homer's asking too."

"That girl's very beautiful too."

"Ms. Mirsadiqi?"

"She looks like her mother, only darker."

Woody nodded.

"You're very good friends with the mother." The dean had a way of putting things flatly so that Woody didn't know if she was asking a question or just making a simple observation.

"She was my girlfriend for a while at Michigan. We were in the same Persian class, and she was one of the Latin tutors. Who've you been talking to, anyway?"

"She taught here for a couple of years, didn't she?"

"That's how I wound up here. When she decided to go off to Iran with Alireza Mirsadiqi she called Mac from Italy and told him that she had a friend in the job market whose mother was a St. Clair alum . . ."

"And that was it?" the dean said. "No national search? Just the old-boy network at work?"

"That's right, Jane." Woody started to unfasten the snaps on his guitar case.

"She always sings your praises," the dean said, "when she's here for the trustees' meeting in the spring."

"You know something, Jane?" Woody closed one of the snaps he'd just opened. "I was thinking you and I could become good friends too."

"And?"

"There's this aura of disapproval about you. Not of what I do, but of who I am."

"Who are you?"

"I've always thought of myself as a liberal, on the right side of major social issues—I mean on the left side: racism, poverty, sexism. I voted for Kennedy, Carter, Mondale, Dukakis . . . I'm a member of Amnesty International and Common Cause. I like to think I'm someone who wants to hang on to some things that we're in danger of losing, ideals that go back to Athenian democracy and English liberalism. But from your point of view I'm an obstacle in the path of progress, an anachronism."

"Athenian democracy was a male-dominated institution based on slavery."

"That's one way of looking at it. What about English liberalism?

Locke, Hume, Mill . . . Self-determination, natural rights of the individual, constitutional limits on the powers of the state . . . No, don't answer. I don't want to hear it. You give new meaning to the word WASP, Jane."

"How's that?"

"White Antediluvian Sexist Patriarch. Do you remember when Elizabeth Feinstein was here?"

"I found her offensive."

"Right. The preeminent feminist literary scholar in the country comes to St. Clair to talk about the canon of Western literature, and you find her offensive. You know what *I* liked about her? I liked the fact that she said, 'I value the same things you value, I got into this business because I love literature, not because I want to expose its corrupt ideological assumptions; but I want to find a place for some other concerns too.' She made me want to be on her team. Even Mac wanted to be on her team, and that's saying something."

"And you don't want to be on *my* team?"

"You haven't picked me." A pause. "You know what she said about you? Afterwards? Out in the hall?"

"No, what did she say?"

"She said, 'That woman's not coming for dinner, is she?' She meant you, Jane. For what? Why do you have to be so ready to take offense? And to give offense?"

"Is there anything else? Should I expect a formal complaint? Are you going to get up a petition to send to the Board of Trustees?"

"Do you know what I had in mind? What I was planning to do? To say?"

"*Should* I know?"

"I was going to ask you to stick around after the party. I was going to ask you to . . . I was going to ask you to, oh, I don't know, just stick around."

"Is that a proposition?"

"I was just . . . eroticizing you. You know, Jane, you could be a good-looking woman, if you'll excuse me for saying so. A little makeup, a little lipstick, a little eyeliner; let your hair hang down. You don't have to look like Elizabeth Cady Stanton to be a feminist."

"I'm going to pretend I didn't hear that."

"I just thought . . ."

"You thought, She's a single woman, she'll be grateful if I make her an offer."

"Why put such a negative spin on it? How is a man supposed to proposition a woman these days? I tell you what's on my mind. You say yes or no. I don't know how else to communicate. I don't know how else men and women are going to communicate."

"What about your wife?"

"Ah, yes, my wife. I haven't seen her for two years. I can't get ahold of her. She doesn't have a phone. She doesn't answer my letters. We haven't . . . made love since Cookie's death. It did something to her. She *got* religion; I lost it."

"And now you're horny?"

"Yes, I am."

"And you want someone to service you?"

"Forget it, Jane. All signals are red. No go. I haven't been paying attention. I'm sorry." Pause. "Your hands are shaking, though. You're tough, but your heart's pounding, isn't it? You're upset. Don't be embarrassed. My hands are shaking too. Look. And my heart's pounding. It's all right. I know I'm alive."

Woody took her hand but she pulled it away.

"I'd better go."

"If that's what you want."

"That's what I said, isn't it?"

"I'll walk you to your car."

"I can make it on my own," she said, but Woody walked with her to her sensible little Corolla.

"She really said that," the dean asked when they got to the car, which was parked at the end of the drive, "about my coming to dinner?"

"She said it, but I shouldn't have told you. I'm sorry."

"And what did *you* say?"

"I said to her, 'You're a big girl, Elizabeth; you can look after yourself.'"

"And what did she say?"

"She didn't say anything. I was kidding her, because I thought *she* was kidding, but she was serious. I didn't realize how upset she was."

"All I did was . . ." She opened the car door and slipped into the seat.

"It's all right, Jane; you were just being your own good-natured self. *Shalom.*"

She said something in Hebrew that Woody couldn't follow. "Reply to a fool as his folly requires," she said in English, pulling the door closed. He wasn't sure if she was referring to him or to Elizabeth Feinstein.

The party was starting to break up. Younger faculty were packing up their children; students were standing around in groups. Woody looked for Turi Mirsadiqi but couldn't find her. He didn't want her to drive home. But there were still a few people around the fire, and Curtis was playing "Amazing Grace" and Larry Taylor was blowing on a harp and Nora Stout was playing her hammered dulcimer. Woody hurried to join them.

Curtis, who could play the banjo in any key without using a capo, was playing in D. Woody tuned the low string of the National Steel down from E to D. He knew a dozen versions of "Amazing Grace," but D was a great key. G was too, and as Curtis was finishing a banjo solo after the second verse Woody shouted, "Let's go to G." G was a little high for "Amazing Grace." You had to sing right out to hit the high notes, but that was good too.

> Through many dangers, toils, and snares,
> I have already come;
> 'Twas grace that brought me safe thus far,
> And grace will see me home.

Woody took a solo up the neck, and then they shifted back to D. Woody played the melody on the high strings but left the low D open, like a drone of a bagpipe. He looked around him. A handful of students were left, but no one was listening. The tables were empty; the beer was gone. Blind Bob Martin's wife was at his side, tugging at his arm. He had his mandolin case in one hand and was shaking hands with the other, holding his hand out for whoever would take it. He was always glad to be at these parties, always among the first to arrive and among the last to leave, and everyone was glad to have him. Mac was lying down on the couch in the living room; he'd need a ride home too. He didn't know how to drive anyway, had never owned a car, had never been married, and there was a third thing, too, that he'd never done or had; Woody forgot what. Someone else could give him a ride, but Woody wanted to get away for a minute. The party hadn't gone as he'd planned. He'd hardly played his new guitar at all, hadn't held an audience in the palm of his hand, hadn't shone as a star. But it was better this way. For a few moments he'd lost himself, lost his self, in the music, in the community of students and faculty, men and women, young and old; but now an inner bell tolled him back to his sole self, and he felt a stab of melancholy.

WOODY DROVE Mac to his apartment on Simmons Street, a block from the campus, and turned around in the lot, but instead of driving straight home he turned down Grove and went over to Seminary Street to avoid the strip. The tires of the pickup hummed on the brick streets. The humming stopped when he hit the edge of town and turned onto 150, heading west to Kruger Road. Corn stubble on his left, soybean stubble on his right. But his fit of melancholy persisted, and instead of turning off 150 onto Kruger Road he kept on going, circling around the moraine and then driving up to the cemetery. A "hard pipe of igneous rock," Terry Baylor had called the moraine, a "glacial turd." But the dean had gotten rid of the Geology Department, and Terry was now working for the U.S. Geological Survey at the University of Illinois.

There were half a dozen cars—their windows steamed up—parked in a row near Cookie's grave, but Woody found a spot between an ancient Packard that belonged to a farmer on the other side of New Cameron—at least Woody'd seen the car in the drive once on his way to Burlington—and an '85 Chevy Impala with big shocks and the struts jacked up and chrome Cragar wheels. Since Sara and Ludi had left he'd gotten into the habit of talking things over with Cookie, up in the cemetery. Just letting things come out. Not talking exactly, but directing his thoughts towards her. He'd gone over the details of the memorial service, for example, and of the reception at Lowell House; he'd described the guitar to her, and the encounter with the black clerk/owner at Crossroads Music; he'd told her that the dog had disappeared for three days, and that when she'd come back they'd driven over to see a white buffalo calf that had been born out in a field just east of New Cameron. Laska had barked and the buffalo elders had lumbered over to the fence to investigate, shaking their great heads from side to side.

Sometimes he thought she answered him, but not in a way he could really be sure of. He listened for her voice in the wind, in the leaves. The books on grief that he'd gotten from the public library after her death had told him to expect small hallucinations—her step just behind him as he entered a room, her hand on his arm, her smell in a closet or even in the bathroom—but so far this had never happened, and now it had been six years. The grief books had also led him to expect a second good-bye, a final parting or letting go, probably in a dream. But this hadn't happened either, and Woody didn't want it to happen. He dreaded the moment, in fact.

After her death he'd gone to mass for a while with Hannah. He'd grown up in the Methodist Church, and the mass seemed strange and mysterious. Incense, mystery, drama, statues, genuflecting, holy water, celibate priests. Old Father Davis, who from a distance looked like a young man, though he was older than Woody, had an Irish accent so strong that Woody couldn't understand him, even when they were talking face to face. Later Woody learned that it was a speech defect, not an accent. But after a month the mystery was gone. At least Woody's sense of mystery was gone, dissipated in the coffee hours after mass, in the incessant harping on money, in the letters from the bishop warning against birth control, till finally the mass itself seemed just a bunch of mumbo jumbo—more mumbo, more jumbo, than he could take. His body revolted even before his mind. The prospect of going to mass made him twitch. He couldn't do it. It became physically impossible.

But then what did he *really* believe? Did he have *any* convictions, anything that went beyond the sense, shared by almost everyone he knew, that life was accidental and meaningless, totally without a larger purpose? And that this didn't really matter anymore, as it had mattered for Kierkegaard and Camus, because everyone knew it and continued to live, nonetheless, just as earlier generations had lived, worrying about money, about their children, about getting laid? For years—before the new dean had done away with the freshman preceptorial program—he had lectured on Tolstoy's *Death of Ivan Ilych* to the entire entering class. You will all, he told them, live lives more or less like Ivan Ilych's. You'll finish your degree at St. Clair and have a little celebration at Jumers or the Old Mill with your parents, and maybe your girlfriend or boyfriend; you'll find a job, and you'll have an affair with a milliner and there will be carousals and visits to places in outlying districts where everything will be done *comme il faut*, in clean linen (that's clean underwear); like Ivan you'll get married, and like Ivan you'll soon discover that there's more than bed to marriage. And you'll learn to exercise power over your subordinates and to be obsequious to your boss, and to your boss's spouse; and you'll discover that you would be happy if only you had more money and a larger house.

"It's only when Ivan gets cancer, only when he begins to suffer," Woody would go on after a long pause, "that he begins to transcend this existence. Is that what it takes? Cancer? Who needs it? Are there any alternatives?

"I'll tell you one alternative, one that will cause some suffering, though it's not as bad as cancer." Pause. "That's this class that you're taking right now." Laughter. But Woody was serious. And so were his colleagues. They read Plato and the story of Abraham and Isaac, they read Sartre and Martin Luther King, and Simone de Beauvoir, and they read the great explainers of the modern world: Freud, Marx, and Darwin. They read Colin Turnbull's account of the BaMbuti in the Ituri Forest, to see if the ideas that they'd been exploring made sense in a radically different culture. It was a great course. Woody loved it. It made a kind of sense out of human life. He had great faith in books and book-learning. He was an old Gutenberg man. His life had been a life of books, and not just academic books. He'd learned to garden from a book, *The Ruth Stout No Work Gardening Book*; he'd learned to play the blues out of books by Happy Traum, Jerry Silverman, and Stephan Grossman; he'd learned to cook out of books—Julia Child, Marcella Hazan, the *Time-Life* series; he'd learned to make love out of a book too—Alex Comfort's *Joy of Sex*—or at least he'd learned a lot of things he would never have thought up on his own.

But in the end, of course, something eluded him. That he would die, and that his children would die, that everyone was subject to the laws of entropy, no longer bothered him. He had no desire to live forever. If life isn't meaningful now, in the present moment, it won't become meaningful by being prolonged indefinitely. Death, in fact, is a condition of meaning. Without it human beings, like the Greek gods, would make no significant choices, confront no limitations. Most of the people who clamor for immortality don't know what to do with themselves on a rainy Sunday afternoon. That's what he'd learned from books, and that's what he tried to get across to his students. No, it wasn't death in general that he couldn't grasp, it was Cookie's death in particular. It was Cookie who was dead, Cookie whose first sentence had been "Piggies run in houses," Cookie who'd asked "Whobody comin'?" whenever she heard someone at the door. "Where's the light?" he'd ask, and she'd point at the ceiling: "Uppy dere." And later, when she was eight or nine, she'd wander through the house repeating her favorite phrase, "a bronze head of giant proportions"—something she'd picked up from a Tiny Tim comic, one of those old ones that were about three inches square and an inch and a half thick. Cookie, whose great adventure had just begun. Death had given her life a shape. But it wasn't the shape he'd wanted. It was an ugly shape, brutal, violent. As if someone had ripped the pages out of a beautiful book so that you couldn't finish the story. Death was fine with him. But not this death.

He'd thought he was getting over it. A man can grieve for only so long. Grief wears itself out. But the arrest of Angela Strappafelci had upset him more than he'd realized. He tugged against the news like a fish tugging against a hook. Whichever direction he swam in, the hook kept tugging him back. He looked for more news. There wasn't much. The Italian government was demanding immediate extradition, but there were inevitable delays. Woody was afraid. Like a cancer patient in remission, he was alert for symptoms of recurrence. He didn't want to go through it again, through the old pain. He thought he'd gone through it and come out the other side. There were articles on della Chiave in the *New York Times* and *Newsweek* and *Time*, but there wasn't much information about Angela, except that she'd grown up in Rome and had been involved in the formation of right-wing youth groups, and that with her boyfriend, Niccolò Bosco, she'd murdered Judge DiBernardi and had shot and seriously injured seven women who worked for a radio station with left-wing leanings, and that she'd met Bosco at a neo-fascist youth camp in the Abruzzi.

You have to wonder—Woody directed his thoughts at Cookie. *Just your age.* He was thoughtful rather than angry, like a man working out a chess problem. He wondered if Cookie had ever parked up here, necked. *Did you? No, don't say anything. I hope you did. I hope you didn't miss out on anything. But it doesn't make sense, does it? Killing a judge while he's waiting for a bus to go to work. Shooting seven women at a radio station. She and her boyfriend. The neo-fascist youth camp, up in the mountains, was called Camp Hobbit. Camp Hobbit! Murdering their friend Bevilacqua. Threatening to kill Filippo Forti's son. He was their friend too. No, better not to think about it.*

Woody rolled down his window and wiped off the front window with a rag. If you sat here every morning and watched the sun come up, you'd see it gradually move across the horizon, from the Lundquist silo in the northeast to the Warren hog barn in the south-east. After a year it would come back to its starting place. But if you were a careful observer you'd see that it didn't come back to exactly the same starting place. You'd be observing the precession of the equinoxes. The problem is, you'd have to watch closely for about a thousand years before you could notice that the sun didn't come back to exactly the same place year after year. So how would you notice? How did the Greeks notice? They had Babylonian records that went back two thousand years. But how had the Babylonians noticed in the first place?

He got out of the car to pee, walking past Cookie's grave so he could pee down the slope of the moraine. From where he was stand-ing he could see the farm, a light on in the kitchen window, the campfire still flickering faintly.

"Pops." He heard a voice. He thought for a minute it might be Cookie, but she called him Pop, not Pops. The other girls called him Dad, or Daddy.

Someone else was peeing, next to the big Packard, his pants pulled all the way down to his ankles. Woody hadn't heard the car door open. A kid. No, not peeing, peeling off a rubber, looking down at what was left of an erection, having trouble hooking his thumbs under the rubber rim of the condom. When he finally got it he pulled the rubber down and tossed it high into the air where it caught on the branch of the white oak. The boy looked at Woody. "*Hey*, Pops," he yelled, and then he let out a loud whoop and hopped back into the car without pulling his pants up.

In about sixty seconds the engine started and the Packard backed out onto the road. Time to go home.

Sunday
Morning

The students had done a good job of cleaning up, but Woody's guitar was still out, sitting by what was left of the fire. He took the guitar out of the hardshell case and played a Taj Mahal song from a tape that Ludi had given him for his birthday:

> I got the blues so bad one time
> It put my face in a permanent frown;
> But now I'm feeling so much better,
> Think I'll cakewalk into town.

He looked around for the dog but there was no sign of her.

> I want to go on a picnic in the country,
> Mama, want to stay all day;
> I don't care if I don't do nothing,
> Just while my time away.

Just while my time away. Maybe it was just as well that the dean had turned him down. Turned him down flat. Hadn't thought twice; had seemed eager, in fact, to inflict pain. In his second or third year at St. Clair he'd had an article turned down by *Classical Philology*. At the bottom of the form rejection one of the referees had written "Pompous and illiterate even among our rejections," and Woody remembered how the tears had sprung to his eyes. *Pompous and illit-*

erate even among our rejections. But he'd gotten over that disappointment, and in fact the article—on the fragments of Philolaus and
Archytas—had subsequently been published in *Classical Studies.*
He'd get over this disappointment too. In fact, he was over it
already. The prospect of beginning a new life with the dean of the
college was already beginning to seem faintly preposterous. Woody
and Jane. Seasoned campaigners in the wars of love? Like Anthony
and Cleopatra? He smiled and gave a little snort. He looked around
at the tractor standing in the open door of the empty barn, and
beyond the barn at the faint line of the horizon, the rim of an
inverted bowl, a red-figure *kylix* in which the painter had laid out the
constellations, or Nestor's four-handled *depas.* He gave another
snort. Tomorrow he'd put the new float chamber in the tractor and
plow up a garden plot for the spring. And then he'd go over his
lessons for Monday. It was a truly wonderful thing, he reminded
himself, that a man could earn a living talking to young people
about Homer and Ovid and Horace. *What if the old love should
return?* But the old love would not return. He would put the
thought out of his mind. He would sink down into his old life like
an old man sinking down into an overstuffed chair. Like Nestor at
home in Pylos, or Phoenix, who had held the baby Achilles in his
arms. Old warriors.

But he wouldn't forget how the hot tears had started to his eyes
whenever he'd looked at the rejection slip, even a week later, when
he'd finally showed it to Hannah, tossing it down in front of her at
the kitchen table, casually, on top of the evening paper she was pag-
ing through, and how she'd stood behind him and kneaded his
shoulders and told him it must have been a mistake.

He went into the house, poured himself a paper cup of retsina
from a half-full bottle, glanced around for the bat, and went back
outside. He'd made light of the bats in front of the students, but in
fact he was frightened of them himself. He didn't panic the way he
used to, but he found them very upsetting. He didn't like getting up
in the night knowing there was a bat in the house, swooping around.
He couldn't rest till he'd killed it. That's why he'd spent so much
time looking for the third bat. He told himself that the students had
been excited, that Carol Nelson might have been mistaken. Maybe
there had been only two bats. But he knew he was kidding himself.

They roosted in the attic and got down into the house through the pocket door. He'd sealed up the door once, but Ludi, who wasn't afraid of anything, had unsealed it because she'd wanted to close it to keep the dog out of the dining room while she worked on one of her projects. Then when Woody and Sara came back from taking her to school, Sara opened the pocket door and a bat fell out. Taken by surprise, it must have had its sonar turned off because it fell halfway to the floor, then took off and smashed into the wall in the back of the dining room closet, landing in a Waterford crystal tumbler. Exterminators wouldn't touch them because they were an endangered species. Woody'd tried everything: insect bombs one year, mothballs the next. Two ultrasound devices, guaranteed to rid your house of mice, rats, roaches, and especially bats, had been emitting their ultrasonic sounds in the attic for two years, but so far they'd had no effect. Last year Woody tried to plug up all the holes, but he hadn't managed to find the bats' entrance.

He'd finished the glass of retsina, put the guitar in its case and carried it into the house. He found his badminton racquet—an expensive graphite racquet weighing less than three ounces that one of his students had bought for him in Indonesia—where he'd left it in the front hall. Most of the lights were still on in the house, but he walked around with his shoulders hunched, like a man leaving a crowded auditorium in the middle of a concert. The only thing to do was turn all the lights off and wait in the dark till it started flying around again. He sat in the dark in the living room and waited a few minutes. Then he took out his guitar again and played softly: "Woke up this morning feeling so good I lay back down again. Roll your big leg over me, Mama; I may not feel this good again." He didn't like the repetition of "again," though it didn't bother him when Taj Mahal sang it. Taj Mahal played a National Steel guitar too, a tricone like Woody's.

He waited, a hunter in a blind. He took the guitar strap off so he could put the guitar down in a hurry. The badminton racquet was on the couch beside him. It was dark, but not so dark you couldn't see. The song ran through his head and through his fingers. When he stopped playing and listened he could hear lots of noise. A regular racket. Things in the walls. Things from the surrounding fields, looking for a winter home. He put down poison once a year, right after the first frost. It was the price you paid for living in the country. Snakes. Rats. Mice. All looking for a home. They didn't really bother him, not even the snakes. But the bats spooked him.

He was startled by footsteps. It was the dog walking around upstairs. He waited for her to come down. The click of her nails on the hardwood stairs drowned out all the other sounds except the sound of Woody's heart. He forgot about the bat. The dog came running into the room, and Woody patted her head; but he could still hear footsteps upstairs. He put down the guitar and picked up the badminton racquet. He was standing behind the piano, fiddling with the lamp switch, when a dark figure came through the pocket door, wrapped, or tangled, in a sheet.

"Distinguished Professor . . ." the figure said, in Persian. It was Turi Mirsadiqi. Her speech was a little slurred.

Woody managed to turn on the lamp, which had a defective switch.

"Ms. Mirsadiqi?"

"Distinguished Professor . . ." she said again, and then, in English, "I thought you'd never come back."

"Shame on you," he said. "A good Muslim girl, drunk as a skunk."

"I've never been drunk before."

"How do you like it?"

"But I've smoked a *huqqu* . . ."

"Which do you prefer?"

"I don't know yet."

"I saw you eating pork, too."

"That's another thing I've never done before."

"Was it tasty?"

"It was delicious. It was heavenly. But it upset my stomach."

"Where's your car?"

"Shahla drove it back."

"Does she know you're here?"

"No one knows. I told her I'd get a ride with someone later on."

"I see."

"There's something else I've never done too."

"I'm sure there are many things."

"Do you want to know what it is?"

Woody wasn't sure he wanted to know. "Look," he said, "you can sleep on the couch. I'm tired. I'm going to bed."

"Don't you want to know?"

"I can guess."

"Go ahead."

"But if I guess wrong, I'm in trouble; and if I guess right, I'm in bigger trouble."

"You won't get in trouble. Guess."

"You're too rich," he said. "You've been spoiled all your life. You expect everyone to fall in with your wishes."

"Wrong," she said. "Baba was always very strict, especially with me. My brothers could do anything, but I . . ." She seemed to lose her train of thought.

"And what would he do if he could see you now?"

"But he can't see me now. Anyway, I don't want to think about that."

"Maybe you should. It might cool you off."

"Why are you angry?"

"I'm not angry."

"You're shouting."

Woody took her by the arm and forced her down on the sofa.

"I'm frightened when I lie down."

"Why?"

"Because everything moves. Like on a ship." She stuck her hands out and tried to sit up.

"Do you need to use the bathroom?"

She nodded.

"This way." He helped her through the dining room into the kitchen. There was a toilet and sink in the laundry room off the kitchen. He closed the door behind her and within seconds could hear her throwing up. What an unpleasant sound, he thought. And then he thought, What funny noises our bodies make. How they betray us. And then he thought, No, it's the other way around. We betray our bodies by our ridiculous behavior, and by our imagination . . . He was still trying to work this thought into a satisfactory shape when she emerged from the laundry room, white as a sheet, white as her makeshift chador.

"Feel any better?"

"I'm sorry." She started to cry. "It's so embarrassing."

He could see that she was naked under her chador.

"Where are your clothes?"

"In your bedroom. On the floor."

Woody maneuvered her back to the couch and went upstairs to get a pillow and a comforter and a pair of loose-fitting pajamas, fastened round the waist by a string, that he'd brought back from Esfahan over twenty-five years ago and which he'd worn on Sunday mornings.

"Put these on," he said. "I'll get a bucket in case you have to throw up again." He left a light on in the kitchen and one in the front hall so she wouldn't have to stumble around in the dark. A little while later, while he was making a final check for the bat, he heard her making her way to the bathroom again.

WHEN WOODY woke at about six-thirty he thought for a minute that his wife was pushing up against him, and then he thought that the dog had climbed up onto the bed again, and then realized that it was Ms. Mirsadiqi. Turi. He froze. He could feel her at his back. He turned his head slowly but couldn't see her. He seemed to be wrapped up tight in his own flannel sheet. Like a mummy. Or a child in swaddling clothes. He waited for a couple of minutes before trying to extricate himself, slowly, without disturbing her. He could feel her breath on the back of his neck—not too nice. Fetid. He couldn't pick out parts of her but thought he could feel the pressure of her breasts on his back, small but firm. Or perhaps he was just imagining the pressure.

She put an arm around him, and it took him a minute to realize that she was awake, deliberately holding on, that she wasn't going to let him go. Next to the alarm clock, which now said 6:42 in large red numerals, he noticed a box of spermicide suppositories and a bright yellow box of Ramses lubricated condoms. She had come prepared. But he had to go to the bathroom. He pulled away from her.

In the bathroom, standing at the toilet, he wished, for the thousandth time, that the well water wasn't so full of sulfur, wished that they didn't have to drink bottled water. At the same time he was considering his position, trying to imagine what Plato would advise, or Aristotle, or Tolstoy, or C. S. Lewis. His leading moral lights. About sexual intercourse with a young woman he neither loved nor cherished, though she was in fact his best student; and, coincidentally, the daughter of his oldest friend, his first lover.

What he had told the dean about Turi's mother, Allison Mirsadiqi, was not strictly true, for he had in fact made love to Allison in Bologna, after the *strage*. Several times; more times than he could count. In his hotel room and in hers. While Hannah was in the hospital, thinking she was Mary Magdalene, offering herself to the doctors as a prostitute for Christ but becoming hysterical when Woody came into the room, blaming him for sending Cookie away, to Harvard, to Italy; and Cookie herself in the morgue, in a sealed lead vault, waiting to be shipped home. He had never spoken of this to anyone, not even to Allison, not even to himself, for it violated his sense of who he was, deep in the core of his being, his sense of himself as a man who had been faithful to his wife for almost thirty years, as a man who had always brought reason to bear on his passions and desires. He told himself that it had been an aberration, that he'd been half-crazed with grief, that he'd turned to Allison as another man might have turned to wine, that he'd knelt between her thighs as another man might have knelt before the holy virgin in San Petronio. And maybe he had. But so what?

So what? he asked himself now. Why had he struggled so hard for so long to deny what he suddenly could see as clearly as he could see his reflection in the mirror over the sink: that she had saved his life, and even his soul, had kept him from following Hannah over the edge of madness? The fact was so simple that it stunned him, as if someone had slapped his face. The gift of her body was what she'd given him, all that she had, no small thing. Why had he never spoken of it to her, afterwards, back in St. Clair? Why had he pretended for seven years that nothing had passed between them?

And now, though he had not experienced real lust for a woman since that time in Bologna, he wished that he had paid more attention to the debate over the new sexual harassment policy, which had occupied hundreds, perhaps thousands, of hours of faculty time. But so what? he asked himself again, knowing that this truth too was perfectly simple and clear. He turned on the water and waited till it ran hot. This truth was that he wasn't worried about what Plato or Aristotle or Tolstoy or C. S. Lewis would say; he wasn't worried about the new policy on sexual harassment; he was worried about—well, he was just worried. After seven years he wasn't sure that he even knew what to do. It was true that in the last few weeks, ever since the memorial service, his libido had mysteriously begun to reassert itself, but at this particular moment, contemplating his own face in the mirror as he dried his hands, he felt no particular desire. If Ms. Mirsadiqi had been more experienced, then it would be a different matter. She would know what to do, what to expect. His wouldn't be such a grave responsibility. He thought about the dean. It was hard to know about the dean. For all her gruff ways she seemed less threatening than Turi Mirsadiqi. But perhaps that was because she was far away, or at least at a safe distance, whereas Ms. Mirsadiqi was waiting for him in his bedroom.

When he went back to the bedroom she was sitting on the edge of the bed, and he thought for a moment that she was going to get up and leave, and at that moment he knew his own mind, his own heart. He could count the number of women he'd made love to on the fingers of one hand—a prostitute in Chicago who'd later married an alderman from the Third Ward, a one-night stand on the torn leather sofa in the basement of Adams House at the U of M, and then Allison, and then Hannah. He was flooded with memories of these women, their touches and tastes, borne downstream on a powerful current. And so when Ms. Mirsadiqi slipped off the pajama bottoms he had given her and lay back with her head on the pillow, he was overwhelmed. He could see that her breasts, under her pajama top, were lopsided, like her mother's, but what reminded him most strongly of Allison was not her appearance but her matter-of-factness, the matter-of-fact way she raised her knees, the matter-of-fact way she inserted one of the bright blue suppositories before pulling up the flannel sheet, waiting now, he thought, for him to show her the way.

"Would you mind?" she said, sticking her hand out from under the soft blue sheet. She was holding a condom in a yellow foil packet between her first two fingers. He had an erection now. Full and hard, straining. He couldn't imagine what he'd been afraid of. He took off his robe so she could see it, to establish the fact of it, so that in case it went away later, they'd have a point of reference.

"Ramses," he said. "I wonder if it's Ramses the First or Ramses the

97

Second? Probably the Second. He lasted such a long time. Maybe that's why they named these Ramses. I never thought of that."

She patted the bed beside her.

"During the reign of Ramses the Second," he said, "Egypt enjoyed a period of unprecedented splendor." She's been playing with herself, he thought; she's ready to go. He tore open the foil packet, rolled the rubber over his prick. "You're not taking any chances, are you!" He knelt between her knees, nestling the tip of his penis, sheathed in smooth lambskin with a reservoir tip, between her lips for almost a full minute till the sensation became almost unbearable. Why do we attribute such importance to these sensations, these pricklings? A little bit of skin, hardly a square inch, touches another square inch of skin . . . not even actually touching, in this case. A tiny bit of friction overwhelms us. Remolds us. Makes us new.

Aristotle?

Plato?

Tolstoy?

C. S. Lewis?

The poets knew better; at least Sappho did: *I'm covered with cold sweat; my limbs tremble.*

"Are you OK?" she asked.

"Yes. Perfectly fine."

She pulled him into her, squeezing his buttocks with her hands.

He was Zeus fucking Hera on Mount Ida; he was Ares, Anchises, Odysseus, fucking Aphrodite, Venus, Calypso. He was Catullus fucking Lesbia, Ovid fucking Corinna—what shoulders, what arms, what breasts, what firm young thighs. But it was another line from Sappho that occupied his mind, from a fragment addressed to Eros: λέπτον / δ᾽ αὔτικα χρῶι πῦρ ὑπαδεδρόμηκεν—a subtle flame has gotten under my skin. But this flame wasn't so subtle. The suppository, in fact, was red hot, literally hot. He felt as though he'd dipped his prick into a bowl of warm lye. Ms. Mirsadiqi began to flop around like a fish in the bottom of a boat, or like a rodeo bull coming out of the chute. It was all Woody could do to hold on.

The suppository really *was* hot, really hot. He couldn't be sure that his penis was still there, or that he even had a penis. He pulled it out a little to check.

"How do you like this, Distinguished Professor?" she said in Persian. "Are you enjoying yourself?"

The dog had come into the room and was fussing around the bed, nudging Woody's leg with her head and whining. The more Woody tried to hold Ms. Mirsadiqi steady, the more she thrashed. He let all his weight fall on her and held her wrists up over her head. It was like holding someone underwater. Like trying to drown a strong swimmer.

She finally settled down. "What's the matter?"

"*Niente*," he said, "but slow down. *Piano, piano.*"

The fire was dying down a little. He could feel his prick again, get a sense of its shape; no permanent damage had been done. The alarm clock went off. He reached over to turn it off and knocked a book onto the floor, a Dick Francis novel. He was still holding her down, trying to look into her eyes, like a fighter pilot trying to lock in on enemy radar. You can't really look someone in the eyes. Only in the eye. You can't focus on both eyes at the same time. Woody jumped back and forth, from one eye to the other.

"What are you looking at?" She smiled, and her smile triggered a more abundant eruption of . . . what? Love? Affection? Endorphins? That was something else Woody had learned from a book— *endorphins.*

She struggled free and began thrashing around again. Woody couldn't hold out any longer, but the heat of the suppository was still so great that he could hardly feel himself coming. He would have moved gently on top of her to bring her to a climax, but she jerked too violently, like a bucking horse, and tossed him off.

He went into the bathroom to flush the Ramses down the toilet and then went downstairs to let the dog out. When he came back into the bedroom she was up on one elbow, looking very pleased with herself.

"Well," he said, "you can check that off your list of things you haven't done before."

"Oh," she said, "I've done it lots of times, quite a few times, any-way."

Woody was surprised. "Last night you said . . ."

"You never guessed what *it* was."

"I assumed . . ."

"I've done *it*, but I've never . . . *abam nemiyad;* I've never had a . . . you know."

"I see. Then I would have guessed wrong."

"So you see, I still have something left to experience. Now do you mind if I ask you a personal question?"

"Go ahead."

"Did my mom . . . *abesh miyad* right away?"

"Ms. Mirsadiqi!" he said.

"You can call me Turi," she said.

"Turi," he said, but he still didn't know what to say.

"Well?"

"Turi," he said, "you just don't *talk* about some things."

She put her hand under her pajama top and scratched one of her breasts. "Why not?"

"You just don't."

"I just want to know," she said.

"Your mother didn't tell you about . . ."

"No," she said, "just that you were friends in Ann Arbor. But I have ears. I hear things. And Baba Joon is always asking about you. He's very curious. I put two and two together. Now tell me, did she . . . *abesh miyad* right away?"

"No," Woody said, "it took a while. But we were both pretty inexperienced. At least I was. I didn't know what to do, how to . . ."

"How long?"

"Well, two or three months before you could count on it."

"I don't want to wait that long."

"You've never come?"

"I have, yes, but not with a man. In the bathtub. The spray from a hose. I let it run over me."

Woody didn't know what to say.

"Do you think we could do it again?"

"I think you'd better go home."

"That's it? Slam bam thank you ma'am? Are you kidding?"

Woody was sitting on the edge of the bed, running his hands over her. She had the sheet pulled up to her chin. "Did you see *Something Wild*," he asked, "when they showed it in the Union in September?"

"Yes."

"Is that where you learned to . . . be so active? You're trying to be like Melanie Griffith?"

Turi sat up and pulled her pajama top up to her neck, exposing her breasts. "Is anything wrong with that?"

"Not exactly *wrong*."

"Tell me."

"You might want to slow down a little. Take it easy. Did you see Sonia Braga in *Dona Flor and Her Two Husbands*?"

"No, but we could get it and watch it this afternoon."

"I don't have a VCR."

"We could rent one."

"I don't have a TV."

"We could watch it in the dorm, or . . . or you could tell me all about it, every detail."

Woody didn't go to the temple for his Hebrew lesson at ten o'clock. Instead they made love again, with a lubricated Ramses, but without a suppository, and though she didn't come to an earth-shattering climax, she experienced a pleasant tingling sensation, like the sensation she felt when she let a jet of water play over her in the tub, that augured well. They were both pleased with themselves, flushed with the sense of well-being that follows the sudden satisfaction of long-dammed-up appetites.

WOODY FIXED bacon and eggs on a griddle and she sat at the kitchen table, wearing his robe over the pajama top and a pair of panties, and told him about the first chapter of her honors thesis, "The Ring of Gyges." Woody had put on a pair of jeans and a white shirt. An earlier version of the story—earlier than Herodotus or Plato—had been discovered in 1972 by Russian archaeologists at a dig at Al-Qurnah, in southern Iraq, near the ancient city of Nineveh. The story of Gyges was a small part of eleven clay tablets that had been transcribed and published by Professor Farzad Dihqani at the Oriental Institute in Chicago, and Professor Dihqani had agreed to be Turi's outside honors examiner. A number of scholars had commented on the significance of the discovery, but the only thing they agreed on was that the magic ring discovered by Gyges, which is not mentioned by Herodotus, was not, as had been previously thought, Plato's invention.

Woody was pouring the last of the coffee from the pot into his cup when he looked out the window and saw the dean's little red Corolla coming up the drive.

"Holy shit," he said. "You better get upstairs. The dean's here. Just leave the paper."

"I need something to read."

"There're plenty of books upstairs. Just get out of here."

She ducked up the back stairway, closing the door behind her. Woody rinsed out her coffee cup and stuck her plate, unwashed, up in the cupboard above the sink, out of sight.

The dean was wearing jeans and a ragg sweater and carrying a large grocery sack from the Eagle. She'd let her hair down.

Woody had slipped on an old hunting jacket and was trying to open the door as she climbed up the back porch steps and looked in the window. He fumbled with the deadbolt, as if it were the combination to a safe—his fingers were trembling—and opened the door, afraid he wouldn't be able to speak. But he opened his mouth and words came out: "Are you the truant officer? I'm sorry, I skipped school this morning." He remembered how hard she'd been the night before, and the expression on her face when he'd asked if she wanted to stick around. He couldn't tell her that he was not the same person who had propositioned her; couldn't tell her that everything had changed. "I was just heading in to the office," he said. His voice seemed unnaturally high to him, but the dean didn't seem to notice.

"In your slippers?"

"Yes," he said. "I was going to put on my shoes."

"Truce," she said. "I don't blame you for skipping school. I brought a peace offering." She held out the paper sack, which contained a large can of tomato juice, a lemon, and a small bottle of vodka. "I hope you've got some Worcestershire," she said. "I had it out on the kitchen table, but I forgot to put it in the sack." She was a little nervous too and kept on talking. "We started pronoun endings this morning. You know, some of those women don't have a clue, and Mrs. Goldfarb's daughter is going to drive me up the wall. Today she said, 'You're a doctor, but not the kind that does anybody any good.' I could have slapped her." She looked at the table. "How'd you manage to get the *New York Times*? I've always thought that was the worst thing about this place: you can't get the *Times* on Sunday morning."

It was time to decide; time to stick boldly to his lie; time to carry the grocery sack back outside, to suggest that they get together later, maybe go out to dinner, but later, after he'd graded a set of papers, after he'd gone over the readings for Monday's classes. But he couldn't think quickly enough and the moment passed. He put the sack down on the counter by the sink. He thought he might just tell her that . . . But what could he tell her? He needed time to think. "It's last week's," he said. "I pick it up on Tuesday and then save it for Sunday morning."

She turned to face him. "You don't mind being a week behind?"

"Most people think I'm more than a week behind! Maybe a couple of millennia." He couldn't tell her that it was too late, that youth and beauty . . . And yet that wasn't what he meant.

"I've been thinking about what you said," she went on, "about the English liberals . . . and about Elizabeth Feinstein. She really said that about me?"

It was the same question she'd asked the night before. "What's that?" he said. He put his hands in his pockets to keep them from shaking.

"'That woman's not coming for dinner, is she?'" The dean lined up the vodka, the tomato juice, and the lemon on the counter. "Take your jacket off," she said, "stay a while; I'll fix you a drink."

Woody didn't want a drink, but he didn't know how to refuse without making *brutta figura.*

"Glasses are in the cupboard, over the sink."

"Worcestershire?"

He took off his jacket and hung it on a hook by the door. "She was a little upset," he said. "The Worcestershire's on the shelf, to your left. Maybe she's not used to being challenged like that. You can be a little unsettling."

"All I said was that the obvious pleasure faculty take in student bloopers reveals a certain amount of hostility or aggression. 'Magellan circumcised the globe with his clipper.' She even admitted that it probably wasn't genuine. It doesn't *sound* genuine, does it? It sounds made up."

He thought that if he could ask her to leave and come back in an hour . . . "Maybe you've got a point," he said, "but *her* point was obviously something else, and it was pretty clear that she does *not* harbor a lot of hostility towards her students. It's the loss of a common tradition that she was getting at." Woody had thought this through so many times he didn't have to concentrate on what he was saying. "Our students don't have a grasp of their own past, of Western culture. And now everyone is pushing to have them learn about other people's traditions. When they don't know a damn thing about their own. Every culture initiates its children into its own history; it tells them its own stories. This is true of the BaMbuti. It's true of the Chinese. It's true of the American Indians. There's only one culture in the world that would even dream of starting out by telling its children the stories of other cultures before they know the stories of their own. The notion that we should operate this way is unique to the West. The unique thing about our culture is that most of our children know little or nothing about it. No sense of their own past. Blacks and women are right to claim their own histories. These histories tell them who they are. They enrich their lives. The rest of us ought to do the same. When I was living in Esfahan the students *memorized* the Ghoran—young children too. They didn't sit around in a classroom and discuss it or analyze it, as if it were just one voice among many. They *lived* it."

"Good grief, Woody, you're shaking. It's all right; calm down; I'm nervous too; I'm sorry; I didn't come here to argue with you." She paused. "You're afraid, aren't you." She reached out to touch him but he pulled away. "You don't have to be afraid of me, Woody, at least not this morning."

"Why *did* you come?" he said, knowing as he spoke that it was the wrong thing to say, but unable to help himself.

She stepped back and looked straight at him, pursing her lips. "Don't put me on the spot."

"You wanted to tell me that you've changed your mind."

"Yes, I suppose so."

"You're going to replace Mac when he retires? Classics will continue as a full major, not part of World Lit? We'll go back to teaching Tolstoy and Plato and Marx and Freud?"

She looked at him in surprise. "Not about *that*, Woody. Don't be a putz. Don't make me say it. You wanted me to stick around last night and I didn't do it. I was too proud. Well, here I am. Do you want me to eat humble pie? Give me another serving, it's delicious."

He hadn't meant to put her on the defensive. "No no no. Jane. It's just that I never know where I stand with you."

"You can't figure it out now?"

Standing in front of the kitchen window, her face dark, she raised her glass to him and they both drank. The tomato juice stained her upper lip, which she wiped with the back of her hand, and Woody seemed to catch a glimpse of her as a young woman, as she had been twenty years earlier. Vulnerable, but brave, looking ahead, not back. A train went by and they had to raise their voices.

"I wish I were on that train," she said.

"It's a freight train; you wouldn't be very comfortable. Besides, it's going towards Chicago, not California."

"You know what I mean. I've been here four years. You'd think I'd get used to it."

"The Midwest?"

"But I don't. I feel like I'm just passing through; it's not home."

"Some people go native. Others . . ."

"What about you, Woody? Have you gone native?"

"I *am* native. Michigan, not Illinois. But the Midwest."

"This feels like home to you?"

"It *is* home. I raised three daughters here. One of them's buried here. I'll be buried here."

"My parents are buried in Queens." She smiled. "At least they could have built this place on the river."

"The founding fathers were Protestants, Jane, they were WASP farmers. They picked the best land they knew how to pick: flat and rich."

Woody heard footsteps upstairs. The dean looked up.

"The dog," Woody said, alarmed. He turned his back to the dean and poured the rest of his Bloody Mary into the sink. She didn't notice. He could imagine himself in a TV sitcom, or a French farce, or a Restoration drama; but he couldn't imagine what would happen next.

"When President Hanson called to see if I was interested in the dean's job, I thought it was a joke. I thought someone was pulling my leg. I'd lost my job at Columbia. I was suing the university. I was a New York Jew who'd never set foot off pavement, except in Central Park. And then I flew out to O'Hare to meet with your search committee. With you, Woody. You were there. A bunch of friendly midwesterners, inviting me to be their leader. It was impossible to refuse. Ideologically impossible too. We need more women in administration."

"And you didn't have anywhere else to go."

"That's true too, but something would have turned up."

"Do you think we made a mistake? Or that you made a mistake?"

"The nearest bookstore is in Iowa City. One hundred fifty miles. The nearest opera house is the Chicago Lyric . . . It's like living in a foreign country. It loses its freshness after a while. DeKalb Corn signs. Pioneer Corn signs. Pfister. Swanson. Grain elevators. Republicans."

"You can get kalamata olives and good Parmesan cheese at Cornucopia. Two years ago you had to go to Chicago. I used to buy ten pounds of Parmesan at a time, and olives in twenty-eight-pound buckets."

"I know, I know, and good French bread at the new bakery, and challah during Rosh Hashanah and Yom Kippur. 'Man cannot live by bread alone.' Women either, or neither."

"Still a complaining Jew."

"That's my signature."

She hadn't finished her Bloody Mary, but Woody started to make a pot of coffee. The dog was yapping at the door, wanting to come in.

"I think you're the one who's changed *your* mind," she said.

"How's that?"

"Last night you wanted me to stick around. That's the way you put it. 'Stick around.' Not very romantic, Woody, but I like that. I'm not very romantic myself. I think romance is overdone. But here I am . . . and you're not making it easy for me. Payback time?"

"No, Jane."

"What if I *had* stayed?"

"I would have liked that."

"But here I am now."

"Can I make a proposal?"

"I'm all ears."

"I'm a little hungover; I've got a lot of papers to grade; I was just on my way to the office, in fact. Why don't I take you out to dinner, about seven o'clock. Something nice. We'll go to Stephanie's in Peoria. I haven't had a good French dinner in ages. I used to cook French, but now I do mostly Italian, Italian and Chinese."

"And then?"

"And then? Jane, I hardly know what to say, I . . ."

"You seem very cautious."

"A man my age . . ."

At that moment the door to the back stairway flew open, and Ms. Mirsadiqi—Woody hadn't heard her footsteps on the stairs—stood framed in the doorway, stark naked from head to tail.

"Oh," she said. "Excuse me. I didn't know you had company." She stood in the doorway, letting them have a good look. Hers was not one of the bulb-shaped bodies that became popular in the late Middle Ages; hers was a classical body in a classical pose, feet firmly planted, so you could see how her weight was distributed. Her light brown skin looked as if it had been oiled.

Woody was as surprised as Achilles had been when Athena suddenly appeared to warn him not to kill Agamemnon.

"Sorry," she said, and disappeared up the back stairs.

"She spent the night," Woody said, "because she'd drunk too much last night. She was sick. I put her down on the couch." But the dean was already stuffing the vodka bottle back in the grocery sack. "It's not what you think, Jane, really. She was too drunk to go home last night. She was here when I got back from driving Mac home. She slept on the couch . . . I'd forgotten all about her."

The dean was too angry to speak—at least that was Woody's immediate impression—and he didn't blame her; or maybe she was too close to tears. That was the impression he had later, when he replayed the scene, as he often did, in the theater of his imagination. Just before she left she moved towards him and raised her hand, as if to touch his face. He thought later that she'd been on the edge of tears, and his heart went out to her, a complaining Jew who'd lost her job at Columbia and found herself in the Midwest, a long way from home. But maybe it was just a look of anger and disgust. Maybe her hand had been raised to slap him.

He stood at the window and watched her walk down to the drive. He heard the car door slam and then the sound of the engine revving as she backed around in a half circle and drove out the long driveway and without stopping turned left on Kruger Road.

Woody put on his shoes and slipped on his hunting jacket and called the dog. He thought of taking his shotgun; he wouldn't have minded killing something, but he didn't want to clean and oil the gun afterwards. He went west on Kruger Road till he hit Warren Woods and then he walked through the woods all the way to the Spoon River. He followed the old tow path down to New Cameron, a town so small you couldn't get a cup of coffee there unless you knocked on someone's door and asked for one. The cemetery made famous by Edgar Lee Masters was about fifteen miles upriver, in Lewiston. An Italian poet had written an anthology about the bombing, modeled on *The Spoon River Anthology*, in which the victims, identified only by the numbers that had been chalked on their wooden coffins, spoke. It wasn't exactly maudlin, but its intention was to uplift the reader, and Woody had never cared for it. He'd received a copy from the Association of the Families of the Victims, along with the newsletter that came every six months.

He couldn't even remember Cookie's verse in the *Antologia per una strage, 15 agosto 1980*, but he remembered her coffin number: 84. She was one of the last to die.

The dog, unaware of his mood, or else trying to counter it, bounded with joy. She stuck her nose into the cold muddy river; she leaped into the air; she turned and turned on her own tail. Given the chance, who wouldn't want to experience that pure animal joy? Woody *had* felt it that morning, in bed with a young woman, but now he could hardly swallow his anger.

They walked for almost four hours, following the river down to Odell, and then circling back through Warren Woods—a patch of virgin forest, now part of the state park system but without the concession stands—till they hit Township Road 500N. About four o'clock the dog disappeared, but she was waiting for Woody when he came out of the woods behind the Lundquist place, about a mile from his own driveway. It was getting dark. He could see the farm across a field of dry cornstalks—Curtis had switched to no-till planting and hadn't plowed the stalks under this year—but it was fading, gradually disappearing into the night. He looked for a light, but the windows of the house were dark, and he realized he was disappointed. The anger that he'd been nursing all afternoon—anger sweeter than honey—now seemed pointless, wasted.

He still had the bat to deal with. He would eat a little supper and then read his Dick Francis novel in the bedroom, with the door closed, till nine o'clock or so, and then he would patrol the house, looking for the bat. If he didn't find it at nine he'd go back to the bedroom and try again at ten. He stopped to pet the dog, who had run to meet him. He really didn't want to deal with it, didn't want to sit there in the dark waiting. A man shouldn't be afraid in his own house. He thought he might go somewhere, stay overnight with Curtis, or with Mac. But how would he explain? Curtis would laugh at him; and Mac, Mac who loved him like a son . . . Mac would be sympathetic, but he'd tell everyone and soon it would be all over campus.

When he opened the kitchen door, however, he knew at once that she was still there, waiting for him in the dark. He tried to summon up his anger, but in fact he was relieved. She was stretched out on the sofa in the living room, reading a book in the semi-dark. She didn't look up till he cleared his throat.

"I thought you'd be gone by now."

"I don't have my car."

"I forgot about that. You could have called someone."

"How would *that* look?"

"What does it matter now, after that business this morning? What were you thinking of?"

"I wanted to stake my claim on you. I wouldn't have done anything if you hadn't invited her out to dinner. You were going to dump me."

"What was I supposed to do?"

"Think. Think think think think think. That's what you tell us."

"I couldn't think of anything. Besides . . ."

"I think you're what I need right now," she said. We've been reading parts of Goethe's *Conversations with Eckermann* in my German class. Goethe thought it would be a good idea if he fell in love with an older woman."

"So he had an affair with Charlotte von Stein?"

"Right."

"First he has the plan or the idea, and *then* he falls in love? And that's your plan? To fall in love with an older man?"

"Right."

"As part of your educational agenda?"

"Why not?"

"God save us. I'm old enough to be your father."

"Oh, Professor Woodhull, don't be a bore. Think about your Justice Douglas, and your Senator Thrumann . . ."

"Thurmond," Woody corrected her. "They're in their eighties, for heaven's sake."

"Right, and you're only fifty, am I right?"

"Fifty-three."

"So you have another twenty or thirty years to go. And think of your Frank Sinatra. Besides, it's only for a few months, then I'll be gone."

Standing in the dark, Woody turned on the lamp by the piano so he could see her. The switch was defective and he had to wiggle it back and forth between his fingers before the light came on. He saw the bat right away. Not flying, but perching, or roosting, on the wall, clinging to the rough plaster near the ceiling.

"Don't move," he said.

"What's the matter?"

"Just don't move, OK? There's a bat on the wall behind you. I'll get my badminton racquet."

"You're not going to kill it?" She turned to look at the bat.

"Of course I'm going to kill it."

"I don't see it."

"There, on the wall, by the piano, right up at the ceiling. I'm going to close the pocket door so that if it starts flying around it won't be able to get out of the living room."

"It's so small."

"You sound like Ludi," he said.

He closed the pocket door behind him and went to look for the badminton racquet. He'd been the intramural champion at one time, defeating Insiang Xi, a Chinese-Malaysian student, in a match played before an audience of about twenty people in the old

Women's Gym. Not front-page news, but a small triumph. He and Xi had become close friends, and then Xi had been killed by killer bees in Costa Rica. But that was twenty years ago.

It took him almost five minutes to find the racquet, which he'd left on the dresser in the bedroom. When he got back Turi was standing on the piano bench, her arm outstretched towards the bat.

"What are you doing?"

"What does it look like I'm doing?"

"Don't touch it, for Christ's sake."

"Why not?"

"It could be rabid."

"I don't think so."

"What do you mean you don't think so? How the hell would you know?"

"I have my secret means."

"Turi, get down."

"Just a minute." Her hand closed around the bat and plucked it gently from the wall. "There," she said, bringing the bat close to her face and making little cooing noises. "Turi Joon will look after you."

"Jesus Christ, Turi, I can't believe you."

"Don't be upset, Professor Woodhull. I've done this before, you know."

"No, I didn't know. Is there anything you haven't done?"

She was still standing on the piano bench. "Have *you* done it?"

"Picked up a bat? No."

She stroked the bat with her finger. "This little bat wouldn't hurt you. She wants to be friends."

"How do you know it's a she?"

"She feels like she's pregnant. I can feel little bumps on her tummy."

"God almighty, Turi. Take it outside."

"I want *you* to hold her."

"Forget it."

"Really, Professor Woodhull. You have taught me many good things; now I'd like to teach you something. What are you afraid of?"

"I'm not afraid. It's just . . ."

"You *are* afraid, afraid of a little tiny bat."

Woody took a deep breath. "All right," he said.

She stepped down off the bench and came towards him.

"It'll get away when you try to hand it to me."

"Not if you hold her wings, like this."

"I don't know."

"I do. Here, give me your hand."

Woody held out his hand. Turi put her closed fist in his hand and slowly opened her fingers. "Wrap your hand around mine." Woody wrapped his fingers around hers and closed his eyes. She pulled her hand away and he closed his fingers around the bat. At first the bat struggled. He could feel the wings trying to expand.

"Don't squeeze her too hard," she said. "Just hold her."

Woody stood motionless, holding the bat in his outstretched hand.

"There," she said, "that's not so bad."

He didn't know if she was talking to him or to the bat.

"Now what?"

"What does it feel like?"

The bat had relaxed a little. No longer trying to open its wings, it hummed or thrummed in his closed fist, like a little dynamo.

"What does it feel like?" she asked again.

"I don't know. It feels like a bat."

"What else?"

"I don't know."

"Think think think think think."

"I don't know."

"It feels like my *kos* felt this morning," she said. "The second time."

"That's right," he said, laughing a little. "You're right. A cunt; a cunt with wings."

Turi opened the pocket door and they went into the front hall. She opened the front door and they stepped out onto the porch. It was almost dark now, and still warm. Probably not much below sixty. The sky was clear.

"Just let it go," she said. "Gently. Don't throw it; just toss it."

Woody did as she said. The bat dropped almost to the ground

before catching itself and thrusting upwards like a swimmer coming up from the bottom of a pool. It disappeared into the night, and Woody experienced a sudden sinking sensation, as if like the bat he too had been tossed up into the night air and would now have to spread his wings to keep himself from falling.

Christmas
1986

Woody sat down to Thanksgiving dinner with a dozen international students—Thai, Chinese, a tiny Japanese girl who ate twice as much as anyone else, an Indonesian student whose father was a butcher and who had carved the turkey so skillfully that there wasn't enough meat left on the bones for a good soup; an Italian whose parents lived in Argentina, not a strong student, but he spoke eight languages fluently; Samer Al-Nimr, whose father was a sheikh; Turi herself and two other Iranian students from Italy, Turi's friend Shahla Golestani and a young man, Gholam Mordad, who was a Zoroastrian but who didn't eat pork because his mother was a Muslim. Most holidays slip right through your fingers, not much more than excuses for a long weekend, but Thanksgiving's got deep roots; the labor unions and the government together weren't strong enough to root it out and transplant it to a Monday. And yet it's a simple holiday; it doesn't carry all the emotional baggage of Christmas—a good American holiday. Besides, Cookie had spent her last four Thanksgivings in Cambridge, so Woody wasn't reminded of her every time one of the students walked into the kitchen.

Woody served turkey and mashed potatoes, but not sweet potatoes or pumpkin pie, which he'd never cared for; two kinds of stuffing, one with pork and one without, the one with pork cooked separately from the turkey; lots of gravy, which Woody always called sauce; and cranberry relish, which the international students never ate. Even the Chinese, who seemed to have a taste for everything under the sun, never ate more than tiny token portions. Some of the students had been coming for four years. For others it was the first time.

He served some nontraditional dishes, too: *bulgogi*, kimch'i, Iranian rice pudding, litchi nuts in syrup. It all seemed easy and pleasant to Woody, and satisfying. He didn't know why women complained so much about cooking. The rice pudding was not to his taste—too sweet—but it was gratifying to see the students dig into it.

Woody and Turi had been spending weekends together, discreetly. Her father had taught her to shoot, so he'd taken her duck hunting down by Oquawka, just above Lock and Dam Number 18. Twice they drove down to Iowa City in her Alfa Romeo. Woody tried to pretend that he didn't love driving the car, with its lovely Latin lines and its five-speed, all-syncromesh gearbox, but Turi knew better and always insisted that he drive at least halfway. They stayed at Iowa House, in a room overlooking the river, and ate both nights in a Vietnamese restaurant near the Guitar Foundation, and then browsed through the Prairie Lights Bookstore before going back to their room. She was experiencing orgasms on a regular basis, but instead of moaning and crying *aaah aaah O O O*, she sounded like some kind of tropical bird, *ki ki ki ki kikikikiki KE'E'E'E'AA*, which just goes to show, despite Diogenes Laertius, that the language of love is not universal. He taught her how to prepare eggplant Imam Bayaldi, using whole cherry tomatoes instead of chopped-up tomatoes—she'd never done any cooking, since her family always had cooks. And he taught her how to adjust the idle on the Alfa Romeo.

But the term was almost over; the students were anticipating the long break. Some were going home; others would be spending the holidays with relatives or friends; a few would be staying in St. Clair; and Woody was looking forward to being alone again. In his imagination he had already begun to look back on the affair as a completed thing. Finished. Like a model airplane. Something to be admired, like a work of art. He would take her to the airport in Moline or Peoria; he would keep a stiff upper lip, like Humphrey Bogart in *Casablanca*. She would get on the plane. He'd wait, maybe see her through the window, settling into her seat. There would be no long kisses, because the airport was a public place. He would feel a pang—more than a pang—because he was genuinely fond of her. But he hadn't lost his head, like the old professor in *Der Blaue Engel*, which he and Hannah had seen in Ann Arbor. Maybe he'd stop at Mac's for a cup of coffee on the way home from the airport, not saying anything about Turi, because Mac wouldn't approve. Then he'd go home and put a new set of strings on his guitar.

The next afternoon, however, he heard her telling her father that she would be spending Christmas with a friend. When he came into the kitchen she mouthed the words "I'm using my credit card," as if he would begrudge her a phone call to Rome. She was speaking to her father in Persian and Woody had trouble following, but he gathered that she'd already sold her ticket, and that her father wasn't at all pleased. "How do *you* know what Allah wills?" she said, more than once. "I know, Baba Joon, but maybe Allah wants me to experience a traditional American Christmas. That's what he seems to be telling me."

It wasn't till after she'd hung up the phone—he was putting a spoonful of coffee into a little one-cup espresso maker—that he realized that *he* was the friend she'd been talking about, *his* house the farm in the country where she was going to spend a traditional Christmas.

"You can't stay *here*," he said, alarmed.

"Where else am I going to stay?"

"You should have thought of that before you sold your ticket."

"I did think about it. I thought I'd stay here. I thought you'd be glad to have me. I thought . . . I thought you'd be happy. I thought we were friends . . . more than friends, lovers. You're my lover. Doesn't that mean anything to you? I don't get it."

"It was a misunderstanding. I'm sorry. My children are coming home, I thought . . ."

"If you ask me to leave, I'll leave. But you have to come right out and say it. I'm not going to volunteer."

"Of course I won't kick you out."

"I'll go if you want me to," she said.

"No," he said. "I don't want you to go."

"Then it's settled," she said. "Let's not talk about it anymore. Let's just pretend that we love each other."

•　　•　　•

Two DAYS before Christmas Woody went to pick up Ludi at Grinnell, about an hour on the other side of Iowa City. He'd meant to tell her, and Sara too, about Turi, but for one reason or another he'd never gotten around to it. It had never seemed like the right time.

He'd written regularly, and she'd written too, long letters with sketches—birds, dogs, the view from her dorm window, and detailed "studies" of her boyfriend. Some of these were semi-nude, very close to nude, in fact. She was letting him know something—that she was in love. Woody already knew it because he'd gotten a bill from the College Health Service for a diaphragm *and* birth control pills.

Well, he'd briefed her. She was on her own, and he was glad that she was in love because he thought that now she would understand his position. Even so, he never got around to telling her in his letters. He'd go on about his classes, about the dean, about Thanksgiving—which she'd spent with Saul's family in Minneapolis—and about Sara, who was working as a waitress in a Greek restaurant on Halstead Street in Chicago. On the phone he told both the girls that one of the international students might be spending the holidays with them, but he hadn't gotten down to the real issue, and neither of them asked him any questions.

His last chance to explain passed on Thursday night, the night before he went to pick up Ludi. He was just about to say something on the phone, to explain, when Turi came into the kitchen, and he didn't want to explain in front of her. He'd already told her that it was OK, that there wasn't anything to worry about, and she didn't seem to see that there *was* a problem, didn't seem to appreciate the delicacy of the situation. But after all, Woody told himself, he was a grown man. After all, he didn't need his daughters' permission to go to bed with someone.

LUDI HAD a chemistry exam in the afternoon. Woody loaded her things in the truck, covered them with a tarp, and waited for her in her room, looking through some of her books. *Civilization and Its Discontents*, an Intro. to Sociology text, I. A. Richards's translation of *The Republic* using a vocabulary of six hundred simple English words. Pretty remarkable. Woody read the section on the cave. What a powerful metaphor for . . . for what? Woody was a Platonist by inclination; like Plato's philosopher, he longed to break out of the cave of appearances into the blinding light of Beauty and Truth. But he was an Aristotelian by trade. The metaphor of the cave was powerful, but it cut too many ways. Better to live in the world that one actually experiences—a Thanksgiving turkey on the table, a young woman in his bed, his daughter walking into the room with a smile on her face—than pine for another reality behind this one.

> Plato thought nature but a spume that plays
> Upon a ghostly paradigm of things;
> Solider Aristotle played the taws
> Upon the bottom of a king of kings.

On the way home Ludi snoozed, propping Woody's jacket between her head and the window of the pickup, till they got to Iowa City; then she sat up and started to tell him about Saul.

"We talked it over for about a week," she said, "and decided we were mature enough for a sexual relationship."

"Good," Woody said. "Did you remember what I told you?"

"About making him take it out right away so the condom doesn't slip off?"

"Well, yes, that too. About being careful, about . . ."

"Saul doesn't have that problem."

"It's not a *problem;* it's just common sense."

She was a little feisty at first, but she slid over closer to him. She was in love and couldn't stop talking about the beloved.

Every lover is a poet, says Plato. Woody thought so too, but he didn't say it. He didn't want her to stop talking.

"You remember what you said about the dean?" she asked him. "Or what she said about herself?"

"What's that?"

"That she was a complaining Jew in New York, and that she's a complaining Jew in St. Clair, and that she'll always be a complaining Jew?"

"Yes."

"Saul's mother's a complaining Jew too."

"What does she complain about?"

"Everything. Saul says it drives him crazy."

"Well, as long as Saul doesn't complain."

She gave him a look to show that this was out of the question. "He's a poli-sci/math double major," she said, as if being a double major precluded complaining. "And he sings. He's going to give a recital next term—Dvořák *Liebeslieder*—and I'm going to accompany him. Senior recital. Maybe you could help me with them . . ."

"Did you bring the music?"

She patted her backpack.

"Are they in Czech or English?"

"German."

He was going to tell her about Turi, but she fell asleep, snuggling up against him, dreaming of Saul.

He'd been planning to stop at the McDonald's in Davenport, but he didn't want to wake her up. Christmas, he thought, was more complicated than Thanksgiving. It was hard to go wrong on Thanksgiving; Thanksgiving is plain sailing. But Christmas is a dangerous strait; you're lucky to get through it without encountering some rough seas, without getting knocked around a little or even shipwrecked. Woody'd been trying to live in the present moment, but he couldn't let go of the past. It had too powerful a hold over him. Every bump in the highway jolted his memory, as if he were literally driving down Memory Lane. *You can't escape us,* this chorus of memories seemed to say—memories of almost half a century of Christmases. *This is your life; this is it; we're all you have.*

Ludi woke up and stretched just as they hit the Centennial Bridge across the Mississippi. "You know what I dreamed?" she asked. "I had two dreams."

Woody came back to the present moment. They were getting low on gas.

"No," he said, and he started to scold himself for not getting gas in Grinnell, which he could have done while he'd been waiting for her to get out of her chemistry exam, and now they'd have to stop in Newport, but as she started to speak he suddenly thought that even if they were low on gas, even if they'd have to stop in Newport, a man could do a lot worse than to be driving sixty miles an hour through the dark on Route 80 in a pickup truck with his daughter on the seat next to him, a young girl in love and about to tell him her dreams.

•   •   •

LUDI HAD been dreaming about Saul, about how much she loved him, and later, when she finally figured out the situation at home, she was especially hard on Woody because her own love was so pure, so wonderful, and so uncompromising that she couldn't comprehend the sordidness of Woody's purely human predicament. And Sara, who came home on the train on Tuesday night, was hard on him too, but for different reasons, which Woody could only guess at: because she didn't have anyone to love her—no lover, no boyfriend, no one special—and because she didn't like her job at the Mount Parnassus, and because she'd been putting on weight. And Turi was hard on him because he'd told her that he'd explained everything to his daughters, when what he'd really meant was that he was *going to* explain everything.

The house was full of anger, ill will, petulance—like the house of Agamemnon at the beginning of the *Oresteia*—and Woody had to go through the motions of Christmas alone. He got a tree, which he put up on the morning of the twenty-fourth; in the afternoon he built a fire in the fireplace and put up the lights around the living room windows; he set up a card table in the living room with a jigsaw puzzle on it. He didn't like jigsaw puzzles himself; he was too impatient and didn't have the knack. He knew, of course, that you had to start with the border, but he couldn't recall ever fitting two pieces together. But he liked the idea of other people sitting around working on a puzzle, and the girls had always been good at it. The attic was full of puzzles, mounted on plywood and shellacked. It was a regular art gallery—Vermeers, Rembrandts, Botticelli's *Primavera*, Picasso's *Three Dancers*, a five-thousand-piece version of Seurat's *Un Dimanche à la Grande Jatte*, which they had seen several times at the Art Institute in Chicago.

That evening he made pizza. He'd tried for several years to get his family to eat *spaghetti alle vongole* on Christmas Eve, but he'd never been able to get the girls to eat the *vongole*, so he'd switched to making special pizzas from recipes from an article in *Gourmet* magazine that he'd seen in the public library. Four different kinds of pizza. He chopped up the ingredients for each one separately and put them in little glass bowls, which he arranged in a row on the kitchen table: pepperoni, anchovies, red peppers, green peppers, chunks of feta cheese, black olives, peas, red onions, artichoke hearts, grated mozzarella, sliced mushrooms . . .

He turned on the oven and sat down at the table, at a loss. He was tired of female voices. Or female silences.

Sara and Ludi had made common cause against him and Turi, but then they'd had a falling-out and gone their separate ways; they weren't speaking to each other, or to anyone else. Turi was threatening to leave, but she had no place to go. The weather was bad—storms and storm warnings. The Peoria airport was closed. O'Hare was socked in. There were weather advisories on the radio. He looked out the window. The yard light was on and he could see snow falling in huge flakes, so big and slow you could almost count them.

He poked at the jigsaw puzzle in the living room, made from a slide he'd taken of the palazzo they'd lived in, in Rome, near Piazza del Popolo, during his sabbatical in 1974. Cookie had been sixteen, Sara ten, and Ludi only six, just old enough to start *scuola elementare*. No one else knew what the puzzle was. It would be a surprise.

While he was sitting in the kitchen, waiting for the dough to rise, he taped a program he'd heard an hour earlier on a different station. An NPR reporter on his way back from the Middle East had stopped in Paris, where he'd recorded a street musician singing the blues. The singer sounded like someone from the Mississippi Delta, but he was an Englishman, fifty-six years old, older than Woody. A policeman came and chased him and his two French sidemen away; the NPR reporter followed them to a bar where a band was playing "Sweet Georgia Brown." Later on, back on the street, the singer and the two sidemen played an instrumental version of "Amazing Grace" that blew Woody away. Three guitars. Three Fender Stratocasters. It was December and the Englishman was fifty-six years old. The NPR reporter asked him if he ever got tired of playing the blues on the streets of Paris. "I wouldn't know what else to do," he said.

TURI, who had moved her things into his study—there was no other place available—was propped up on a daybed, reading, a comforter pulled up to her neck. The room was cold.

Woody poked his head in the door. "Everything OK?"

Her clothes were scattered over everything. Dirty clothes. Books and papers were everywhere. Stacks of magazines: *The New Yorker, Harper's, The Atlantic, The New York Times Book Review.*

She didn't answer him; she was too busy reading. She didn't even look up.

"What do you want on your pizza? Anchovies? Artichoke hearts? Peas?"

"Whatever."

"Look, Turi. I'm sorry. How many times do I have to say it? I'm sorry."

"It's all right." She turned a page.

"It's not all right."

She turned another page, as if she were speed-reading.

"Want me to do a wash?"

"I'll do one later."

"I don't mind."

"I said I'll do one later."

"What are you reading?"

"A book."

"I see."

"Look, Distinguished Professor. It's my fault. I shouldn't be here. I should have known better. I'm a fourth wheel. In Italy we say *terzo incomodo*. Maybe I should say *quarto incomodo*."

"A fifth wheel," Woody said. He was trying not to lose control. He didn't want to give way to depression, disappointment, remorse. He was blaming himself. He'd been living in a fantasy world. He started to pick up her clothes.

"Look, Woody. I said I'd do it later. I don't want you pawing my stuff."

"It stinks in here."

"I thought you liked my smell."

SARA WAS in Cookie's old room, her clothes spread out on Cookie's workspace—a long table, a sheet of plywood on two filing cabinets. On the bed she'd made a nest out of old sleeping bags. She was reading too, lying on one side, the way Woody did, holding the book out, one edge on the floor. There was no register and the room was cold.

"You'd be warmer downstairs. I've got a fire going."

She was twenty-two, working as a waitress in a Greek restaurant in Chicago.

He recognized the novel she was reading, one of his paperback copies of *Anna Karenina*.

"*Anna Karenina*? Do you want me to leave the door open?" Woody waited for an answer, but she kept on reading. "The world's greatest human achievement," he said. "Next to Homer. I'd rather read Tolstoy than Shakespeare."

"Dad. If you've said that once, you've said it a thousand times."

"Just trying to break the ice. What's happening now?"

He could see she was about a third of the way through. She must be getting close to Levin's rejection by Kitty.

"Oblonsky's got a chorus girl lined up." She didn't look up, but at least she'd spoken.

"Is that so bad?" he said. But not meaning it. What he meant was, Do you see me as Oblonsky? He'd always thought of himself as Levin, not Oblonsky. He'd always found the story of Levin and Kitty more interesting than the story of Anna and Vronsky.

He didn't try Ludi, who was alone in her room. They still hadn't practiced the Dvořák *Liebeslieder*.

He got the bowl holding the pizza dough out of the warm closet in the pantry. Half the fun of it was *assembling* the pizzas. He thought about tomorrow. He'd bought chestnuts for the stuffing, but he didn't feel like peeling the chestnuts by himself, or making the stuffing, and he didn't feel like decorating the tree. He didn't feel like doing any of the things he'd thought they'd do together. What he felt like was putting a new set of phosphor-bronze strings on his National Steel guitar and trying to figure out the version of "Amazing Grace" that the Englishman had been playing in Paris. But before he could get his guitar out the phone rang. It was Hannah.

"Merry Christmas."

He didn't recognize her voice at first. He hadn't talked to her in almost two years.

"Aren't you going to wish me a Merry Christmas?"

"Hannah, is that you? Where are you?"

"At the Amoco station in Newport." She sounded like a woman unsure of her welcome. "I have a present for the girls, I want to drop it off. And I want to talk to you. I want to say hello to the kids."

"We haven't eaten yet. You want some pizza?"

"Sister Judy's with me. I'm not really supposed to call you, but we're so close. We're going up to the Mother House in Dubuque, but the weather's so bad we decided to stop at a motel."

"You could stay here."

"It's not a good idea, Woody."

Woody was surprised by his own feelings. What right did she have to do this to them on Christmas Eve? He had enough troubles without this. And yet anger almost immediately gave way to a feeling too complex to be comprehended in a single word. He thought he had hardened his heart against her, but now he experienced a tremendous upsurge of feelings, painfully intense, that left him so short of breath he could hardly run up the stairs.

He didn't knock on Ludi's door, just barged in. "Mama's coming home," he said. "She'll be here in an hour."

Ludi looked up from the table where she was drawing. "What about Turi?"

"She'll have to move her stuff in here. She can be *your* friend, from Grinnell."

Something about his tone of voice prevented any of the girls from challenging him.

Turi was still propped up, reading. "Listen," he said. "My wife's on her way. You're going to have to move in with Ludi. You want to get your stuff out of here, OK? Look, I'm sorry, but you've got to do this for me."

"It's all right, Woody," she said. "I can handle it."

The girls seemed to sense what Woody was going through. No one crossed him or made problems. Comforters were fluffed, blankets flapped and folded. In a cupboard that Woody had built in the bedroom, sheets, blankets, and pillowcases were all neatly folded and labeled. Woody picked out a queen-sized sheet, forest green with a flower pattern, that they'd bought in Rome, and matching covers for the two comforters. He put the sheet on the wrong way and tried to pull it loose, but it caught on a corner and Turi had to pull the elastic band to release it.

"Take it easy, Woody," she said in Persian. "It'll be all right."

She helped him with the comforter covers, which were tricky. You had to hold the corners of the comforter in one hand and push them up into the cover while the other hand grabbed the corners on the outside.

"You want to throw this stuff in the washing machine?" he said, gathering up the old sheets. "Better keep your stuff separate."

The house was full of bustle and commotion, as it should be on an important holiday. People were calling to one another. Upstairs, downstairs. Woody could hear the gentle rumor of the washing machine and the hum of the dryer.

Woody coached them in the kitchen. "There's going to be a moment," he said, "when someone is going to have to lie directly. Turi is here from Grinnell, OK? Don't say anything about her mom, OK? Remember, Allison and Mama were friends. Mama was one of her students at Michigan. Turi's Ludi's friend. You don't have to say anything else. Ludi, where is Turi from?"

"Tehran, then Rome."

"What's her major?"

"Classics."

"How did you meet her?"

"She lives in the same dorm."

"You can ad-lib the rest."

HANNAH CAME to the back door. Woody had heard the car in the driveway and was waiting for her, had watched her under the yard lights, getting something out of the backseat of a black Cadillac. An old one. It was hard to be sure of the color. It was still snowing heavily and snow blew into the kitchen when he opened the door to wait for her. She had a package in her hand, wrapped in plain paper, probably a book. The air on the back porch was sharp and cold.

She was wearing a long, loose black skirt and a puffy down jacket. Alone with her in the kitchen, Woody was suddenly frightened and called for the girls. "Mama's here," he shouted at the bottom of the stairs. "You look . . . elegant," he said to Hannah. "Prosperous."

"I don't know about prosperous. But I'll settle for elegant. You look pretty good yourself."

"Let me take your coat."

"Don't I get a hug?"

Woody hugged her. He was agitated, so full of feelings that he found it difficult to formulate a plan, consciously. There were so many things to think about.

The pizza ingredients, in glass bowls, gave the table a festive look. Preparing food was what Woody felt most comfortable at. He should have been a cook, a chef, instead of a teacher. Hannah sat down at the table. Woody offered her a glass of cider and poured a glass of red wine for himself. He was worried that someone would give the game away, but when the girls came into the kitchen Hannah just assumed that Turi was someone's friend and didn't ask for an explanation.

Woody tore the pizza dough, which he'd punched down for a second rising, into five equal blobs and spread each blob out on a nine-inch pizza pan.

"Tehran and Rome," Hannah said. "How exciting. It was always nice to have the girls' friends here during the holidays. Is this your first Christmas away from home?"

"Yes, it is," said Turi.

"You must be lonely."

"No. Not too lonely. It's nice to see a typical American Christmas."

Sara and Ludi sat next to their mother on the opposite side of the table, facing Turi and Woody. Woody smeared a little olive oil over the dough on each pan, except Hannah's, and then spooned on the tomato sauce, and they began to assemble their pizzas. Hannah didn't like olive oil on hers, though it made the crust crisper, and she always put the mozzarella on first and then the tomato sauce, and Woody couldn't remember now why he had once found this so irritating. What difference did it make?

"You know," Hannah said to Turi, "I wrote a letter to Woody when he was living in Esfahan, and he found it lying in the street. Facedown. I've always wondered if this happens regularly in Iran."

Turi laughed. "It's no more likely to happen in Esfahan than in St. Clair," she said.

"That's not very likely, then, is it? It's hard to understand."

"Ashraf Khanom was sure it was a miracle," Woody put in. "That's the family I was living with. She made Ebrahim Agha furious with all her talk."

"What do *you* think?" Turi asked Hannah.

"I used to think it was a miracle, fate, destiny, something like that."

"And now?"

"Now I think the postman couldn't read the address and dropped the letter on the street."

The pizzas were like works of art, or beautiful flowers. Woody put them in a five-hundred-degree oven and set the timer for ten minutes.

"That's what I used to think," he said, "but now I agree with Ashraf Khanom. I think it was a miracle."

AFTER SUPPER Woody put another log on the fire, to keep it going, and then he and Hannah went up to the attic to get some books that she wanted to take with her to the convent.

"They grow up fast, don't they," she said, climbing up the narrow stairs behind Woody.

"Too fast."

He'd packed her books in large cardboard tomato cartons and stacked them in the east end of the attic. Nine cartons, covered with bat droppings. Hannah was afraid of the bats and kept her head hunched down, as if she expected them to dart at her. Behind the boxes were the jigsaw puzzles, mounted and shellacked, almost two dozen of them, souvenirs of Christmases past and summer vacations.

"They're hibernating," Woody said. "They're out cold."

"You never know. Sometimes they wake up."

"They won't hurt you." Woody had always pretended he wasn't afraid of the bats; but now, having held one in his hand, he really wasn't afraid anymore and didn't have to pretend.

"I don't like them, Woody. I don't like being afraid."

"You shouldn't be afraid in your own house."

"But I am afraid."

There were bat droppings everywhere. Woody could see the bats up in corners of the rafters. The two electronic sonar devices—guaranteed to rid the house of mice, rats, and bats—blinked on top of old steamer trunks that had been in the attic when they bought the house. They'd been blinking there for over a year, no more effective than the mothballs and the insect bombs; Woody'd gotten up on a ladder and caulked every opening he could find on the outside of the house, but nothing had worked.

Hannah started taking books out of boxes.

"What are you looking for?"

"I have to design my own study program."

"What are you studying *for*?"

"It's all very advanced, very liberal, not what I expected."

"I'm not following you," Woody said, though he thought he was following her.

"I'm joining the convent," she said. "I should have written to you, but I wanted to tell you myself. It's the best thing," she went on quickly. "It's what I want. I have to design a program of study to prepare myself."

Woody wanted to shout, to wake up the bats so that they'd fill the attic air with their cries, with their dark wings, and frighten some sense into her. Instead he swallowed and went "huhhhhhh," letting the air out suddenly.

"There are some things we'll have to settle," she said.

The stack of books grew rapidly: Thomas Merton, Hans Küng, C. S. Lewis. Some other old favorites too, from the University of Michigan—not what he'd expect her to take to a convent: *Faust*, the *Duino Elegies, Either/Or.*

Woody was glad to see her set aside the self-help books she'd accumulated after Cookie's death. She handed him the books she wanted to take and he put them in one of the tomato cartons that he'd emptied out. He didn't know what to say. He knew better than to argue with her, but he wanted to say something, let her know . . . As a family they—he and Sara and Ludi—had never really acknowledged that the present arrangement was permanent, that Hannah wasn't coming back. They hadn't exactly expected her to come back, but they hadn't closed the door on the possibility. They hadn't ever discussed, in fact, what they would do if she did come back; but they'd always left the door open, as if they were waiting for her to get over it.

"We're going to have to get a lawyer," she said, handing him a copy of C. S. Lewis's *Four Loves*. Woody had always admired C. S. Lewis, but after reading A. N. Wilson's biography he thought there was something creepy about the man. "In the eyes of the Church we're not really married, since we weren't married by a priest, and you weren't a Catholic."

"But legally . . ."

"Right, that's why we have to get a lawyer. The convent lawyer can take care of it if you want her to, or you can get your own lawyer."

Woody let this sink in. "What sort of arrangement do you have in mind?"

"Fifty-fifty, right down the middle."

"What about the girls? How about a four-way split? We each take twenty-five percent?" (Woody had actually thought about this.)

"I don't think so."

"Don't forget that the college loans are part of the estate; they just about balance off the farm."

"I need the money, Woody. What about a loan for me? I worked hard all those years. I'm sorry if it seems hard, but . . ."

"What do you need the money *for*? I mean, if you're living in a convent . . . ?"

She handed him another C. S. Lewis book, *The Screwtape Letters*. "Nuns have to eat too. There are a lot of expenses. The upkeep on the physical plant is enormous; the furnace is going to have to be replaced, tuck pointing . . . Besides, it's my dowry."

DOWNSTAIRS, the girls had cleaned up the kitchen, including the pizza pans, and were sitting quietly in the living room, working on the jigsaw puzzle. Hannah and Woody carried two boxes of books out to the car. Woody still had something he wanted to say, but he didn't want to say it in front of the girls. He put a hand on Sara's shoulder, and she understood him immediately. The puzzle was starting to take shape; the border was almost finished.

Hannah looked at it and guessed right away. "It's our apartment in Rome, isn't it?"

Woody didn't say anything.

"It is, isn't it? I can tell. I just have a feeling."

"I'm not saying."

"You'll have to write to me, Sara," Hannah said, "and tell me that I'm right."

Sara got up from the table and hugged her mother. Ludi hugged her too, and then Turi, not quite knowing what to do, got a hug too. The three girls went upstairs. Woody and Hannah stood staring at the unfinished puzzle.

"I'm right, aren't I?" she asked.

"You're always right, Hannah," he said. "Via Savoia 33," he said, and then he said, "Sit a minute, in front of the fire. Just for a minute. I don't want to see you go yet, not like this. It's been two years, and you've hardly talked to the girls."

"I can't, Woody; I've got to get back to the motel; Sister Judy will start to worry. I wasn't supposed to come here alone, but I talked her into it. I said I needed the books."

"We need to talk about the tombstone," he said, reaching for a topic that would keep her there. "I think we ought to get that settled too."

"All right, Woody, but just for a minute."

Woody sat down by the side of the fireplace and stretched out his legs. He didn't say anything till Hannah sat down on the couch. He wanted her to relax, but she sat on the edge of the couch, ready to leave if he didn't have something good to say.

"Have you changed your mind?" she asked. "Frankly, I don't see how we could do better than *La sua voluntade è nostra pace.*"

"Did I write to you about the memorial service at Harvard?"

She nodded.

"On the way back something came to me, out of the blue. I thought it might work: *Quid si prisca redit Venus.*"

But she knew her Horace too well. "Oh, Woody," she said, "not *that* kind of love. Don't you see?"

Woody stalled for time. "Hang on a second."

He went to the back porch and got a package of cigarettes and an ashtray. He lit the cigarette but kept it concealed in his hand as he entered the living room. She could smell it, though.

"Woody," she said, "what are you doing?"

"Do you know what I do on Saturday nights?"

"No."

"I make pizza and drink a six-pack of beer, and then I light up one of your cigarettes. You left six cartons of Pall Malls, you know. I smoke them out on the back porch, like you used to do, when Cookie was still living at home, or in front of the fireplace, like now."

"And then what do you do?"

"The smoke reminds me of you, Hannah. I pretend that you're upstairs reading, or sewing. And I get out my guitar—I've got a new guitar, a National Steel, a tricone, you've got to see it." He set the cigarette down on the hearth, got up, and pulled the guitar case out from under the piano. He opened the case and took out the guitar, which he had just polished. The German silver reflected the firelight like the blade of a sword.

"Do you still play that song, 'Now she's gone gone gone and I don't worry'?"

"'Sittin' on Top of the World'? That's the first song I learned in open D."

"You sang that over and over, Woody. I thought you wanted me to leave."

"Hannah, don't say that. It's ironic, you're missing the irony. 'Now she's gone gone gone *and* I don't worry, 'Cause I'm sittin' on top of the world.' It's not '*but* I don't worry.' That would be different."

"I'm not sure I see the difference."

"Hannah, let's have a cigarette together."

"I haven't had a cigarette in two years."

"Just one, for old times' sake." He put the pack down on the floor next to her and picked up his own cigarette from the hearth. "Are nuns allowed to smoke?"

"No," she said. "It's funny, but that's the hardest thing."

"Not smoking?"

"Mm-hmm."

"Then I think you ought to have one now. A last fling." He blew smoke in her direction and strummed a chord, keeping the cigarette in his mouth while he played. The guitar filled the room with a huge metal sound.

"It's beautiful," she said.

"Just one," he said, "for old times' sake. Remember how we used to sit in front of the fire and have a glass of wine and a cigarette. Would you like a glass of wine?"

"No," she said. "Woody, I don't want a glass of wine."

"But a cigarette?" He put the guitar down on its side.

"All right," she said.

He patted the floor. "Here, in front of the fire."

She took a cigarette from the pack and jigged it against the back of her hand before putting it between her lips. Woody held out a lighter; the flame glowed. She took a puff, coughed, and threw the cigarette into the fire, but Woody held out what was left of his own cigarette and she took it, held it to her lips, and drew in deeply.

"Oh God, that tastes good," she said. "It's been two whole years."

She pulled in deeply again.

"What did you do in the convent?"

"I did without."

"Why are you doing this?"

"Smoking?"

"Joining up; enlisting."

"Not so easy to explain."

"Try."

"When I was in eighth grade at Trinity there was a special day when all of us had to consider whether or not we had a vocation. Nobody really wanted one, and if you thought you might have one, you had to be careful not to say anything or you'd wind up on a track and not be able to get off."

"And you didn't feel anything?"

"Nothing, Woody. And when it did come it wasn't what I expected. Now I think it never is."

"What did you expect?"

"I expected I'd put up a tremendous wall of resistance; that I'd be dragged kicking and screaming, against my will, overwhelmed. Remember the Donne poem, 'nor ever shall be chaste except thou ravish me'? Or the last chapter in C. S. Lewis's autobiography, when he's practically dragged into belief; *compelle intrare*, I think he says. 'Compel them to come in.'"

Woody shook two more cigarettes out of the deep red pack of Pall Malls. They lit up.

"But you were expecting *something*?"

"I think so, Woody. I think I'd been expecting something for a long time."

"Since Cookie's death?"

"I don't know. Honestly, Woody. It just seemed that after she died this life was over. It wasn't real anymore. Without Cookie, there was a big hole. Everything reminded me of her. I couldn't go back to it, or *come* back to it. Real life was somewhere else. The life we had—*I* had—wasn't enough; it wasn't the real thing. The hole wasn't just a hole; it was an opening."

"This is when you were in the hospital?"

"Yes. When I went crazy."

"You still taking your lithium?"

"I've switched to Eskalith; it's better for my eyes. Four hundred fifty milligrams in the morning, four hundred fifty at night, for the rest of my life."

"Good girl."

"I saw something when I was in the hospital. I know I was crazy, but I saw something, felt it. I thought I was alone, then I wasn't alone anymore. I could feel it in the ward."

"And you still feel *it—him*?"

She pulled on her cigarette. "Maybe it's not a 'him.'"

"A 'her'?"

"I don't know, Woody. It's like having a dog in the house. The dog doesn't have to be doing anything. You don't even have to see it. It's just there. It makes everything different. You're not alone."

"We *had* a dog in the house, Hannah. Two dogs."

"You're right, Woody; I guess maybe it isn't like a dog."

Woody put his cigarette down on the hearth and played a Steve Goodman song, one of her favorites, "The Dutchman."

"You're sleeping with that Iranian girl, aren't you?" she asked when he finished.

"I wouldn't if you came home. Do you ever think about it? I mean, seriously?"

She tossed her cigarette into the fire and then lit another, and Woody knew that she'd thought about it.

"I don't blame you, Woody. I guess that part of my life is over." She stood up. "I don't blame you at all, Woody, and I hope the girls don't blame you, though they seem to be getting on all right. And I hope you don't blame *me*, Woody. This is what I have to do. It's what I *want* to do. Now I have to go to the bathroom."

"She's Allison's daughter." He hadn't meant to tell her this, but he thought it might keep her a while longer.

"Allison Mirsadiqi?"

Woody nodded.

"Woody, you're kidding. That's incestuous."

"Don't be ridiculous."

"Does Allison know? I mean . . ."

Woody shook his head. "It's difficult to explain. Well, maybe it isn't. I don't know. It wasn't my idea. It's just . . ."

"Does Turi know?"

"Know what?"

"That you and Allison were lovers?"

"She's got a pretty good idea. We haven't talked about it. She knows that we're old friends."

"What if . . . ?"

"Don't worry, Hannah."

"I'm not worried; I'm just amazed."

"It's not such a big deal."

"It will be if her father finds out." She laughed. "I guess it's pretty funny; I guess I'm glad you've finally got somebody. I don't have to worry about . . . I don't have to feel so bad about . . . leaving. Now I really *do* have to go to the bathroom."

"Finish your cigarette," he said, but she flipped the butt into the fire.

He could hear her in the bathroom at the top of the stairs, brushing her teeth for at least two minutes, washing her hands over and over. The water ran for three or four minutes. He heard her go into Ludi's room, heard voices—the girls must all have been in the same room, listening at the register—to say good-bye. He played another song on the guitar while he waited for her—"Corinna, Corinna"—and then he improvised for a while. When she finally came down he could still smell the cigarette smoke on her clothes.

"You're all right, aren't you?" he asked.

"Do you mean am I having another nervous breakdown?"

"I guess that's what I mean."

She smiled. "Not to worry. I told you, I'm taking my Eskalith."

"Did you know," he said, "that they've arrested the woman who put the bomb in the train station?"

A look of pain crossed her face. "Oh, Woody," she said, "I don't want to know. I've made my peace with it. Let it go. Just let it go, Woody. Believe me. I'm sorry, I'm sorry you have to deal with this by yourself."

"It was in the *Times*," he said, but before he could go on she put her hand across his mouth. He could smell the cigarettes on her fingers.

"Let it go," she said again. "Really, Woody, that's the best thing. 'All shall be well,' remember, 'and all shall be well, and all manner of thing shall be well.' You have to believe that, Woody. I wish I could *make* you believe it. I wish you could believe it as deeply as I do."

"Maybe I do," he said, without really knowing what he meant when he said it.

THAT NIGHT Turi came into his room and sat down on the chest he'd built to hold sheets and blankets. She sang a song in Persian, a sort of lullaby, about a nightingale. Woody couldn't follow it all.

"I used to sing that to Babak," she said, "when he was sad." Babak, her younger brother, had Down's syndrome. She kept a picture of him in her wallet: Oriental eyes, short broad hands, a flat nose, low ears. "It's about a boy," she said, "who can whistle like an *usignolo*—a nightingale—and people come from miles around to hear him. My older brother, Behruz, taught Babak how to whistle, and then we could never get him to stop. He whistled all the time for almost a year."

The chest was under the window on the west wall. Woody could see Turi's silhouette, black against the soft charcoal of the night.

"When Cookie came to Rome," she said, "I fell in love with her. I thought she was so beautiful and so sophisticated and so American, and she spoke with a good Roman accent."

Cookie had been staying with Turi's parents, of course; but Woody hadn't thought of Turi as *knowing* her. It had never occurred to him to imagine them together.

"I wanted to go with her everywhere. She wanted to see the Baths of Caracalla, where Shelley wrote *Prometheus Unbound*. It's only a fifteen-minute walk, but Baba said he'd have Shapur drive us. I never went anywhere without a bodyguard—people were getting kidnapped right and left—but we wanted to go by ourselves, so we gave Shapur the slip. There's an old mule track that goes down the hill to near Piazza Bocca della Verità."

"Did something happen?" Woody asked.

"No. Nothing special. We didn't go to the Baths of Caracalla; we took the Metro from Circo Massimo to Piazza del Popolo, near where you lived for a year. We looked at your apartment and then went over to the *liceo*, and then we sat and talked with our feet in the fountain. Cookie said you'd never take your shoes off."

"I'd take them off now," Woody said.

"Then we walked all the way down to Esfahan—that's the name of one of Baba's stores—to see my aunt. We ate some artichokes first, in a Jewish restaurant. Cookie seemed so grown-up to me. I loved being with her, without Baba or Shapur. Tanteen Minoo—Baba's aunt—lived over the shop, in the old ghetto, and we went up to see her and had *biscotti* and tea. Tanteen Minoo was dying of cancer and kept the shades drawn. She had the most beautiful rug in her room, with yellow flowers on it, on a maroon base, with a pool in the center, and a faun and pheasants. It's really the most beautiful rug, an antique Nain, silk. It was going to be mine, but Cookie loved it so much that Tanteen Minoo told me she'd leave it to Cookie. Tanteen Minoo never learned to speak Italian, so she talked to Cookie in French and to me in Persian. But I didn't tell Cookie what she said about the rug." Turi leaned back against the window and crossed her legs. "I'm sorry," she said. "I've always been sorry. I wish Cookie could have had it."

"Where's the rug now?" Woody asked.

"Baba has it in his study. Tanteen Minoo died two years ago."

Woody closed his eyes in the dark and tried to imagine the rug. Pheasants and a faun, and a pool. No wonder Cookie liked it.

"On the afternoon before she went to Bologna, we went to the Protestant Cemetery, by the pyramid. It's only five minutes from our house. Ten minutes. She wanted to see Keats's grave, and Shelley's. Where Shelley's heart's buried. She said they burned his body on the beach at Spezia and that one of his friends pulled the heart out of the fire. I think she was in love, because she said her soul was an enchanted boat, but she was very mysterious about it. 'My soul is an enchanted boat.' It's a line from one of his poems. When it started to get dark the caretaker rang the bell for us to leave. He knew we were still in there, but he couldn't see us, and Cookie wanted to copy down the inscription, and she couldn't find anything to write on. I was afraid we'd get locked in. She finally wrote it down on a candy-bar wrapper. Maybe we could look it up tomorrow, Woody. If you'd like to. With all your books I'm sure we could find it somewhere."

But Woody didn't have to look it up. He'd been there himself; he'd sat on the bench where Cookie and Turi had been sitting; he'd emptied his loose change into the little collection box for food for abandoned cats. *Nothing of him that doth fade but doth suffer a sea change, into something rich and strange.*

Power Suit

In June 1986 I graduated from St. Clair College, *cum laude*, with honors in psychology. Congratulations were in order, and my father, as was the custom when faculty children received their degrees, rose from his seat to greet me and give me a kiss on the cheek as I crossed the platform to receive my diploma from Dean Feldman and a handshake from President Hanson. The speaker, Ted Koppel, was whisked away in a private jet immediately after the ceremony so he could give the same speech again at Dartmouth that afternoon. President Hanson, back from a trip to the Far East, brought the ceremony to a close and we marched out to the tune of Purcell's "Gordian Knot Unty'd," running a gauntlet of faculty members on our way to the Fine Arts Center, where we had assembled earlier that morning. We were happy and sad at the same time, happy that it was over and we were going out into the real world at last, sad that it was over and we were leaving old friends behind. There was champagne for the graduates, and a jazz band played on the lawn in front of Clair Hall; but the mood was subdued. I'd been on the dean's list for four years; I'd graduated with honors; but what was I going to do *now*?

At the Career Services Office we'd learned to prepare our résumés, we'd been videotaped doing practice interviews, and we'd learned networking skills; but those of us who weren't on clearly defined tracks that led to graduate or professional school, or who didn't want to work for Arthur Andersen, were at a loss. A few people had been recruited, of course, but many of us were just waiting around for something to happen, and it was a little embarrassing. Faculty members knew better than to ask what our plans were, because they didn't want to know. But parents of classmates were intensely interested. They did want to know. You had to put a good face on it and conceal the fact that not only didn't you have a job, you had no prospects, and you weren't even sure what the next step was.

Daddy's faith in the value of a liberal arts ideal was so complete that he never felt the need to justify it, and I suppose that's why I'd never had any doubts myself. "Liberal" arts are the arts that make you free, he used to say. They liberate. From Latin *liberalis*. I was free; but I still didn't know what I was going to do.

I'd majored in psychology because I wanted to understand what makes people tick, but I'd learned more about what makes rats tick than about what makes people tick. I was no longer sure, in fact, that there was something that *made* people tick; I was starting to think that people just ticked. Just for the record, though: I did have one job offer, from a motel chain headquartered in Cincinnati, but I turned it down. I didn't have anything against Cincinnati, I just didn't want to live there. I didn't want to be an administrative assistant. Later I was sorry, because being someone's administrative assistant in Cincinnati would have been better than waitressing at the Mount Parnassus restaurant on Halstead Street on the south side of Chicago. Anything would have been better than standing at the bus stop on Halstead and Green at two o'clock in the morning waiting for a bus downtown so I could wait for the IC to take me to Hyde Park, where I shared an apartment with three University of Chicago students, two blocks from the Museum of Science and Industry. I bought a *Career Guide for College Graduates* and made a list of everyone I knew who had a job, so I could start networking. But it turned out I didn't know very many people, and the people I did know were in no position to help me, though a friend of one of my roommates had a cousin who knew someone who worked at the Museum of Science and Industry, and this cousin had told her about a job opening at the museum for an assistant exhibit developer. One Friday afternoon on my way to work I stopped at the museum and picked up an application at the personnel office, though the position hadn't even been advertised yet. Besides, what I really wanted to do was go home, not to my apartment, but to my real home. The city was too boring and too frightening at the same time. I wanted to be back in my old room, to lie in bed all day reading a trashy novel, or maybe *Pride and Prejudice*, and not come down till suppertime. Daddy and I would fix pasta . . . Of course I couldn't *say* this to anyone because I was supposed to be having a big adventure—a single girl on her own in the big city. I couldn't *say* this to anyone, but when I found out I had to work on Christmas Eve, I quit, just like that. Nikki Mariakakis, the manager, was pretty nice about it and let me work the last two weeks before Christmas, which was good, because I was making quite a bit in tips. He said he understood how important it was to be with your family at Christmas, that I could take a week off, come back for the New Year's rush. But I didn't want to come back. I wanted to go home and stay home. I wanted to stay with Daddy; to take care of him. I thought he needed me.

Usually during the holiday season there comes a moment when someone decides to remind everyone else of the true meaning of Christmas—that it's not expensive presents, not material possessions, and so on, but spiritual treasures. Nineteen eighty-six was no exception. This time it was Mama, who stopped to see us on her way to the convent's Mother House in Dubuque, Iowa. It wasn't a good time for a visit. Or maybe it was. We were all in a disciplinary mood. Daddy had to be punished for sleeping with one of his students. Well, sleeping with her was OK, I guess, but what wasn't OK was that she was spending the holidays with us. A girl my age. We'd refused to help Daddy decorate the tree or put the lights up, or chop up the stuff for the pizzas. And then, about six o'clock, Mama called, and Daddy started rushing around to get the house ready. The thought of Mama swooping down like an avenging angel gave Ludi and me a certain satisfaction—Daddy was going to get it now—but only for a minute or two. We hadn't seen Mama for almost two years, and even though we blamed her for moving away, we still had an idea that she might come back home, like the woman in the song that Garrison Keillor sang on the radio every Saturday night:

Look who's comin' through the door
I think we've met somewhere before
Hello Love, Hello Love.

I think we still had an idea of how things were supposed to be, so we got moving—Turi too—and by the time Mama arrived there were clean sheets on the beds, and lights on the tree, and Turi had moved all her things into Ludi's room.

I'd talked to Mama a couple of times in Chicago, on the phone, but I didn't have a car, and hers wasn't working, so it was difficult to get together. She lived in Oak Park, and I lived in Hyde Park, and there wasn't any easy way to get from one Park to the other. I'm not sure, actually, that we really *wanted* to get together. I was too angry, and she was too . . . I didn't know what she was. She had retreated to a place where my anger couldn't touch her. Ludi and I had always been on Daddy's side. But now things were more complicated. It was still hard to get my imagination around Turi. I couldn't imagine her in Daddy's bed. I recognized my own Elektra complex. Turi had stepped into my mother's shoes, into my father's bed. She had him all to herself. (But did I really believe this stuff, deep in my heart? I don't think so. None of my professors in the Psych. Department would have believed it. They thought Freud ought to be taught in the English Department.)

We ate pizza at the kitchen table and talked about things, stuff, and later Mama and Daddy talked in front of the fireplace. And smoked, the smoke drifting up through the register into Ludi's room. Turi was reading on the bed, but Ludi and I sat hunched over the register and listened, the way we'd done when we were kids. But Daddy and Mama kept their voices down, so we couldn't hear what they were saying. I guess they knew a trick or two too.

"What do you want to happen?" Turi asked, looking up from her book.

I'd hardly said two words to Turi since I'd figured out what the situation was, and I didn't say anything now because I was afraid to put an answer into words. But suddenly I stopped seeing her in symbolic terms. She was just a girl, like me. Only she was a long way from home.

I remembered fucking Aaron Gridley, the funeral director's son—Cookie's old boyfriend—in Cookie's bed, while Mama and Daddy were in Italy; while Cookie was in coffin no. 84, stacked up in the morgue in Bologna. We drove out to the farm to see the dogs, but they weren't around. Curtis was feeding them and they were probably over at the Warren Farms. How tragic Aaron had looked afterwards; how serious we were, afraid too. I'd never told *anyone*, and I don't think Aaron had either. But I told Ludi and Turi now. It was a peace offering. I wanted to reveal something about myself.

"Why do you think you did it?" Turi asked.

"I've never been able to figure it out. I mean, I was starting to feel the urge, but it wasn't overwhelming."

"I mean right after Cookie was killed."

"That's why I never told anyone," I said. "I suppose it was because Aaron loved Cookie too, even though she'd broken up with him when she went to Harvard."

"Did you keep doing it?"

"No, that was it. That one time. I would have done it again, but Mama and Daddy came home. We had a couple of chances to do it in the funeral home when Aaron was baby-sitting the telephone, but we just talked. He and his mom were Christian Scientists and didn't believe in death. There were copies of Christian Science magazines in the living room, with testimonials in the back."

"How could they not believe in death?"

"Death and sin are illusions...I don't know. He tried to explain, but I could never quite figure it out. He wanted me to talk to his mom; he said she could explain it better. But I didn't want to. Maybe that's why we didn't do it again."

"What do you think Mama and Daddy're doing now?" Ludi asked. She was softening too. She was hard-nosed, but she was in love.

"What about your mysterious Saul?" I asked. "You haven't said much about him. You're on the phone with him all the time, but you haven't said much about him."

"Saul's in another category," she said. "Absolutely and finally fantastic. He's going to be a civil rights lawyer."

"And you're going to be the head of the EPA." I laughed at my own joke, but it wasn't all a joke. "What a pair you'll make."

"Is this your first boyfriend?" Turi asked.

"'Boyfriend'?"

"Well, you know . . ."

"'Boyfriend' is hardly the word for it."

"You're in love."

Ludi gave her a look of disdain, as if "love" were as inadequate as "boyfriend" to the depth and breadth of her experience. But the look turned into a grin. It was hard *not* to like Turi, once you got past the fact that she was *sleeping with Daddy*.

"Do you remember how Mama and Daddy used to do it on Sunday mornings?" I asked.

Ludi nodded. "Awesome."

"They made love other times too," I said, for Turi's benefit, "but Sunday mornings was when we were most aware of it. They kept the bedroom door closed and locked, and we knew better than to knock on the door or to make a fuss, but we used to camp outside their door at the end of the upstairs hallway, by the back staircase that went down to the kitchen. We'd make a nest with pillows and blankets and comforters, and play with our dolls. My doll had eyes that opened and closed, till Cookie broke it open because she wanted to see what was inside. And we had a set of little plastic figures with arms and legs on pivots, and a set of doll furniture that included a double bed. The furniture was built to a slightly smaller scale than the dolls. The dolls were too big for the beds, but we used to put the Mama and the Daddy in the bed together anyway, with the Daddy doll on top, and make little fucking motions.

"When the door *finally* opened they'd always be surprised to find our camp—they never seemed to catch on—and then Daddy would fix a big breakfast for everyone. Bacon, eggs, ham, pancakes. They'd still be in their robes, with no underwear on, so that when they crossed their legs you could sometimes see things."

"Was it scary?" Turi asked.

"No," I said, "it wasn't scary." But I could see how it might have been. Freud says that children are frightened of the primal scene, but that wasn't my experience. We outgrew the dolls, and we probably broke camp for the last time when I was seven or eight. Cookie would have been thirteen or fourteen. But the memory of the sounds my parents made was part of my growing up. Strange and exciting, but comforting too, as we waited for those cries and moans, and then subdued laughter, as if what they'd just done was the funniest thing in the world. And then in a little while the door would open and they'd stalk through our camp like a couple of wild bears or elephants.

"Daddy knew a thousand ways to fix eggs," I went on, "and was always coming up with new ones. He'd cook the yolks and the whites separately, for example, and slip slices of cheese and tomato between them, so that it looked kind of like a fried egg, but different; or he'd poach them in vinegar and then roll them in Parmesan cheese and serve them in a nest of bacon and tomato on buttered toast. Whenever we'd bite into one of these new concoctions Cookie would start to moan in ecstasy. Uuuuuugh; ooooooooohhh; oooooooooohhh that's good; O O O. Oh Jesus that's good. And Ludi and I would join in: O O O. Oh Jesus. Daddy was always pleased that we liked his cooking. 'You girls,' Mama would say, lighting up a cigarette. I don't think they realized we were imitating them."

"I wish we'd had a tape recorder," Ludi said.

"You couldn't have been more than two or three years old," I said.

Turi spoke: "Did you know that Cookie was staying with us in Rome?"

I'd known it, of course, but I'd never really made the connection before.

"I had a crush on her right away. I must have been about sixteen. We went to the Keats-Shelley house in Piazza di Spagna; there were some letters he wrote to his girlfriend. Fanny, I think her name was. We had artichokes in a Jewish restaurant in the old ghetto and then we went to see my tanteen Minoo. Tanteen Minoo knew about a movie theater on the outskirts of Tehran where they used to show a curse on the screen at the beginning of every film to keep the men from pissing right in the theater; and she used to make 'tea' out of she-donkey turds, back in Tehran, for bronchitis. They don't do this in Italy, she told Cookie. That's why everyone's coughing all the time in Rome. She thought it must be worse in the north, where it's colder. Baba had Shapur collect some donkey turds from the street, but it wasn't the same as finding them dry and firm in the apothecary's."

We wanted to hear more about Tanteen Minoo, and about

Cookie, who seemed to have another life that we knew nothing about; but we could hear Mama coming upstairs.

It was about nine o'clock. Mama went into the bathroom, and we could hear her brushing her teeth and washing her hands. She took a long time, but when she came in to say good-bye you could still smell the smoke on her clothes, and I hoped she'd get in trouble at the convent, or with Sister Judy, whoever it was she was staying with. I didn't know much about nuns, but I thought they probably weren't supposed to smoke.

The Garrison Keillor theme song was still running through my head:

> It's wonderful now, you're back with me
> And things are like they used to be
> Remember Love, Remember Love.

But I knew that Mama was leaving, and I knew that things would never be the way they were supposed to be. Maybe I'd known it all along, and I was glad Turi and Ludi were there too, for moral support. Mama came in to say good-bye, and I held myself very stiff when she put her arms around me to give me a hug. She was holding a present, wrapped in plain blue paper, in one hand, and I could feel a sharp corner pressing against my back as she held me tighter and tighter, and I could feel her tears too, warm on my neck, and then I could feel myself loosening up, could feel my anger draining away, could feel myself thinking that maybe even now it wasn't too late, if only I exerted my will.

Turi started to leave and Mama put the present down on my desk and gave her a hug too, and then she sat down on the edge of the bed.

"I've come to say good-bye," she said to Ludi and me. "I didn't want to just go off."

I didn't know what to say.

Turi closed the door behind her.

"I know we haven't been best friends," Mama said, "since Cookie died. The way we were. The three of us. I know I've disappointed you." She patted the bed, and Ludi and I sat down on either side of her. "I'm sorry for that," she said. "You don't know how hard this has been for me, and I don't know if I can explain, but this will be our last Christmas together and I wanted to say something to you."

"Nobody's sending you away, you know," Ludi said. "You don't have to go."

"It's not too late, Mama," I added.

She lowered her head and then tossed it back, like a horse tossing its head. "I know that, sweetheart, but it's not so simple."

I started breathing deeply, holding myself together. I'd always admired nuns from a distance. Kristin in *Kristin Lavransdatter*, which Daddy read aloud to us, all three volumes; Sister Sara in *Two Mules for Sister Sara*—Clint Eastwood and Shirley MacLaine. Even Sally Field in *The Flying Nun*. But this was different. This was my mom.

"Do you remember the old song 'You are my sunshine, my only sunshine'?" She paused, waiting for a response, and then started to sing, softly:

> You are my sunshine, my only sunshine,
> You make me happy when skies are gray;
> You'll never know, dear, how much I love you,
> Please don't take my sunshine away.

"You'll never know, dear, how much I love you," she said. "Sometimes I worry that you'll never know how much I love you. But I want you to think of the old poem by Richard Lovelace, do you know the one I mean?—'I could not love thee, dear, so much, Loved I not honour more.' That's not quite what I want to say to you, but it's maybe as close as I can come right now.

"On the night that Cookie died, when Daddy and I went to Bologna . . . Daddy was so angry. He just wandered around. He couldn't sit still. We went to see the body, and I knew it wasn't Cookie—"

"But Mama, it *was* Cookie," I said.

"Let me finish. Later that night I walked out of the hotel—I think Daddy and Allison had gone back to the hospital, or else to the morgue, I'm not sure now, and it doesn't matter anyway. I needed to walk. I thought that if I could only get out and walk I might be able to pull myself back together. It was hot and the streets and piazzas were full of people, because of the heat, and because of the bombing. The churches were open. I went to a church called Santa Maria della Vita. The churches were all open. There were people everywhere, even though it was the middle of the night. People praying. Listening. There's a terrible pietà, terrible or wonderful, by Niccolò something or other, that shows the real horror of the crucifixion. You can see it in the faces. That's what I felt too. There was a lot of unrest, a lot of anger. You could feel it in the air. I didn't know where I was going, but later I must have gone outside the old city walls. When I looked at a map later I thought it must have been the Porta Castiglione, but I can't be sure, it doesn't matter. But I do remember that someone was following me, a young person with shining blond hair, almost golden. I couldn't get away from him, or her, and after a while I stopped trying. Finally I sat down on a park bench, and whoever it was sat down next to me, and I started to talk about Cookie. About how her first sentence was 'Piggies run in houses.' I remember that because I had to translate everything into Italian. My Italian was never all that good, but I didn't have any trouble at all: *Porcellini corrono in case.* I could see that he wanted to say something, but I couldn't stop talking. The more he tried to interrupt me, the faster I talked. I told him everything I could remember about Cookie.

"Now what I want to say to you is this: it's taken me a long time to realize that I should have been listening instead of talking. It was a messenger, and I wouldn't let him or her deliver the message. I can still remember how beautiful this person was, and how kind, to listen to me. Turning towards me, sitting on one leg. I can see the lips parting, but I never stopped talking. What did the messenger want to say? Will I ever know? Did I miss my chance? I don't know, but that's what I'm learning in the convent. To listen instead of talking. To be quiet."

"Do you think it was an angel?"

She flared up, tossing her head back again. "I didn't say that."

"Mom, you were sick, you were having a psychotic break. It was just a nice young person who wanted to help."

"I know I was sick, Sara." Her face softened. "I've never pretended that I wasn't. I was very sick. But that doesn't explain everything. I had seen something, I had heard something, I'd been caught up in it. You know the story about the Sufi that your father used to tell—hears about the fire . . . sees the fire . . . feels the warmth of the fire . . . is consumed by the fire."

"I always thought Daddy was talking about sex."

"He was talking about a lot of things. Sex, music, God. I was consumed by the fire, Sara. I don't know how else to put it. It took a while to sort it out. At first I thought it was the sickness, but it was something deeper. Something in the anguish of that pietà in Santa Maria della Vita that gave it a shape, and then being followed like that. I couldn't escape. I was being hunted down. Down alleys, narrow streets. Afraid of being mugged. I *was* mugged."

"Mama," I said, "remember the scene in *The Sound of Music* where the mother superior asks Julie Andrews if she's running towards something or running away from something? Do you think you might be running *away* from something?"

"And what would that be?"

"Cookie's death, dealing with it. Accepting it. The tombstone thing, I don't see why—"

"Why?"

"Why it had to become such a life-and-death struggle. All-or-nothing."

"I don't blame your father," she said, "if that's what you mean. I don't blame him at all. I'm glad to see he's all right. I'm very glad, and I don't want you to blame him either. Not for anything. It's been hard for both of us."

"It's not over," I said.

"You're as stubborn as ever," she said. "Come on, don't you want to open your present? It's not much, but it's all I could manage. Ludi, do you want to open it?"

Ludi sat up and tore the blue paper off the package, which was, not surprisingly, a book, fairly large, not too thick, bound in ugly white leather.

"The other day in the library," Mama said, "we were culling some books and I came across a Dutch translation of *Pilgrim's Progress*, which seemed odd to me, though there are lots of odd things in the library there. It's leather-bound, but not especially nice. One of those late Victorian arty-type bindings; but the inscription spoke to me—this time I was listening instead of talking—and maybe it will speak to you too. Sister Judy helped me translate it. It's almost like German."

> *Voor Mijn lieve kinderen,*
>   *Ter herinnering aan de dagen, toen wij gegaan zijn door het Dal der Schaduwe des doods, in 't bijzonder aan de donkere dagen van Dec. 1907. Lees het gedeelte van dit boek blz. 59–64. In het licht van God's genade bereiken wij evenals Christen het einde der vallei.*
>
> *A. van Rijn*
Amsterdam 24.12.07

"Once you know what it says, it's easy, you can *see* it." She pointed at the words and we followed her finger across the page with our eyes: "'My dear children, In memory of the days when we went through the Valley of the Shadow of Death, and especially of the dark days of December 1907. Read the something or other in this book, pages 59–64. In the light of God's grace may we, even as Christian, reach the end of that valley.'"

"December 24, 1907," Ludi said. "That's seventy-nine years ago tonight."

"That's another reason I had to come tonight," Mama said. "We've gone through some dark days together, but maybe now we're coming to the end of that valley."

It was Ludi who broke down first, which surprised me, since I'm the sentimental one. She didn't say anything; she just put her head in Mama's lap and cried softly to herself.

"Are you going to get in trouble for smoking?" I asked.

"I'm always in some kind of trouble," she said.

"We didn't get any presents for you; we didn't know . . ."

"You couldn't know, sweetheart. No one can know. But let me tell you one more thing, if you can bear it. Sometimes I hear Cookie's voice, at night, just when I'm falling off to sleep. I hear her call my name. And I wake up a little and I whisper her name: 'Cookie, it's all right, I'm still here, I'm still your mama.' And I whisper *your* names too: 'Sara, Ludi, it's all right, I'm still here, I'm still your mama.' That's what I wanted to say to you. I'll always be your mama. That's why I came tonight. And now that I've said that, I have to go."

After she left, Ludi and I waited for a few minutes—we heard doors opening and closing, and we could see the car through Ludi's window as Mama drove off—and then we went downstairs and worked on the jigsaw puzzle with Turi. Daddy sat on the couch and played his metal guitar: "Now she's gone gone gone and I don't worry, 'Cause I'm sittin' on top of the world."

I DIDN'T get around to telling Daddy I'd quit my job till two days after Christmas. I thought he'd be glad to have me back home, but he didn't seem thrilled, and so I made more of the opening at the Museum of Science and Industry than it deserved. I changed my story a little so Daddy wouldn't think I was a total failure. He read the job description—an assistant exhibit developer, it turned out, was in this case a sort of props person—and got all excited about it. We went to the public library together and got books on the history of computers and on how to do the kind of research I'd have to do: finding old photos, locating information about costumes and clothing (what people would have been wearing in the Social Security Office in Washington in the fifties, when the first Univac was set up). One of the books had several bibliographies, and Library of Congress headings for different areas; and there was a section called "Invention, Scientific Discovery, and Exploration." Daddy seemed to think I already had the job and was getting ready for my first day at work. I'd led him to believe that I had an interview set up, but actually I hadn't even sent in the application. All week he'd been trying to get me to call. I kept putting it off. I was dreading it, and the book *How to Have a Winning Job Interview*, which I was supposed to be studying, didn't make things easier.

Sitting alone in the living room, which was the warmest place in the house because of the fireplace, I alternately poked at the jigsaw puzzle and paged through the interview book. I didn't mind the first part so much: "Understanding the Purpose of Interviews" (chapter 3: "Preparing Your Brain"; chapter 4: "Preparing Your Body"). It was the interview itself that worried me. We were going to have a practice interview that afternoon, and I was dreading that too. The practice interviews I'd gone through in the Career Services Office at St. Clair had never been very successful. At least this interview wouldn't be videotaped. The video camera had made me freeze. I thought I'd be OK in a real interview, but I was too self-conscious in practice situations. But then, that's the way I'd felt about swimming too, and dancing: that I couldn't when people were staring at me, but that I could if no one was watching. But I'd been wrong both times, so I'd agreed to a practice interview. Daddy was going to interview me that afternoon.

Daddy had already read the book and insisted on walking me through the steps. He'd insisted that I get dressed up for the practice interview, but I didn't seem to have the right clothes or the appropriate accessories, so I'd borrowed a skirt from Turi and an Anne Klein blouse and an old suit jacket from Mama's closet. The skirt was too tight and the jacket too big, and my hair, which I'd washed twice, refused to settle down and lie flat. The goal was to have a winning interview. You didn't dress to express yourself; you dressed to make the interviewer feel that you were neat, clean, and— this was the main point—the same sort of person as the interviewer himself, or herself. You didn't wear sneakers or six-inch heels. You had your clothes dry-cleaned or washed. You didn't wear flashy bracelets or dangling earrings that might distract the interviewer. You carried a businesslike handbag, or better, a briefcase. You didn't go into the interview carrying bundles or boxes or shopping bags, or with papers sticking out of your purse or your pockets.

I went back to the jigsaw puzzle. Mama had guessed right. Daddy'd sent in a slide of the apartment we'd lived in in Rome, Via Savoia 33. There was a strip of blue sky across the top of the picture, and the color of the palazzo was just the way I remembered it, almost coral, maybe ochre. You could see the window of the room that Cookie and I had shared. Ludi and Turi, who had decided to make Duck à l'Orange for New Year's Eve—with ducks that Turi and Daddy had shot—worked in short spurts, coming into the living room every few minutes to see what was emerging; but I kept working steadily, adding one piece at a time, waiting for the rusticated stones at the bottom to appear, and the sky-blue arch of the Autofficina next to our front door, and our front door too, varnished so heavily that it sparkled like glass.

I wanted to do the interview alone with Daddy in his study. But he had already brought some straight-backed chairs from the dining room into the living room. Ludi was going to be the receptionist, and Turi was going to observe. Out in the front hall I got into a comfortable position and imagined a cord running from my spine down into the earth and spreading out like the roots of a tree. Then I imagined all the energy of the earth flowing up from the roots, through the cord, up my spine, and into my head. But it wasn't working. I waited in the front hall while the interviewers got themselves situated. Carrying Daddy's briefcase, which was out of shape from all the books he stuffed in it, I looked in the mirror on the back of the front-hall closet door. I looked perfectly normal, except for the briefcase. Like a college student, or a recent graduate. But I couldn't stand it, couldn't stand *me*. I'd been careful about eating, but still . . . I couldn't see the real me, and I couldn't feel the energy of the earth flowing up through my spinal cord and into my head. Of course, I hadn't really given it a chance. I'd worked on the puzzle instead.

When I was finally summoned into the living room I was more nervous than I would have been at a real interview. At least in a real interview I'd be dealing with strangers. If I flubbed, I wouldn't have to see them again. The pocket door slid open and Ludi called my name in a fake German accent: "Ms. Voodvull?"

Ludi, the receptionist, sat on a dining room chair at the card table, which served as her desk. Daddy was sitting on an identical chair in front of the fireplace, the piano bench pulled up in front of him. Turi was lying on the couch, ready to document the interview with Daddy's old Pentax.

"I have an appointment with Mr. . . . Bradley," I said. "My name is Sara Woodhull."

Ludi opened a hymnal and studied it for a moment. "I'm sorry," she said, "but I don't see anything for this afternoon. Mr. Bradley is terribly busy."

"The appointment was for three o'clock."

"Now let me see . . . Ms. Voodvull?"

"Woodhull," I said. "Sara Woodhull."

"Yes, here it is. Miss Voodvull. I'm terribly sorry, but your appointment vass for yesterday afternoon. I'm afraid Mr. Bradley's schedule is full today. He has a very full schedule, you know. I really am terribly sorry, but your appointment vass for yesterday afternoon."

"But I'm sure," I said, trying to be decisive, "that the appointment was for *this* afternoon."

"No no," Ludi said. "It's quite impossible; I have it written down right here, you see. Tuesday. Wednesday is on the next page, you see?"

"But I have to see him; it's terribly important."

"But isn't everything?"

Totally flustered, I was glad when Turi butted in. "Let me play you, Sara. You're too nice." She put the camera down, grabbed Daddy's briefcase, and faced Ludi.

"All right," I said. I could see that Daddy was not any happier than I was with the way things were going.

"I'm sorry, Miss Simmons," Turi said, "but if you'll recall, you called me back to change the appointment from two-thirty on Tuesday to two-thirty on Wednesday. I remember it distinctly. The message is on my answering machine. Look, I've brought the tape with me. We can listen to it together on *your* machine."

Now Ludi was flustered. "I don't think that will be necessary," she said. "I've just remembered a cancellation. Yes. How silly of me. I forgot to mark it out. Mr. Bradley will see you in just a moment."

Daddy intervened. "Turi, let Sara do the interview herself. She's the one who's looking for the job."

"I was just trying to protect her," Turi said, relinquishing her role. "Don't take any B.S. from anybody," she said, putting an arm around me. "You hear? You have to assert yourself."

"Let me handle it," Daddy said. "Ms. Woodhull, won't you sit down. I've been looking forward to seeing you. I've got your résumé right in front of me, in fact. St. Clair College. Did you know that our director of development went to St. Clair? It's a fine school."

"Yes," I said. "My father teaches there."

"He must be very proud of you."

I was at a loss for words. "He used to bring my sisters and me to the museum," I said, "when we were little. And we came on school trips too."

"And did you enjoy your visits?"

"Oh, very much."

"About this job, now. You've read the job description?"

"Yes, and it sounds like something I'd be interested in."

"That's good; that's good. It's going to be an important exhibit. The history of computers, you know. A series of milestones marking important moments in the history of computers."

"Yes, but what exactly does an assistant exhibit developer do?"

"Well, now. Say I told you we needed a photo of a nineteen-fifties office. Could you come up with one by tomorrow? What would you do?"

This was stuff we'd gone over, so I knew what to say: "First I'd check in Hilary Evans's *The Art of Picture Research: A Guide to Current Practice, Procedure, Techniques, and Resources,* and if that didn't turn up anything, I'd look in McDarrah's *Stock Photo and Assignment Source Book: Where to Find Photographs Instantly.* There are other sources too, of course, but these are the ones I'd start with."

"Well, that sounds pretty resourceful to me. I wouldn't have the faintest idea where to look myself. Now, let's try something a little tougher. Let's say you had to put your hands on a Univac."

"Oh, Daddy," I said, "you're making it too easy. You're asking stuff that you know I know. Let Turi and Ludi try it."

They were glad to oblige, and we changed places.

"Ms. Woodhull," Ludi said, lowering her voice to indicate that *she* was Mr. Bradley now. "We have over two hundred applicants for this position. Can you give me any reason to single you out? What *exactly* are your qualifications?"

Turi was now playing my part again. "The way I see it, Mr. Bradley, you're looking for a scavenger hunter. Am I right?"

"Something like that, I suppose," Ludi said.

"It's a game," Turi explained. "Usually you play with teams, but not necessarily. You start with a list of items. The first one to get everything on the list wins. I'm a champion."

"Yes, I understand the analogy, Ms. Woodhull, but analogies have a habit of cutting two ways. Like parallel lines, they may never intersect. Childish parlor games are hardly the best form of preparation . . ."

"If the lines are on a sphere, Mr. Bradley, they *will* intersect."

"I'm afraid you've lost me."

"Say you're looking for something really off the wall, a pair of panties with a heart on the seat, or a bright blue suppository; you have to—"

Daddy intervened again. "Look, this isn't a joke," he said. And then to me: "Don't pay any attention to them, Sara. You have to remember that most people will want to help you if you get them in the right frame of mind. If they think they're on your side, or you're on their side. A good cause. If you can get them to enter into the spirit of the game. That's the challenge. You have to ask them . . ." But Daddy was running out of advice.

Ludi and Turi were too quick for me. I went upstairs and lay down on my bed and waited. I knew that in a few minutes—after a decent interval—Daddy would come up. I was lying facedown when he finally came in and sat on the edge of the bed. I told him that I'd quit my job at the Mount Parnassus and that I'd already packed all my things in Chicago, and that I thought he would have wanted me to come home.

He rubbed my back for a while without saying anything.

"You've got Turi," I said; and Mama's got someone, even if it's only God; and Ludi's got Saul. I'm so lonely in Chicago. My roommates . . . They're nice enough, but . . . Why can't I be more like Turi? Look how she made everything come out her way. I couldn't even get an appointment. And Ludi. I don't know how they do it. I can't be like that."

"There's nothing wrong with being a waitress," Daddy said, but he couldn't help adding, "for a while. You probably learn more about life than . . ." But he didn't say than *what*. "Look what *I* did."

"You went to Iran, and then you went to graduate school."

"I guess you're right. I don't really know how people survive in the *real* world. But look, Sara, you're twenty-two years old; your life is not over. It's just beginning."

"Why doesn't it feel like it's just beginning? I want to come home, Daddy. I want to stay with you for a while."

He pretended not to hear me. Like the dog, when she didn't want to come inside or get in the pickup.

"You don't need a man to complete you," he said, but he was starting to sound like the articles in *Redbook* and *Cosmopolitan* that he read standing in line in the grocery store. I read them too.

"What happened with you and Mama?"

"Christmas Eve? We smoked some cigarettes in front of the fire-place."

"I could smell the smoke on her clothes. Do you think she'll get in trouble?"

"Mama's always in some kind of trouble."

"Did you think she might stay? I mean just for a minute, maybe? Were you hoping?"

"I don't know what to say, Sara. Maybe I was hoping a little."

"Is that why you had a *Prairie Home Companion* tape on? Maybe subconsciously?"

"Maybe subconsciously."

"Do you ever wish you could go back and be a boy again in Grand River?"

"It's not something I give much thought to."

"Were you happy when you were a boy?"

"I guess I was pretty happy."

"Are you happy now?"

"Not too bad."

"Are you happy with Turi?" I could see he didn't want to talk about Turi.

"I'm glad you're hitting it off," he said. "Remember when your uncle Roy brought his dog for Thanksgiving that time, when Argos was still alive? Just after we got Laska?"

"I wish I could be more like her," I said. "Like Turi, I mean, not Laska; and like Ludi."

"You're like you, Sara. You don't have to be like anyone else."

"They're toucher." I meant to say "tougher" but it came out "toucher." "I'm not very touch," I said, making the same mistake again.

"You're nicer; they're pretty aggressive."

"Do you think Mama figured out about Turi? Who she really is?"

He nodded his head. "Mama's pretty sharp," he said.

"Do you think she might have been planning to stay, but when she figured out about Turi she changed her mind?"

"Sara, nothing is easy, nothing is ever simple."

"Because I couldn't bear to think *that*."

"Sara, you have to remember that other people have lives to lead that don't revolve around you, and that includes me. You have to stop feeling sorry for yourself. Things are never going to be the way they were. There isn't any 'supposed to be.' I read in the Cahill Catalog the other day that . . . an ad for some of the Garrison Keillor tapes . . . something about life in Lake Wobegon being the way we desperately hope against hope it's still being lived in small towns across the country, something like that. But I thought that was totally wrong, couldn't be more wrong. You know why those are good stories? Not because they're nostalgic. Because they're not. They're good stories not because they give us life the way it's supposed to be but because they don't."

NIKKI MARIAKAKIS let me have my old job back at the Mount Parnassus, which really wasn't so bad; and when Mr. Bradley called from the Museum of Science and Industry, two weeks after I'd sent in my application, to set up an interview, I almost turned him down. I still hadn't fully recovered from the practice interview, even though Ludi and Turi had apologized. They were just trying to toughen me up, they said. I was too nice. I had to learn not to let people push me around. But I didn't know how to explain this to Mr. Bradley, so I said yes, I'd be delighted.

I bought my own copy of *How to Have a Winning Interview* at Kroch's in Hyde Park and studied it on the IC and then on the bus to Halstead Street. The interview was on Friday. Daddy came up on the train on Wednesday night, and came right to the restaurant, where he got special treatment from Nikki—a glass of ouzo on the house, and a plate of flaming saganaki. The next morning we bought a new attaché case at a luggage store on Wabash, across from Kroch's downtown store, and then we went to Marshall Field's to buy a suit. Daddy'd been reading about power suits in the women's magazines in the grocery story and thought that was what I needed, and he'd brought along a book called *Dressing for Success* from the public library.

I knew he meant well, but I was dragging my feet, blaming him now for pushing me to go to college when I'd wanted to become an airline stewardess. I'd even sent away for material from a training school, but I wasn't old enough at the time. The material, which was very glamorous, had ignited all sorts of fantasies that still flared up a little whenever I saw a pair of stewardesses walking down an airport corridor, chatting with a pair of pilots, of course, and dragging their little suitcases behind them on wheels.

ON THE Jeffrey Express, on the way downtown, Daddy reread the "How to Buy a Suit" chapter. It was a wintry day, in the teens, but Field's was crowded. I wanted to go to the women's department on the second floor, but Daddy wanted to see top-of-the-line suits, which were on the third. "You want to get yourself a really good suit," he said several times. "It's the beginning of your business wardrobe. You can wear the jacket with another skirt or with a dress, or you can wear the skirt with another jacket . . ."

We'd gone over my basic wardrobe. According to *Dressing for Success* I should have three suits (black, tan, burgundy), three colored blouses, two dresses, and three silk scarves. Instead of three suits I had three pairs of jeans, half a dozen white blouses, and my waitress's uniform, which I had bought at a uniform supply place on Halstead, not far from the restaurant. It wasn't exactly a Greek peasant costume, but it was on those lines.

We stepped out of the elevator on the third floor into a different planet, occupied solely by middle-aged women.

Daddy had put his copy of *Dressing for Success* in his briefcase.

One of the women approached us: "Is there something particular you're looking for?"

"Yes," Daddy said, "we're looking for a good-quality single-breasted wool suit. Something with a simple rolled collar and three-inch lapels." It was funny to hear him talking this way, because I knew he didn't know anything about clothes.

I'd made him promise that he wouldn't ask for a "power suit," but I was still slightly embarrassed. The saleswoman didn't bat an eye, however. She was handsome and looked as if she did this for fun, because she loved clothes. She was wearing a blazer over a blouse with some kind of bow on it, and an A-line skirt that skimmed over her body. (I tried to imagine her with Daddy, but I'd gotten sort of used to the idea of Turi.) This woman was too smooth for Daddy, who was . . . well, sort of rough.

I wanted to get in and get out; I wanted to get it over with, but Daddy was taking charge, letting the saleswoman know that *he* was the authority figure, so that she wouldn't try to unload on us clothes that she was having trouble getting rid of. Daddy was prepared to become annoyed if this happened, but perhaps the woman sensed this and didn't try anything; or perhaps it never occurred to her. Maybe she was just a nice woman.

Daddy was wearing a suit himself. His only suit. Navy blue. Nondescript. And a blue St. Clair tie. He looked nice. I hadn't seen him in a tie in ages. "Wear a suit to buy a suit," he said. I didn't have a suit, so I had to make do with a blue wraparound skirt and my one patterned blouse. But I was carrying my new attaché case.

The saleswoman took us to the 8–10 section and stood by while we looked through the suits, which were on large plastic hangers with the skirts folded over inside the jackets. I thought that *she* was appraising *us*, wondering if we knew what we were doing, but she didn't faze Daddy, who felt the material of each suit, looked at the label, examined the lining, checked the stitching behind the collars, tugged at the buttons. If the suit had a pattern he checked to make sure that the pattern matched at the seams. And finally, he took one of the sleeves in his hands and twisted it as if he were wringing out a damp cloth. I glanced up at the saleslady each time this happened, and each time she smiled. "If the wrinkles stay in the material when you do *this*," Daddy explained, "then they'll stay in it when you wear it."

I was too uptight to really look at the suits, or to look at myself in the store's five-panel mirror. The suits all looked the same to me, but we finally settled on one with shoulders that weren't too pointy, a straight skirt that was neither too long nor too short (slightly below the knee), neither too loud nor too quiet (navy blue). I stood in front of the five-panel mirror, holding my empty attaché case, while Daddy checked the hemline to make sure there were no dips. The skirt was a little tight, but I was planning to lose weight.

Daddy told the saleslady that the adjustments would have to be made today, and that he wanted them done by the head fitter.

"I don't know about today," she said.

"It has to be today," Daddy said. "My daughter has an important job interview tomorrow afternoon."

"Let me see what I can do."

When she disappeared Daddy told me to slip on a size-10 skirt.

I didn't want to, but I did. "The jacket's perfect," he said, "but the skirt could be a little roomier; you'll be more comfortable."

"You can't switch the skirt," I said.

"Of course you can. Just keep the jacket on," he said. "Do it now." He hustled me into the dressing room.

"Daddy," I whispered, "you can't *do* that. Really."

But he did it. He put the size-8 skirt back on the hanger with the size-10 jacket.

"Daddy," I hissed.

"Shhh," he said. The saleslady was coming back with the head fitter in tow. "It'll be perfect for *some*one."

The head fitter wasn't looking too pleased, but Daddy slipped her a ten-dollar bill (another trick from the book), which totally surprised her; but it did the job, just as the book said it would.

"How does it *feel?*" she asked. "Move around, there, let me see you sit down."

The jacket didn't lie absolutely flat around my neck and the head fitter said she'd have to remove the collar in order to fix it, but the skirt fit perfectly.

THE NEXT morning I filled out the "Rational Thinking Worksheet" in the back of *How to Have a Winning Interview.* The point was to counteract *all* irrational thoughts (not just irrational thoughts in interview situations). In the left-hand column I listed all my irrational thoughts and fears; in the right-hand column I listed "facts." Then Daddy and I went over a list of questions from a different interview book, one endorsed by the *Wall Street Journal.*

There were two sets of questions—questions I could expect to be asked, and questions I should ask the interviewer. The first list included "Behavior-Based Questions," and I was prepared to tell the interviewer about a time when I had worked effectively under pressure (getting the food booths ready for the International Fair at St. Clair), and about how I had handled a difficult situation with a co-worker (my suitemates); about a time when I had been unable to complete a project on time (term paper), and a time when I had "anticipated potential problems and developed preventive measures" (warding off sexual advances from Nikki at the Mount Parnassus); a time when I had to deal with an irate customer (the Mount Parnassus again).

"Well," Daddy said approvingly, "you've got all your ducks in a row."

And I was armed with questions about the "organizational mission" of the museum and about the "most difficult problems I'd face in this position" and about the "culture" of the organization.

But in the afternoon I reverted to the relaxation techniques of the first book, which focused more on emotional preparation. I knew that I needed a positive attitude, that's just common sense. But the book went further, suggesting that energy is magnetic and that it attracts energy of similar vibration. Positive thoughts will attract positive events. Skyhawk Osborne, author of *The Spiritual Imagination*, writes: "Every woman brings to birth in her own life whatever she conceives in the depths of her spiritual imagination." I tried once again to imagine that my spine was a cord reaching down into the earth, and that the energy of the earth was flowing upwards into my head. But it still didn't work. I sat in a quiet place (my bedroom) and repeated: "My arms and legs are heavy. My arms and legs are heavy and warm. My heartbeat is calm and regular. My breathing is relaxed and effortless. My stomach is warm. My forehead is cool. My right arm is heavy. I am at peace. My right arm is heavy. I'm relaxing. My right arm is heavy . . ." I felt a little better, or at least a little heavier. I said to myself, slowly: "I am the best person for the job. People like me. I'll make a very good impression in the interview. I get along with new people easily." And suddenly I knew where I was. I was watching Richard Simmons squirm on *Late Night with David Letterman*.

James Bradley's office was on the second floor. It wasn't an office, really; more like a workspace, separated from other workspaces by room dividers. There was a metal desk, and on the desk there was a computer. The young man who had escorted me up to the second floor and down a long corridor with doors opening into real offices left me standing there, though there was no one in the workspace. From where I was standing, in my power suit, I could look down on the electric trains. The secretaries I'd noticed on the way were dressed casually—no power suits—but not *too* casually.

Bradley showed up in five minutes with a cup of coffee in a

museum mug, one of those insulated mugs that keep your coffee warm for up to an hour. He put it down on a coaster on top of the desk. He was wearing jeans and a white shirt with the sleeves rolled up.

"You're here for an interview?" he asked.

I opened my mouth, but nothing came out, so I nodded.

This was the moment in which I was supposed to create a good first impression. According to *How to Have a Winning Interview*, I had about five seconds. I had my attaché case in my left hand—hanging down at my left side, not in front of me—so I was ready to shake with my right. Trying not to look like a wind-up toy, I held my rib cage upward, kept my head up, and smiled. I wanted to suggest that I had a good reason for being there, that I hadn't just wandered in. And then suddenly I began to speak. "A friend of one of my roommates," my voice said, "has a cousin who works here." *Irrelevant personal information.* This was one of the first things on the "Do Not" list, but Bradley seized on it.

"Who's that?"

"I'm not sure exactly."

"Do you know what department he works in?"

"I think it's Development or something," I said.

We spent a lot of time trying to figure out who *exactly* it was, my roommate's friend's cousin. I thought his name might be Grady, but Bradley called Development and there was no one named Grady. Or Brady. Or O'Grady. Then he called Personnel and ascertained that no one named Grady or Brady or O'Grady worked for the museum at all. And then he asked me about the dates of World War II.

I admit I should have known the dates of World War II, but I didn't. I could see the newspaper header:

SEVEN OUT OF TEN AMERICAN HIGH SCHOOL
STUDENTS DON'T KNOW DATE OF PEARL HARBOR

And I'd gone to college. If he'd asked me about the first Automatic Sequence Controlled Calculator, the Mark I (1944), or about the first Univac (1951), or about Edward Lorenz's use of computers to predict weather (couldn't be done) (1961), or about the difference between analog and digital computers, I could have told him. Or if he'd asked me to tell him about a time I had worked effectively under pressure (voter registration drive *and* being in charge of the food at the International Fair at St. Clair), or had handled a difficult situation with an authority figure (dealing with police when two roommates were arrested for substance abuse), or had been creative in solving a problem (bottom-pinching at the Mount Parnassus), or had anticipated a potential problem and developed a preventive strategy (bottom-pinching at the Mount Parnassus), I would have been fine. But he hadn't read the *Wall Street Journal National Business Employment Weekly Interviewing* book. "What the hell do the dates of World War II have to do with your goddamn computer exhibit?" I wanted to shout. But instead I managed to recall that a lot of basic computer research came from the demands of the military. "There was the Whirlwind Computer at MIT," I said, "right at the end of the war, for keeping track of bombing missions. That might make a good 'milestone.'" (The exhibit was going to be organized around a series of "milestones.")

"That's not a bad idea," he said, writing something down on a notepad.

For the first time I was glad that I'd studied the *Wall Street Journal* book. Strategies that had seemed stupid or academic suddenly made sense. Like "taking control of the interview by asking your own questions."

"Could you say a little bit," I said, "about your organizational mission?"

At least this got him off the subject of World War II and onto the purpose of science museums. I'd always thought the Museum of Science and Industry was unique, but it turned out there are similar museums in Paris and Munich, to name only two.

"Does your corporate culture encourage risk-taking?" I asked when we'd covered the "organizational mission." "How much freedom will I have to do things my own way?" And so on.

Bradley hadn't given much thought to these questions, but we stumbled along. When I left his cubicle I didn't feel like a total failure, but I couldn't generate any success fantasies either, like calling Daddy to tell him I got the job (though Daddy was waiting in my apartment, two blocks away—why would I *call* him?), and when I walked out the front door and saw the parking lot full of cars and the rows of yellow school buses, I felt as helpless as a child. I remembered the school trips from St. Clair. Four hours in a bus with fifty third-graders, or fifth-graders, or seventh-graders. We seemed to go every other year. There would always be two or three mothers, including my own. I can remember them sitting up next to the driver and smoking. And leading us in singing rounds: *Scotland's burning, Scotland's burning, Watch out, Watch out. Fire Fire Fire Fire. Pour on water, Pour on water.*

WHEN I got back to my apartment I made it sound worse than it really was. I wanted to make it impossible for Daddy to put a good face on it. We were sitting next to each other on the bed in my room, with the door closed. One of my roommates, a Chinese woman named Li Chi, was cooking something with a dozen cloves of garlic.

"Well," Daddy said when I'd finished my tale of woe, "chalk it up to experience." My power suit was on a hanger on the doorknob. It really was a nice suit, but it had cost over five hundred dollars.

That night we browsed through Powell's Bookstore, which was practically underneath my apartment, but we didn't buy anything, and then we ate at the Medici, just down the street, and then we went with my roommate Betsy to a party at her cousin's apartment. It had been snowing all afternoon and about two inches had accumulated. The plows were out but hadn't gotten to the side streets. I still hadn't unpacked all the boxes that I'd packed up before Christmas, because I didn't feel like packing them again, and trying to see into the future was like trying to see into the dark through the snow that had started falling heavily again.

There were plenty of U of C types for Daddy to talk to at the party, but it was a younger crowd; the music was loud and the dancing a little on the wild side. Daddy wasn't a good dancer, but he pushed me around the floor every time a slow dance came on, Billy Joel's "This Night" or Madonna's "Crazy for You," or Clarise Killion's "Say Good-bye," which someone kept playing over and over.

James Bradley was at the party. Well, why shouldn't he be? I thought. He had just as much right to be there as I did. But I tried to avoid him. I knew now that the Japanese attacked Pearl Harbor on December 7, 1941, at 7:55 A.M. local time, and that the German military leaders surrendered unconditionally to General Dwight Eisenhower on May 7, 1945, at three o'clock in the afternoon. I did know the date—I realized—of the first atomic bomb, because it was August 6, one day after Daddy's birthday, but it hadn't registered that afternoon.

Daddy went back to my apartment about eleven o'clock. I was ready to go too, but I didn't want to walk back alone with him. I wasn't ready for another retrospective. I didn't exactly blame him for the fiasco, but it had been crazy to spend five hundred dollars on a suit. I could have lived on that for two months. He couldn't afford it either. I was thinking now that the smile on the saleslady's face had been one of amusement. She'd been smiling *at* us, not *with* us. And that was on top of a hundred dollars for an Italian leather attaché case.

I tried to steer clear of Bradley. He seemed to be content to sit in a corner drinking beer and talking intently to a girl with long black hair. He was still in jeans and the same white shirt. I didn't know if he'd seen me or not. Maybe he was trying to avoid me just as much as I was trying to avoid him.

But that wasn't the case. When I walked by him to get to the bathroom, he called out, "Miss Woodhull?"

I ignored him, but he called out again, "Miss Woodhull?"

I looked around and pretended not to see him, but he leaped to his feet.

"Can I ask you something?" he said. "I almost didn't recognize you."

"More dates?"

"No, seriously." He followed me into the bathroom and shut the door.

"What would you like to know?" I said.

"How did I do?"

"How did *you* do?"

"Yeah," he said, "I've never interviewed anybody before. I think I made a mess of it."

I was at a loss. It was like looking at one of those 3-D pictures. You can't look *at* it, you have to look *into* it, to see the picture. I relaxed my eyes, and then I saw it clearly for the first time.

"I guess I shouldn't have followed you in here," he said, as if he were noticing for the first time that we were in the bathroom.

"No," I said, "that's fine."

"Thanks," he said. "I'm more of a computer person than a people person, if you know what I mean."

"Right," I said. "That was your first interview?"

"Yeah."

"Really," I said, "for your first interview I think you did a terrific job. You threw me off a little there at first, with those questions about World War II, but then you pulled yourself together."

"Well," he said, "thanks. I guess I better get out of here."

I'M NOT much of a drinker, but suddenly the beer tasted the way it's supposed to, not heavy and filling but subtle and hoppy and malty, and I was a little dizzy when I got home. After two o'clock. Daddy was asleep on the couch in the living room, and I didn't want to wake him up, but I made a little noise anyway, just in case he was on the edge of waking up. My power suit was still on a hanger on the doorknob in my bedroom. I slipped the jacket on over my blouse. I didn't put on the skirt, but I held it in front of me and danced around in front of the cheap mirror that I'd fastened to the back of my closet door. I was still hearing the music from the party.

> Three o'clock, the party's done,
> All the rivers have run dry,
> Not a star left in the sky,
> Still it's hard to say good-bye.

In the mirror I thought I caught a glimpse of myself as my father saw me, in my suit. Beautiful, strong, capable, desirable. I thought he'd been wanting to make me into someone else, but he'd just wanted to make me into me. I knew I'd get the job, and I did, but I never wore the suit to work. I wore jeans and men's shirts or sometimes a skirt and a nice blouse. But it was nice to know that it was there, in my closet, like a suit of armor, just in case I ever needed it again.

The Ring
of
Gyges

St. Clair College
2 South St.
St. Clair, Illinois 61401
Department of Classics

17 January 1987

Graduate School of Arts and Sciences Admissions Office
Harvard University
Byerly Hall, Second Floor
8 Gardner Street
Cambridge, Massachusetts 02138

Dear Admissions Committee:

I am writing to recommend Ms. Turan Mirsadiqi for admission
to the graduate program in classics. Ms. Mirsadiqi has been in two
of my classes at St. Clair, and I am directing her honors project. I
know her work well and can recommend her enthusiastically.

The first of these classes, Classical Mythology, was a large one
by St. Clair standards—42 students—but Ms. Mirsadiqi, though
she was only a freshman, made her presence felt from the very
beginning. She is an intelligent and thoughtful reader who sees
more than the average student and who is able to articulate her
perceptions clearly in the classroom discussions and in her written

work, which consisted of daily written assignments and two formal papers. I have kept copies of many of her daily assignments because they serve as examples of the kind of reading I want to encourage. I've also kept copies of her formal papers, both of which demonstrate a firm grasp of the ambivalence of much literary experience.

Her first essay, "Is Helen a Slut, or What?" in which she offered a sympathetic reading of the dilemma Helen faces in the encounter with Hector after the duel between Paris and Menelaus, was imaginative if not brilliant. Her second paper, however—on the role of Psyche in the late Greek mythology—was truly exceptional. The idea that Psyche represents something new in the erotic imagination of classical antiquity is not itself a new one, but by approaching the question from a woman's perspective Ms. Mirsadiqi was able to see things that Neumann and Behnke overlooked in their magisterial treatment of the subject. The essay was awarded the college's Davenport Prize for the best essay in the humanities.

The second course was an upper-level seminar in Ovid. Ms. Mirsadiqi attended the Liceo Classico Machiavelli in Rome for several years, and her command of Greek and Latin is probably stronger than that of most graduate students. She is unassuming, however, and brings out the best in other students. She has published several translations in the college literary magazine, and a revised version of one of the translations she did for this class has been accepted for publication by the Atlantic (Ovid, Amores II.4, Non ego mendosos . . .). I have also encouraged her to revise her seminar paper—on the problem of "sincerity" in the Amores—for eventual publication, though she will need to take a closer look at Propertius and the other Roman elegists.

Ms. Mirsadiqi is one of those students teachers count on to keep the class discussions alive. She has learned to make connections between the texts and her own personal experience without simply using the texts as jumping-off places for private reveries, and her frankness and openness in the classroom help other students to be equally frank and open.

This ability can also be seen in her honors project, "The Ring of Gyges," in which she examines two familiar versions of the story of Gyges: Herodotus i:8–14 and Plato, Republic 359, and a third version, in Old Pahlavi, from an unpublished transcription of three of the clay tablets discovered in 1972 during the Russian excavations at Al-Qurnah in southern Iraq. This version is especially important because it helps us define Plato not simply as a philosopher, but also as an historian of consciousness. The story of the magic ring—the prototype of a whole series of magic rings that includes the ring of the Nibelungen and Sauron's ring in Tolkien's The Lord of the Rings—did not originate with him, but he recognized in it a powerful symbol of the divided self, a problem he placed at the center of philosophy.

In its present form "The Ring of Gyges" suffers from the problem of many undergraduate theses: that is, it is largely a compilation of information, though in this case the compilation is quite significant, for it includes information that was unavailable to the nineteenth-century German scholars—Müller, Schugert, Gelzer, Kroll—who dealt with the story of Gyges. It promises to go beyond a compilation, however, and to become a remarkable piece of scholarship.

The major difficulty at the present moment is that Ms. Mirsadiqi, though she has a gift for languages, has only recently begun studying German. I've been helping her wade through Müller's article on Gyges in Pauly-Wissowa, and that will probably have to suffice. Professor Dihqani of the Oriental Institute of the University of Chicago, who provided us with a transcription of the Al-Qurnah tablets, as well as his own translation, has agreed to serve as Ms. Mirsadiqi's outside honors examiner.

And finally, Ms. Mirsadiqi grew up speaking Persian with her father, English with her mother, and Arabic with the servants. When she was twelve she moved with her family to Rome, attended Italian schools, and was graduated near the head of her class at the Liceo Classico Machiavelli, where she studied French as well as Greek and Latin. She is a very sophisticated young woman, and a good person—charming, unpretentious, full of fun. I can't think of a student in my twenty-four years at St. Clair who would have been a stronger candidate for a fellowship at Harvard. I hope you will give her application serious consideration.

Sincerely,

Alan Woodhull

Alan Woodhull
Chair, Classics Dept.

In Plato's version of the story, the Lydian shepherd Gyges discovers a magic ring that makes him invisible. He uses the power of the ring to seduce the queen, murder the king, and take over the kingdom. "What would keep us from behaving like Gyges," Plato asks, "if like Gyges we had a magic ring that concealed our evil deeds from other people?"

As a boy Woody had often fantasized about possessing a magic ring that made him invisible. He and his friends, in fact, had often debated the relative advantages of invisibility versus the ability to fly. If you could fly, you could hover outside Diana Carlson's bedroom window and watch her undress, but she'd see you as soon as you entered the room, or even as you were hovering outside the window, and start yelling for her mom. If you were invisible, on the other hand, she wouldn't be able to see you, but how would you get into the room in the first place? Those were the issues. Perhaps you could slip into the house during the day, when the front door was unlocked, and hide out till bedtime. But what if someone bumped into you? Or what if you had to use the bathroom?

As a boy Woody had never figured out what to do, but as a man he now felt that in fact he did possess such a ring, that he was in fact invisible. That no one could see him. Not the train conductor who punched his ticket—he was on his way back to St. Clair after a visit to Sara in Chicago. Not the other passengers. Not the women who rang up his groceries at the Eagle or the Hy Vee. Not his colleagues, who were gearing up for the new term. Nor the students who had come back to campus to work on their honors projects during the January break. What *they* saw, or thought they saw, was a middle-aged man riding on a train or buying groceries or carrying books from the library to his office on the third floor of Clair Hall.

What no one could see was a man whose whole body was filled with joy at the prospect of the evening that lay before him, whose imagination was filled with fantasies that would have disgusted and appalled his fellow passengers. Turi had been working her way through *The Joy of Sex*, which she'd found in the bottom of Woody's underwear drawer—it had been there so long that he didn't even see it anymore—and had gotten to the chapter "Sauces & Pickles."

"As part of my education," she'd say—calling him Distinguished Professor and using Persian words for their private parts—"I think we should try . . ." And whatever it was—*anal intercourse, armpit, bathing, big toe, bites, blowing, bondage, boots, chains, chastity belt, Chinese style, clothed intercourse, corsets, dancing, discipline, exercises, feathers, femoral intercourse, feuille de rose, florentine*—they would try it. Woody enjoyed these high jinks enormously. But they were part of the visible world. Someone looking in the window—someone who could fly, or hover—could have seen Turi lying on her back, her legs up in the air, or on her knees, her butt sticking out, could have seen Woody touch her little puckered anus with the tip of his tongue (*feuille de rose*). A voyeur could have observed them trying out "Wailing Monkey Clasping a Tree" or "Wild Geese Flying on Their Backs," just as Woody could see the young man in the seat in front of him on the train turn to the window from time to time and mouth the most terrible curses at his own reflection in the window, articulating clearly but silently, moving his lips so that Woody could understand every word. It was the reflection of the young man's face that Woody could see, not the face itself, as it distorted itself in soundless anger. *You goddamn fucking bitch*, the face would mouth at the window. *You goddamn bitching cunt*. Then the young man would go back to the book he was reading.

Woody had to laugh. This young man *thought* he was invisible, but he'd forgotten about his reflection in the window.

Had Woody forgotten something too? His reflection in a window? He didn't think so. No voyeur could have observed "Birdsong at Morning," in which the lovers (Woody and Turi, that is) whisper to each other their most secret fantasies, the desires that are so embarrassing that a person would not reveal them to another soul even under the severest forms of torture. Yet Woody found himself revealing these things, whispering them in her ear, touching her with nothing more than the tip of his middle finger, feeling the current flow, completing a circuit. As he murmured these things into her ear—things that couldn't possibly be acted out—she would encourage him by crying out, just as the book said she would, like an exotic bird. The Indians, he read, believed that parrots and mynahs had in fact learned their cries from the cries of human lovers. Maybe so.

Where do these things come from? he wondered. From the turbulent ocean of sexuality that underlies conscious experience? Well, that didn't really matter. What was disconcerting, though, was

Plato's problem, the discontinuity between the inner and the outer man. He could see no basis for these fantasies in his waking, conscious life, in his experience of the world. No connection. They were two separate worlds.

And there was another world too, another set of fantasies, that he concealed even from Turi, and that he tried to conceal from himself, but they were too powerful, too insistent. They generally took place in Cookie's room. In these fantasies there is a bucket of water on the floor, and a towel under the bucket to protect the floor, and Angela Strappafelci is in the room with him. He shows her pictures of Cookie. Cookie's scrapbook. Cookie's copy of *The Wind in the Willows*, with its homemade library sticker—drawn freehand with a soft, dull pencil—taped on the inside of the front cover:

KENNETH GRAHAME
THE WIND IN THE WILLOWS

Out		In
12/1/66	Pop	12/15/66
2/14/67	Ludi	4/20/67
4/20/67	Mama	

They look through Cookie's things, taking their time, and then he takes her in his arms and leads her to the bucket of water as he might lead a lover to bed and forces her down, forces her head down into the bucket. He can feel her struggling. His whole body trembles too, like hers. He holds her in such a way that he can keep an eye on his watch. Ten seconds. Fifteen seconds. Twenty seconds. Twenty-five seconds. Thirty seconds. It takes all his strength to keep her from overturning the bucket. One hand on the back of her neck, one farther down in the bucket, grasping her hair. He lets her head up for a breath of air, one second, and plunges her head back into the bucket. Water splashing on the towel. On the hardwood floor that he and Hannah refinished themselves. All the time he's talking to himself. Watching the seconds tick by. Holding his own breath. Another thirty seconds. Lets her up again. Talks to her. Murmurs things in her ear as she sucks in the needed air. *Shall we try it a little longer next time? Maybe a full minute? Do you think you could last a full minute? Sixty seconds?* "No, *per favore*," she begs him, "*no, per favore,* I'm sorry, I'm sorry, I'm sorry." *But not as sorry as you're going to be. Maybe seventy seconds. Do you think you could last seventy seconds?* Before she can answer he pushes her head back down into the bright yellow plastic bucket. *I think seventy seconds might be nice. Just think about it. Your head in the cool water. We have all day, so we can just take our time. Would you like to try for ninety seconds, or shall we stay with thirty seconds for now?* And without warning he plunges her head back into the water. She kicks, tries to straighten her body out. He'd strike her, but he's afraid to let go of her head. He has to remind himself that she has not yet been extradited from Argentina, that the first phase of the trial in Bologna has been proceeding without her.

Goddamnmotherfuckingsonofabitch.

Woody looked up at the reflection of the young man in the seat in front of him, and then at his watch: 7:30. The trial of the terrorists would be starting in Bologna on January 22, less than a week. He'd received another letter from the Association of the Families of the Victims. Letters came two or three times a year, describing the efforts of the Association to prod the government to repeal *Segreto di Stato*—"Top Secret Classification"—in cases of terrorism, to make Judge DiBernardi's tapes available. The earlier letter had contained an invitation to testify at the trial on behalf of the *parti lese*, the injured parties. Probably not till after the summer recess. But this was a new development. The defense attorneys were objecting strenuously. Franco della Chiave and Angela Strappafelci were still in Argentina, their extradition inexplicably delayed. The Association was agitating against suspected right-wing sympathizers in the government and in various branches of the secret services, SISDI and SISMI. The acronyms meant nothing to Woody.

Goddamn miserable motherfucking cocksucking bitching bitch.

It was like a tic, thought Woody. Maybe the young man suffered from Tourette's syndrome. And then he thought of Angela Strappafelci, living in a suburb of Buenos Aires. He could almost feel her head twisting and turning in his hands as he held it underwater. *Ninety seconds was too long, he didn't want her to drown, not yet; but he'd let her think "ninety seconds," let her anticipate ninety seconds. With no air.*

Water already in her lungs. Holding her so she can get just a little air in her nose, along with some water. But he thought too of Socrates' prayer at the end of the *Phaedrus.* As a young man at the University of Michigan, Woody had committed this prayer to memory, had inscribed the Greek words on the tablets of his heart, as Aeschylus advises, because he wanted to have it with him always, to have it become a part of him.

> Dear Pan, and all ye other gods that dwell in this place, grant that the inner and the outer man be as one. May I count him rich who is wise, and as for gold, may I possess so much of it as only a temperate man might bear and carry with him.

He had written these words to Hannah from Esfahan, writing them out in Greek and then in English. He had believed with his whole heart that this was what he wanted, that this was how he wanted to define himself. "Let the inner and the outer man be as one." Or, "be one and the same." Or, simply, "be one." He'd tried different ways of translating it, hoping to get it exactly right someday, just as he'd hoped to get it exactly right in his own life. Someday. He'd never abandoned this hope; he'd just stopped thinking about it.

You goddamn miserable cunt. The young man opened his mouth wide but made no sound as he articulated the words. Woody turned his head so that the person sitting behind him wouldn't be able to see the reflection of his own face in the window, wouldn't be able to see that he was crying.

The train stopped at Kewanee, Hog Capital of the World. A few people got off; a few got on, though this train, the Illinois Zephyr, went only as far as Quincy. Forty-five minutes later it crossed over the Santa Fe tracks just outside of New Cameron and he caught a glimpse of the farm—all the lights were on (once a light was on, Turi never turned it off)—and then it stopped in St. Clair at the Burlington Station on North Seminary Street. Turi had wanted to take him to the station so she could pick him up when he got back, but he'd told her she'd better not. It wouldn't do to be seen together in public. Now he wished he'd said yes, because he was lonely, because what he'd learned from her was that even though the inner and the outer man could never be as one, or be one and the same, or be one, two people could bridge . . . He tried to work it out in his head—his inner man and her inner woman, his outer man and her outer woman—but before he could figure it out, the train pulled into the station. He took his coat down from the overhead rack, slipped it on and zipped it up, picked up his overnight bag, and followed a line of three or four people out into the winter night. Martha Renbarger from the Anthropology Department was waiting for someone; just as well that Turi hadn't come to meet him, just as well that she was waiting for him at home. Not that Martha would have cared.

WOODY HAD assumed that Turi would move back into the dorm at the beginning of the new term, which began on Monday. They could see each other on weekends, take little trips to Iowa City, St. Louis, maybe Chicago, though Chicago was dangerous—too many St. Clair alums. On campus they would meet as teacher and student. No little games. No little pats, no secret glances, no Ovidian monkey business, just business. But Turi stayed put. She brought her new Macintosh computer out to the farm, set it up on the dining room table, and spread out her notes and papers around it. Woody was a little put out, but secretly he was pleased. It didn't matter if they couldn't use the dining room because they ate in the kitchen anyway.

"If you want me out of here," she said, "all you have to do is say so."

"It's not that . . ."

"I like it here, Woody; I like pretending that we love each other—most of the time I'm not even pretending, really—and I like your cooking; but if you're worried . . ."

"It's not that . . ."

She called her parents in Rome every Saturday morning—Saturday afternoon in Rome—so they wouldn't call her, and her roommate had explicit instructions about what to say if one of her parents ever *did* call. Woody would hear her in the kitchen, talking in English to her mother and in Italian to her brother Babak, and in Persian to her father. He had trouble following the conversations with her father, but he'd listen as she chatted with her mother—about her classes, about her honors thesis, about other students who had spent time with the Mirsadiqis in Rome, about other Iranian students— waiting for his own name to come up, as it always did. "He's doing fine," she'd say. "We had a meeting last week . . . Yes, yes . . . Yes, I will." And later she'd give him the love that Allison sent. The phone bills were astronomical, but she had plenty of money and always insisted on a reckoning at the end of the month.

TURI'S TRANSLATION of Ovid's *Amores* II.4 caused quite a stir when it appeared in the February issue of the *Atlantic*. The PR department at St. Clair acted as if she'd won the Nobel Prize. Press releases were sent out. There was talk of starting a translation program. Interviews appeared in the local paper, the *Register Mail*, and in the student paper, the *Clarion*. Not everyone was happy, though. Two or three letters of complaint were written to the *Clarion*: the poem perpetuates sexist stereotypes, the speaker is a male chauvinist pig, and so on. And some spirited defenses appeared too. In his Ovid seminar Woody defended the poem on the grounds that it articulated male fantasies and made them manageable by placing them in a humorous context:

> Why am I always in love? A hundred reasons.
> Does she lower her eyes? I burn.
> Is she pushy and aggressive? I'm caught.
> No country girl, she won't restrain herself
> Between the sheets.

But he didn't write a letter to the newspaper. Turi didn't need anyone to defend her. The magnitude of her success rendered her indifferent to criticism, and she pretended to be indifferent to praise, too. But she kept asking Woody about ways the translation might be improved—perhaps *procax* should be translated as "saucy" rather than "pushy"—and her face gave her away, glowing, as if a candle were burning inside her head.

The excitement lasted about a week, and then the serious work of the semester began. Woody always assigned a set of papers on the first day of class to be handed in at the end of the second week. Now he had to grade them. He was trying to get on with his own work too, *The Cosmological Fragments*. But he was more interested in Turi's thesis. Plato had really hit upon something—the birth of consciousness. Julian Jaynes had visited the campus two years earlier and Woody encouraged Turi to write to him at Princeton.

His own sense of being invisible was stronger than ever, stronger even than it had been on the train coming back from Chicago. Standing in front of his mythology class, talking about Hesiod— about Gaia's parthenogenesis, about the divine marriage of Earth and Ouranos (Woody accented the first syllable: OU-ranos), about the castration of Ouranos by his son Cronus, about the shift from a patriarchal to a political conception of power—he felt as if he were standing behind a one-way glass, that he could see his students but they couldn't see him.

Several years ago he and Hannah, while moving some furniture around upstairs, had turned up a big metal box that they'd bought for important papers. As far as Woody knew they'd never put any-thing in it, but when they opened it, there were three letters written by Woody's mother while she was a student at St. Clair. They were written to *her* mother in Chicago. Woody had no idea where they had come from. The really amazing thing was that in one of the let-ters Woody's mother talked about the classical mythology course she was taking, which was the course that Woody was teaching at the time. Some of the things she'd said made him think that the course she was describing must have lasted a full year rather than just a semester. How else could they have included not only the *Aeneid* but the *Argonautica*? He meant to look it up in an old college catalog but never got around to it. Sometimes, in the classroom, he imagined his mother sitting there, one of his students, sitting in the back row, as he talked about the castration of Ouranos by his son Cronus, a pas-sage that over the centuries has lost none of its power to startle, even in the feeblest translation:

> Then did come great Ouranos, bringing with him might. Longing for love he covered Gaia and straightway spread himself in every direction. Then from his hiding place did his son reach out with his left hand, and with his right did he hold the monstrous pruning hook, long and jagged, and eagerly did he prune his own father's genitals and hurled them back to be carried away behind them.

"The severed members landed in the ocean," Woody would say, "and from this act, my friends, was born . . . ?" And he'd wait for an answer. The students had read the material, but they couldn't make the connection, couldn't overcome their resistance.

"Remember Botticelli," Woody would prompt, holding up a print of *Venus Rising from the Sea*. "You've all seen this, right?"

It would take a while, but eventually all but the slowest students would figure it out.

"That's right, my friends, the goddess of love, born from the severed genitals of Ouranos. You thought Freud was joking, but there it is right in front of you, the Oedipus Complex in its most powerful form. Right at the beginning of time the son and the mother conspire against the father." And then he'd pause for questions.

Would his mother have asked a question? Would old Professor Hartley, who, according to her letter, had a lot of things to "get off his chest," have broached the matter so directly? Had they even read Hesiod? This was something else he might check, though he doubted that the old catalogs would include a reading list.

But he was invisible even to his mother.

He wasn't entirely invisible, however. By the middle of March someone had caught a glimpse of his reflection in a window, the way he'd caught a glimpse of the young man's reflection in the window on the train. That was how he interpreted a memo from the dean telling him to come to her office after his second-hour class on Monday. He tried to tell himself that she wanted to talk about the college's role in the Italian minister of agriculture's visit—Woody, because of his beautiful italic handwriting, and because he was the only one on the faculty who spoke Italian, was going to present the minister with a letter from the college—but he knew that that wasn't it. He was fifty-three years old, but when the memo appeared in his mailbox on Friday morning, he felt like a boy who's been summoned to the principal's office. He was nervous all weekend. He hadn't spoken to the dean on a personal level since Halloween. He'd stopped going to Hebrew lessons. He'd wanted to apologize, or at least explain. But he wasn't sure he'd done anything wrong, and he couldn't come up with an explanation that did justice to the complexity of the situation. Their relationship could not go back to what it had been—ironic, joking—but neither could it go forward. Woody got a copy of the new sexual harassment policy from the office of the dean of students and read it carefully. The language was bureaucratic and mildly alarming—it might have been amusing under other circumstances—but he could find nothing that applied to him. He had not subjected anyone to unwanted sexual attention; had not attempted to coerce anyone into a sexual relationship; had not punished or threatened to punish anyone for refusal to comply; had not implied that sexual favors might be a basis for grades in a course; had not engaged in conduct that had the purpose or effect of interfering with anyone's performance; had not created an intimidating, hostile, or offensive work or learning environment.

IT WAS now the third week of the term. The mythology class was reading books v–vii of the *Odyssey* in Robert Fitzgerald's translation. On the previous evening Turi and Woody, sitting at the kitchen table, had read the first three hundred lines of book v aloud, in Greek. The story of Calypso. It was Woody's favorite passage, and he was looking forward to teaching it in the morning, though he was a little uneasy about the coming interview with the dean. He was uneasy, but he didn't say anything to Turi, because he didn't want to spoil the evening.

The class was a strong one that included Jay Miller, the editor of the college literary magazine, and Rebecca Sunderland, who'd played Dulcinea in *Man of La Mancha*, and Barbara Holmes, Jenny Pratt, Alex Tuotuola, and others who hadn't done anything that he knew about but who were good students.

There were some loafers, too, and some fraternity/sorority types. But that was OK with Woody. Some new feminists, trying out their wings, were eager to expose the sexist assumptions of the old stories. That was OK too. And a couple of fundamentalist Christians, who made a nuisance of themselves. And even that was OK. And there were the students who looked at their feet when he asked them a question. That wasn't so good.

On the blackboard Woody wrote:

A) Live in a tropical paradise with a luscious sex partner who is ready and eager to gratify your every fantasy, and who will make you immortal.

and

B) Go home to your aging spouse and grow old and die.

He brushed chalk off his hands. "Let's see a show of hands. How many of you would choose A?"

Hands shot up. Everyone chose A except the two fundamentalists and two or three others who suspected a trick.

"What's the catch?" Betsy Ridenour asked.

"No catch," Woody said.

"It's not like Tithonus, is it?"

"Not like Tithonus. You don't grow old. You don't get sick. No doctors, hospitals, nursing homes."

Betsy's hand went up again.

"Let's see those hands again." He counted thirty-seven.

"How many of you would choose B?"

No hands.

"Everyone has to choose."

Four hands.

Woody was always curious about the B's. One was Arthur Tipton; Arthur was a loner, not liked by other students because he wasn't very likable. Woody sometimes saw him walking by himself across the campus, his short hair combed straight down over his forehead. Heavy glasses magnified his small eyes, but despite his weak eyes, he was not a strong student. Woody didn't want to embarrass him, but Arthur, who'd been looking down at his shoes, glanced up, and Woody called on him.

"Mr. Tipton," he said, "would you give us a minority opinion? Here's an opportunity to gratify our deepest human fantasies: sexual gratification and overcoming death. You're not buying into it. How come?"

Arthur blushed.

Other students were eager to talk. The room was full of laughter, movement, exchange of glances.

Arthur: "It doesn't seem right."

"Can you elaborate a little?"

Apparently not.

Ms. Saunders spoke without waiting for Woody to call on her. "It's not a real choice."

"I'm aware of that, Ms. Saunders, but we can pretend."

Ms. Saunders: "But what's the point? I mean, if it's impossible . . ."

"Maybe we can learn something about ourselves by pretending, by the way *we* choose."

"It's immoral." Ms. Jackson, who was always ready to throw herself into the breach, tireless, couldn't contain herself.

"Ms. Jackson?" he said.

"Odysseus is already married."

It wasn't a cruel class, but there was a certain amount of groaning. "What's moral?" someone asked.

"Moral is not cheating on your wife, for one thing," Ms. Jackson replied.

"I don't see how he could turn it down. I mean . . ." Wendy Johnson, a natural leader, always concluded her responses with "I mean."

"What exactly *do* you mean?"

"Well, we're talking about Odysseus, right? I mean, getting it off with a goddess, and not having to die. I mean, for guys, if it was me, I'd go for it."

"Isn't this sort of a male thing?" said Judy Kramer.

"You mean it's not a female thing too?" Woody asked.

Laughter. A sign of general agreement. The issue was settled.

"Let's look at the text," he said. "Let me read the passage aloud."

The students scrambled to find the place.

"No, no," Woody said. "Close your books. Just listen to the words. Calypso first:

> "Son of Laërtês, crafty Odysseus,
> Descended from Zeus.
> Even now you can't wait to get back home,
> To your own dear country.
> May good luck go with you,
> Though if you knew what suffering lay ahead
> you would stay here with me in this house
> And live forever, though you longed for your dear wife.
> Not that she is as desirable as I,
> For what mortal woman can compare with a goddess
> in beauty and grace?"

"That's her offer: 'I'm better-looking than Penelope. Sexier. More interesting; not inferior'—οὐ δέμας οὐδὲ φυήν. And immortality. You wouldn't have to die. How could you turn it down? Sex and immortality. What a deal. Now listen to what Odysseus has to say." Woody read from his own Greek text, an Oxford onionskin edition that Hannah had given him. He translated as he went:

> "Don't be angry my lady goddess.
> I know that gentle Penelope is no match for you
> In beauty and grace, for she is a mortal woman,
> Unlike you, a goddess
> Who will never grow old and die.
> Even so, I long for the day that I can return home.
> And if some god overturns me on the wine-dark sea,
> I will endure this fate too,
> For I have suffered much on the sea and in battle.
> Let one more trial be added to my story."

> He spoke; the sun went down and darkness covered the
>   earth.
> They withdrew to the inner chamber
> to take their pleasure in each other's arms.

"What is he saying here? Why is he choosing to do this? Can you find the reason within yourselves? Can you connect it to our discussion of the Homeric gods in the *Iliad*? To the choice of Achilles?"

A hand went up. Another.

"Ms. Vollman?"

"Being human is more meaningful than being a god."

"And why is that?"

"Because you have to confront limits, you have to make choices."

"And why is this important?"

"It's what gives your life meaning. Odysseus is choosing the human condition. He's saying he'd rather be a human being with all its limitations than be a god."

"Very good. Mr. Achepol?"

"But it's not really a choice, is it? I mean, no one could really be a god, be immortal."

Ms. Jackson's hand went up. Woody ignored her, but she was determined to be heard: "We *are* immortal whether we want to be or not."

Woody never knew what to do with this sort of remark, the sort of remark that could stop a discussion on a dime.

"I think," he said, brushing by her, "that it's a question of what attitude we take towards our fantasies, towards our deepest wishes. We want sexual gratification; we want to escape death. That seems to be the bottom line. But then we find another line below that one. And to me this is the most important thing of all. Better to live out your life with a real woman, or a real man, than with a sex god or goddess. Better to choose reality over fantasy, not to let fantasy have the last word. This passage is very important to me. I used to worry about death all the time. I thought that if we could live forever, life would be meaningful. But now I see it's the other way around. If we lived forever, life would be meaningless. That's what Odysseus knows."

Ms. Vollman: "Do you really believe that?"

"I do."

Ms. Vollman: "And what about sex. Do you believe that too?"

"Believe what exactly?"

"That it's better to go to bed with a . . . an old woman, an unattractive spouse, than with a sex goddess, or god."

"That's tougher, isn't it. I guess I think it's better to choose reality over fantasy. Reality resists us. Fantasy . . . Calypso suggests fantasy to me. Penelope, reality."

Woody looked at his watch. The class was almost half over and he wanted to get on to Nausicaa and Phaeacia. He called for another vote: "A or B? Gratification of all your sexual fantasies and you get to live forever, or B, live in the real world, work things out with a real person, grow old and die?"

He could sense some uneasiness now.

"Let's see a show of hands."

This time the B's had a clear, though not overwhelming, majority. Woody was satisfied. He'd accomplished something. He'd persuaded roughly twenty people to vote against their deepest instincts. Ready to go on to the landing in Phaeacia, or Scheria. But someone in the back of the room had a question.

"Ms. Taylor?"

"But Odysseus keeps right on screwing Calypso, doesn't he? After he decides to dump her? I mean, that's what this is all about, isn't it?—'they withdrew to the inner chamber to take their pleasure in each other's arms.' And he's been screwing her for how many years, seven years?"

"It's not very clear how many years he's been on Ogygia."

"OK, whatever, but several. So he's just been using her, right? So how's she supposed to feel now?"

"Good question, Ms. Taylor."

"I mean, isn't the *Odyssey* the archetypal patriarchal text? Odysseus encounters a series of women or female figures and . . ."

"And?"

Woody imagined his mother sitting at one of the desks in front of him. What would she have made of this exchange? When Woody was twenty-one—his first year in Ann Arbor—a lover had appeared in his mother's life, and she'd been happier than he'd ever known her, happier than she'd been before Woody's dad had died. But then the lover, whose name was Andy, disappeared, and his mom had kept on teaching Latin at the high school till she was sixty-five. Woody had called her and had written, but not often enough; but he'd never asked her about Andy—he couldn't remember his last name—and she'd never explained.

"Athena appears to Nausicaa," he said, ignoring Ms. Taylor's question. "'Maidenhood must end.' Athena tells her to prepare her wedding chest, to wash all her wedding clothes. Nausicaa goes to her father the king and asks him to send the mule cart around so she can take the laundry down to the river pools. He's going to need some clean clothes, and so are her brothers, for when they go to the dancing. 'See what I must think of!' she tells him. And the beautiful thing about the story is that she doesn't tell her father everything. She doesn't say a word about her own wedding, but her father knows. She doesn't have to tell him."

Standing in front of the class Woody could hardly keep back the tears, because he was thinking of his own daughters. He read aloud from the Greek text, forgetting to translate at first, till the students' laughter brought him back to reality:

She was too modest to mention her own wedding,
But her father understood everything:

"I would not deny my lovely daughter mules,
    or anything else.
Go on now; the stablemen will bring out a wagon
With smooth wheels and a box for your things."

A hand went up.

"Ms. Taylor?"

"Don't you think he's being patronizing?"

"Well," Woody said, "he is her father."

"I mean, she's just doing laundry for the men. Why don't her brothers wash their own clothes?"

Woody started to say something about honoring the otherness of the text, but he stopped himself. It was a legitimate question. Why don't they wash their own clothes? But he wasn't in the mood to explain.

"Just look at this scene on the beach," he said. "Look at how tactful Odysseus is. Naked, grizzled; he doesn't want to frighten them, but the girls run away. Except Nausicaa." Time was running out. "Just listen to this," he said. Once again the students scrambled for their books. "You don't need your books," he said again. "Just listen, and while you're listening I want you to think of something. I want you to think about your parents, because this is the way they think about you, and you don't even know it. You may not know it till you have children of your own, but here's a chance, a sneak preview.

"Ms. Taylor," he said to the girl who'd asked about Odysseus screwing Calypso and about the brothers failing to wash their own clothes, "would you come up here and play Nausicaa for us?"

She made her way from the back of the room, looking straight ahead but not at Woody. "I'll be Odysseus," Woody said. "All you have to do is listen:

'I need your help princess; whether you are a goddess
Or a mortal woman. If you are a goddess,
Then of those who dwell in the broad heavens

You are most like Artemis, the daughter of great Zeus,
In form and stature. But if you are a daughter of mortal
    parents,
Then your father and mother are thrice blessed,
And your brothers too. Surely they glow with pleasure
When they see you begin to dance—
Such a beautiful flower among young women.'"

The bell on Clair Hall—a recording of a bell, actually—had begun to ring. But Ms. Vollman had her hand in the air.

"One more question," Woody said. "Ms. Vollman?"

"About Odysseus," she said. "He really does keep on screwing Calypso, doesn't he? Just like Sherry said? I mean—even after . . ." She shook her head to indicate that she couldn't get over it.

The students were getting their books together; there was no restraining them now.

"Yes," Woody said. "It's called having your cake and eating it too."

MYTHOLOGICALLY speaking, the dean was Artemis or Athena, probably the former, since Athena was helpful whereas Artemis was jealous of her honor. Her virginity, Woody told his students, when they read the *Hippolytus*—Artemis's virginity, not the dean's—could best be understood as a manifestation of her fierce independence. No man could control her. She was not subject to Aphrodite. She (Artemis) was the sort of woman to win the Tour de France, or the first woman to sail round the Cape of Good Hope or Cape Horn. She was the sort of woman you'd expect to meet coming down the Matterhorn as you were on your way up.

There were two people ahead of Woody in the dean's office—he was fifteen minutes early—but there was never any waiting. The dean kept two secretaries busy, their desks separated by a freestanding partition to muffle the sound of their typewriters and to discourage them from talking to each other.

"Busy today?" he said to one of the secretaries, Diana Carter, whose daughter had taken his mythology class several years earlier.

"Always busy," she said, nodding toward the closed door of the dean's office.

Woody looked over a copy of the letter to the Italian minister of agriculture that he'd brought with him—*È con un sentimento di grande onore in occasione della Sua visita negli stati uniti ci permettiamo di presentarLe questo medaglione quale espressione di sentita gratitudine da parte di tutto il Collegio di Santa Chiara e, in special modo, da parte dei Sui studenti che hanno proseguito i loro studi in Italia . . .* —in case that was what the dean wanted to see him about. He put the letter down without finishing it and picked up a copy of the *Chronicle of Higher Education.*

The dean's door opened; the vice-president for finance came out and Edna Hautman from the German Department went in.

Woody looked at the ads in the *Chronicle.* Lots of jobs for administrators. Nothing for classicists. In Woody's first year in grad school at Ann Arbor there were plenty of good jobs; in his second year, everybody got a job; his third year not everybody got a job. His last year almost nobody got a job. He'd been lucky. Actually, he noted, there was an assistant professorship in Utah, a one-year position. And a full professorship at Yale. Substantial publications required.

The dean's overall agenda had been to relieve the faculty of excessive committee work by appropriating all power to herself. It had seemed like a good idea at the time, but then the Geology Department had been eliminated, and now the dean didn't want to replace Mac; she wanted to turn Classics into a branch of a new World Literature "concentration," though no one knew exactly what a concentration was.

Edna Hautman came out of the office, nodded at Woody, and John Fields, Physics, who agreed with the dean on everything and even tried to imitate her style, went in.

At ten o'clock sharp, John came out and Woody went in, the letter in his hand.

The dean—tall and craggy—sat behind her desk. Woody could think of many famous craggy men but not many famous craggy women. She wore no makeup. Her gray hair was pulled back and tied in a bun.

"Well, Jane," he said, "what can I do for you?"

She was writing something. "Have a seat," she said without looking up. Her desk was not bare, but it was uncluttered.

She picked up the phone and pushed a button. "No calls," she said.

Woody always found it difficult to understand why a student might feel nervous sitting in his office. For what? He wasn't going to bite anyone's head off. Did the dean feel this way now?—feel that there was no reason, in her mind, for Woody to be nervous?

Woody was older than the dean but not *that* much older. They had both lived through the sixties and shared some of the same political landmarks, landmarks that the students were too young to remember: the Kennedy assassinations, LBJ, the assassination of Martin Luther King, the war on poverty, the war in Vietnam, Nixon, the first moon landing, Kent State, busing, Watergate. This year's freshman class had been starting kindergarten when Nixon resigned.

The dean made a few remarks about the nature of the liberal arts college, which seemed uncharacteristically indirect. "This has got to stop," she said finally.

Should he ask what, as if unaware of any problem? Not to ask would be tantamount to acknowledging that there was in fact a problem.

"The dean finds this situation very painful."

The dean's habit of referring to herself in the third person when discussing official business always made Woody a little nervous. "I don't care for these visits myself," he said. "Sometimes I'm sorry I ever learned to write an italic hand; if I hadn't I wouldn't have to do these damn letters."

The dean looked startled. "What on earth are you talking about?"

"Passamonte's visit. Next month. I've got the letter here."

"I'm not talking about Passamonte," the dean said. "I'm talking about the situation that's developed."

"What situation is that?" Woody asked, regretting this gambit as soon as he'd used it.

"The situation you've created. It puts the college in a very embarrassing position."

"I'm not sure what you're getting at."

"You remember the case of Ivan Meadows?"

"Of course."

"The dean would hate to see a similar outcome. It's not good for anyone. And it's not necessary." The dean didn't want to spell it out, and Woody wasn't willing to discuss the matter till she did.

"What's not necessary?"

"Don't make this difficult for the dean."

"Jane, tell me what this is all about."

"Don't be so dense, Mr. Woodhull."

"And please stop calling me *Mr.* Woodhull."

"All right. Woody." She pronounced his name as if it were distasteful. "But you're going to have to face up to this thing; you're going to have to do something about it, and you're going to have to do it now."

He could see that she wasn't going to give in. "You mean about Ms. Mirsadiqi?"

"Of course. What did you think I meant?"

"Hard to be sure, since you weren't willing to tell me. But this is hardly parallel to Ivan's case."

"Not an exact parallel, but close enough from an administrator's point of view. A big headache for the dean. The same kind of headache."

"But Ivan wouldn't leave that girl alone. He even went into the dorm after her. She didn't want anything to do with him. She asked for police protection. Her father threatened to sue the college . . ."

"From the point of view of the administration, the fact that you are cohabiting with Ms. Mirsadiqi boils down to the same thing: a major headache."

"Has Ms. Mirsadiqi complained?"

"You know she hasn't. That isn't the point."

"Well, then, what is the point? *Cui malo?* Who's being harmed?"

"The situation has been brought to the dean's attention."

"By whom?"

"That's immaterial at this stage."

"It's not immaterial to me." Woody didn't like the word "stage."

"This is a community, Mr. Woodhull. We have to consider the good of the whole. That's why we developed a policy on sexual harassment after the Meadows episode."

"I haven't harassed anyone."

"You're looking at the small picture; the dean has to look at the big picture."

The dean took a folder from her desk drawer, took out a piece of paper from it, and began to write something on the paper. She picked up the phone, pushed a button, and told the secretary not to hold her calls any longer. Woody was still sitting there. It took him a while to realize that the interview was over.

THE VISIT of Fausto Passamonte, the Italian minister of agriculture, originally scheduled for the first week of March, had to be postponed indefinitely. The Italian government—itself an interim government—was on the edge of collapse. And then, almost without warning, the visit was rescheduled for the first week of April. It wasn't the sort of occasion Woody enjoyed, but he wanted to speak to the man about the extradition of Angela Strappafelci and Franco della Chiave. Why hadn't they been extradited? Woody experienced a sense of outrage when he thought about it. He didn't expect anything much from an encounter with a minister of agriculture, but he wanted to make a personal gesture. He'd been reading with greater care the bulletins from the Association of the Families of the Victims in Bologna. The Association was not a self-help group, as he'd initially assumed, but a political organization.

They were already halfway through the term, and the pressure to get rid of Turi was increasing. He'd received an official letter from the dean, and the faculty was debating a new policy on amorous relations that would supplement the recently enacted policy on sexual harassment. Woody had been given a deadline—April first. In the event that he was still cohabiting with a student over whom he exercised power, the dean would convene a special commission consisting of the Executive Committee and three members of the Judicial Board. Enclosed in the envelope with the letter were copies of the sexual harassment policy and a draft of the new amorous relations policy.

The April first deadline passed. Woody still hadn't said anything about it to Turi. *Her* position was perfectly clear. If Woody *asked* her to leave, she would leave. Otherwise, she'd stay. Woody's position was perfectly clear too: she could stay or go as she pleased. He was not going to *ask* her to leave.

Whenever he thought of his position, he found himself short of breath. But alive. Maybe that was why he was acting against his own best interests.

"She's not mine to give up," Woody said to Mac, who'd finally got wind of the matter and confronted him in his office, "or to hold on to, for that matter. She's not a prize, a *geras*. This isn't Briseis and Achilles."

"You've got to think of the good of the whole," Mac said, sitting on the edge of Woody's desk, playing with a pencil.

"And you're not Nestor either."

"Her father's going to get an honorary degree in June. They're hoping he'll kick in ten million for the new capital fund drive. With ten million dollars . . ."

So that's it, Woody thought. "You're afraid her father will back out of the deal if he finds out his little darling is cohabiting with a faculty member?"

"Not to put too fine a point on it, yes."

"So all this stuff from the dean's office is smoke and mirrors?"

"I don't think the dean actually sees it that way, but that's what it boils down to."

"Mac," Woody said, laughing, "I never thought the day would come when you and the dean would find yourself on the same side of an issue."

"It's no laughing matter."

"In one of those books on grief that I read after Cookie's death, it said that the dead person often appears to say good-bye, in a dream. That's never happened with Cookie; I'm still waiting, Mac, but my dreams . . . I'll dream that I go downtown and that I see Larry Taylor drive by in his van, and I wave to him, and then I buy some toothpaste in Osco's. Too boring. Hannah wouldn't listen to them. But I feel Cookie's come back in another way, like Socrates' *daimon*, not exactly appearing, but . . . You know, she never urges me to do anything; but if I start to take a wrong turn, then I can feel this resistance, almost like a voice telling me to turn back. But I don't hear that voice now; that's why I'm sticking to my guns."

"You're shooting yourself in the foot, that's what you're doing. You're playing into that woman's hands."

Sitting alone in his office, after Mac left, trying to read Euripides' *Hippolytus*, Woody tried to remember a time when Mac had been angry at him, but he couldn't. He knew that Mac had the good of the Classics Department at heart, and his own good too, Woody's good; and he knew that he himself had made up all the stuff about Cookie coming back as his *daimon;* but even though he'd made it up, right off the top of his head, he knew that it was true.

WOODY REWROTE the letter several times in Italian on sheets of good parchment till he got it just right, and then he put the final copy in a St. Clair diploma folder, which he put on the corner of his desk, along with a medallion in a velvet-lined box, an image of Clair Hall, one of two remaining sites of a Lincoln-Douglas debate.

St. Clair College
2 South St.
St. Clair, Illinois 61401

Il 27 marzo 1987

Signor il Ministro di Agricultura,

It is with a feeling of great honor that on the occasion of your visit to the United States we present to you this medallion as an expression of the gratitude sincerely felt by St. Clair College and by our students who have pursued their studies in Italy.

It is to be hoped that these exchanges will contribute to the good relations between the United States and Italy and that they will continue to bear the fruits of peace and amity.

Please accept, Signor il Ministro, the homage of our profound respect.

Presidente del Collegio

Woody added his own note, also in Italian, on a half sheet of paper, which he stuck in the diploma folder along with the official college letter. He intended to hand it to the minister of agriculture personally, if he got the chance:

27 marzo 1987

Signor il Ministro di Agricultura,

Although I speak as a foreigner, I also speak as one who loves Italy, or who has loved Italy in the past. From my point of view it is astonishing not that the Italian government has failed to discover all the "facts" about the *strage* of 15 August, which are complex, but that the government has failed to act upon what it knows. As the father of Carolyn Woodhull, who was killed in the bombing of the train station in Bologna in 1980, I urge you to do everything within your power to expedite the extradition of Angela Strappafelci and Franco della Chiave from Buenos Aires, Argentina, and to release the tapes made by Judge DiBernardi in the course of his investigations, and to abolish *Segreto di Stato* in cases of terrorism.

Sinceramente,
Alan Woodhull

They drove to the Warren Farms in a college car. Turi had insisted on going with Woody to the ceremony because her father, who knew Passamonte personally, had asked her to, had told her that the minister would be expecting her. Woody didn't care. At least he'd be sure to meet the minister.

There were secret service agents everywhere, but not as many as there had been for Mitterrand, in 1984, or for Khrushchev, in 1962, Woody's first year at St. Clair, a year before Kennedy's assassination. Woody hadn't written the college letter for Khrushchev—his talents as a calligrapher had not yet been recognized, and in any case he didn't know the Cyrillic alphabet—but he could remember the secret service agents who had come to the farm, and who had blocked off Kruger Road completely for two days so that not even school buses could pass. Woody'd had trouble getting into the college. Other leaders had come too: Benazir Bhutto, King Olaf V of Norway, South Korean president Chung Hee Park, King Charles XVI Gustavus of Sweden, whose cousin lived in Bishop Hill, and even a delegation from Iran. Woody had not attended all these affairs, but he'd been to the Iranian one, since he was the only one around who spoke Persian. The drill was always the same: roast hog, potato salad, lettuce salad, three-bean salad, and lots of pie. The Iranians, who had no interest whatsoever in hog farming, refused to eat the pork, but if the State Department learned a lesson, it had forgotten it by the time Pinky Bhutto came. Didn't anyone realize that Pakistanis were Muslims? Woody always thought of her as Pinky—her nickname at Harvard—because she'd spoken to one of Cookie's international law classes, about a year after her father was overthrown by General Zia; and she'd been present too, sitting on the speakers' platform, when Cyrus Vance, who'd just resigned as Carter's secretary of state, spoke at Cookie's graduation.

A large, striped canopy—which Woody recognized as belonging to the Davidson Funeral Home—had been set up near the entrance to the hog barn. There were still patches of snow around the foundation on the north side. Although it was April it was chilly and large heaters had been hooked up to a special generator that chugged softly off to one side. About a hundred folding chairs had been set up under the canopy. Woody looked around for Curtis, who had developed a knack for managing these affairs, but he was nowhere in sight.

The minister of agriculture upset his security guards by leaving the roped-off area under the canopy and mingling with the crowd, shaking hands as if he were an American politician on the stump. Woody shook his hand but didn't have a chance to hand him the letter.

There were a few shortish speeches, by the U.S. secretary of agriculture, and by the assistant secretary of agriculture, and then by Dick Warren, a former U.S. secretary of agriculture, who presented his Italian counterpart with an oil painting, framed in barn siding, of an Illinois farmhouse.

Various other presentations followed, during one of which the assistant secretary called Woody aside and told him that the governor, Big Jim Thompson, who had forgotten to bring something to give to the minister, would present the letter and the medallion from St. Clair. He introduced Woody to the governor as the head of the Italian Department.

The governor held out a huge paw: "Pleased to meet you, Mr. Head."

Woody handed over the diploma folder and the medallion. Reluctantly. He was somewhat annoyed, but he was relieved too. Politics made him nervous. He was glad to be a spectator rather than a participant.

After dinner, which was the same as always, except that someone had thought to provide several large bottles of Gallo Hearty Burgundy, the governor made a speech in which he praised St. Clair College, about which he clearly knew nothing, as a quality institution, which could be justly proud of its record, etc. The translator translated for the minister. The governor was enjoying himself; Fausto Passamonte was not. Woody thought about leaving as quickly as possible. He had papers to grade. But Turi—where was she?—would want to say hello to the minister.

At the end of his speech the governor pulled out the letter from the diploma folder. "Senior Minister-o di Agriculture-a," he said before realizing that it was in Italian. He handed it to the translator. Woody realized that the governor had pulled out not the official college letter but his personal letter.

The translator, who had been translating English into Italian, for the benefit of the minister, now translated Woody's Italian into English, for the benefit of the audience:

"Signor il Ministro di Agricultura, Although I speak as a foreigner . . ."

Woody rose to leave. He thought he'd like to go back home and loosen up the soil in the garden that he and Turi had put in—lettuce, arugula, cilantro, peppers, tomatoes, two rows of beans. Or just cut the dead wood out of the grape arbor, something he should have done two weeks earlier. But the assistant secretary, who had been sitting next to him, grabbed him by the elbow: "What the hell is this?"

". . . astonishing not that the Italian government has failed to discover all the 'facts' about the *strage* of 15 August, which are complex, but that the government has failed to act upon what it knows. As the father of Carolyn Woodhull, who was killed in the bombing of the train station in Bologna in 1980, I urge you to do everything within your power to expedite the extradition of Angela Strappafelci and Franco della Chiave from Buenos Aires, Argentina, and to release the tapes made by Judge DiBernardi in the course of his investigations, and to abolish *Segreto di Stato* in cases of terrorism."

The *New York Times* printed the letter the next day. St. Clair College was front-page news, but no one thanked Woody, who declined to be interviewed. If the minister of agriculture was upset, he said nothing about it to Turi, who stayed behind to chat after Woody left. A month later the interim Italian government collapsed and Passamonte returned to his villa in Umbria in order to spend some time with his family before returning to public life.

THE EXECUTIVE Committee, along with three members of the Judicial Board, met in the Alumni Room on the first floor of Clair Hall. No one was sitting down when Woody entered the room. It had been several years since the college had disciplined a faculty member—the Ivan Meadows case—and there was a good deal of the excitement that sexual scandals always generate. Someone was in trouble. Woody. Woody could remember the feeling from high school, from grade school, when someone was going to be paddled in the principal's office. How did everyone know?

A table ran almost the entire length of the long room. On one side, an old rectangular piano, a sheet of glass over its blackened ivory keys, blocked the door to what had once been a small kitchen. On the opposite side of the room stood a desk said to have been used by Abraham Lincoln, on what occasion Woody couldn't remember. But he remembered Dean Acheson speaking in that room, standing at one end of the table, primping in the big mirror on the wall at the far end of the room, adjusting his tie, running his fingers through his silvery hair, still trying to justify his support of U.S. military commitments in South Korea back in the fifties. This was the place that had been reserved for Woody. Acheson, a handsome man, hadn't been able to stop admiring himself. Woody admired himself too, but only briefly. He was too nervous. He had jotted down a few remarks on the back of an envelope, but couldn't find the envelope in the pocket of his jacket.

According to the sexual harassment policy, which he had studied very carefully—especially Division IV, section 9, c, "Protection of the Accused"—someone would have to file a formal complaint, and as far as he knew, no one had done so. It was clear, moreover, that he hadn't physically assaulted anyone (Division I, section 3, a), nor had he threatened anyone that submission to his sexual advances would be "a condition of employment, status, promotion, grades, or letters of recommendation." Nor had he engaged in a pattern of "conduct intended to discomfort or humiliate by making comments of a sexual nature or by sexually explicit statements, questions, jokes, anecdotes, or speculation about sexual activity or previous sexual experience." No, the problem was the new amorous relations policy, which had been hastily drawn up to supplement the sexual harassment policy. The faculty had not yet approved the amorous relations policy, so Woody wasn't sure how it would be applied in his case.

There was none of the small talk that generally precedes committee meetings. No joking around. The dean sat silently at one end of the room, Woody at the other, like parents presiding at a large, unhappy dining room table. Woody had been hoping to see a musician or two, but he was disappointed. The two men, Frank Simpson, Chemistry, and Gerald Franklin, French, sat together on one side of the table: Frank had won several teaching awards but had never spoken a word in public; Gerry, who spent two years out of three directing the college's program in France, might bring a European perspective to the proceedings, but he'd never stand up to the dean. The women, on the other side of the table, were made of sterner stuff. Woody didn't expect any sympathy from any of them: Alice Arnold, the campus Marxist; Evelyn Davis, who'd been hired to teach medieval history but who had thrown out all her history books the minute she got tenure and now taught courses in Women's Studies; Muriel Brooks, never married; Heather Schuman, Sociology, unhappily divorced, who'd made a pass at Woody about a month after Hannah'd taken the job in Chicago.

In her opening remarks the dean made extensive use of the passive voice: a disturbing situation had arisen; it was hoped that the facts could be established, that a solution could be found, that the community wouldn't be jeopardized; it had been determined that there was sufficient evidence to require a hearing. The issues were serious; sexual harassment was reprehensible and could not be tolerated by the community. "This is a community," the dean said several times—as if that made everything clear—before inviting the group to look closely at Division II, section 10, k of the sexual harassment policy: "Sexually explicit statements, questions, jokes, or anecdotes."

Evelyn Davis was the first to speak. (The dean took notes on a yellow legal pad.) "I just want to get something straight, Woody. Is it true that you encourage students to talk about their sexual fantasies in class, and that they're forced to translate some pretty sexually explicit material? Actually, that's not what bothers me; I've got nothing against sex. What worries me is that a lot of this material is demeaning to women. It was a different world. I understand that. But aren't we trying to put that behind us?"

Woody was astonished. "What on earth are you talking about?"

"I'm talking about Classics 203, and about Classics 395."

"We've been reading Ovid's *Amores*, if that's what you mean; but I never thought of it quite that way."

"How *did* you think of it?"

"My uncle didn't learn to read till he joined the army."

"He learned Latin?"

"Not Latin, English. They gave the students pornography to read. It was amazing how fast they learned. No time at all."

"And this is the principle you're operating on at St. Clair College?"

"More or less. You know the trouble with the high schools? They give the kids Caesar's *Gallic Wars* to read instead of Ovid and Catullus."

"And you think the pornographic material is suitable for St. Clair students?"

"I'd object to the term 'pornographic.'"

"You introduced it."

"I was drawing an analogy. Do you really think Ovid and Catullus are pornographers? Is that what this hearing is about? Who's on trial here anyway? Ovid? Catullus? Homer?"

The dean intervened. "No one's on trial, Mr. Woodhull. This is a hearing to establish the facts so we can determine what's best for the community. There's reason to believe that there may be a serious conflict of interest." The dean returned to her legal pad. "When did your relationship with Ms. Mirsadiqi begin?" She spoke without looking up.

"About the middle of the fall term."

"Can you be more precise?"

"All Saints' Eve."

"You mean Halloween?"

"Yes."

"And Ms. Mirsadiqi has been living with you ever since?"

"More or less."

"And have you given any thought as to how this might affect the community?"

"Frankly, I don't think the community gives a damn."

The dean paused. "The dean thinks that may be a misperception."

"Look at Martha Renbarger," Woody said. "She was screwing half the guys in the Beta House, and what did *you* do? You told her to move farther away from campus. Come on, Jane, give me a break." Woody was starting to feel more combative.

"We're not here to discuss Professor Renbarger."

"*Farther away from campus.* Good lord. I'm sorry you didn't appoint *her* to this committee, or the commission, or the board, whatever it is."

"Would someone please read Division III, section 4, e."

Evelyn Davis already had the relevant passage at her fingertips: "'A faculty member who fails to withdraw from participation in activities or decisions that may reward or penalize a student with whom the faculty member has or has had an amorous relationship will be deemed to have violated his or her ethical obligations to the student, to other students, to colleagues, and to the college.'"

"Why not add the town of St. Clair?" Woody said. "The state of Illinois, the United States, the entire community of civilized society?"

When the dean spoke again she seemed to Woody to be speaking through a long tube, from a great distance away. "This is not a time for jokes," she said. "The dean has made it abundantly clear, verbally and in writing, that unless you terminate your relationship with Ms. Mirsadiqi you will be subject to disciplinary action. You were given a deadline . . ." Blah blah blah. She kept using the word "see." Can't you *see*? Don't you *see*? How can you not *see*?

Woody finally interrupted her. "What is it I'm supposed to see?"

It was the dean's turn to be astonished. "Mr. Woodhull, this is a serious matter. Your professional career is at stake here."

Woody's head was spinning. "May I say something?"

"Could you please wait until the dean has finished."

"No," he said. "I can't wait. I can't wait any longer. The simple truth is this: I was lonely. I hadn't made love to a woman since my daughter was killed in the bombing in Bologna. Ms. Mirsadiqi insinuated her way into my bed, and I didn't kick her out. And I don't intend to. I thought that my ability to love had been impaired. I couldn't remember what an erection felt like. What harm have we done? Whom have we injured? Now you've constructed a story that goes like this: 'A dirty old man takes advantage of an innocent student. It's not about sex; it's about power. He's having a midlife crisis and wants to reassure himself. He loses his head. He becomes infatuated. He behaves like an adolescent.' Well, why not? Look at Saul Bellow; look at Picasso, look at Frank Sinatra, look at Justice Douglas. You don't like their stories. You can't stand them. You can't stand them. You can't stand it. I'm sorry. You can't stand to see someone come alive. You hide behind your new morality: 'may be deemed to have violated his or her ethical obligation to the community.' What kind of language is that? You talk about community. 'This is a community.' What's that supposed to mean? You value a certain kind of propriety over human feelings. Yes, things can go wrong. Professors shouldn't be allowed to take advantage of students. But you can't regulate love."

"Are you telling us you're in love with Ms. Mirsadiqi?"

"No, I'm not, actually. Let's just say I have the highest respect for her. Let's just say *omnibus historiis se meus aptat amor, me nova sollicit, me tangit serior aetas.* That's Ovid, ladies and gentlemen; if you want to know what it means, you can read Ms. Mirsadiqi's translation in the latest issue of the *Atlantic.* Extra copies are available in the PR Office."

Commencement

Sometimes Woody felt that Sara and Ludi and Turi and even Hannah were following a straight line into the future. Sara was working on a Chaos exhibit at MSI—part of the larger History of Computers exhibit—and her position was no longer funded by soft money. It was a real job. Ludi, though she was only a freshman, was going off to work with a woman at the Minneapolis Zoo on developing a method of harvesting tiger ovaries. Turi was going back to Italy for the summer and would be starting graduate school at Harvard in the fall. And Hannah. Hannah had completed the first portion of her self-study program and had been accepted as a postulant at the convent. Divorce proceedings were nearing an end; she still wanted her half of the estate; Woody was going to have to remortgage the farm to come up with her share.

On the other hand, Woody felt that his own life was going in circles. Like a hunter lost in the woods, he kept circling back to the same point, just as he circled back to the cemetery on his way home from campus. Not every night. But two or three times a week. Where Cookie was waiting for him.

When he pictured her, it was as he'd last seen her, in the old International Terminal at O'Hare, in jeans and a bright yellow blouse with a steep white collar. There'd been a last-minute problem with her ticket and he'd been trying to sort it out while she and Hannah put the tags on her luggage—his old duffel bag, and a lightweight nylon bag for the overflow—and a tote bag that she would carry on the plane with her. He could see her standing in line outside a door marked ALITALIA, bending over to get a drink at the water fountain just outside the door, looking up, scanning the room for him and Hannah, waving as she disappeared through the door.

When he'd told Mac that he'd begun to hear her voice, like the voice of Socrates' *daimon,* he'd been speaking figuratively, but now he wasn't so sure, so strong was the sense of her presence, her voice, a voice that came not from "out there" but from within him, but that was no less real than the voice of the young man who'd called him Pops after the Halloween party.

One evening, about six o'clock, he was standing at her grave, watching one of Curtis's men drag a five-bottom plow across a low-lying field that had been too wet to plant all spring, when he saw Turi's car pull into the drive. She got out of the car, went in the back door, and came out almost immediately wearing nothing but a straw hat that he sometimes wore when he was working out in the sun. Woody's heart flip-flopped. What the hell! She walked out to the back of the garden, where she'd planted some arugula, and bent over from the hip, so that her butt stuck up in the air, and cut the arugula leaves near the ground with a pair of kitchen scissors. Woody couldn't actually see the scissors, he couldn't actually see the green leaves that she held in her clenched fist when she stood up, but when she turned around to face the cemetery, he could see her bush, a black dot between her legs. She took off the straw hat and waved to him, waving the hat back and forth over her head, and then holding it out in front of her and pulling it back towards her head, signaling him to come home. She'd known he was up there all along, even though he'd parked the truck on the other side of the road. She'd caught a glimpse of him when he thought he was invisible.

"It would be so simple," he said to Cookie, "just to ask her to go back to the dorm. Commencement's only three weeks away and then she'll be gone anyway. It would simplify things. She wouldn't mind."

"You know you're not going to do it, Pop."

"The dean wants to get rid of me," he said; "that woman is obsessed. She's calling the trustees. I'm getting phone calls. Fay Dawkins called last night from Massachusetts. Shardlow Anderson called me from Chicago. He's the chairman of the board. Jerry Balthus called from New York. It's not easy to get rid of someone with tenure, but it's not impossible. Moral turpitude. That's all they've got to go on, unless I do something criminal. Turpitude. Well," he went on, quoting Turi's translation of *Amores* II.4, "I'm not perfect, I'm the first to admit it. Why tell you a string of lies? No, confession's good for the soul, so maybe I'm crazy, but here goes."

"Pop, take it easy; you haven't done anything wrong."

"She's brought in a gender consultant, to do workshops for the whole faculty; she wants me to have a special session with her."

"Are you going to do it?"

Woody shrugged. "I guess I could hear what she has to say." He looked at his watch. Six-thirty. Time to go. But he wasn't quite ready to leave.

"You know that letter I gave to Passamonte, the Italian minister of agriculture, that was printed in the *Times*? It's been in the Italian newspapers, all over Italy, *Il Resto del Carlino* in Bologna, *La Repubblica* in Rome, *Corriere della Sera* in Milan. I got two letters today, in one envelope. From the president of the Association—you know his son was killed—and from the vice-president. He was coming back from Switzerland; his wife and son were waiting for him in the station. They were standing on the platform just outside the waiting room you were in. His wife was killed. His son lost an eye; he was in a coma for three months. He's an artist now. They wanted to thank me for what I did, for writing the letter. The testimony on behalf of the injured parties—the *parti lese*—has been rescheduled till next fall, after the summer recess. They hope to have Angela Strappafelci and Franco della Chiave extradited by then. It's complicated. I've been invited to testify. All the family members have, relatives of the victims."

"Are you going to go?"

Woody shrugged his shoulders. "School starts at the beginning of September."

"You could ask for a leave. How long would it take? You'd only have to be there one day."

"What could I say?" he asked. "What could I say that I haven't already said? I already said what I have to say, at the memorial service, remember?"

"You'd think of something, Pop. You always think of something."

THE WORDING of the new amorous relations policy, which had been adopted at the last faculty meeting, was crucial. The dean's proposed amendment to change "strongly discouraged" to "prohibited" had failed by a single vote. Martha Renbarger, one of the few faculty members who'd spoken out against the policy, had called for a secret ballot, or it would undoubtedly have passed. "Strongly discouraged" was one thing; "prohibited" was another. Woody was prepared to be strongly discouraged. Woody was even prepared to submit to a counseling session with Ms. Tara Hillman, the gender consultant. What he was *not* prepared to do was ask Turi to move out until the last minute, the terminus ad quem represented by the arrival of her parents. She'd gotten wind of his predicament and had moved some of her things back to the dorm, but he'd asked her to stay.

In the seminar room on the second floor of Clair Hall, which had been converted into a temporary office for Ms. Hillman, the heavy table had been moved to the back of the room. All the padded seminar chairs had been removed, but a dozen large, colorful cushions were lined up along the wall and a large, thick rug, also colorful, had been laid out on the floor. Ms. Hillman, a small, athletic woman with short blond hair, wore jeans and sandals and a colorful blouse. After a brief introduction she asked Woody to bend over to pick up several objects—a pencil, a paper clip, a three-hole punch, an empty coffee cup—which were arranged in a circle on the rug.

"Bend your knees," Ms. Hillman said, "so that your rear end doesn't stick up."

Woody bent his knees and retrieved the various items, including the coffee cup, on which was printed, in brightly colored letters, "If you harass me, I'll pour scalding coffee on your crotch." Above the inscription a cartoon woman smiled gleefully.

"Now let's try it again. This time I want you to hold on to the front of your shirt."

"Why?"

She took the items from him and put them back on the floor, bending her knees. "So you don't expose your breasts if you're wearing a low-cut dress."

Woody clutched the front of his shirt. He handed the pencil, the paper clip, the three-hole punch, and the coffee cup to Ms. Hillman, holding his shirt all the time so he wouldn't expose his breasts.

For the second exercise she wanted him to sit on the rug.

"I've got a bum knee," he protested. "Torn meniscus. There's a little piece that sometimes flips out, flips up . . ."

But she wasn't interested in excuses.

Woody sat on the floor and pretended he was wearing a short skirt, which Ms. Hillman, while walking back and forth, pretended she was trying to look *up*. Every time he shifted around to ease the pressure on his knee, she clicked her tongue to indicate that she'd caught a glimpse of his panties. After two minutes of this Woody stood up without permission. He was in a murderous rage and could hardly control himself. His knee buckled and he lurched forward. Ms. Hillman sprang back and assumed a combat position that Woody had seen on posters for kung fu films, her left arm extended in front of her, her right arm raised horizontally to deliver a disabling blow to his Adam's apple. Woody grabbed on to the edge of the table.

"I hope your anger," she said, when she saw that he wasn't going to attack her, "will lead to a measure of understanding. I want you to think about what just happened, and I want you to sit down and make out a list of your own gender-specific behaviors and think about how they may affect the women you come in contact with on a daily basis. And I want you to monitor these behaviors for a few days because a lot of them are unconscious. At the next session we'll talk about some of these behaviors to see how you can change them."

But there was no next session. The next session had been scheduled for Friday afternoon, but Woody refused to go. The next morning he got a phone call from the dean. He and Turi had gotten up early and taken down the storms from the second floor and put up the screens. Turi was upstairs in the shower; Woody could hear the water running.

"Jane," he said after a brief silence. "I didn't recognize your voice at first. You're working on Saturday." Woody held the phone between neck and shoulder and started to doodle on a small notepad. Of course, he thought; she always worked on Saturdays. Sundays too, after Hebrew lessons at Temple Sinai.

"Mr. Woodhull," she said again, and Woody knew that push had come to shove.

"Jane, it's me, Woody."

The dean was all business: "Professor Thomas Hunter from the University of Iowa will be taking over your Ovid seminar, and a graduate student from the University of Illinois will be doing Greek II."

Like a man crossing a deep gorge on a swaying footbridge Woody was afraid to look down.

"Jane, I'm coming down to the office right now. This is ridiculous. We can work something out."

"What do you think the dean has been trying to do?"

"What about Ms. Mirsadiqi's honors project?" he said, trying to keep his voice steady.

"We're working on it," she said. "Professor Hunter is willing to—"

"We need to talk this over," Woody interrupted.

"The dean doesn't think that that would be a good idea."

Woody shook his head and nodded at the same time. "Mac's good for another ten years," he said. He tried to make a chuckling sound, but it sounded more like a man choking on a piece of gristle. "But you really need another person. A one-man department, I mean a one-person department, it's not a good idea."

"I'm sorry, Mr. Woodhull, but you haven't given the dean any choice."

"The amorous relations policy says 'strongly discouraged,' not 'prohibited.'" He waited for her to say something.

"It's an abuse of power," she said after a pause.

"It's not an abuse of power; it's a mutual arrangement. What the Italians call *un piccolo amore*." The dean started to interrupt. "Yes, yes," Woody said, "I realize we're not living in Italy."

"This *piccolo amore*, or whatever you call it, is not in the best interests of the community."

"Is this a unilateral decision, Jane? The president was in Nepal last I heard."

"They have telephones in Nepal."

"So this is the president's decision?"

"In consultation with the chairman of the board."

Lying in bed at night, after making love, Woody had sometimes tried to anticipate this moment. It was like imagining a bridge collapsing—a big bridge, like the Golden Gate Bridge, or the Centennial Bridge over the Mississippi—as you drive over it. You can frighten yourself a little, but then you get to the other side of the bridge and you forget all about it. But now the bridge was trembling, and he remembered that his Cub Scout troop—or was it a "pack"?—had always broken step when they marched across the two-lane bridge that crossed Spring Creek just outside of Grand River, so that their marching feet wouldn't set up a rhythm that might cause the bridge to start vibrating. That was the problem; he and Turi had forgotten to break step, and now the bridge was vibrating; soon it would start to shake, and then to twist violently; and then it would collapse.

Woody shook himself. The dean was still talking. Outside the kitchen window a cardinal sang, over and over again, *What cheer? What cheer? What cheer?* He could smell hogs . . . He wasn't thinking clearly, but he wanted to keep the dean on the line. He'd been trying to live in the present moment, trying to resist his inclination to project himself into the future so that he could look back on the present, as if it were the past, in order to sort out the meaning of what had happened, or what was happening. But now he couldn't help himself. *Count no man happy until he is dead.* Solon's words to Croesus, the richest man in the world, which Croesus recalls as he is about to be burned at the stake. Woody'd never believed it. What if you were happy all your life, and then unhappy for, say, the last couple of days before you died? But now he believed.

"Is there anything else, Jane?"

"No," she said, "that's all. You'll get a letter on Monday."

Woody hung up the phone and tried to breathe deeply and deliberately, to pump his system full of oxygen. Turi was still in the shower. He stepped out onto the porch and then walked briskly down the long drive to check the mail. The cardinal was still singing: *What cheer? What cheer?* There was a bill from the power company and a copy of *Acoustic Guitar* and a letter from Sara in an MSI envelope. She'd called two days earlier to say she'd just been promoted to exhibit developer, and he was expecting a full account. He tore open the letter as he walked back to the house. Fear and anxiety were turning to anger, and anger restored his strength: *Ac vim susci-tat ira.* Weak in the knees, like Entellus, he had fallen; but like Entel-lus he would return to the battle keener than before.

He was reading the letter from Sara when Turi appeared in the kitchen door, wearing a light bathrobe. He had himself under con-trol. She had a pink towel in her hand, and when she reached up to dry her wet hair the lapels of the robe parted like clouds to reveal a constellation of moles between her breasts, which were small and delicate, like the breasts of the Ludovisi Aphrodite under their *draperie mouillée.*

She tied the towel round her head and opened the refrigerator. "Would you like a soft-boiled egg?" she asked.

"I'd love one," he said. He didn't know whether he was trying to destroy himself or to save himself.

He didn't tell her about the dean's phone call till they'd finished their eggs. First she was angry, and then she started to cry. "I'll talk to the dean myself," she said. "I guess I'd better move out."

"*Alea iacta est,*" he said. "The die has been cast." He put his arms around her. "I've been a teacher all my life," he went on. "I've never wanted to be anything else, except maybe a blues singer. I've never wanted to fly an airplane or captain a ship; I've never wanted to be a writer or a movie star. I've never wanted to be rich; I *am* rich. I don't even care very much about *The Cosmological Fragments of the Early Greek Philosophers.* I just want to stand in front of a class and talk about Ovid and Homer, or go over the *mi*-verbs till the students really *get* them: ἵημι and ἵστημι and τίθημι. So they're not afraid of them. But I don't want you to leave, so there must be something else I want too, something I want more, even though I'm not exactly sure what it is."

She was still crying a little. He could feel her tears on his shoul-der. "Do you want to go upstairs?" she asked.

They'd finished the "Sauces & Pickles" chapter—*south Slav style, stockings, substitutes, swings, Turkish style, vibrators, Viennese oyster, voyeurs, wetlook*—and had developed a repertoire of moves that would have served them for years. Turi was very practical, and totally unsentimental. Which was a good thing, because Woody was sentimental enough for two. He remembered anniversaries, picked wildflowers, read *Les Fleurs du Mal* aloud to her in bed, in French and

English. His French wasn't very good, and she laughed at him, but she always wanted him to keep reading, and to keep rubbing her back or, when she rolled over, her breasts and stomach.

"You remember the passage from Goethe you told me about? About wanting to have an affair with someone older, as part of his education?" She was climbing the stairs in front of him.

"You mean in *Eckermann*?" She stopped on the landing and turned to face him.

"Right. Before he takes up with Charlotte. But it's you I'm talking about, not Goethe. Did you get what you wanted? Are you satisfied? Has it been a good learning experience?"

Pause. Woody wished he hadn't said "learning experience."

"You know how I imagine things, Woody?"

He didn't answer.

"I think that when this is all over we're going to be good friends. I'm going to write to you from Cambridge, and you're going to keep teaching me things. You're never going to be far away from me, Woody. When I get a job, you'll be the first person I call; and when I'm humping some Harvard grad student who thinks he's hot stuff but doesn't know what the hell he's doing, I'll think of you, and if he asks me why I'm smiling, I'll tell him, 'I just thought of something funny.' And that'll be you."

WOODY'S SUSPENSION for the remainder of the term was confirmed by the chairman of the board, Shardlow Anderson, who called to make sure that Woody understood that the dean had the support of the board. "Sorry, Woody, but we've got to have our ducks in a row when the parents show. If they get wind of this . . . Her mother's been a trustee for fifteen years, and her dad's got more money than God. Ten million dollars. That's a hell of a way to kick off the capital fund drive. And there's plenty more where that's coming from. But these Middle Easterners, they're mighty jealous of their womenfolk's honor. You ought to know that, Woody. You've shot yourself in the foot, and you're not doing the college a damn bit of good, not a damn bit. We want you out of the picture."

"She'll be back in the dorm when her parents show up."

"I want her back in the dorm now, not tomorrow or the next day. Now. Then we'll see."

"What will we 'see'?"

"That'll be up to the board."

Woody toyed with the idea of resigning. He'd had enough. He'd become invisible in a new way, the way a junior faculty member who's been denied tenure becomes invisible, the way a man who's lost his job becomes invisible. People still say hello, but they keep their distance, they look past you. But the idea was too frightening. What would he do? He hadn't published enough to find another job, not at his age. There might be a place for him in the prison-education program at the junior college. Or Curtis was always looking for extra help. He could drive a tractor; he could probably learn to run Curtis's new no-till drill, with its heavy-duty coulter and computerized seed-delivery shoe. Or he could line up gigs at the local roadhouses. A man with a guitar could actually earn a living in downstate Illinois. A single guitar player was cheaper than a band. But he'd have to play more country. It wasn't that he didn't like country, but his heart wasn't really in it. He wasn't a country singer crying in his beer; he was a bluesman who'd rather drink muddy water and sleep in a hollow log than let the bastards dog him around; who'd rather make himself a pallet on the floor where he could close his eyes and let a kindhearted woman ease his worried mind. But when he got out his guitar and started to play, it was a song of parting that came to his fingers, one of the simple images at the heart of the music he loved:

> Standin', standin' in the station,
> Suitcase in my hand,
> Suitcase in my hand,
> Doggone.

The dean canceled the Jelly Roll Baker program—Woody had been calling it a "demonstration"—that Woody had been planning for the Black Student Union program in the third week of May. The dean invited a speaker from the University of Chicago instead to talk about the relationship between blacks and Jews on the south side of Chicago; but BSU threatened to stage a different kind of demonstration, threatened to hold the blues demonstration off-campus. The dean had to back down.

Woody'd been working with Lori Teller, the vice-president of BSU, a senior chemistry major who sang so softly that he could barely hear her, even when he stood right next to her and played as softly as he could. It was the second week of his suspension, and he was surprisingly calm most of the time, though he experienced moments of panic that came predictably, at the ring of the telephone, at the sound of the mailman's truck on Kruger Road. His offer to meet with the board at the trustees' meeting had been rejected. Turi's mother was one of the trustees. It would be best if Woody were to make himself invisible.

"I'll sing loud all right when the time comes," Lori said.

"Why don't you sing loud right now?"

"It doesn't feel right."

"You think it's going to feel better in front of a crowd."

"Yeah, I do."

Woody shrugged his shoulders. What could he do?

Woody was going to give a little history of the blues, complete with slides of some of the old bluesmen, and blueswomen; he was going to demonstrate some of the different styles, Mississippi Delta, Texas, Piedmont; and Lori was going to sing three songs, "Easy Street," "Man of My Own," and "Crazy Blues"; and then they were going to do the old Otis Spann song that Cookie had sung in the talent show in Sanders Theater—"Mr. Jelly Roll Baker." Only they were going to add more languages, Russian, German, Swedish, Chinese, Japanese, Arabic, Turkish, Marathi, and several African languages: Shona, Twi, and Amharic. And of course Persian. Lori rounded up the international students, collected translations, and organized the rehearsals.

Woody, who stayed away from the campus during the day, had been rehearsing with small groups of students in the living room of International House. "You don't really have to *sing* it," he said, "just get the words out somehow. Now let's take it from the top," and he'd hit the opening E7 chord and the sound of the National Steel guitar would fill the room, and the students would egg each other on in a dozen languages.

In the Common Room the chairs were arranged sideways rather than lengthwise, so that the audience faced the large window, vaulted like a church window, on the south wall. The light was not good—too bright, leaking in between the old damask drapes that were about to fall apart—but the seat below the window was long enough to accommodate all the singers, and Jessica Lowden from the Philosophy Department, who was going to back Woody up on Dale Peterson's washtub bass, and Larry Taylor, who was going to play the blues harp. And for the guitars—Woody's National Steel, and Larry's Martin and Jessica's Gibson, which he'd borrowed for the occasion. All in different tunings: open D, open G, and regular. Woody didn't want to take up time tuning during the demonstration.

The three of them stood in front of the large window. Woody had brought some percussion instruments in case anyone wanted to join in: rattles, bongo drums, spoons, bones, an old washboard and a metal scrub brush.

At their final rehearsal they'd spent most of the time learning how to go out together. With four measures left Woody would say, "Let's all go out together," or "Let's go out together now," and they'd know it was time to stop. (Starting was no problem. Woody would start. The others would come in when they felt the spirit move them.)

Ben Greenburg, the dean's speaker, introduced himself to Woody before the demonstration.

"This is a surprise," Woody said.

"Your dean," Greenburg said, "decided to call off the lecture; but she neglected to call *me*. Hey, I figure a deal's a deal. If she'd called a week ago, that's one thing. But today, after I drive four hours?"

"Actually," Woody said, "I heard you lecture on Genesis at the Midwest Faculty Seminar a couple of years ago. Maybe three. You talked about Abraham jewing down God over Sodom and Gomorrah. 'How about ten good men? How about it, God, would you save the city for ten good men? How about five, five good men . . .' Very funny. Really. I'm not joking. You were hysterical."

"If you think that was funny," Greenburg said, sitting down in one of the comfortable chairs in the front row, "you should hear me on the Book of Job."

The Common Room was packed with people, students and faculty and some townspeople, who might not have come to hear a lecture on the ongoing relationship between blacks and Jews in Chicago but who wanted to hear Woody demonstrate the blues. Woody looked around for the dean, not expecting to see her. Two years ago she'd walked out while he was interviewing John Jackson—whom Woody had billed as the last of the old bluesmen—slamming the Common Room door behind her. Later she said they'd been exploiting him.

"The man couldn't read or write," Woody said, "and we were paying him a thousand dollars to answer a few questions. Who was exploiting whom? I heard him give the same answers, verbatim, on NPR."

"That's what I'm talking about."

The demonstration was going to be broadcast live on the college radio station, and two microphones had been set up on either side of the makeshift stage. Woody was worried that not everyone would be able to see the screen, which was to the right of the window, but there was no other place to put it. Turi was going to run the slide projector during the first part of the demonstration, and then she was going to sing "Mr. Jelly Roll Baker" in Persian, right after Samer Al-Nimr, whom Woody hadn't seen since Thanksgiving, sang it in Arabic. Samer was the only one who hadn't shown up for a rehearsal. But he was there now, a political science major, very confident. Like Turi, he spoke several languages and was going to Harvard in the fall. Woody imagined them getting together in Cambridge, imagined them becoming lovers, imagined them looking back on this moment. Woody didn't know Samer very well, but he liked him.

Woody began with two songs that the oldest bluesmen remembered from a time before the blues, "John Henry" and "Poor Boy, a Long Way from Home." He was a little nervous at first, but the washtub bass steadied him and the harp filled his heart with courage and longing, so that he forgot he was simply demonstrating and began to sing, putting everything he had into the songs, not worrying about what people would think.

"Eighteen eighty-seven," he said before the applause died down. He waited a minute and then started again: "Eighteen eighty-seven. Charley Patton and Blind Lemon Jefferson were both born in the same year. One hundred years ago. Your great-grandparents would have been born about that time." He nodded to Turi and a slide of the Dockery Plantation near Cleveland, Mississippi, flashed on the screen. "Most historians say the Delta blues were born on this huge, five-thousand-acre plantation. It's where Charley Patton worked. Charley's father was a preacher, but Charley disappointed him by taking sides with the devil and playing the blues. When Patton lived on Dockery in the twenties there were as many as a thousand black people working the cotton fields on the Sunflower River." Woody nodded to Turi and another slide flashed on the screen. "That's Son House," he said. "Actually Son was born in Louisiana, but he came up to work at Dockery. Next slide, please."

A slide of Robert Johnson appeared on the screen. Johnson was holding a National Steel guitar, with f-holes, just like Woody's. A couple of people made the connection and started to laugh, and pretty soon everyone was laughing.

Lori Teller, whom Woody introduced as St. Clair's own Memphis Minnie—Turi showed a slide of Memphis Minnie with her band—amazed Woody by belting out her songs just like her prototype; and if "Mr. Jelly Roll Baker" was not a great success musically, it was a triumph nonetheless, a triumph of the human spirit, as people like to say when someone overcomes a disability. Lori sang it through in English, and then Woody sang the first verse in Italian, and then one by one the students came up to the microphone and sang or chanted or simply demonstrated the first verse in sixteen different languages.

Woody didn't want to call it a triumph of the human spirit because he didn't care for that sort of language. What was so triumphant about singing the first verse of "Mr. Jelly Roll Baker" in sixteen different languages? Maybe "singing" wasn't the right word. "Demonstrating" was better, though some of the students sang with a real flair, especially Samer, who hadn't bothered to rehearse. There was nothing musical about his singing; he didn't pay any attention to Woody, who strummed a chord now and then, just to remind the audience that they were hearing the blues chanted in Arabic.

Lori sang it in Shona, and Manual Moratu sang it in Twi, and then Turi sang it in Persian. She sang softly, and everyone stopped laughing and became very quiet, straining to hear her, as if they understood Persian, as if she were delivering an important message on which the fate of the college depended, as if it were crucial not to miss a word. Woody could see that her hands were trembling. It was the first time he'd seen her nervous. And then everyone sang it again in English, and the noise level rose again, like the tide, lifting all boats equally. The washtub bass thumped beneath their feet; the sound of the harp soared over their heads, like a bat darting around the ceiling; Woody's fingers plucked the strings of the shining National Steel without effort. The guitar itself sparkled under the chandeliers that dangled from the high ceiling.

> Mr. Jelly Roll Baker,
> Let me be your slave;
> When Gabriel blows his trumpet
> You know I'll rise from my grave,
> For some of your jelly,
> Some of your sweet jelly roll;
> You know it's doing me good
> Way down deep in my soul.

They went out on Taj Mahal's version of "Sweet Home Chicago." It was five o'clock Friday afternoon; the room gradually quieted down and emptied. A student from AV had come to pick up the screen and the slide projector. The kids from the radio station rewound the tapes and packed up their microphones. Woody put the guitar in its coffinlike case. For a few minutes the inner and the outer man had been one and the same. Woody's inner self had become visible for all to see. He hadn't realized it while he was singing, but maybe that was the way it had to be. You had to lose your self to find it. Hidden in the moment itself, in the instant—less than an instant—between past and future.

Ben Greenburg remained behind. "That's the easiest six hundred bucks I ever made," he said.

"Glad you liked it; you driving back to Chicago tonight?"

Greenburg nodded.

There had been a time when Woody would have invited him to have dinner and to spend the night, but for reasons that he didn't fully understand, that time was past. He was tired. Turi was waiting for him. He wanted to go home.

•   •   •

ON FRIDAY morning before Commencement Woody discovered a pair of Turi's bikini underpants in the bottom of the bathroom hamper. He held them to his nose for a moment before tossing them into the washing machine with his own underwear.

She'd moved her things back to the dorm on Wednesday. On Thursday she'd gone up to meet her family at O'Hare. They were driving down this morning in two rented Mercedes holding bodyguards, Alireza's personal secretary, Turi's aunt and uncle from Milan, and Turi's younger brother, Babak, who understood Italian and Persian but rarely spoke himself. They were going to stay at the Ramada Inn on the square, which was not as nice as Jumers but more convenient—a five-minute walk to the campus. Turi's two older brothers, who'd gone to Harvard, had stopped to see friends in Cambridge and were coming later.

When the wash was done Woody put the clean clothes in a laundry basket, put the dark clothes in the washer, and hung the first load out on the line. It was a beautiful day, bright but not too hot; he needed something to do, and he liked the sweet stiffness of clothes that had dried in the sun. When he came to the bikini panties he held them to his nose again. Her smell was gone. He fastened them on the line next to one of his T-shirts.

What no one had counted on was that Alireza didn't speak English. Italian, yes. Persian, yes. Arabic, yes. English, no. The president's secretary called Woody at home shortly after lunch. Mr. Mirsadiqi's personal secretary—the one who knew English—had become ill and had remained in Chicago.

Woody'd done three loads of laundry and was just fixing himself a salami sandwich.

"Allison can translate for him," he said. "Or Turi. Or her brothers."

"Her brothers aren't coming till tonight. Mrs. Mirsadiqi's at the trustees' meeting; Turi's at the commencement rehearsal. The president wants you down here now."

"He's back from Nepal?"

"Woody," she said conspiratorially, "do yourself a favor and get down here. The president wants to talk money; the chairman of the board wants to talk money; Mr. Mirsadiqi wants to talk money. Jorge Serrano is here. When he speaks Spanish, Mr. Mirsadiqi can sort of understand him, and when Mr. Mirsadiqi speaks Italian, Jorge can sort of understand him. But it's not easy. Besides, Mr. Mirsadiqi is asking for *you*. He wants to see *you*."

Fuck 'em, Woody said to himself. *Fuck 'em*. It felt good. *Fuck 'em*. "Why doesn't the president call Ms. Hillman?"

"Ms. Hillman?"

"The gender consultant."

"Get serious, Woody. What do you want me to tell the president?"

"Tell him I'll be right down."

TURI HAD taken the train up to Chicago. Woody'd taken her to the Seminary Street station, and then, sitting at the kitchen table, he'd written out a list of chores. He rearranged the living room furniture, putting the Castro Convertible back in front of the window, where it had been before Turi moved it in front of the fireplace one Saturday afternoon while he was at the office. He cleared early drafts of her honors thesis off the dining room table. He called Sara, but she wasn't home. Ludi would be home soon for a week before going up to Minneapolis for the summer. She was going to work with a research biologist at the zoo, figuring out how to harvest tiger ovaries. But he'd already called her several times to reconfirm her plans.

He was troubled by the longing for a new life that always came over him at Commencement. If he was angry at Hannah, at least he understood her motives. She'd discovered her vocation. She'd been called to a new life by something, or someone. Sometimes he felt that he too was being called to a new life. But by what? By whom? By Turi? Much as he loved her—yes, he'd begun to use the word "love" for his feelings—she would soon be gone. Besides, he had already experienced his calling. Teaching had been his vocation. He had never tired of it, had never become cynical about students, or about the power of great books to inform and enlighten. But you had to open yourself to them. That's what he tried to teach his students. Not to do things to the books, but to let the books do things to you. To fill you, to change you. This is what he had stood for at St. Clair. This is what he had fought to hang on to in the classics program.

He parked his pickup in the lot on Cherry Street, across from

Clair Hall. The president was waiting for him on the steps. President Hanson was tall, six feet three; he had white hair that was neither too thick nor too thin; and he had the sort of large, squarish head that Woody associated with college presidents. Like Harlan Hatcher, who'd been president of the University of Michigan when Woody was a student there, or Derek Bok at Harvard. He traveled all over the world, heading up conferences on the future of higher education. In the sixties he'd predicted that most of the funding would come from foundations, a policy that had led the college to neglect its alumni. The fact that he'd been dead wrong had done nothing to undermine his prestige, and he was still much in demand, though the college was now trying to make up for lost time by courting its alumni.

"You remember that letter to the editor?" the president asked, putting an arm around Woody and holding the door open for him at the same time. He had to reach in front of Woody and give the door a swing. "Challenging you to a cock show in the Common Room?"

If the president had observed the drama of Woody's suspension, or firing, he'd observed it from afar, from Washington or New York or Berkeley or Katmandu. (Washington, New York, Berkeley Woody could understand, but what did the president do in Katmandu?) Woody, who had never been one of the "key men" (or, moving with the times, "key persons") whom the president had groomed for key positions, was surprised that he remembered the cock show challenge.

In his second year at St. Clair Woody had written a mildly unfavorable review of the college literary magazine for the student newspaper, of which he was the advisor. The incensed editor of the literary magazine had written a scurrilous letter to the newspaper challenging Woody to a cock show. There was a big fuss. The president, who happened to be on campus, took an interest in the matter. The letter was libelous. Lawyers were consulted. Woody could sue the college. Woody assured the president that he had no intention of suing the college, but that didn't matter. Who would be held responsible? That was the question. It turned out to be Woody, as advisor to the newspaper. He should never have allowed the paper to print such a scurrilous letter. He was in a position to sue himself, but he passed up the opportunity.

"You backed away from that one," the president went on. "Now you've got another chance to lay it out on the table."

"I'm not sure I follow you."

"You're in a position to do yourself some good," the president said. "We've got a big fish on the line; we've got him right up at the edge of the boat, do you understand? The papers have been drawn up for months; I just don't want anything to go wrong at the last minute."

They entered the president's inner office through two outer offices. The first, a little room where Abraham Lincoln had gone over his notes for the fifth debate with Stephen Douglas, was furnished in the style of the Italian funeral home where Woody'd made arrangements to have Cookie's body shipped home: black damask drapes, a black horsehair sofa and a Queen Anne chair, and an antique cherry writing desk. In the second room the president's secretary stood at a portable metal rack, like something from a clothing store, on wheels, sorting through special robes used by the trustees, by Commencement speakers, and by honorary-degree recipients. She was looking at the labels inside the collars, checking the sizes. Mortarboards were stacked on a coffee table.

At a round table in the inner office sat the chairman of the Board of Trustees, the director of development, and the dean, smiles congealed on their faces. Turi's brother Babak sat at the table too, a crayon in his short, broad hand, coloring on a tablet of yellow legal-sized paper, and on the president's library table too. A little fold of skin covered the inner corner of each eye, giving him a pronounced Mongol look, but Woody could see the resemblance to Turi. Babak, who made a soft burring sound as he swept the crayon across the paper, and his father were the only ones who seemed at ease.

"Jenab-e Agha-ye-Mirsadiqi," Woody began in Persian, addressing himself to a handsome man on Babak's left. It was exciting to see the man, his high, burnished forehead, his dark skin, his Italian silk suit—so much money alters a man's appearance, gives him an aura. "It is a moment of great excitement for all of us—" but Shardlow Anderson, the chairman of the board, held up a hand. Woody was addressing Alireza's bodyguard, who was filling in for the personal secretary and translator, who was recuperating in the O'Hare Hilton. Alireza was using the small private bathroom, a converted closet, in the president's office. When he appeared, he reminded Woody that the super-rich have no need to worry about appearances, though the casual clothes he wore were clearly expensive.

"Jenab-e Agha-ye-Mirsadiqi," Woody began again. "It is a moment of great excitement for all of us . . ."

Alireza Mirsadiqi looked at Woody for a moment, as if he were making a decision, and then stepped forward and embraced him, gave him a big bear hug. There was a manly smell to him. He held Woody up for the others to see, as if he were displaying him.

"I know this man," he said in Persian, and stopped.

Woody realized that he was waiting for him, for Woody, to translate.

"I know this man," Woody translated. "But it might be easier to speak Italian," he said, in Italian, to Alireza. Alireza Mirsadiqi raised a hand and continued in Persian.

"My daughter is fortunate to have had his wise advice and counsel."

"My daughter is fortunate to have had his wise advice and counsel."

"Over the years."

"Over the years."

"You too are fortunate."

"You too are fortunate."

"To have his great wisdom."

"To have his great wisdom."

"At your disposal."

"At your disposal."

"When he speaks."

"When he speaks."

"You can feel the river flowing through you."

"You can feel the river flowing through you."

"And when he is silent."

"And when he is silent."

"It is as when the rain stops."

"It is as when the rain stops."

"And in the orchard."

"And in the orchard."

"The trees draw moisture up into themselves."

"The trees draw moisture up into themselves."

Woody recognized snatches of Rumi. Or maybe it was just a flowery way of talking that Iranians used on occasions like this. Or perhaps Alireza was having them on.

"Humor is very important, don't you think?" Alireza went on, as if reading Woody's thoughts.

Woody translated. Everyone nodded.

"I wanted to be a Sufi," he said. "My teacher told me that I would need a sense of humor, that a man who has suppressed his sense of humor is like a camel on the roof—he has no capacity for wisdom. I had a sense of humor . . . I wanted to pursue the Sufi way, but my father wanted to send me to the United States. My mother said it was too far away, and I had an older brother in Italy, so I went to Italy to study geology, so I could work for British Petroleum."

Woody translated.

"I am only a poor businessman. I left my studies at the university to become a rug merchant. My professor at the university—this was in Rome—asked me could I get him a rug, so I wrote to my father, who was a professor at the university, saying I wanted a rug, a blue Kashan—they think that the design is everything—about two by three meters. He wrote back and told me that my job was to study geology, not to think about selling rugs. So I wrote to my friend Idries—may Allah have mercy on his soul—and told him to go to the bazaar and buy a rug. The professor's friends all liked the rug; they wanted rugs too. So I wrote to my friend and asked him to buy five rugs, such and such colors and so on. Five rugs, ten rugs, a hundred rugs . . ." He shrugged. Woody translated.

"From rugs I branched out to other things . . ." He waved his hand to indicate the breadth of his business interests. "But nonetheless I have the highest regard for education. Where there is a spring of sweet water, people will be attracted. And the animal kingdom too, of course. St. Clair College is such a place."

The president smiled, as if acknowledging a joke or a special bond. "The papers are all in order," he said to Woody, who relayed the message to Alireza. Everything was laid out on the large round table. Handsome folders, like large menus in a fancy restaurant, held copies of the proposal, which included a four-million-dollar renovation of Alumni Hall, the creation of endowed centers for Creativity Studies and Interdisciplinary Studies at a million dollars apiece, and five million in unrestricted giving that would go into the endowment. Also on the table: endowment figures, architectural drawings of the proposed renovation of Alumni Hall, charts, budget figures, projections for the new capital campaign, and records of previous conversations. Alireza seemed more interested in his son's crayon drawing.

"The only thing that's really up in the air," the director of development said to Woody, "are the centers for Interdisciplinary Studies and Creativity Studies. You've got to make him understand that these positions have to be surrounded with another two hundred thousand dollars."

"Why's that?"

"That's just the way it's done. The million is for salary, the rest for support."

"You mean a million isn't enough for an endowed chair?"

"These aren't endowed chairs, Woody; they're centers. There'll be a lot of administrative work."

"Shouldn't this have been explained earlier, in the original proposal?"

"Don't argue, Woody; just translate."

"What on earth *are* these centers?" Woody asked. "This is the first I've heard of them."

No one said anything. The director of development looked at the dean, who hadn't spoken since Woody's arrival, and the dean glanced at Woody. Their eyes met for an instant like bullets colliding in midair. She had rolled her hair up on the back of her head in a French twist and was wearing a little makeup. There had been times when Woody'd thought that the differences between them were like the differences between Beatrice and Benedict, or Audrey Hepburn and Cary Grant in *Charade*, which he and Turi had seen in Iowa City—comic devices used to delay the inevitable. But now he saw that—despite the hair, despite the makeup—this wasn't so, that their differences were irreconcilable, that they were moving along on different tracks that would never intersect.

"The description is here somewhere," she said. "They represent an interdisciplinary approach to higher education that will reference every division of the college." She stopped. "Are you going to translate?"

Woody started to translate but couldn't find the words in Persian, so he switched to Italian.

Alireza nodded, asking a question every now and then, still in Persian, as Woody explained, in Italian, the need to surround the centers with another two hundred thousand dollars.

"These centers," Alireza asked, "I don't quite understand; they will be places that scholars will visit, or places of study?"

"I don't think that's it," Woody said in Italian, speaking rapidly. "They'll just be offices run by more administrators. Frankly I think you'd be better off endowing two chairs in classical studies, one in Latin, one in Greek. Your daughter was a classics major, after all."

"Of course," Alireza said. "I had something like that in mind originally, but I thought . . ." He shrugged his shoulders. "I thought perhaps I was too old-fashioned. I'm a simple businessman . . ."

"Please, Jenab-e Agha-ye-Mirsadiqi, there's no need for that."

Alireza smiled. "Well, my friend, I leave it up to you. I lean on your great wisdom."

Woody wrote out the terms of Alireza's gift on a sheet of Babak's yellow legal paper. Alireza dictated in Persian, switching to Italian when Woody couldn't understand, and Woody wrote in English. He wrote slowly and neatly with his Parker Duofold pen. The two men conferred from time to time, and Woody was glad that no one could understand them except the bodyguard, and he couldn't tell.

THAT NIGHT they had an impromptu dinner—Turi's idea—at Woody's. Turi's older brothers had arrived; Allison had to eat with the president and the trustees and the candidates for honorary degrees; Alireza, who was receiving an honorary degree, was supposed to eat with them too but declined because he couldn't speak English.

Woody was uneasy at the prospect of sitting down to dinner with all these people. Turi's brothers, for example, looked like the kind of brothers who would be jealous of their sister's honor. Though they were very attractive too. And her uncle, Alireza's brother, a tall man with a pencil-thin mustache, looked as if he might be concealing a knife under his cloak. They were all a bit awkward at first, standing around in the Common Room, not knowing what language to speak; but there was nothing standoffish about them, and there was no denying Turi. Besides, Woody loved a good dinner, loved playing the role of the generous host—Chaucer's franklin, or Homer's Alcinous. So the matter was settled.

Woody served an American dinner. Corn on the cob, three dozen ears of young field corn that he and Turi's brothers—Behruz and Sohrab and Babak—poached from the field that butted onto the back of Woody's property, two enormous steaks that Woody cooked on the grill, and a big salad with lots of Turi's arugula. Alireza had never eaten corn on the cob before, but his brother and sister-in-law had eaten it at the American consul general's residence in Milan and made a point of turning their ears over and over, lengthwise, on the stick of butter in the butter dish before sprinkling them with salt and pepper. Turi helped Babak butter his ear of corn, which was so hot that he kept dropping it. They sat at a long picnic table on the Italian patio Woody had built with Purington Pavers, the same bricks, he explained in Italian, that had been used to line the Panama Canal. Some streets in Paris, he'd been told, were paved with Purington Pavers. He'd sunk treated four-by-fours in the ground, poured cement around them, and nailed two-by-fours around the top to support the grapes that he planted at the four corners. He'd seen a picture of something like this in an Italian cookbook.

They were all drinking red wine except Alireza, who drank Coke, but the Coke seemed to affect him like wine. "I have three things to tell you," he said to Woody. "First, not everyone was happy with you this morning." He laughed. "Did you see their faces? We gave them a little surprise. There's something you haven't told me, don't try to deny it. Second, the Holy Prophet said that the ink of a scholar is holier than the blood of the martyr. Third, 'God provides the food; men provide the cooks.' We are in your debt, Jenab-e Agha, especially my daughter."

THEY HAD finished dinner by the time Allison arrived. Turi had brought out Woody's guitar so that he could sing the little Persian song about the nightingale that she'd taught him. He stumbled over the words, but everyone applauded enthusiastically, especially Babak, who was fascinated by the shiny guitar. Woody, who had never let anyone else play the guitar, let him hold it and showed him how to strum an e-minor chord by holding down the fourth and fifth strings over the second fret. It took him a while, but once he got it, he got it. "That's enough, Babak," Alireza said once or twice in Italian, for Woody's benefit, but Babak kept on strumming. Swallows circled above the barn; bats darted after mosquitoes; a flock of crows flew overhead, and Woody cupped his hands over his mouth and gave a four-hoot owl call: "Hoo hoo hoo hooauagh; hoo hoo hoo hooauagh." The crows scattered and cawed and then disappeared behind the barn.

Woody called again: "Hoo hoo hoo hooauagh; hoo hoo hoo hooauagh."

They waited in silence.

"Do they ever answer?" Alireza asked.

Woody called again: "Hoo hoo hoo hooauagh; hoo hoo hoo hooauagh. Sometimes," he said. "There's a pair of barred owls that roost in the cemetery. You never know when they'll come."

"Hu hu hoo hu," Alireza tried softly.

"You can't hold back," Woody said. "Cup your hands. Like this."

Alireza cupped his hands and hooted loudly.

"Not quite," Woody said. "I don't know how to explain. It's like whistling. You just have to keep doing it."

Woody demonstrated again, and then again, and pretty soon everyone was hooting, including Turi's aunt, Homa, who made a delicate little hooting sound. Everyone except Babak, who continued to strum Woody's guitar.

They were all hooting so intently when Allison arrived that they didn't hear her drive up. Woody was the first to see her, standing at the corner of the house, watching them in amazement.

Woody stopped hooting, and then the others stopped, one by one, till there was only the sound of Babak strumming his e-minor chord.

"What on earth are you guys doing?"

"We're calling owls," Behruz said in Persian. "*Boofha-ra seda mikoneh*. Jenab-e Agha-ye-Voody is very good. You should hear him."

"An unexpected talent," she said. "Woody Khan is very versatile."

Behruz translated for his aunt and uncle, and for his father.

"I knew I should have invited old Shardlow Anderson out here after the dinner," Allison said. "Wouldn't that be something. The chairman of the board. You should have come to the dinner. We could have used a little hooting to liven things up."

"Maybe you could release some owls at one of those meetings," Woody said. "Diodorus says that Agathocles the Tyrant of Syracuse released owls before he attacked Carthage. The owls sat on the soldiers' shields and on their helmets, got them all fired up. I suppose because the owl was sacred to Athena."

"Did it work?"

"Almost," Woody said, "but not quite. Do you want something to eat?"

"I'm stuffed, but I'll have a glass of wine."

"I'll get you a clean glass," Woody said.

"Don't bother; I'll use Alireza Khan's."

"It's got Coke in it," Woody said.

She shrugged, emptying the dregs of her husband's Coke on the ground.

"You know, Agha-ye-Voody," Alireza said, "that to hoo is an important part of the Sufi rites. Hoo," he said again. "One syllable, one hoo, is often enough to sustain the novice who has been well trained, to set him dancing, to bring him to the desired state."

"I had no idea," Woody said.

"Hoo for Babak," Allison said.

"Not now."

"Why not? *I'd* do it but I can never get it right."

Alireza said something quickly to her in Persian that Woody couldn't understand.

"You were hooting like an owl," she said; "you can hoo like a Sufi."

"All right, all right." And Alireza began to sing or chant: "Hoo; hoo; hoo; hoo."

"You have to do it louder," Allison said. "There's a Persian saying," she explained to Woody. "*Divana-ra hoo'i bas ast.* To a madman, it is enough to shout hoo!"

"'Hoo' is short for *houwa*," Alireza explained. "That's *he*, that is, God. And 'madman' is a technical term. When the Sufi calls himself a madman he means that what looks like madness to the ordinary person may be sanity or insight to others who can *see*. Any fool can drop a rock down a well; but a hundred professors can't get it out again without a 'madman,' like my son Babak." He threw his head back and shouted, "Hoo, hoo, hoo; hoo, hoo, hoo." After a moment or two Babak put down the guitar and began to caper around, shuffling his feet, dancing.

"Hoo, hoo, hoo," Alireza shouted. No one seemed to find it odd, so Woody didn't find it odd either.

"Baba Joon," Turi said. She and her brothers were preparing to leave.

"Hoo, hoo, hoo."

"We're going to the reception now, out at Jumers; and then we'll probably go to the dance with Sheryl. My roommate, remember? You met her this afternoon. Babak's going with us." But Babak didn't want to go with his sister and brothers; he wanted to play the guitar.

How did the madman or Sufi get the rock out of the well? Woody wondered, but he didn't ask. He was happy. He'd sat next to Turi at the picnic table; he'd spoken Persian with her father, who sat across from him, and with her aunt and uncle, and Italian with her brothers. He couldn't have imagined a better ending to this chapter of his life, but now he was sorry to see the evening winding down. He got up suddenly and carried a tray of dirty dishes into the kitchen. He turned on the water in the sink and opened the dishwasher. Time marches on; πάντα ῥεῖ, *tutto scorre*. Everything passes. *In niz migozareh.*

In a little while the door to the back porch opened and Allison came into the kitchen. Time had not touched her beauty, which was still ripening. Woody could see that she was not only beautiful but happy.

"A *succès fou*, Woody," she said, "especially the owl calling. What an idea!"

Woody lined the plates up in their slots in the dishwasher.

"Well," she said, "another year."

"Another year," he said.

He poured a little wine into a glass. Allison held out her glass and he poured some for her, emptying the bottle.

"Another year," he said again, turning off the water.

During Allison's yearly visit, they would always stumble into a moment like this, a moment in which they found themselves together, face to face, with ten minutes or so to say everything that needed to be said, but what needed to be said could never be said. At least it never *had* been said.

Allison hadn't been the first woman he'd gone to bed with, but she'd been the first woman he'd made love to more than once, for free. There hadn't been a lock on the bedroom door in her apartment on Hopewell Street, behind the Nichols Arboretum, and every now and then while they were making love her roommate would come in and rummage through her drawers or poke around in her closet. "Sorry," she'd say, tiptoeing around. Woody had never dreamed such things were possible, the miracle of fucking and the anti-miracle of the roommate opening and shutting drawers—he couldn't put them together; but Allison didn't seem to mind, and sometimes she'd speak to Nancy, the roommate, telling her where to look for a scarf, or a sweater, or shoes.

Woody put a glass in the top tray of the dishwasher. As a general rule, he imagined, old, experienced lovers took advantage of moments like this one to go over old times, to summon back old ghosts, maybe to touch each other, just to let each other know that they hadn't forgotten; and he and Allison occasionally spoke of Nancy or of dinners at Metzgers and the Old German restaurant or of the time Allison was elected to tell the old-man-of-the-mountain joke at the Classics Department Christmas party. She was the first woman ever to tell the joke, and her version was so raunchy and disgusting that she was elected to tell it again the next year.

"Hannah fixed the dishwasher just before she left," Woody said. "The soap dispenser didn't work and she ordered a new one, but when she took it apart she found that it was just a bad connection." He paused. "Now it works perfectly."

"How long has it been, Woody?"

"Four years since she moved to Chicago. Two years she's been living in the convent. Right now she's at the Mother House in Dubuque. She stopped by at Christmas."

"I came with Turi in eighty-three. I think she'd just started teaching then."

228

"We're divorced now," Woody said. "Officially. May seventeenth."

"And you and I are models of decorum—no sly glances, no winks, no subtle allusions to our secret past."

"There's something right and proper about it, don't you think? Something admirable."

"Yes, I do, Woody," she said, "but sometimes I think we're squandering something, dropping a precious stone into the sea."

"You're right," he said, seeing an opening. "It's not as if nothing has ever passed between us." He started to look back and then checked himself. "What is the span of a man's life anyway?" he asked, trying to think of Turi and Allison together. His imagination was full, not with a secret sense of triumph but with a sense of the mystery of things, and a sense of well-being too. He could hear Babak's e-minor chord through the kitchen window, and the rumble of Alireza's voice telling a story in Persian. And then the sudden hooting of an owl, up close: Hoo hoo hoo hooauagh; hoo hoo hoo hooauagh. It took his breath away. "Jesus," he said, "it's right outside. Listen."

Hoo hoo hoo hooauagh; hoo hoo hoo hooauagh.

He tiptoed to the screen door and opened it softly. "It'll be up in that big locust tree on this side of the drive," he said, waving at her to follow. "Don't let the door slam."

Standing on the porch step he looked up into the moonlit sky, a field of dark blue beyond the light of the yard light. Then laughter. Alireza's.

Alireza cupped his hands to his mouth and called again: "Hoo hoo hoo hooauagh; hoo hoo hoo hooauagh. Maybe I didn't fool an owl," he said, "but I fooled Voody Khan, didn't I!"

"Very good, Alireza," Woody said. His heart was still pumped up. He noticed that Alireza was holding the guitar on his lap. Babak was playing with the dog, who had returned after a mysterious absence. Babak buried his face in her mantle and then looked up as if he were surprised to see everyone. Woody got her bowl and filled it and put it on the back step, and then he and Allison went back into the kitchen.

He put the glass of wine up to his forehead.

"I'm happy that you and Alireza hit it off so well," Allison said.

"He's very kind," Woody said, "and very generous. More than kind; more than generous."

"You never know how things will turn out," she said. "I think he was worried."

"Worried?"

"Worried."

"That we *wouldn't* hit it off?"

"I told him what happened in Bologna," she said. "I mean what happened between you and me. It's something we need to talk about."

"'Something we need to talk about,'" he said, echoing her words. "I don't like the sound of that." But he smiled.

"Is that an enigmatic smile?" she asked. "Or is it the real thing?"

"It's the real thing."

She was standing with her back to the sink. She smiled. "Woody, if I can't talk to you, whom can I talk to?"

They heard footsteps on the stairs and then the porch door swinging open. Alireza came into the kitchen bringing Woody's guitar. He put his arms around Woody and gave him another embrace, still holding the guitar in one outstretched hand.

"Voody Khan," he said in Persian, "we are in your debt."

"It is we who are in your debt, Alireza Khan. Your kindness will be spoken of for many, many years; your generosity will be felt by students and faculty alike for years and years to come."

"And especially by those who study the ancient languages." Alireza put his hands on Woody's shoulders and looked him in the eye and laughed. "There's still something you're not telling me," he said. "That dean . . ." He made an Italian gesture, flinging his fingers sideways as if he were trying to shake off water.

"Especially," Woody said.

"Allison Joon," Alireza said, "Shapur and I will take Karim and Homa back to the motel now. They are very tired. You stay and talk to Jenab Voody. Old friends are best." He looked at Woody. "You can give her a ride into town later? The children have taken the other car, I'm sorry . . ."

"Of course," Woody said, his heart pounding.

He went outside with Alireza and Allison to say good-bye to

Turi's aunt and uncle and to Babak, who held out his hand for Woody to shake. He kissed everyone on both cheeks, Persian style, and walked with them down to the Mercedes, which was parked in front of the barn.

Shapur drove. Alireza sat in the backseat with his brother. Babak and Homa rode in front.

As soon as they had gone Woody opened another bottle of wine and lit one of Hannah's cigarettes. There was a pack on the back porch, hidden under the box holding the dog's toenail clippers.

"I didn't know you smoked, Woody."

"I don't."

"I see."

"Not during the day. Never. But sometimes at night, when I've had some wine, a cigarette tastes good. These are Hannah's. She left six cartons when she went to Chicago."

Allison poured some wine for herself. "You thought for a minute," she said, "that you'd get out of our little talk. But you were mistaken."

"*Spes sibi quisque*," he said. She laughed. "Let every man's hope," he went on, "be in himself."

"I know what it *means*," she said. "Must be a battle scene."

"Latinus, king of the Latins. Just before the battle with Aeneas." Woody looked around him at the dirty dishes stacked on the table. "So you told Alireza everything?"

"I told him that it was nothing," she said, "not worth talking about. That's what I told Alireza. That it was nothing. A reflex. We were both desperate, you especially. I don't know if you know how desperate you were. You told that story to Hannah in the hospital and you thought she was going to be all right. But then she'd turn on her side, away from you, whenever you came into the room. She was hearing voices that said she was a handmaiden of the Lord, and she was angry. I'd never seen anything like it. She hadn't wanted Cookie to go to Italy and she blamed you, and that priest who kept coming around only made things worse, dragging up things from her child-hood. When you saw him coming you'd get so short of breath you couldn't breathe; you'd start to hyperventilate. You'd breathe faster and faster till your whole body was trembling, and sometimes I had trouble getting you back to the hotel."

"How did he react?"

"He was very angry. I thought it was all over between us. We were up in the garden. I thought he might throw me off the roof into the street. I've never seen him so angry. And then a funny thing happened. I told him the truth. I told him that it wasn't nothing, that it was everything. That I loved you and couldn't bear to see you suffer so. I had to take you inside me, Woody. Into my cunt, my *kos*, and into my soul. I'm sorry, Woody. I didn't mean to be so emotional, but it's been seven years and you've never said a word. You've acted as if nothing happened. I just had to let you know."

She wiped her eyes on her sleeve.

Normally Woody smoked only on the back porch, because he didn't want the smell in the house; but tonight he let the smoke fill the kitchen while she talked, and when he'd finished the cigarette he ground it out on a dirty plate on the table. It was true; he'd been desperate; and she'd taken care of everything, made all the arrangements—insurance, doctors, calling the children, finding a place to store Cookie's body till it could be shipped back home on the plane with him and Hannah. The trips to the morgue were the worst thing. He couldn't remember; he'd blocked them out; and he'd blocked out the long nights in the hotel, on Via . . . Via . . . Via—he couldn't remember the name, but now he remembered a wide street closed to traffic, people walking up and down all night, beggars, street musicians; and he remembered how Allison lay next to him, holding him against her chest, till he quieted down enough to make love. Woody hardly knew how to think about it. But now that a third person, a stranger, knew, he had to think about it, had to make a special effort, like Alireza.

"It was a wonderful story," she said, as if she were continuing an earlier conversation. "In the hospital I mean, about the little lights on the mountain, the little girls going to the mountain with the wandering minstrel. And I remember the doctor squirting the sedative up into the air out of the hypodermic, like stars in the Milky Way."

"Hannah went to sleep," Woody said. The moment had passed, but it would come again. "I thought she was going to be OK."

"And now?"

"Now she *is* a handmaiden of the Lord."

"It's hard to understand," she said. "Leaving everything behind."

"It's not so hard," he said, "if you think about it. I could see it—the impulse, I mean. To leave everything behind."

"Where would *you* go? A monastery?"

"That's just it, isn't it? I don't know where I'd go. That's why I'm still here."

"I can't imagine you anywhere else, Woody."

"I can't either," he said, standing up. He started to clear the table, but the dishwasher was full, and there wasn't much room in the sink. "So Alireza knows everything," he said again, trying to adjust to the idea.

She nodded.

"And he's not jealous? He leaves you out here alone with me?"

"He's very jealous, Woody. You don't understand what this means to a man like him. Why, in Iran . . ."

"I don't want to know."

"You don't know how much this has cost him, Woody Khan." She smiled. "More than ten million dollars. Much more."

"He's very kind."

"More than kind, Woody. Good. Like Plato's just man. I read through Turi's thesis last night, you know. I was thrilled, Woody. You know, she's really flourished here. Alireza wanted her to go to Harvard like the boys, but I thought St. Clair would be better, and I was right. You've taken good care of her. It really was thrilling to read that thesis. I never could have written something like that when I was an undergraduate. It made me want to go back and read Plato in Greek, but Plato's too hard. I can still read Homer, but Plato . . . How do we behave when we're invisible, when no one can see us? How would you behave, Woody? Would you be the same as you are anyway?"

"I sat behind a guy on the train," Woody said, "coming back from Chicago. He kept turning his face towards the window and really chewing someone out. He thought he was invisible, but I could see his reflection. He'd read his book for a while, and then something would get to him and he'd turn his face.away to the window and start in again."

"Some of the men Alireza does business with are like that,

Woody. You should see them—Italians, Iraqis, Iranians, Indians, Arabs from the Gulf states, and Saudis too."

"No Americans?" Woody interrupted.

"Not many," she said, "because they don't know the languages and they don't trust the translators. They all think they're invisible; they all think they're wearing Gyges' ring. But Alireza can see them, just like you saw the guy on the train. You'd think Alireza would need a magic ring too, to deal with these people, to make so much money when they're trying to cheat you every time you turn around . . ."

As she went on talking Woody tried once again to grasp his own position, to explain it not to others but to himself. The metaphor of the ring, which had seemed so clear at one point, now seemed impossibly complex. No, not complex; muddled.

"Gyges saw the queen naked," she was saying when Woody started to pay attention again.

"In Herodotus's version," Woody said. "But there's no magic ring in Herodotus. Everyone thought Plato invented the ring till the discovery of the tablets at Al-Qurnah."

"In Herodotus, though, the king *wants* Gyges to see the queen naked. He arranges it. But Gyges isn't invisible. The queen sees him. Have I got it right?"

"She catches a glimpse of him." Woody poured more wine, stepped out onto the back porch, and lit another cigarette. The smoke made him dizzy.

Allison was sitting at the kitchen table. She was the queen and Alireza was the king, and he was Gyges.

"He must either kill the king," Woody said, "and marry the queen, or lose his own life."

"That's what I've never understood," Allison said. "Why does she tell him that? 'Either you must kill the king and marry me, or I'll have *you* killed.'"

"I suppose she was mad at her husband for arranging for Gyges to see her naked."

"Yes, I suppose, but it still seems excessive."

"What cost him more than ten million dollars?" Woody asked suddenly.

"Alireza?" She poured a little more wine. "Coming here; seeing you. But this is the funny thing, Woody. The more I told him it was nothing, that it meant nothing at all to me, that it was just a reflex, the madder he got. But it wasn't nothing, Woody. I don't think it's ever *nothing* when two people come together, no matter how . . . no matter what . . . I don't know; it doesn't matter. But I needed you too, Woody. I hadn't wanted Cookie to go alone; I'd told her I'd go with her later in the month. If I'd insisted . . . If Shapur had driven her . . . If she'd taken a later train, or an earlier train . . . I loved her, Woody, and I loved you too."

Woody emptied his glass and poured more wine. "What's the funny thing?"

"The funny thing, Woody, is that when I stopped pretending, when I told Alireza the truth, that I've always loved you—you know that—but in a good way; I never made myself crazy over you—but you're my oldest friend, Woody. You and Hannah, and now Hannah's gone. You're the only link with my old life. My parents are both dead. You never knew them. I talk to my brother at Christmas and Thanksgiving. I think you met him once in A-Square, and I come back to St. Clair, Woody. I come back to see you."

"And the funny thing?"

"Yes, I keep forgetting. The funny thing is that when I told Ali that it was something rather than nothing, and that I loved you, then he stopped being angry, and I think he started to love you too, a little bit at a time."

Woody swirled the wine in the bottom of his glass. "I don't know what to say," he said.

"It was a challenge, but to tell you the truth I think he's rather pleased with himself."

"For being so forgiving and understanding?"

"Yes, he likes a challenge; but it's not an act. He really *is* forgiving and understanding. He never held it against me. And he wanted to meet you."

She sat down next to Woody and scooted her chair around so that her back was towards him. "Rub my shoulders, will you?" Turi liked this too, he thought, as he kneaded Allison's shoulders. She would turn away from him in bed so that he'd rub her shoulders with one hand while he was reading. He could smell Allison's perfume. The bottle of wine was almost empty, but there was another bottle in the cabinet under the sink. He couldn't put the two things together, the two women, Allison and Turi. They were two magnets with poles reversed, like the little Scottie dogs he used to play with when he was a kid, one white and one black. Magnets on the base. At his aunt Esther's. "Let the inner and the outer man be one," he said.

"Socrates' prayer."

In the distance an owl called, a real owl.

"Listen," Woody said.

"It's Alireza," she said, her eyes wide open.

"I don't think so."

"It's just the sort of thing he'd do."

"Listen, it's too far away."

"That's what I'm saying. If he could fool you up close, then he could fool you from far away."

"He'd have to be over on Kruger Road, on the other side of the cornfield. We'd see car lights."

"He could have turned the lights out."

"It's been half an hour since they left. Do you really think he'd sit there in the dark for half an hour with Karim and Homa? And the driver? And Babak?"

They were standing outside on the porch steps.

"You never can tell."

They listened closely. The owl was silent and then hooted again.

"Let's sit out here," Woody said. "I'll bring out another bottle of wine." He got the last bottle of wine from under the sink, cut the wrapper with a small knife, and screwed a corkscrew into the cork. He popped the cork and went outside. They sat on the top step with the fresh bottle of wine between them, and Woody smoked another cigarette, blowing the smoke sideways, away from Allison. The wine was loosening his tongue; he wanted to tell her that she had been his first love and that Turi had been his last. But what did it mean? Coincidence? Pure chance? Like finding the letter in Esfahan? Or was Turi a substitute for his own daughter, Cookie? Or maybe a simple midlife crisis? Or Jung's innocent maiden? But it had been Turi who had sought him out, after all. Deliberately.

"How about you, Woody?"

"*What* about me?"

"Was it nothing for you?"

He didn't say anything.

"Are you sorry?"

"No, never sorry," he said.

"Does Hannah know?"

"About Bologna?" He shook his head.

"I'm glad," she said. "I've always been afraid that that was something that had come between you."

Woody kept shaking his head. He could feel the tears smarting behind his eyelids.

"Do you think I could see her?" she asked. "I mean do they have visiting hours at the convent? Do you have an address?"

"St. Hilda's, RR2, Dubuque, Iowa. I don't remember the zip. It's beautiful, really. A bluff, actually, overlooking the river."

"You've been there?"

"Just driven by. You can't see the convent from the road, but you can see the main building from the parking lot at Lock and Dam 11."

"Do you go there very often?"

"No," he said, "not very often. It's a two-and-a-half-hour drive. It's been a while. You can see the nuns going in and out, but you can't make out who they are."

"When was the last time you heard from her?"

"Two years, and then she came at Christmas to say she wanted a divorce."

"I'm sorry, Woody." She put her hand on his leg.

"Did you see Bernard Knox's article on *Oedipus* in the *Hellenic Review*?"

"No, Woody. I don't keep up anymore. The school takes all my time. International conferences; new developments in language teaching; the teachers want this and that; and the paperwork for the students . . . A lot of Iranians. Not all of them legal. But they can't go back. The Ayatollah has declared them traitors—any who've done their military service. If they lose their student visas they're in real trouble."

"I used to think that *Oedipus* illustrated the working out of a divine plan," he said. "The will of the gods."

"Isn't that what most people think?"

"Yes, but then I looked at Waldock again—remember, everyone was reading him in graduate school: nothing but the 'terror of coincidence.' When I think about it, it makes sense. Τύχη or μοῖρα, it's got to be one or the other. But if it's a divine plan, it's not much of a plan, is it? You'd think the gods could come up with something better."

"What about the tragic flaw?"

"Impetuosity? I can't see it. Sure, he's a little impetuous, but who wouldn't be under the circumstances? But the 'terror of coincidence.' Like finding Hannah's letter in Esfahan. But this year I had another idea. You have to ask why the play has such an impact. That's what really interests me, as a teacher. I can't go with Freud or Jung; they just don't ring true. But I think Freud was on the right track: everyone has a secret self that he may not even be aware of. Oedipus thinks he's a good guy, a good king. And he is. Everybody thinks he's a great king. But he's also a man who killed his father and married his mother. It's the collision of these two identities that gives the play its oomph."

"How did that go over in class?"

"It went over pretty well; it opens up the play so you can see yourself in it. You sometimes catch a glimpse of this other self when you hear people talking about you behind your back, or from children."

"I don't know, Woody. It seems to me you've got a lot of loose analogies."

"Aristotle says that the greatest thing of all is to be a master of metaphor."

"You always were a Platonist, Woody, always looking for the real reality behind this reality."

"I can't help it."

"And now you're an Aristotelian? Never mind. You can be whatever you want. Do you know what I'll remember about tonight?"

"What?"

"Everyone calling the owls. Even Karim and Homa. You guys didn't even notice me drive up. I couldn't figure out what was going on. And Alireza. Wasn't he good?"

"He was very good. I thought it really was an owl. He had me fooled."

"That was nice of you to let Babak play your guitar."

Woody shrugged.

"Woody," she said, "tell me what's going on."

"We're sitting here talking and drinking too much wine."

"I mean with you, at the college. Why do I have the impression that you're in hot water?"

He shrugged again.

"Tell me why old Shardlow changes the subject every time I mention your name. I wanted to tell him what a great job you've done with Turi, and he starts talking about the bond issue. Something's up, Woody; out with it. You haven't been a bad boy, have you?"

They picked up their glasses and drank some more wine.

"I got involved with a student," he said.

"A little bit on the side?"

"It was more than that."

"You didn't fall in love, did you?"

"No," he said, "I didn't fall in love."

"How about her? Did she fall in love with you?"

"Maybe I did fall in love," he said. "They wanted to can me. The dean especially. She was living out here. The girl. She said she'd move back to the dorm if I asked her to, but that she wouldn't go if I didn't ask her."

"And you didn't ask her?"

"No."

"I see."

The owl called again, and then another owl answered from Warren Woods. "There're two of them," Woody said. "It can't be Alireza."

"No, it's not Ali," she said; and then she said, "Woody, this is very exciting news. This makes sense of everything. I guess old Shardlow didn't want it to come up because he knew I'd take your side; and he wasn't the only one avoiding the subject. Does everyone know except me?"

"I think it's on a need-to-know basis. They did can me, though. I was out of here. Till your husband showed up. If his secretary hadn't gotten sick in Chicago . . . If they hadn't needed me to translate . . ."

"Call the owls again, Woody. I love it when you hoot like that."

Woody cupped his hands to his mouth and hooted: "Hoo hoo hoo hooauagh. Hoo hoo hoo hooauagh. Hoo hoo hoo hooauagh." He waited a moment and then tried again: "Hoo hoo hoo hooauagh. Hoo hoo hoo hooauagh. Hoo hoo hoo hooauagh."

Allison dug her fingers into his leg.

Woody got up and turned off the yard light and then sat back down again. Allison put her hand back on his leg. He hooted again: "Hoo hoo hoo hooauagh"; and then again: "Hoo hoo hoo hooauagh." There was an answer from the cemetery: Hoo hoo hoo hooauagh. Hoo hoo hoo hooauagh.

Woody hooted again, and the owl hooted back. They kept it up for several minutes, and then the owl was silent.

"He's flying now," Woody said, putting his hand on top of Allison's. "They can't hoot and fly at the same time."

"Will he come here?" she whispered.

Woody nodded. "He might." She moved her hand under his, hooking her thumb around his thumb. Waiting. "You won't hear him till he lands," Woody said. "You won't hear a thing. Their plumage is so soft they don't make any noise. Watch the locust tree."

The owl, however, landed not in the locust tree but on one of the two-by-fours at the top of Woody's grape arbor, hardly twenty feet from them. They didn't see it till it hooted—Hoo hoo hoo hooauagh—and then what they saw was a black rectangle about eighteen inches high and six inches wide. And two bright eyes, looking at them. The owl adjusted its feathers and hooted again: Hoo hoo hoo hooauagh. Woody had never heard one so close.

"Answer him, Woody," Allison whispered. She stood up and moved away from the steps, closer to the owl. Woody followed her.

"Shhh. Don't go any closer."

"Fantastic." She whispered in his ear.

The owl continued to hoot: Hoo hoo hoo hooauagh, hoo hoo hoo hooauagh.

"He wants you to talk to him. I wish Alireza and Babak were here. Call him, Woody. Talk to him."

"Jesus Christ, Allison, just be quiet."

"Call him, Woody. I want you to call him. This is too fantastic."

The owl knacked its beak, making a loud snapping sound, and hooted again: Hoo hoo hoo hooauagh.

This time Woody answered—"Hoo hoo hoo hooauagh"—and the owl flattened its ear tufts against its square head, tilted forward, and suddenly was gliding directly at them, a great, dark shape, silent on enormous wings. Woody dropped to the ground, pulling Allison down with him; he waved his arm over his head, punching at the owl so that it couldn't grab their heads. They heard nothing, but they felt the sweep of the great wings passing over them, disturbing the night air. The owl landed in the locust tree, knacked its beak again, hooted two or three times, and flew away.

Lying on the damp ground, Woody kept his arm around Allison, who was breathing in short little gasps. They lay beside each other for a while without talking. Above them the great constellations—Canis Minor, Taurus, the great bear—grazed across the Illinois sky as they had grazed over the ancient civilizations of China and Greece, imaginary configurations by which mariners still navigate, as if the universe were in fact a system of concentric spheres and not a mathematical description of a finite curve with unimaginable coordinates. Boötes the Herdsman was rising over the grape arbor. We draw the lines, Woody thought; we create the monsters, but the dots, the stars, are there. But he kept his thoughts to himself. It seemed to him he'd come to the place he'd been looking for all evening, a place where prayers are answered in unexpected ways, which is just the way prayers are *supposed* to be answered. You might get what you want, but it won't be quite what you expected. They'd been calling owls all evening, after all. And then the owl had come out of nowhere. How frightening it had been; how mysterious. Like Hannah's letter in Esfahan, like the chain of events in *Oedipus*, it cried out for an explanation, an interpretation; it was hard not to reach for one. But Woody reached instead for Allison. He kissed her neck and her eyes and her mouth.

"You still haven't said anything, Woody. Seven years, and you haven't said a word."

"I tried to pretend, too," he said, "that it was nothing. Just what you told Alireza. It's just taken me longer to tell myself the truth." He pulled back so he could see her face. "You saved my life," he said. The words came easily because he'd said them to himself before. "You gave me all that you had, the gift of your body. No small thing."

She started to laugh. "Well, I'm glad we finally got that settled."

Woody laughed too. "Don't you want to hear the rest of it?"

"Maybe next year," she said. "We'll have to make this an annual event. Woody Woodhull's Annual Owl Call."

He took her by the hand and pulled her up. She got her purse from the kitchen and they walked over to the pickup, which he'd pulled into the barn so that there'd be plenty of room for the Mirsadiqis' two rented Mercedes. He let the tailgate down so the dog could jump into the back.

On the way into St. Clair, sitting beside him in the cab of the truck, she asked him, "Do you think it was a sign?"

"Of what?"

She smiled at him. "You old fox."

"Seriously. A sign of what? You mean like a burning bush?"

"More like an epiphany."

"More like an owl," he said. "*Strix varia*. When in doubt always use Latin names."

THE COMMENCEMENT speaker was Malcolm Cowley, a literary critic whose work on Hemingway and the lost generation Woody had admired as a young man. Cowley, sitting in the front row on the platform, two rows in front of Woody, looked as if he were pushing eighty. He'd visited St. Clair two or three times to look at some early editions of Hemingway and Dos Passos in the Lombard Collection in the library. Woody wrote out Cowley's name in capital letters on his program:

M A L C O L M C O W L E Y

And then he started to work on an anagram, which is what he always did at Commencement, while the president introduced the candidates for honorary degrees, all distinguished and influential. Woody didn't pay any attention to the first two, but the third candidate was Alireza, who stood stiffly, hands at his sides, while Richard Young from the Economics Department described his many accomplishments in the field of international business, bringing the nations together, establishing goodwill wherever he did business, extending the hand of friendship . . . The hooding committee placed a yellow and azure hood over Alireza's shoulders and the president motioned to him to sit down. The fourth candidate was Cowley, whose demeanor suggested that he already had a string of honorary degrees.

The first word that leaped out at Woody was OWL. Another coincidence? He shuddered, feeling again the sweep of the owl's wings and the fear and the wonder in his own heart. The second word was MAY. He crossed off the letters.

M̷ A̷ L C O L M C Ø̷ W̷ L̷ E Y̷
MAY OWL   LCOLMCE

He searched for more words, crossing off letters as he went along.

M̷ A̷ L̷ C Ø̷ L M C O W̷ L̷ E Y̷
YOWL LAME   COLMC
M̷ A̷ L C Ø̷ L̷ M C O W L E̷ Y̷
MOLE MAY LCCOWL

And then back to O W L:

M A L C O L M C Ø̷ W̷ L̷ E Y
OWL

Woody had heard a lot of Commencement speeches delivered from this very platform. In general, he thought, his preference would be to ask someone at random from the audience to talk off the top of his or her head for ten minutes; but Cowley's speech, which he had some trouble hearing, was actually pretty good—anecdotal, an old man reminiscing, but the anecdotes were interesting. Cowley told about struggling to make a living as a writer in New York and Paris in the twenties; he told about meeting Hemingway in the lobby of the Ritz in Paris in 1932 when he was finishing *Exile's Return;* he told about working with Faulkner—or trying to work with Faulkner—on the Vintage Portable edition that eventually turned Faulkner's reputation around.

Woody didn't start working on the anagram again till the speech was over and it was time for the students to march across the stage as the dean read their names, to shake the president's hand and get their diplomas from the registrar.

M̷ A̷ L̷ C̷ O̷ L̷ M̷ C O̷ W̷ L̷ E̷ Y̷
CALM MOLE LOW   CY

But he liked the idea of the owl.

M̷ A L C̷ O̷ L M C O̷ W̷ L̷ E̷ Y̷
COME OWL   LLAY CM

He was getting close.

M̷ A̷ L̷ C̷ O̷ L M̷ C̷ O̷ W̷ L̷ E̷ Y
COME OWL CALM   YL

He knew he had it:

COME CALMLY, OWL

He drew a circle around it on his program and wrote YES.

The students were still traipsing across the platform. No one tripped; no one buzzed President Hanson as he shook their hand. People whistled and applauded despite the dean's repeated admonitions to hold all applause till *all* the degrees had been awarded. Jessica Lowden got up to greet her daughter as she walked across the stage—an old St. Clair custom—and a few minutes later, as Turi approached the platform, Woody left his seat to explain the custom to Alireza, who rose to embrace *his* daughter.

Woody was enormously moved. To see his students crossing the stage. To be a part of this. He had been invited to the lunch afterwards for the platform party—a buffet in the reading room of the library—but he wanted to be alone; and he didn't want to say goodbye, not to Turi, not to Allison, not to Alireza.

So instead of joining the platform party for lunch, the new Alireza Mirsadiqi Professor of Greek found himself driving up to the cemetery. The weather had cleared up for a while—the decision to stay outside had undoubtedly been a tough one—but now it was threatening to rain again. Woody could see his clean laundry flapping on the line.

"I ought to get back down and take in the clean clothes before it rains," he said out loud, as if addressing Cookie. And then after a while he said, "But I'm not going to. If they get wet, they'll dry again. It doesn't matter."

The owl's roost was not far from Cookie's grave. He couldn't see the owl, but he could see the owl's hole, about three big branches up, and he could see where the ground was littered with owl pellets. "Come calmly, owl," he said aloud. "That's good; that's really good, one of my best efforts." He thought he might send the results to Cowley himself. He could get the address from the president's secretary.

Commencement, Cowley had observed at the end of his speech, was not only an ending, it was a beginning. How many times had Woody heard that same sentiment, on that same platform? About once a year, he thought. He didn't disagree; and yet something in him resisted the idea, wanted to turn it around. Of course Commencement is a beginning; that's what the word means. But Commencement isn't only a beginning; it's an ending. That's the real paradox. The end of your old life. You can *look* back, but you can't *go* back.

When Woody looked back on this moment, as he often did, he couldn't remember exactly when he'd made up his mind, or when his mind had been made up for him. Was it before or after he saw the two dark blue Mercedes, carrying Turi and her parents and her brothers and her aunt and uncle, coming down Kruger Road? Was it before or after they turned in the driveway that he knew that his old life was over, knew it in a new way, knew that he couldn't go back to it, not even as the Alireza Mirsadiqi Professor of Greek? Someone else would have to fill that role. He watched the two Mercedes turn into the driveway and pull up to the house. He was neither happy nor unhappy. His wife was gone; his children were gone; Turi was leaving; the farm was a dream of Eden. It was time for him to go out into the world.

Down below, in another world, he saw Turi get out of the first car. He saw her look around for his truck, saw her walk up to the door and knock halfheartedly, saw her bend over and whisper some-

thing to the dog, who was jumping up on her. She opened the door
and went inside, and then she came out again. She walked over to
the clothesline and took her panties down. She glanced up at the
cemetery, but he couldn't tell if she saw him or not; and then she got
back in the car. The two Mercedes turned around in front of the
barn and drove off.

House
for Sale

"Love and work," Daddy used to say; "that's what it's all about. If you've got someone to love and to love you, and you've got meaningful work, that's all you can ask for."

By the end of the summer of 1987 I had both, and for the first time in my life I felt like an adult. At least like an adulteress, for I was having an affair with a married man, a consultant whom *I* had hired myself in my new position as an exhibit developer in charge of Chaos, six hundred square feet of floor space to be organized down to the last inch by the fifteenth of December.

My parents, on the other hand, had been behaving like children. I thought I was in a position to give them some advice, just the way they'd always given me advice when I was a child. But they weren't interested.

I didn't know whom to blame more, Mama or Daddy. It was Mama who set things in motion, i.e., the divorce proceedings. Daddy dragged his feet for a long time, wouldn't talk to the convent lawyer on the phone, wouldn't sign the papers that were sent to him. But then he caved in and signed everything without looking at it. I thought he was too soft. He could have fought more. For Ludi and for me. I was starting to learn about money. It wasn't something we'd talked about at home. I'd always assumed we were rich, and of course we were, because we had a nice house, one that was full of books, and good clothes and plenty to eat. But Daddy's lawyer— Doris Brett, a St. Clair fixture—seemed to think we were poor, that eighty thousand dollars, including the house, wasn't much of an estate for a man in Daddy's position. Of course there was Daddy's TIAA-CREF, but that wouldn't amount to much if he started drawing on it now, and Social Security, which he couldn't touch till he was sixty-two. I'd been driving down to St. Clair every weekend since June to help with the paperwork and to help get the house ready to sell. Daddy and Mama had paid only eighteen thousand for it, but Daddy thought we could get at least forty. Of course there would be a capital gains tax . . .

Daddy had proposed a four-way split: Mama, Daddy, Ludi, and I. We'd each get a fourth once the house was sold. But Mama wanted half for her dowry, and Daddy said that was fair.

My sympathies had been with Daddy all along, until I found out that he hadn't *really* lost his job, though that's the way he talked. If Turi hadn't told me the whole story, I might never have found out. I didn't blame him for the affair with Turi, especially now that I was conducting an affair of my own and thought I understood a thing or two about love that I hadn't understood before; but when I found out he'd turned down an endowed chair in classics—that he could have become the Alireza Mirsadiqi Professor of Greek—so he could go to Bologna to attend the trial of the terrorists who blew up the train station, that's when I put my foot down. But put it down on what?

"We wouldn't have to sell the farm, Daddy," I told him on the phone. "What can you accomplish in Bologna? Cookie's dead. Those people will be convicted—or not convicted—whether you go to Bologna or not. It doesn't make sense." It wasn't just the end of our life together as a family; it was the end of my expectations about what our life was going to be in the future. It was like reading a short story and thinking it was a novel. You think you've got a couple of hundred pages to go, but all of a sudden you're at the end. The story you were reading is over. That's it. The rest of the book is other stories. What was I supposed to do for Thanksgiving, for Christmas? I couldn't very well spend it with Richard, who had a wife and family of his own.

When you're reading a novel, you have a sense of where you are in the story because you know roughly how many pages are left. But when you're reading a collection of short stories, you don't know. Unless you're on the last one. And even then, you can't be sure it's the last one until you get to the very end. Unless you look at the table of contents, of course; but where's the table of contents for the story of a family?

"It's too late," he said. Nothing could be done, but he didn't say he was sorry, and I don't think he was.

"The last time I saw you guys together was Christmas Eve," I said. "I thought it might be a new beginning. What happened? What went wrong?"

"It *was* a new beginning," he said, "but every new beginning is also an ending."

THE HOUSE had been sold to a young couple, right out of graduate school. In psychology. Idealists, they weren't able to conceal their enthusiasm for country life. They wanted to have a big garden, and horses. But they weren't able to conceal their ignorance either. They didn't know a sump pump from a septic tank. They didn't understand how things worked, how a house worked. They didn't seem to realize that they couldn't simply hook up to city water and gas, that the motor on the old furnace blower had to be oiled regularly, that you couldn't just order the bats to vacate the attic. Instead of minimizing the bat problem Daddy pointed his flashlight up at the joists under the roof, so they could see the bats clustered on top of each other, and started telling bat stories until he realized that they were having second thoughts. And then he promised to get rid of them— the bats. They had it written into the contract! Ludi and I were indignant, but Daddy didn't seem to mind. "Mama and I didn't know any more than they do," he said, "when we bought the farm."

That was the last week of June 1987, about two weeks after St. Clair's Commencement. Daddy had called a family conference to tell us what we already knew, more or less: that the divorce was final and that he was going to Italy for the second phase of the trial in Bologna. *He* had plunged us into this mess, but he talked as if we were all acting in concert. Ludi didn't seem to mind so much, but she was openly scornful of the new owners. She was going to be a vet. She *liked* bats—eighty percent of the world's plants are pollinated by bats—and was gratified to learn that the exterminators wouldn't touch them because they're on the endangered species list.

I wasn't so happy about the bat situation. In fact, I was sort of like the new owners: unnerved by the bats. Every weekend we tried something new, or something we'd tried before but maybe hadn't done right: more mothballs, different settings on the electronic ultrasound devices, patching up the holes one by one. We tried opening the windows in the evening so the bats could go out, and then Daddy would go back up and close the windows in the middle of the night so they couldn't get back in. But it didn't work. They had secret entrances. We had to discover them. Ludi and Daddy were going to do it that night, were going to watch the bats to see where they went out. They were going to plug up the holes with pads of steel wool that Ludi had sewn together. She'd also collected some bugs, which she had in a paper sack. She wanted to see if she could feed the bats.

From a distance it looked as if everything was in order. Ludi was a great organizer; organized-looking piles of stuff grew in the barn; stuff for me, stuff for Ludi, books for the college library, books for the public library, stuff for storage, stuff for the Salvation Army. Like my old bike, a balloon-tired monster—country roads were too hard on English bikes. Did I want it in Chicago, where I'd have to carry it up three flights of stairs? I'd decide later.

We'd taken things at an easy, slow pace. The piano (which had belonged to my grandmother) had already been put in storage for Ludi. It was valued at nine thousand dollars and there was a corresponding nine thousand dollars for me in Daddy's will.

I'd called Daddy to tell him we should go out to eat, but instead of packing up the kitchen stuff, he and Ludi had planned an elaborate dinner. Daddy had tossed several handfuls of olive pits on the grill and the air was fragrant with olive-pit smoke. We'd been saving olive pits for years, and since we generally forgot to put them on the fire, we'd accumulated several bushels of them.

From a distance it may have looked like everything was in order, but up close it looked like chaos. In every room of the house closet doors and dresser drawers stood open, empty; but in every room there was a pile of stuff that no one could decide about. Hard-core stuff. My old college notes; Daddy's papers from when he was an undergraduate at Michigan. He'd never looked at them, not once, but he couldn't bring himself to toss them. No value to anyone. And there were still books in every room. I'd learned a lot about chaos in the last few months at MSI. I'd learned that under certain circumstances perfectly ordinary phenomena start to behave chaotically: cigarette smoke dispersing, for example, or ripples in a stream. I'd also learned that a certain kind of mysterious order eventually emerges from these chaotic systems. But I wasn't so sure that that was going to happen in the life of our family.

The books were the real heartbreaker for me because I knew how much they meant to Daddy. They were his life. "Gutenberg man," he used to call himself. "Reading and writing," he'd say, "just like love and work. I'm living the life I want to live." Teaching was his vocation. The books were a symbol of that vocation.

The kitchen stuff that was too good to get rid of—I'd already taken quite a bit—was going into storage: Daddy's pots and pans, copper and cast-iron; my grandmother's roaster and china, which was Japanese. Ludi and I divided the knives—Sabatier and Wüsthof, all old-fashioned carbon steel—between us, except for an eight-inch chef's knife with a broken tip. Cookie had dropped it once and then tried to straighten the tip with a pair of pliers. Daddy was going to take it to Bologna.

I blamed Daddy and Ludi, but I was just as bad. I still had boxes of my own stuff to sort through. The thinginess of things was getting to me, binding me to the past. My grandmother had been different. If she didn't use something in a year, she threw it out. She taped lists to the insides of closet doors so she knew what was on each shelf. The butcher's table in the kitchen stayed. The young couple who bought the house fell in love with it and offered five hundred dollars. Daddy let them have it for twenty-five, which is what he paid for it at an auction.

Our lives were exposed, torn open by the tremendous power of things, possessions. I didn't see how it could happen. To us. This was the last weekend, and on top of everything we still had to deal with the bats. Ludi was directing that operation.

AT TIMES like this my mother used to take up elaborate ironing or mending projects. When we were about to leave for vacation, for example, she'd start darning socks. It drove everyone crazy, but I wished she were here now, instead of living at the convent in Oak Park, where she was taking a course of study in preparation for convent life. A special course for people with a late vocation. In the middle of the summer I'd taken her out to dinner, which I'd thought of as another adult thing to do. Dinner at the Greek restaurant on Halstead Street where I had worked as a waitress. The Mount Parnassus. I picked her up in Oak Park in her old Chevy Monte Carlo, which she'd given to me. I'd spent half a month's salary getting it running again. I stopped for gas and she asked me to buy her a pack of cigarettes. Pall Malls.

At the restaurant the people I'd worked with—Alexa, Cassie, Angie, Nikki, the busboys—treated me like a big shot. Nikki M., the owner's son, brought us each a complimentary glass of ouzo. American born, he still spoke with a thick accent. Mama poured a drop of water in her ouzo, so that it turned cloudy, and then took a small, nunny sip.

"Your father and I drank ouzo in Athens," she said, "before you were born. Hand me another cigarette, would you?"

Mama smoked and I made small talk about MSI—the exhibit, Lorenz's discoveries about weather, chaos.

Mama resisted the idea of chaos. "Just because you can't predict something doesn't mean it's chaotic. It just means that you don't have enough information, or that it's too complicated." I tried to tell her that it was something different from that. That no matter *how much* information you had, you still wouldn't be able to predict. Like the waterwheel I'd been working on, trying to duplicate the one Lorenz was said to have built in his basement to illustrate his theory. No one seemed to know if he'd actually built it or not. Maybe it had just been a thought experiment.

But Mama liked the idea that order arises spontaneously in these systems—chaos and order together. "See," she said, "there really is order after all." I didn't quite know where to go from here, but Alexa, our waitress, brought two plates of flaming saganaki. Mama left her cigarette burning in the ashtray while she ate.

The couple at the table on our right started to exclaim over *their* saganaki. At the table on our left six girls and an older man, talking a mixture of Italian and English, were having trouble ordering dessert. The man was explaining something in Italian to the girls. When the man went to the bathroom, the girls paid the bill. Somebody was having an adventure.

Alexa brought kabobs for me and moussaka for Mama. I offered her a taste of my lamb, which was delicious, but she shook her head.

"Have you become a vegetarian, Mama?"

"No, I just don't eat meat anymore." She sat back in her chair and lit another cigarette.

She smoked naturally, unself-consciously, and I thought of all the times we'd criticized her for smoking, pinning up cancer articles on the refrigerator or taping them down to the table or the bathroom mirror. But now the smoke connected us, linked us to the past, and I breathed it in greedily, and then Alexa brought us a plate of *kourabiedes*, and then it was time to go.

DADDY AND Ludi were in the kitchen. It was in the nineties, but Ludi was baking an elaborate hazelnut cake. She'd unpacked kitchen stuff that I'd packed the night before. She didn't believe in giving in to the weather. She and Daddy were making common cause against me. Not exactly, of course, but sort of. I was the one who was angry, who wanted to have things out, who wanted an explanation. I was the adult and they were playing in the kitchen, making a fancy dinner instead of packing up the stuff. We should have gone out for pizza, but that wasn't good enough.

It was Saturday night and they were listening to Garrison Keillor's *Prairie Home Companion* on a small radio in the kitchen. Daddy had taped the "News from Lake Wobegon," including reruns, every week for years. There were hundreds of tapes, many of them not labeled. But he wasn't taping it tonight; the stereo and tape deck were in their boxes out in the barn. I was outside, setting the picnic table on the patio, which Daddy had made out of old bricks that he'd hauled out to the farm when they were tearing up one of the streets in town. There weren't many grapes on the vines that covered it. Not enough sun. But there were a few, and the effect was very Italian. I'd brought out plates and glasses on a tin tray with rigid handles that kept it from tipping: pasta bowls, regular plates, the green and black tablecloth and matching napkins, wineglasses, glasses for seltzer, a bottle of wine, already half empty. Montepulciano d'Abruzzo. On one side of the grill: onions, eggplant, zucchini, mushrooms. On the other: an *arista* studded with garlic and tied with sprigs of rosemary.

Ludi came out to pick arugula and basil for the salad. She

snipped off the leaves with a pair of kitchen scissors and put them in another pasta bowl. She wore shorts and a bandanna to hold back her long red hair. She was sweating, but she liked the heat. She wanted to move to the South. She wasn't sentimental, like me. I've never wanted to move anywhere.

Daddy's birthday presents were at one end of the picnic table—a set of guitar strings, a new Shubb capo for the metal guitar, which had a flat fingerboard. These were from me. They were what Daddy had asked for. Ludi didn't operate this way. I got Daddy what he wanted; she got him what she wanted him to have.

I poured myself a glass of the wine and added a little seltzer. The dog was outside with me. She didn't know what was happening; didn't know she'd have to move to Grinnell with Ludi, who'd moved out of the dorm and into her own apartment. And there was no way to tell her, no way to explain.

Daddy came out, poked at the roast with a fork, closed the top vent on the cooker, adjusted the three bottom vents.

Seven o'clock.

Seven-fifteen.

I had another glass of wine. The bottle was almost empty, but there was another bottle inside, on the kitchen table.

A river of corn separated us from the moraine, from the cemetery. Daddy'd fixed up Cookie's grave, planted a few bulbs, tulips and daffodils, that would come up in the spring. I'd never thought he was the type.

Seven-thirty. Ludi carried out another tray, pasta in a white china bowl from China. Penne with cream and *pepe verde*, little green peppercorns, hot, but not too hot. It was an old favorite, Daddy's own invention. You were supposed to put a little *speck* in it too, but you couldn't get *speck* in St. Clair, and Cornucopia was out of prosciutto. Daddy brought his glass and the second bottle of wine. Ludi was drinking iced tea. She never drank more than half a glass of wine. We were all together, but Daddy called out in a loud voice, "*Si mangia*," as if he were summoning Mama and Cookie from a long way away.

Ludi said the bats would start to fly around about eight-thirty. We had to be at our posts before that.

During supper Daddy and Ludi tried to make up to me. I'd been playing the role of the disapproving adult. I finally got a chance to tell them about the Chaos exhibit. But I didn't care. It was our last meal together in this old house, and I was too sad to care. And I was dreading the bats. Ludi said we all had to go up in the attic. We'd have to be quick to spot the secret entrances.

Dad played his guitar for a while:

> Come on in this old house
> Ain't nobody here but me.
> Come on in this old house
> Ain't nobody here but me.
>
> Come on upstairs, turn the light down low,
> Come on, babe, make me a pallet on your floor.
> Come on in this old house
> Ain't nobody here but me.

We drank champagne with the hazelnut birthday cake; Daddy opened his presents—the guitar stuff from me, a membership in the Sierra Club and a Sierra Club calendar from Ludi—and then we did the dishes. By the time we were done it was after eight, starting to get dark. I dreaded going up to the attic, but Ludi was determined that we were all going to work together. Daddy and I were just a tiny bit drunk and trying not to show it. Ludi was perfectly sober. I couldn't argue her out of it. If I wouldn't go with her, she wouldn't do it. Then we'd still have the problem of the bats. And the Spring-fields had been telephoning to make sure the bats were gone.

Daddy brought the rest of the champagne up to the attic, and three glasses. The attic fan was broken; squirrels had nested in it and one of the blades had broken off. But we couldn't deal with everything, and the Springfields, who had a long list of things we had to do—part of the contract—had overlooked the attic fan.

The attic was hotter than hell, but I'd put on a long-sleeved shirt (for protection) and turned the collar up. I had a scarf over my head, too, and long pants. The musky odor of the bats and their shit was almost overpowering in the heat. Daddy plugged in an old electric fan that was missing the protective wire cage. (It was in the attic because the wire cage was missing.) It looked dangerous, but it gave us a little breeze. Daddy propped it up on a steamer trunk.

Ludi had fixed up a special light so we could see, and Daddy had a flashlight, but I was afraid. The image of bats swooping down, getting tangled in my hair, biting my neck, made me sweat even more. I was dizzy with the heat. It was like a sauna. I held the cool champagne glass to my forehead, ran it over my arms. Ludi touched my arm accidentally and I almost cried out.

The attic was empty except for some old steamer trunks that had been there when we moved in. We'd played with them. They were like regular closets. You'd stand them up on end and open them up, and there were little drawers and sleeves for shoes, and one of them had a special compartment for a top hat. There were rods for coat hangers too and special hangers with O's rather than hooks, like the kind you see in some motels now, so you can't steal them. But in these the O slipped over the rod and was locked into place by a catch at the end. It was the first time I'd seen the attic this way, empty, and I was reminded of the nave of a cathedral. At the head of the stairs was the place where we had our clubhouses. It was framed in so we could have two-story clubhouses. The boards were still there, over the open rafters. The chimney went up at an angle, behind the stairs. My heart was beating.

Ludi said we could talk, but quietly.

Daddy pointed his flashlight up at the peak of the roof. You could see three quivering masses, like black holes, but alive with movement, changing shapes slightly, like shadows on water. Three clusters with twenty-five to thirty bats in each.

"When Odysseus is caught in Charybdis," Daddy said, "a wave tosses him up and he grasps on to a great fig tree, up above the whirlpool, and Homer compares him to a bat clinging to a limb, τῷ προσφὺς ἐχόμην ὡς νυκτερίς." Daddy never missed a chance to quote Homer. I thought of Odysseus clinging like a bat over the whirlpool of our family life and then rejected the image.

"Look," Ludi said, "they're washing themselves." The flashlight revealed tiny pink tongues as the bats licked their fur, tiny claws as they cleaned their ears and combed their bat hair.

"I wonder what it's like to be a bat?" I said.

Ludi was more scientific. "You can't imagine what it's like to be a bat," she said, as if she wanted to prevent me from even trying.

"It'd be like being a mouse with wings."

"Don't be silly. You can't imagine what it'd be like to be a mouse."

"I can imagine flying," I said, "and having webbed fingers and hanging upside down, and eating insects. Remember the time that fruit fly flew right in my mouth. Yuck."

"That's what it'd be like for a human being trying to act like a bat. That's not what it would be like to *be* a bat. There's nothing comparable to echolocation in human experience." I could never win an argument with Ludi. "There's a special tube in a bat's inner ear," she said, "that registers supersonic tones just before it dies."

"How on earth could anyone know *that*?"

"Somebody did some experiments back in the thirties, when they were trying to develop radar. They measured the voltage; it shoots way up just before death."

"Did they kill the bats? And if they did, how did the bats know they were going to kill them?"

I had Ludi stumped. "I don't know," she said.

I knew she wouldn't approve of killing them, even in the name of science. "I wonder if Cookie heard anything different just before she died," I said, thinking out loud.

Ludi didn't say anything for a while, and then as she was about to say something a bat suddenly dropped into view and began to circle the attic. Then another, and another.

"At the end of the *Odyssey*," Daddy said, "Hermes conducts the souls of the dead suitors down to the underworld. Homer says that the dead souls squeak like bats in an underground cave, flitting around, crisscrossing in the dark, and that once one of them falls the 'rock-hung' chain is broken and they all start to fly around."

The rock-hung chain had been broken. The air was filled with bats. I was terrified, but fascinated too. They didn't fly in patterns or formations the way birds do. What had looked like a solid but quivering mass was now totally individuated. There were no leaders, but they never collided. They were perfectly free. Ludi started making a clicking noise.

"Stop that," I said. The sound attracted the bats, which swooped around our heads. I could feel air from their wings on my hands, which were covering my face. I held on to Daddy, but Ludi stood up and walked right into the center of the whirlpool, holding her paper bag of bugs. I held my breath. I closed my eyes too, but not all the way. I had to see. I was expecting the bats to fly right into Ludi, to get tangled in her hair, bite her neck, all the things I was afraid of. When she put her hand in her sack of insects and held it out, palm up, I almost screamed. There was a dark blur of wings and the insect was gone. She took another out of the sack and did it again. Another dark blur of wings. And then something happened that frightened even Ludi. Without warning a bat began to circle the electric fan. Ludi let out a scream. "Oh no. Turn the goddamn fan off! Daddy, turn it off! Pull out the plug. Do something!"

Daddy scrambled towards the fan, which had worked its way to the edge of the steamer trunk.

"Be careful of your hand!" I yelled.

"That was so stupid," Ludi yelled. "What were you thinking of? Why didn't you fix the damn fan instead of just junking it up here? Why didn't you throw it out?"

The fan was plugged into an extension cord that was plugged into a light fixture on one of the rafters.

"Watch your hand," I yelled again. I'd been waiting for the ping or the slap that the bat would make when it hit the blade of the fan, but there was no ping, no slap, no sound of metal impacting on bat flesh. The bat had pulled away from the fan and then flown right through the whirling blades without being hurt. The bat circled and flew through the whirling blades a second time, and soon there was a stream of bats flying through the blades of the fan, like a string of schoolgirls taking turns jumping rope.

Ludi calmed down. "I'm sorry, Daddy," she said. It was a rare thing for Ludi to apologize. I was impressed.

After about ten minutes the bats started to go outside. We counted three exits down under the eaves. There was some in-and-out movement, and then suddenly, as though an inaudible bell had sounded, there was a great rush of wings and within thirty seconds the bats were gone, and we were plugging up their doorways with Ludi's pads of steel wool, shoving them down with a broom handle into the secret openings beneath the eaves.

The next morning Ludi got me up early. We went up to the attic. No bats. No dark, shadowy clusters up in the rafters. We went outside. It was about five o'clock, and I was almost too sleepy to care. We could see the bats circling the house, darting under the eaves. Ninety to a hundred bats, though it was hard to count. They circled for about half an hour, and then left, first one, then another, then the entire colony, heading off in the direction of the Warren Farms, and then they were gone. I'd never been able to win an argument with Ludi, but this time I thought she was wrong. I thought that I wasn't just imagining it; I thought that at that moment I knew what it was like to be a bat.

Part Two

Christmas
1987

Daddy left for Bologna at the end of August. He'd arranged, through an editor at the *Chicago Tribune*, a former student, to cover the trial for the *Trib*. One article a week. On spec. The editor was going to see what he could do about syndicating the articles. Apart from a few notices in the *Times*, there had been almost no coverage of the trial in the U.S. The checks were going to come to me, and I was going to deposit them in the joint account that Daddy had opened with the money from the farm so that I could write checks for Ludi's tuition and living expenses and to the convent for Mama's share of the divorce settlement.

Daddy spent the night on the couch in my new one-bedroom apartment on the third floor, and I drove him out to O'Hare in the morning in Mama's Monte Carlo, which I'd had fixed up. I pulled over to the curb outside the TWA terminal; we unloaded the car and said our good-byes. At no point had I ever felt so strongly that I was the adult and my parents were the children. I was pretty steamed up, in fact, because I could see so clearly that they were setting off on wild-goose chases, abandoning their responsibilities. It was like watching people in a movie when they're about to make some fatal mistake and you want to warn them but you can't, or like shouting at the dog when she doesn't want to do what you want her to do. Daddy struggled to get through the automatic door, which wasn't working properly, with his big new suitcase and his guitar and his heavy briefcase, the one I'd carried to my practice interview in our own living room. He turned and waved, like the dog looking over her shoulder before she took off on one of her jaunts. "Come back, come back," I wanted to shout; but I waved too, and then I pulled out into the stream of traffic and headed north on 294. I was waving good-bye not only to Daddy but to my old life. It was time to get on with my new one.

Bernie, my boss at MSI, had quit; gone to the new Tech Museum in San Jose. Jim Bradley had taken over Bernie's job, and I was now an exhibit developer, which was fine, except the "milestone" I'd inherited—the Chaos milestone—was in trouble. IBM, the major corporate sponsor, was not happy with the plan to replicate Edward Lorenz's "discovery" of chaos, in which visitors (we called them patrons or clients) would be invited to alter one or more of twelve variables on a simulated weather program and then observe what is known in the trade as the Butterfly Effect. "Does the Flap of a Butterfly's Wings in Brazil Set Off a Tornado in Texas?" Lorenz had asked in a famous paper. In our simulated weather model a tiny change in one place—raising the temperature one degree in Chicago, say—would cascade exponentially through a series of meteorological variables (humidity, ocean surface tempera-ture, atmospheric pressure, wind velocity, the behavior of the jet stream, etc.). No matter how much data you gathered and fed into the computer, you'd never be able to predict the weather more than three or four days in advance. I'd even located Lorenz's original Royal McBee computer at the Fermi Lab and had persuaded MIT to donate it to MSI—all we had to do was pay the shipping costs—when the IBM execs started making unpleasant noises. The prob-lem, in the eyes of the IBM executives, was that this particular milestone highlighted the *failure* of computers. They had something more *positive* in mind. The problem, in my eyes, was that if the Chaos milestone was scrapped, I'd be out of a job.

Richard, the consultant I'd hired from the University of Chicago, was helping me work out an alternative plan—a Lorenzian waterwheel—but Richard's wife had found out about our affair, and Richard had resigned. I wasn't even allowed to talk to him on the phone. Besides, he'd gone to a conference in Geneva, and Sally, his wife, had insisted on lunch so we could have a "talk." I'd told Daddy the whole story on the way out to O'Hare, and he explained to me

that "adult" and "adultery" come from different Latin words—
adolescere, which means to grow up, and *adulterare*, which means to
adulterate.

"The waterwheel sounds good to me," he said. "Just explain it to
IBM the way you explained it to me. And about the other . . . Buy
yourself a nice hat," he said, putting his arms around me; "have a
nice lunch, and don't tell any more lies. Don't try to justify yourself;
just tell the truth. But maybe not all the truth. You don't need to go
into the details."

WHEN I'D visited MSI as a child, on school trips or with my parents
on one of our jaunts to the big city, I'd never given a thought to
exhibit development. The exhibits had seemed to me to be
immutable: the World of Mathematics, the Electric Trains, the Coal
Mine, the Whispering Gallery (where I'd propositioned Richard),
the baby chicks in the Farm. They were just there. It never occurred
to me that somebody had to think them up—and not just think them
up. Somebody had to draw up plans and confer with designers and
senior scientists and with carpenters (or fabricators, as we called
them). And somebody had to pay for them. Or rather, somebody had
to persuade somebody else to pay for them. That is, I had to persuade
somebody—an IBM executive—to pay for the Chaos milestone.

At the progress meeting on Monday I was ready to go with Plan
B—the waterwheel. The idea was simple, at least in theory. A stream
of water flows into buckets on a large wheel, like a millwheel. The
buckets have holes in them, so that if the water is turned on very low,
nothing will happen. The water will leak out of the holes in the top
bucket faster than it flows in, so there will never be enough weight
to overcome friction and set the wheel in motion. If you turn up the
water a little, the buckets will start to fill up and the weight of the
water will cause the wheel to turn, and it will go round and round.
But then if you turn up the water a little more, something funny will
happen, at least according to the theory. As the buckets take on
more water (and more weight), the wheel will turn faster. But then
the buckets at the bottom won't have time to discharge all their
water, so they'll be carrying some water back up with them on the
opposite side. At the same time, since the wheel is turning faster, the
buckets at the top won't take on as much water. Pretty soon there'll

be more weight on the right-hand side than on the left, and the wheel will reverse direction. And then the same thing will happen again and the wheel will reverse itself again. Common sense tells you that the wheel will eventually reach a steady state, but in fact that never happens. The reversals are as unpredictable as the reversals of the earth's magnetic field. Chaotic. You can know the rate of the flow of water, and the capacity and dimensions of the buckets, and the number and size of the holes in each bucket, and the weight of the wheel and of the buckets, and the torque of the wheel, but you still can't predict the direction in which it will turn after a dozen revolutions.

But the real beauty of it, as I stressed in my presentation, is that when you graph the motion of the wheel on a computer, using three sets of coordinates to locate a point on the wheel in three-dimensional space at a given time, you *see* a new kind of order emerging. Or rather, the computer can see it and can represent it right on the screen. The pattern will never repeat itself, but it will produce a sort of butterfly shape, with two wings, one for clockwise rotation, one for counterclockwise. Fortunately Richard had been able to locate Lorenz's original paper on the subject, "Deterministic Nonperiodic Flow," which included illustrations of several "Lorenz attractors," as these patterns—or nonpatterns—came to be called. I'd also learned that Lorenz himself actually had built one of these wheels, and so had a Professor Malkus at MIT—the man who'd been willing to unload Lorenz's old computer—and someone in France, and I implied that I had access to the plans, which wasn't strictly true. In fact, it wasn't true at all, though I had spoken to Lorenz's widow, and I'd tried, unsuccessfully, to reach Willem Malkus at MIT. And I had talked to a potential consultant from Stanford. I wondered if he knew as much about women as he knew about Lorenz attractors.

WHY WOULD I buy myself a hat? I wondered, thinking about Daddy's words at O'Hare; I never wore a hat. No one in our family ever wore a hat unless it was ten below zero; I didn't even *know* anyone who wore a hat. But walking down Michigan Avenue on my way to the Cape Cod Room at the Drake I glanced in the window of Tailleurs Nouveaux and saw a fantastic hat, broad-brimmed, floppy, trimmed with flowers, but not flowers of this world. At least not like any flowers I'd ever seen.

I walked on to the Drake, but I was half an hour early, so I went back to Tailleurs Nouveaux. I was wearing a pastel summer dress that I'd bought at an end-of-summer sale in Field's basement and that matched some of the flowers on the hat, which was sort of like the hat that Eliza Doolittle wore at the end of *My Fair Lady*, which I'd seen at the Court Theater in January, right after I got the job at MSI. Like Eliza I was experimenting with a new identity, but without the help of Professor Henry Higgins. Standing in front of the window, looking at the hat *and* at my reflection, I tried to imagine myself as Eliza. I struck an elegant pose and almost burst into song.

I was sorry I hadn't had a chance to talk to Richard, but Sally had probably planned it that way, separating the suspects so they couldn't collude on a story. I hadn't met Sally and didn't know what she looked like, but she'd said she knew what I looked like and would recognize me. Her tone, on the telephone, had been studiedly neutral.

And what was I feeling, about Richard, about the luncheon? I was surprised, actually. I was pleasantly excited. Richard and I had not told ourselves that we loved each other, not even during sex, not even right after sex. He knew a little Italian and would say, "*Ti voglio bene*. You have no idea. *Ti voglio bene*." He wished me well. Well, I wished him well too. But I think I was more concerned about losing him as a consultant than as a lover. I could find another lover, but I wasn't sure I'd be able to find another expert on chaos theory, at least not locally. I was, in fact, already looking back on the affair as something completed—sad that it was over (assuming it was)—but with a great deal of satisfaction. I had had sexual intercourse before, but I'd never really had a proper affair. I'd never been the *other woman*. I was completing my maiden voyage on the rough-and-tumble seas of adult sexuality. And now: landfall; I was coming into port, where Richard's wife, Sally, was waiting for me. Sally, the wronged woman. But this was part of the drama. I wasn't exactly looking forward to the meeting; but I wasn't afraid either. I wasn't going to apologize, nor was I going to explain or justify myself. I was going to speak to her as a woman of the world, an adult—rationally, calmly. No scenes, though the prospect of a scene was exciting.

Richard hadn't told me much about her. I knew they had two children and that she taught a class in life drawing at the School of the Art Institute, and that she painted at home.

Twelve-oh-five. Still twenty-five minutes. Time slowed to a crawl. I was looking alternately at my reflection and at the hat, ducking down so I could line up the reflection of my head with the hat. Till I realized that someone was watching me from inside the store. I could either run away or go into the store. I went in.

An older woman—the woman who'd been watching me—stood behind a counter with bits of things on it. Material. Artificial flowers. Ribbons. A wooden block shaped like a head. She smiled at me and called to someone from the back.

I'd never been in a hat store before. There were black and white photos on the wall. Lots of pictures of the British Royal Family: the queen mother in a toque, Princess Di in a close-fitting hat with a small rolled brim, trimmed with feathers, Princess Anne in a trilby with horses in the background. And a photo of Jackie Kennedy in a cloche. And a sign on the wall:

> *People Notice People Who Wear Hats*
> —YVETTE JELFS

Maybe that was it: I wanted to be noticed.

"Can I help you?" She had a slight foreign accent.

"Just looking, thanks."

"Of course. It's beautiful, isn't it?"

"That hat in the window. Yes."

"By Claire Bouchard. May I show it to you?"

"I've never worn a hat," I said.

"*Every*one wears a hat in Paris."

"I've never been to Paris either."

"Well, there's a first time for everything. Permit me, please."

She got the hat from the window and put it on a wooden hat block on the counter, setting it at a jaunty angle. It looked even more cool and inviting than it had in the window. A woman wearing that hat would . . . Well, she'd be noticed.

"Let me just comb your hair up," she said, "and pin it. You want to see the nape of the neck. Just sit here." She motioned me into a chair. "Your hair won't carry a hat like this when it's hanging over your shoulders." She pinned my hair up and put the hat on my head.

I was sitting in front of a three-paneled mirror that multiplied my image. There were Saras all over the place, just as there had been when Daddy and I bought my power suit.

I was relieved, almost, that it was too big. I didn't really want to spend the money for a hat that I'd probably never wear again. I had to hold my head very steady to keep the hat from slipping off. It was really a wonderful hat, though. The colored flowers were made of silk and held in place by some kind of netting. It was like a painting by Monet.

"It is perfect with your cabbage roses," she said. It took me a minute to realize that she meant the floral pattern of my dress.

"Do you have a smaller size?"

She looked surprised. "There's only one of these."

"This is the last one?"

"No, Madame; there is one only."

I turned my head this way and that, afraid to ask the price.

"It's too large," I said, turning my head quickly so that the hat stayed put, facing forward, while my head turned. (Inertia. I'd been learning plenty about inertia.)

"Not at all, Madame." She lifted the hat off my head and showed me the grosgrain ribbon on the inside, like a hatband. "We will gather the ribbon here, you see"—she pulled the two ends of the ribbon tighter at the back to demonstrate—"and stitch it up like so. A little tighter, that is all. You will see. Will next Tuesday be convenient?"

"Oh no," I said, rather loudly. Emphatically. "I'm going to lunch. If I don't wear it now, there's no point."

"Very well. It is only a few moments."

"How much does it cost?" I asked, finally.

"A hat like this," she said, "by Madame Bouchard, one of a kind, price is not a consideration. Claire," she called, putting the hat upside down on the counter. "Could you come here a moment."

Claire appeared from the back room, a large woman with a slight mustache. She nodded while the saleslady explained the problem.

"*Bien sûr, bien sûr.*"

She reminded me of my mother as she wrapped a length of strong black thread around her finger and knotted it with one hand. It took her less than a minute to stitch up the ribbon. She placed the hat on my head with the needle still dangling from the thread. Perfect. She made a loop, ran the needle through the loop, pulled it tight, made a second loop, ran the needle through backwards, and pulled it tight again. I'd seen my mother do it a hundred times but had never been able to do it myself.

The hat fit perfectly, and cost two hundred twenty-five dollars. Almost half as much as my suit. I did some quick calculations in my head while she waited for Visa to OK the purchase. I was hoping, almost, that the hat would push me over my credit limit, which would have been embarrassing, but I'd have saved two hundred twenty-five dollars. It didn't happen, though, which made me sure that I wouldn't have enough credit left to pay for my lunch. Sally had invited me. *She* would have to pay.

Afterwards I looked at myself in the window, the way Daddy would look at himself in the window of the hardware store next to the barbershop after he got a haircut, wanting to see how it looked but not wanting anyone else to notice. The hat was like a halo, or a crown. Or a helmet.

I WAITED for Sally in the lobby outside the restaurant.

Would she pick up the check? I certainly hoped so. I wasn't sure about the etiquette of these situations. Who paid in *Julia*? Vanessa Redgrave or Jane Fonda?

"You must be Sara," she said. Coming at me from behind, from inside the restaurant. "I almost didn't recognize you with that hat."

I was a little on the nervous side by now.

"I already have a table," she said.

The restaurant was full of women in their thirties and forties, but there weren't many hats—a couple of cloches, like the one Jackie Kennedy had on in the picture in the hat shop. Certainly nothing like mine. I guess I was really making a statement; but I wasn't sure what it was I was stating. And people *were* noticing me. I collected a lot of sideways glances. Were they admiring me, my bold taste? Could they see that I wasn't used to wearing a hat? Could they tell that I was meeting my lover's wife for a "talk"?

Sally was beautiful, but not too beautiful. Like a real person, not a model. Medium height, long legs. She was wearing a summer dress like mine, modestly cut with a large floral print, but she wasn't wearing a hat. We followed the maître d' past leather-upholstered booths to a table in the back. It was dark, and the tables were set so close together that whatever we said to each other we'd be saying to our neighbors as well. There were flowers on the table, and a bottle of white wine and two glasses, one already half full of wine.

"I want this to be civilized," she said, smoothing her skirt under her bottom as she sat down. "But not *too* civilized."

I didn't know what to say to this, but I felt I was in for trouble, in hotter water than I'd anticipated.

"Did you ever see *Between the Devil and the Deep Blue Sea?*" she asked.

"A long time ago."

"That's about as civilized as I want to get."

"You mean where Elaine Carter throws the lamp? And then tries to claw Nicole Ferraro's eyes out?"

"I was thinking of the earlier scene, on the boat . . ."

"I guess it's a good thing we're here in this civilized restaurant with lots of people around us."

"A good thing for you."

She poured some wine into my glass and then topped off her own. I was having some trouble with the hat as I pretended to look at the menu, which I had to hold up straight in front of me because I was afraid to tip my head too far forward. The hat felt strange, like an aura. It weighed my head down. My head seemed to be connected to a large wheel. I couldn't imagine myself shaking it no or nodding it yes.

But nodding and shaking were what was called for.

"Your family was killed in the bombing in Bologna in 1980," she said, "and you were raised by a maiden aunt who sent you to St. Clair College."

I nodded my head cautiously. In the process of creating a new identity I'd told Richard that my whole family had been killed in the bombing. I'd turned myself into a lone she-wolf, on her own, a self-created existential heroine par excellence. My own person. (Maybe that's why I'd bought the hat.)

"You've lived in Chicago since August 1986," she went on. "You worked as a waitress at the Mount Parnassus for six months and then found a job at the Museum of Science and Industry. You started locating things for the computer exhibit and then when someone quit you became an assistant exhibit developer, or a project logistics coordinator, or something like that. You got Richard's name from the U of C because he's into chaos theory and asked him to be a consultant. You've been eff-ing him two or three times a week since April in your apartment on Fifty-seventh Street, which you share with two U of C grad students. That's all I know. Tell me the rest."

Richard apparently hadn't told her that I'd moved into another apartment in the same building—with no roommates—when I got promoted.

"How did you find out?"

"I saw you and Richard leaving the museum together. I was on my way back from the Co-op with groceries. I left my cart on the sidewalk and followed you. When I got back, the cart was gone. Sixty dollars' worth of groceries. Plus the cart. I confronted Richard just before he left for Geneva. We had a big scene."

"I'm sorry."

The waiter came to take our orders. At least he didn't identify himself and tell us that he would be our server.

Sally ordered coquilles St.-Jacques, a cup of watercress soup, and blue cheese dressing on her salad. I hadn't really looked at the menu, so I asked for the same. Sally sipped her wine, and I did the same, though I couldn't tip my head back far enough to finish it off. It was very good wine.

"What do you want to know?"

"I want to know what you think you were doing."

I didn't know how to answer. I wasn't sure I wanted to tell the truth. I wasn't even sure I knew what the truth was. Had I been looking for an adventure? Trying to act like an adult?

"This is the twentieth century," I said.

"What's that supposed to mean?"

"Well, for one thing . . ." But I couldn't think of *one thing*.

"That infidelity is simply a fact of life?"

The waiter brought our salads. I was grateful for the diversion.

"We're both adults," I said. "We made existential choices."

"You and Richard?" She laughed. "I'm sorry about your family, but that's no excuse." She paused. "Maybe there's a rational response, a rational way to behave," she said, "but I'm not sure what it is. Anyway, I'm not one of those women who're going to wait it out, like Maggie in *The Golden Bowl*, Maggie and her prince."

I'd read *The Golden Bowl* in my American Lit. seminar, but I hadn't been able to make much sense of it. "Isn't he involved with her best friend?" The waiter brought our soup.

"Friend and stepmother—Charlotte. *She* waits it out. Maggie does. She plans everything. No scenes. Nothing embarrassing. Charlotte and her father—Maggie's father—go back to America and Maggie has her prince all to herself again. He doesn't even have to say he's sorry. She doesn't *want* him to. It would be too embarrassing. But I'm not like that. I can't be. I don't want to be. Fidelity is like being together in a wonderful house, all by yourselves. You can run around naked. You can stand naked in front of the open refrigerator. You can make love on the living room couch. But you can't do it if there's somebody else there. You can't let yourself go."

The waiter brought our scallops and Sally ordered another bottle of wine. We ate in silence for a while. Basically what I remembered about Henry James was the cover on the paperback edition—a woman with long black hair leaning back, or reclining on a bed without actually lying down—and the comments by Dorothy Parker and somebody else: "Henry James chewed more than he bit off," I said. "Like a hippopotamus trying to pick up a pea."

"That's what people say when they can't understand him. He's beyond their ken."

I speared a creamy scallop with my fork and remembered a little more. "Isn't the problem," I said, "that Maggie and her father thought they could just *buy* the prince, like one of the works of art they're always buying? Doesn't she think she *owns* him . . . ? Doesn't she have to learn . . ."

I hadn't noticed the waiter bring the second bottle of wine, but it was there, on the table, and we were drinking it. I could see I'd hit home. Or at least touched a sore spot.

"I suppose you're going to tell me that if I gave him what he needed at home he wouldn't be sniffing around elsewhere? Something like that."

"I wouldn't put it like that."

"How *would* you put it?"

I felt out of my depth, but I didn't want to be bullied.

"I guess I'd say that Richard and I were attracted to each other . . . We made an existential choice." That was my second "existential choice" of the lunch, but I couldn't think of anything else to say.

"I'm attracted to a lot of people, but I don't take my pants down . . . And what the hell is an existential choice anyway? How does it differ from a regular unexistential choice? You can't have it both ways. Two people can really focus on each other, or they can eff around . . . That's my existential choice. When I take Richard's cock in my mouth I don't want to have to think about you putting it in your mouth, do you understand? Do you even know what it's like to imagine your husband—for better, for worse, in sickness and in health—eff-ing someone else? The image. The picture. Maybe if two people agree that eff-ing around is OK, it *is* OK; but then they can never have the kind of relationship you get a glimpse of when you first fall in love . . ."

I tried to steer the conversation back to *The Golden Bowl*. "Doesn't Maggie get her husband back because she lets him go?"

"If you have a bird," she said in a loud voice, "don't keep it in a cage; let it go free. If you love someone, let him go free; don't try to imprison him and he'll fly back to you. What a crock. Spare me, please."

"Are you going to make a scene?" I asked.

"No," she said; "I'm going to propose a toast." She raised her glass: "Here's to the ladies who lunch." We both drank.

"Did you ever see *Company*?"

I shook my head no, forgetting about the hat, which threatened to tip over into my plate.

"Stephen Sondheim," she said. "Richard and I saw it in New York. I should get a hat like yours, then we could do the scene. 'Here's to the ladies who lunch— Da da da da da. Da da da da da da planning a brunch. Da da da da . . . claiming they're fat . . . looking grim, 'Cause they've been sitting Choosing a hat—'" Sally stood up and raised her glass. "'Does anyone still wear a hat? I'll drink to that.'"

That was our "scene." Some heads turned; and the waiter

brought the check, which Sally paid, without asking if we wanted dessert; but it could have been a lot worse.

OUT IN the street. Michigan Avenue. We didn't have much to say to each other. I thought that after a lunch like that you ought to take a cab, but I didn't want to spend twenty bucks to get back to Hyde Park, so when Sally headed north, I headed south. I looked at myself in the window. The hat wasn't a halo (I wasn't an angel); it wasn't a crown (I wasn't a princess); it wasn't a helmet (I wasn't a warrior queen). It was just a hat, and I was just me. But it was beautiful, and people did notice me as I walked down to the bus stop at Oak Street, where I waited for the Jeffrey Express. I thought things had gone pretty well, all things considered, though I was out two hundred twenty-five dollars for the hat. I took still another look at my reflection in the window of a luggage shop. The hat wasn't a bad hat, it wasn't old hat either; I wasn't about to eat my hat, or to go begging hat in hand; I wasn't going to pass my hat or do a hat trick, or pull anything out of my hat, or do anything at the drop of my hat; I wasn't going to hang up my hat; I wasn't going to keep anything under it; and I wasn't going to talk through it. What *was* I going to do with it? Put it in the closet with my suit until I needed it again?

The bus came in about fifteen minutes. I got on and slipped a dollar bill into the cash box. Sally was sitting in the very back of the bus. I guess she hadn't wanted to spend twenty bucks either. She had her face in her hands and I could see that she was crying. She hadn't seen me; I could have sat in the front; there were plenty of empty seats. But my heart went out to her. I went to the back of the bus and put my arm around her. I took off my hat and put it on the seat.

"I just wanted to bully you a little," she said after a few minutes, "and make you apologize, and then forgive you. You'd be so relieved and grateful; and I'd be so mature and understanding. I thought maybe I could love you like a sister. I had to, don't you see. Because otherwise I'd have to hate you, and it's too terrible. I can't bear it. It's like having a cancer that keeps gnawing at you, it never stops. I can't sleep at night it hurts so bad."

We were on Lake Shore Drive by this time, bypassing the ghetto that separates Hyde Park from downtown. The lake was deep blue, the promenade busy with joggers, cyclists, skateboarders, dog walkers. In the harbor, sailboats, motorboats, and yachts rode at anchor. When we passed the Point, I thought that if I ever got married I'd like to get married out on the Point, with water on three sides. Maybe an Italian wedding.

"Sally," I said, but she was asleep, and maybe it was just as well. I don't know what I was going to say, but it would probably have been sentimental and embarrassing.

The end of the line is the MSI parking lot. Sally was awake by now, her eyeliner streaked, her lipstick worn thin where she'd been pressing her lips together. She gave me a hug; we said good-bye, and I watched her walk across the parking lot, across the Midway, across Fifty-sixth Street to the 1700 Building, a forty-story high-rise with everything from studios to four-bedroom apartments. It was Saturday afternoon. I wanted to go home and sleep, but I had work to do. I had to prepare new text and new visuals for the Chaos milestone. The waterwheel was in, and I was happy about that; but I was afraid I'd promised more than I could deliver.

The museum had been closed for three hours by the time I left my office, or my cubicle. It wasn't dark yet, but it was getting there. I stood on the steps for a while. I could see the lights in Richard and Sally's apartment on the fourth floor. Richard would be back the next day, Sunday. I tried to imagine their reunion, to imagine them working out their differences. Without me. Richard had been an imaginative lover. The first man I ever slept with more than a couple of times. The first man whose cock I'd actually put all the way in my mouth, the first man who'd waited for me to come. Would these couplings, I wondered, cascade exponentially through marital variables, like a change in the surface temperature of the ocean? If you fed every single thing that could be known about Richard and Sally into the world's most powerful computer, would it be able to predict whether or not they'd still be married after thirty years? twenty? ten? five? two? six months?

But it wasn't the thought of Richard that made my heart ache. It was the thought of Sally: Sally proposing a toast in the Cape Cod Room; Sally crying in the back of the bus; Sally who was probably reading a story to her children right now because Richard was in Geneva; Sally who might have loved me like a sister, like Cookie.

•   •   •

My JOB turned into a career; and then my career turned into a vocation. I couldn't give you the exact dates of the changes. There were no dramatic turning points, just a series of progress meetings and progress reports and disagreements with the designers and the fabricators. It was more like the order that gradually emerges out of chaos: even when you learn to expect it, it always takes you by surprise. But once you've seen it, you see it everywhere. In the smoke rising from someone's cigarette; in an oil slick in the parking lot; in the waves breaking on the beach along Lake Shore Drive. I read some of the key papers by Lorenz himself, and by Mitchell Feigenbaum, Albert Libchaber, and the Santa Cruz group, and Benoit Mandelbrot. Most of what I read I couldn't understand, but I wanted to participate in my own small way, and I *could* understand the sense of excitement, the sense that a major paradigm shift was under way. I could sense that after years of increasing specialization, scientists were engaged once again in a common enterprise that would alter our understanding of evolution ("chaos with feedback"), ecology, epidemiology, even the Second Law of Thermodynamics. Everything is winding down? Entropy is irreversible? It simply wasn't true. Or it wasn't true in the old way. I was glad now that I'd taken physics for my lab science at St. Clair, even though I'd chosen it for the wrong reasons. I'd chosen it because at the time it seemed less messy than chemistry or biology; but what could be messier than a nonlinear equation?

A paradigm shift was under way, and I was a part of it. It was all there in the simple waterwheel. Of course, getting the waterwheel to behave chaotically was another matter.

Anyone in the museum business will tell you that four months is not enough time to mount a complex exhibit, any exhibit—the other milestones had been in development for two or three years—but by the end of the first week of December, two weeks before the opening, on the eighteenth, the wheel was up and running. We'd had to replace the original nylon ball bearings, which created too much friction and caused the wheel to move unevenly, and we'd had to replace the nautical wood frame, which had been treated with chromium salt as a fungicide—the chromium salt turned the water yellow. But we couldn't get the wheel to behave chaotically. Richard, whom I'd rehired as a consultant—Sally had skipped over most of her

277

agenda to get to the last part, treating me like a sister—started to make a histogram, quantifying the rotation at 0°, 30°, 60°, 90°, etc., but there was nothing to quantify. The wheel turned smoothly in whichever direction—clockwise or counterclockwise—it happened to start out in and could not be persuaded to reverse itself, no matter how much we tinkered with the flow of water. Maybe the universe was more regular than we'd thought.

A museum opening is not unlike a theatrical opening. Chaotic. Everyone has too much to do. The pace becomes increasingly frantic. The head fabricator, who had built the wheel according to my specs, had run out of ideas. The designer had washed his hands of Chaos. The senior scientist in charge of the exhibit made a big show of accepting responsibility—he should have known better than to entrust an important exhibit to an inexperienced developer like me. I made frantic calls to MIT. I talked to half a dozen people who knew about Malkus's wheel, but no one remembered seeing the wheel actually work. One of the people, in fact, thought that Malkus had never been able to get it to work properly.

The Frenchman was my last hope. I had an address, but I'd been firing off telegrams, which Sally translated into French for me, for almost two weeks without a response. My heart leaped up, then, when I saw an airmail letter curled up in my mail slot from Atelier Bernard Gitton. He wrote in English: "I was a scientific researcher before to turn out badly and to create my studio." An artist, I thought. My heart leaped back down again. "The first difficulty is to find an aesthetic form to the machine according to the place where it has to be set." Finding an "aesthetic form" was the least of my worries. "I have to draw and dream and draw and the beginning of an idea comes. Then I draw on my computer from my sketches. For the chaotic machines I also built a simple model. Then I make industrial drawings . . ." I skipped ahead, past his histogram at the bottom of the first page and on to the second, looking for something useful. "To drill more holes in some buckets," he wrote, "to make faster the flow from each bucket to overcome residual friction."

That night, after the museum was closed—I didn't want anyone to see what we were doing—Richard and I drilled more holes in the buckets to increase the flow. I should have kept out one of the industrial drills from the shop, but we made do with Richard's Black &

Decker, though each hole took almost five minutes of drilling, and the drill got so hot we had to wrap Richard's shirt around the handle. Eight buckets. We drilled four additional holes in the bottom of each of the eight buckets. At ten o'clock Richard drilled the last hole and hung the bucket back on the wheel. I turned on the water, and we waited while the first bucket began to fill (and, of course, to leak at the same time). I wanted to give the wheel a little push but held myself back. For about thirty seconds friction resisted the pull of gravity, and then the wheel began to turn. The second bucket took on a load of water and the wheel began to turn faster. Richard had put his shirt back on but hadn't buttoned it. I was conscious of him at my side. I won't say that I didn't want him to put his arms around me and kiss me, or even put his hand on my bottom, because it wouldn't be true. And I won't say that I didn't want a token, a sign that what had passed between us wouldn't simply disappear without a trace, that it wasn't just a bit of random data that would be canceled out by another bit of random data. Where was the Butterfly Effect, the small variable cascading exponentially through thousands of other variables?

After about a dozen revolutions the wheel, which had been speeding up, suddenly slowed to an abrupt halt and reversed itself. This was exactly what it was supposed to do, but after so many failures I think we were both stunned, as if the true chaotic nature of the universe had suddenly been revealed to us. Was this the sign I'd been looking for?

"Residual friction," Richard said. "It's so obvious when you think of it." Richard took my hand and I looked at him briefly, but I couldn't take my eyes off the wheel. After three revolutions it reversed itself again and I almost jumped out of my skin. Richard pulled away to look. If I'd been wearing my hat I'd have tossed it up in the air, but I'd given the hat to Sally, who'd worn it at least once a week till the end of September. She knew how to carry it off; she didn't have to hold her neck stiff the way I did.

Every time the wheel reversed itself I caught a glimpse of a great mystery; but just as I was about to turn the water off, I hesitated a moment to watch Richard button up his shirt, and I caught a glimpse of an even greater mystery. I caught a glimpse of Sally waiting for us, in their apartment across the Midway, while their children slept, waiting for us to come back with good news or bad. She hadn't tried to bully me into apologizing, and she hadn't made a big production about forgiving me. We'd had lunch together twice at the Medici and once at the little delicatessen that had opened up in the Windermere Hotel, and she'd done some preliminary sketches of me for a portrait. I watched the waterwheel slow to a stop and then reverse direction. I watched Richard unbutton his shirt and start over, because he'd got the buttons lined up with the wrong holes.

What we had to do now was get the wheel hooked up to the computer so that the stream of apparently random data could generate a butterfly, a mysterious Lorenz attractor. What we had to do now was go back to tell Sally the good news and open a bottle of champagne.

THE OPENING, on the Friday before Christmas, was a great success. Important people in tuxedos and evening gowns, holding glasses of champagne and little plates of shrimp and assorted hors d'oeuvres, wandered from milestone to milestone. From Milestone I—the punch-card machinery used at the Social Security Administration in the thirties—they moved on to the huge Whirlwind computer developed under contract for the military at MIT, and then on to the first commercially available computer, Univac I, the first computer to predict the results of a presidential election. Chaos was Milestone XI, and I was gratified to see the crowds gather around the waterwheel. I was flushed with success, in fact, and though I encouraged people to go on to see the rest of the exhibit, I was quite happy to see them stay put, like compulsive gamblers around a roulette wheel.

Richard and Sally were there too, and at the ceremony itself, where speeches were given by an IBM executive—not the man who had nixed the original Chaos milestone but someone higher up—and by the chairman of the museum board, and by a few other people. I thought I could distinguish their applause—Sally and Richard's—from everyone else's when I was introduced by the senior scientist and given credit for the waterwheel. Everyone was looking at me and applauding, and then it was someone else's turn.

The high lasted that night, all day Saturday, and most of Sunday, but on Sunday night, as I settled down to a plate of *penne all'arrabiata* at the Medici on Fifty-seventh Street, the reality of Christmas set in, like a heavy weight around my neck. A chapter in the story of my life had come to a happy ending; but that story was just a small part of a larger story, the story of the family, and I didn't see how that story could be resolved. Daddy called once a week from the station in Bologna—he didn't have a phone in his apartment—and was writing a weekly column for the *Tribune* about the trial, as if the enigma of Cookie's death could be sorted out by the Italian judicial system; and Mama didn't call at all; she'd moved to the Mother House in Dubuque, wasn't allowed to use the telephone, and was discouraged from writing personal letters.

At least Ludi was coming on Tuesday. I'd called her the night of the opening and asked her to come, even though I knew that she'd been planning to spend the holidays with Saul's family in Minneapolis. I couldn't face Christmas alone, but together I thought we could hold it at bay. Like the Horatii at the Sublician bridge, we'd hold off the invading sentiments till the bridge itself had been demolished. (In Daddy's version of the story the bridge had been held by three young girls.) We'd shop together for some nice presents, but we'd dispense with a tree, and we'd listen to Taj Mahal and Ry Cooder and Mississippi John Hurt on my new tape deck while we sorted out the family finances; and on Christmas Day, if it wasn't *too* cold, we'd walk all the way downtown along the lake and have dinner at the Cape Cod Room. We'd have scallops or shrimp or some kind of fish soup, and drink a bottle of good white wine.

I finished my *penne all'arrabbiata*, ate my salad, and treated myself to a slice of white chocolate mousse. Ludi had been eight years old when Cookie went off to Harvard, twelve when she was killed. We'd stayed at the Williamses' while Mama and Daddy were in Italy. Mr. Williams taught German and Mrs. Williams ran a bakery on Seminary Street that made wonderful bread and croissants and lemon bars and chocolate fudgies. She put us to work to give us something to do. We punched a clock just like the regular employees, and we got checks at the end of the week. At night I finished reading *The Lord of the Rings* aloud to Ludi—Gollum falling into Mount Doom, carrying the ring with him; the happy celebrations in Gondor; the return to the Shire. Without Frodo, of course. Daddy had promised . . . And Frodo didn't really die. He went off to the Grey Havens, and that's what I told Ludi about Cookie. That she'd gone off to the Grey

Havens with Frodo and Gandalf and Elrond and Lady Galadriel and the others; and that she and I, Ludi and I, were like Merry and Pippin, coming back to the Shire. But deep in the night I'd hear her crying softly—we were sleeping in the same room though we didn't have to, and Mrs. Williams had let us move the little stand that separated the twin beds so we could put the beds close together—and I'd reach out and hold her hand, because I was her big sister now that Cookie was gone.

RICHARD AND Sally had already gone to spend Christmas with Sally's parents in Cincinnati, which seemed to me as far away and as unknowable as Bologna or the Mother House in Dubuque. My old roommates too had gone to their various homes across the country. I wasn't ready to go back to my own apartment, so I wandered around Hyde Park till I found myself standing in front of MSI. I was tempted to go in. I couldn't get enough of the wheel, couldn't wait for Ludi to see it.

Mama always said—even before she got convent fever—that this world wasn't our true home. I'd never really understood before what she meant. I understood what she *meant*, of course, but I didn't understand the emotional basis for it, hadn't felt it along my pulse, as Daddy used to say. But as I wandered around Hyde Park that night—Harper Court, back up to Fifty-sixth Street, down to the lake, back under the IC tracks at Fifty-seventh Street, up to Blackstone, with its beautiful old houses—I did feel it along my pulse. I thought that maybe I felt what Mama had felt, something inside me whispering that this wasn't my home, that I didn't belong here, that nobody would be waiting for me in my apartment when I got back, that everyone I might conceivably drop in on had already gone somewhere else, or was getting ready to go somewhere else, and that my own true home was somewhere else too.

Maybe so, I thought, as I unlocked the first of three locks on my apartment door; maybe Hyde Park *wasn't* my true home; but it was the only home I had.

LUDI WAS supposed to arrive on the afternoon of the twenty-second. She wasn't an experienced driver, and there had been some light snow, so I was a little worried about her driving Daddy's old pickup. I could remember how timid and cautious she'd been when Daddy was teaching her to drive. But then she'd become . . . not exactly reckless, just overconfident.

I mopped the kitchen floor while I waited. It was an eight-hour drive from Grinnell, and I'd asked Ludi to call if she wasn't going to be here by five o'clock, but calling wasn't her style. Looking out the window I saw gray snow. Powell's Bookstore was still open. The radio said there might be more snow. I hadn't done any shopping because I'd wanted to wait till Ludi got here. Now I didn't want to go because I didn't want to be gone when she arrived. When she finally did arrive it was almost eight; I was afraid the Co-op would be closed.

I buzzed her in and opened the door. I could hear the dog barreling up the three flights of stairs, and Ludi's footsteps behind her. Leaning over the balustrade and looking down, I could see her in a parka that had belonged to Daddy, the hood thrown back, her long, curly red hair—my mother's hair—tumbling around her shoulders. When she looked up, she was smiling.

"I parked on that little street that runs into Fifty-seventh, OK? Do you think it'll be all right to leave it there?"

Laska was sniffing my crotch. I bent down and kissed the top of her head. "No problem."

Ludi knocked the snow off her boots and took off her glasses, which had fogged up. I followed her into the apartment, seeing it through her eyes. When we were children, her room, full of plants and pictures, had always been neat and organized. I was more like Mama, who cleaned behind the refrigerator, and behind the stove. The back of her closet was perfectly clean. But every flat surface was covered with *stuff.* "Look behind the stove," she'd say. And we'd all take turns peering into the narrow crack between the stove and the wall.

My furniture was comfortable but falling apart. I had an old couch and an old armchair. Heavy, like my grandmother's. The same color, too: something between brown and maroon.

Ludi knew about the exhibit, because we talked every week, but I'd held back a little. I hadn't told her how much it meant to me because I wanted to *show* her. I wanted her to be amazed. We could hear sounds from other apartments, and smell cooking smells. Someone was using a lot of cumin.

"You want to walk to the Co-op? I didn't get anything yet. I thought we'd go together, and then when it got too late I didn't want to go myself, because I was afraid you'd get here while I was gone. Or do you just want to sit a minute? You want something to drink? The Co-op's going to be closed in a few minutes. How about some tea?"

"This is nice, Sara." She picked up a copy of *The Two Towers* from a table next to the couch and started to page through it. "Have you got a bowl we can use for Lasky? I've got to get her food out of the truck."

"I've been rereading it," I said. "Daddy never finished reading it aloud the third time. Your time." *I'd* finished reading it aloud to her. I wanted her to remember, but I didn't want to have to remind her.

"I'm glad I came," she said. I was glad too, but I didn't want to press the point, since her original plan had been to spend the holidays with Saul's family in Minneapolis. We left the dog in the apartment and walked to the Co-op to get something for supper. Ludi took after Daddy; she loved to cook and she enjoyed shopping. We bought a pound of shrimp, some rice, an expensive red bell pepper, balsamic vinegar, kalamata olives. And in the parking lot Ludi brushed aside my plan to keep Christmas at bay and we bought a tree.

After supper we made ornaments out of baker's clay—salt, flour, and water—and we made little angels and Santas out of *penne* and *maccheroni*. My favorite kinds of pasta. We didn't have any lights, and we didn't have a stand, so we propped the tree in a corner and wired the top to the curtain rod.

Ludi had lots of stories about Saul, which I was more inclined to listen to now than I had been in the summer because now I had a few good stories of my own about Richard. Besides, Ludi had come down from the peak of the mountain. No longer Diotima or Beatrice, she was interested in the experiences of mere mortals. Like Daddy and me.

"What if you two do it again?" she wanted to know.

"She'd kill me! But I wouldn't. I don't think Richard would either."

"Isn't it weird? Do you ever talk about it? You and Richard?"

"No, we don't talk about it, but it doesn't feel weird either."

"How *does* it feel?"

"It's hard to explain," I said. "She's taken something that hurt her and transformed it. I wish we could do that with Cookie's death."

"Why does everything lead back to that?" Ludi asked. "It's like you're a criminal trying to get around a roadblock. You take some back road and you think you're safe, but then you see the lights up ahead, and the barricade, and you have to turn back."

"When you have an affair . . . somebody gets hurt . . . but you're still alive; you can work something out, keep on going."

Ludi clicked her tongue and Lasky came trotting out of my bedroom. "You can work something out when somebody dies too," she said. "You can keep on going; you don't have to let it tear your whole family apart."

"Remember how we used to pretend that Cookie had gone to the Grey Havens with Gandalf and Galadriel and that whole crowd, and that you and I were like Merry and Pippin, and that we had to clean up the Shire?"

"It would make more sense to clean up your apartment."

"I did clean it," I said. "If you don't believe me, you can look behind the stove."

DADDY HAD left me in charge of family business—about thirty file folders in a cardboard tomato lug. The box was the perfect width, but the lid wouldn't fit on right and had crushed the tabs at the top of the folders.

Ludi had straightened out her own finances at Grinnell, where her financial status had changed because she was no longer a dependent. She'd redone her financial aid forms, which are more complicated than income tax, and had received a full scholarship. Daddy's affairs were more complicated, though for a disorganized person who lost things all the time he had the records in pretty good order. Medical expenses. Federal and state income tax records. A record of old mortgage payments. The bill of sale for the farm. The papers for the divorce settlement. We had to make the final payment before the end of the year. I wrote out a check to the convent for $27,836 on the joint money-market fund that Daddy had set up for us. It was such an astonishing sum of money that Ludi and I kept looking at the check after I'd signed it. (For tax reasons that I didn't fully understand, the check went to the convent rather than to Mama.)

The most problematic document, however, was neither the bill of sale for the farm nor the settlement papers for the divorce, but a three-page photocopy of a modification, dated "27 luglio 1981," of "La legge 13 agosto 1980 n. 466." Ludi and I had talked about it on the phone, but we hadn't decided what to do. The law, according to the explanation in Daddy's folder, extended the category of victims of acts of terrorism who were eligible for compensation from the Italian government to include victims of earlier terrorist bombings, back to 1969, and to include foreigners. All we had to do was establish that Cookie had been killed in the bombing and we were eligible for L. 100.000.000.

"That's a lot of money," Ludi'd said on the phone; and that's what she said now: "That's a lot of money; at least it's a lot of lire."

I had an old *New York Times* under the sink, so we looked up the currency values. On December 14, L. 100.000.000—if I'd done my calculations correctly, 100,000,000 divided by 1,453—would have been worth $68,823.12.

"*Cento milioni per testa di morto,*" I said, reading aloud the terms of the settlement. "Blood money—that's what Daddy called it. He wouldn't have anything to do with it."

"It's a lot of blood money. Almost seventy thousand dollars. That's almost as much as the whole estate was worth."

"Don't even think of it," I said.

"Why not?" Ludi asked. "Is there a statute of limitations?"

I ran my finger down the page. "It doesn't say. There's a *conto corrente* at the post office. The first thing you have to do is send a letter to the Ministro degli Interni."

"It's worth a try."

"You're not serious?" I said. "Daddy would never let us do it."

"Daddy's in Italy."

"He'll have to sign the papers."

"I can sign his name."

"What about Mama? She'll want her half."

Ludi threw back her head and rolled her eyes.

I was nervous, trembling inside. "It's just not right, Ludi; taking money for Cookie's death. The government was trying to buy people off so they wouldn't complain so much about not getting on with the investigation . . ." I raised several more objections, but Ludi, sitting sideways on the couch, her head tilted back—her long red hair hanging straight down over the arm of the couch—kept on rolling her eyes till I wanted to scream. "How can you not care?" I shouted. "How can you not care that Mama's joined a goddamn convent and Daddy's gone off on a wild-goose chase to Italy? Our whole goddamn family is falling apart. If you'd taken my side maybe it wouldn't have happened, if you'd stuck up for me."

"I don't think I've ever heard you swear like that," she said.

"Jesus, Ludi, I don't see how you can just not care."

"You know I care, Sary. You don't really think I don't care, do you? You know better. And who are you to talk, anyway? Fucking Aaron Gridley right in Cookie's bed, before Cookie's even buried? How do you explain that? And telling me that Cookie's gone to the Grey Havens. I didn't know what to believe. But fucking Aaron Gridley, Cookie's old boyfriend. Boy, you are really something."

"You know what I mean," I said. Lamely.

"I know what you mean," she said; "but don't tell me *I* don't care, OK? When we were staying with the Williamses after the bombing . . . Every night, Sara, I went to a terrible place. And every night you reached out and took my hand and helped me get back; but I don't ever want to go back to that place, Sary. It's not a question of caring; it's a question of letting go. You think of yourself as warm and fuzzy, but really you're hard as nails. You want to control everything, everyone. Mama. Daddy. Me. A hundred million lire. That's a lot of money. We need the money, Sary. Maybe you don't need it, but Daddy needs it, and I need it. They don't give out fellowships in vet school. You have to pay your way. I'll have to pay my way. If I get in, of course. It's not cheap."

"You'll get in," I said. "How could you even think you wouldn't get in?"

"Because I still have to do physics, that's why. I can't do the math; I don't like it."

I knew she could do whatever she wanted, but we left it at that. It was time to get on with the business of Christmas.

We listened to Christmas carols on the radio while we decorated the tree with the pasta ornaments. On Thursday afternoon we bought a small turkey at the Co-op and chestnuts for Daddy's stuffing. We made cranberry relish and an apple pie, though I didn't have a spring-form pan like the one Daddy always used. We lit candles, wrapped presents and put them under the tree, and then we took the Jeffrey Express downtown to see the big tree at Field's and watch the kids line up for Santa Claus. The works. And what I realized was that Ludi could do all these things, and carry me along with her, because she wasn't so sentimental. She didn't get all weepy the way I did at the memory of the heroic Christmases of the past. She was the first one of the three of us to stop believing in Santa Claus, the first to stop believing in God. That was my little sister. Amazing. I resolved to be more like her.

The day before Christmas is the busiest day of the year at MSI. People come to see the Trees of Many Lands exhibit, and they come because they don't know what else to do. The gift shops were packed. The line for the coal mine looped around and stretched all the way back to the Rotunda. But best of all, the waterwheel was drawing big crowds. Kids dipped their hands into the water as they watched the butterfly attractors grow on the big TV monitors. I kept going down, from my cubicle on the second floor, to check. When I went home at four o'clock, people were still pouring in through the door.

Ludi, who'd been Christmas shopping, had brought back stuff for pizzas. We drank a little red wine while we fixed the pizzas, and a little more while we ate them, and then we put the dog on her leash and went to the museum. Ludi'd been in Chicago three days and still hadn't seen my wheel. I couldn't take it any longer. We put on our coats and walked to the loading dock on the west side of the building. Mort, one of the security guards, checked me out on the TV monitor before opening the door. "Can't be too careful," he said. A radio was blasting; the cleanup staff was having its own Christmas party; pizza boxes were open on the supervisor's desk; cans of beer and pop had been spread out on a flat truck.

"I didn't see a thing," I said. "I've just got to get some stuff from my office and I want to show my sister the waterwheel."

"We didn't see anything either," one of the men said, nodding at the dog.

We took the staff elevator up to the balcony so I could show Ludi my office first, my office space, that is, in a warren of offices, or cubicles, that I'd never imagined as a child—office spaces for developers, designers, project coordinators, and facilitators. And then real offices for the senior scientists and the big bosses.

I had my original sketches for the wheel pinned up to one of those partitions that can be moved around to form different spaces, along with Daddy's latest column from the *Trib*. I wanted Ludi to see that I was a real person, but of course all she could see was my filing cabinet and my shelves, my desk and my computer.

There are places where the museum feels like a great cathedral, nave and transept and lots of little chapels—the Whispering Gallery, for example, and the pendulum, suspended from a dome modeled after the Pantheon in Rome, where Foucault gave the first empirical demonstration of the rotation of the earth. You could see it here. If you waited long enough. You could see the floor of the museum turning under the plane of the pendulum. And if you had good measuring instruments and a good stopwatch you'd see that the pendulum deviated to the right at every swing; and you'd see that it deviated exactly the same amount at each swing. I liked to stop here—when I was showing someone around—and give a little speech: "The pendulum symbolizes the old order of things—the perfectly regular motion of the universe, the immutable laws of Nature. Whereas my waterwheel symbolizes the new order of things. Chaos." This is what I said to Ludi as we stood watching the pendulum.

"What would happen if you tried to stop it from swinging?" Ludi asked.

Right away I got a nervous feeling in the pit of my stomach. "Don't even think of it."

"What if you just gave it a little push in a different direction? It would be like stopping the universe, or getting the earth to spin in a different direction."

"No, it wouldn't, Ludi. It's just a thing." But Ludi was already climbing down into the pit. "Be careful, Ludi," I shouted. "That thing must weigh a ton. You can't just stop it."

"I can feel it, though."

"Don't touch it, Ludi. I could lose my job."

"Don't be such a fraidy cat. I'm not going to hurt anything."

"I could lose my job."

"Is *that* what you're worried about?"

Now I was ashamed of myself. I really *was* a fraidy cat.

I climbed over the railing and down into the shallow pit, which was about fifteen feet in diameter, and stood next to Ludi. The pendulum swung back and forth on a plane in front of us. Silently. Ludi touched it with her finger as it swung by. I held back for a while, but then I couldn't resist. There was something sexual about it. All that energy that you can pick up on with just the tip of your finger—like touching an electric fence, or an erect penis. You feel it through your whole body.

"This is fantastic," Ludi said.

I had to agree. But I was starting to worry about my waterwheel. Would she like it as much as she liked the pendulum?

The Chaos milestone was just north of the Whispering Gallery. We couldn't go through without whispering to each other. "This is where I propositioned Richard," I whispered from one end of the gallery.

"Shame on you," she whispered back from the other end, but there was no disapproval in her voice.

The valve that supplied water for the wheel was around the corner in the Imaging corridor, which led to the West Pavilion. I opened the valve and waited.

"Nothing's happening," Ludi shouted.

"Are you getting water?" I shouted back. "The top bucket's got to fill up a little before it starts to turn."

"There's water. Can you turn it up a little?"

I opened the valve a little wider but not all the way. The wheel was just starting to turn when I came back around the corner. I turned on the computer that monitored the motion of the wheel. Ludi watched in silence. The wheel turned faster and then seemed to settle into a steady rhythm, drawing loops on one of the overhead computer monitors—there were four terminals and four overhead monitors—and then it slowed down, stopped, and reversed itself.

"Look at that," Ludi said. I could see that she was impressed.

"The computer's graphing three streams of apparently random data," I said, "angular position, angular velocity—"

"You don't need to explain everything," she said; "just let me look."

"I keep looking for a pattern," I said. "The first time we got it to work, it went to the left four times, then right three, then left four, right four . . . Like the combination of a padlock. I kept track of patterns, expecting it to repeat itself, despite the theory. It's hard to believe there really is no pattern."

On the monitor we watched the computer plot the motion of a point on the wheel in three-dimensional space.

"What are these buttons?" Ludi asked.

"If you push this one," I said, "you'll see the pattern for the last two days. Look." I pushed the button, and a butterfly appeared on the monitor, representing about five hundred revolutions of the wheel. "This one will show you the pattern for yesterday's revolutions. This one will show you the day before yesterday. They're all different, look. Richard's working on a program that will show you one day's pattern forming—yesterday's—at an accelerated rate, so you can see the butterfly taking shape without waiting around too long."

"It's always a butterfly?"

"Right. We start the wheel up exactly the same way every day, but the pattern turns out different. The classical physicist who grasped this was Poincaré. It's all explained in the text part, over here."

Ludi pushed the first button so we could see the pattern, our own pattern, emerging, uninterrupted. Every revolution of the wheel added to one wing of the butterfly—to the left wing when the wheel turned counterclockwise, to the right when it turned clockwise. No loop was the same as any of the previous ones. Order emerged out of chaos.

"If it ever repeated itself," I said, "that would be it. It would be like the universe coming back to the same place."

"Didn't the Chinese think it did just that?"

"The myth of the eternal return. That was Nietzsche, wasn't it?"

The text part of the exhibit was laced with meaningful quotations from Hesiod, from Yeats, and from Chinese proverbs, and also included an explanation of Black Monday, last October 19, when the Dow Jones Average dropped over five hundred points: relatively minor bad news had been magnified as it cascaded through a system of interdependent variables.

According to Richard the extra holes we'd drilled had increased the volume of water flowing through the system just enough to overcome the residual friction that had prevented the wheel from behaving the way it was supposed to: chaotically. In spite of this prosaic explanation, however, the wheel always seemed miraculous to me.

"I put my first dog to sleep," Ludi said, looking straight ahead. "I've been interning for Dr. Shepherd. He runs the animal clinic on the way into town. About halfway out to Route 80."

"Oh, my God, Ludi, how could you do it? It'd be like putting Argos down."

"I have to do it, Sary. You have to do it if you're a vet. That's part of the job. If you're a doctor you don't have to do that. But if you're a vet . . . you don't have a choice. It's what you do. One of the things."

"Was it a big dog?" I asked. A dumb question. What difference did it make if it was a big dog or a small dog? But I wanted her to keep going.

" A big dog," she said. "A black Lab, with hepatocellular carcinoma. He couldn't stand up; he could hardly breathe; the cancer had metastasized to his lungs; his stomach was distended. The father and his son were there. A man, not the dog's father. And his little boy. Dr. Shepherd has a theory that it's good for children to see the whole cycle. Life and death. That's the value of pets. But the boy didn't want to be there. 'It's going to be all right,' his father kept saying; 'it's going to be all right.' But the boy started crying and his father took him out."

"What happened?"

"Dr. Shepherd asked me if *I* wanted to do it."

"You mean you weren't planning to? You didn't have any time to think about it?"

"No. I didn't have any time to think about it. You're supposed to have your DVM to do it. Legally. But I said yes. I wanted to do it."

"What happened?"

"I injected the dog with five cc's of pentobarbital and he went to sleep, just like Argos. I put the needle in in the cephalic vein on the inside of his leg and squeezed, and he went right to sleep."

"Isn't that what's supposed to happen?"

"That's what's supposed to happen," she said; "but when Dr. Shepherd went back into the office I put my face down in the dog's neck and started to cry. I thought I couldn't bear it. I was all torn up inside. I wasn't as strong as I thought I was; but I was full of love too."

"I'm sorry," I said.

"Don't be sorry," she said; "that's the way I feel now; that's why I'm here. I needed to touch base."

I'd been hoping for a moment like this, but now that it had arrived, I felt awkward, and I turned away to look at the wheel. I don't know how long Ludi and I stood there, side by side, in front of the computer monitor, but after a while I had the feeling that we were not looking *at* it, but *through* it, as if the monitor were a window, as if we were looking out a window that opened onto the ocean, Keats's magic casement, opening not on fairylands forlorn (or whatever) but onto onto onto . . . what Daddy used to call the *Ding an sich*, the thing itself; the heart of things; the mystery of it all. I couldn't figure out how to put it into words. I wanted to reach out and touch Ludi; I wanted to take her hand and tell her that our paths had crossed at this particular point in space and time and that they'd keep on crossing. I wanted to tell her that I'd never let her go . . . But I knew that that was the wrong thing to say to Ludi, so I kept my mouth shut and watched the butterfly wings grow on the monitor as the wheel turned. We kept watching till I realized that the dog had disappeared. I couldn't remember when I'd seen her last.

"She'll be all right," Ludi said.

But I was a worrier and started shouting: "Lasky, Lasky, come on, girl, Lasky, Lasky."

I shut down the computer and turned off the water. We finally found Laska downstairs at the party, eating a slice of pizza. I was surprised that Ludi didn't say anything, since she *never* let the dog have leftovers, especially pizza, which wasn't good for her. But it was Christmas Eve. Ludi and I ate some leftover pizza with the cleanup crew and split a beer, and then we went home.

CHRISTMAS MORNING wasn't as bad as I'd expected. No more than a slight panic. When I woke up Ludi was already in the kitchen making an apple-and-onion stuffing, since we hadn't gotten around to peeling the chestnuts. She'd already walked the dog.

We weren't expecting Daddy to call till afternoon or evening, morning or afternoon in Italy. Ludi had already typed up a letter requesting the L. 100.000.000. She wanted me to translate it, then decided against it. "Better if it's in English." Then she changed her mind two more times, and then she changed it again. I wrote the letter in Italian, which I'd learned in Italy, but I kept it simple.

"That way they know we mean business," Ludi said.

We included Daddy's Social Security number, which was on the income tax forms, and his new address (my address). Ludi signed Daddy's name.

"Let's put it in the mail now," she said. "The stuffing's supposed to cool off anyway before we put it in the turkey."

I thought maybe she sensed my misgivings and wanted to make it a fait accompli before I balked.

"I'm not sure I have any stamps," I said.

"There are stamps in your desk."

"You want a cup of coffee first?"

It still didn't seem right to profit by Cookie's death. That's what I couldn't get past. But I didn't want to get into an argument with Ludi. Mama always said that once a woman starts to argue, to give *reasons*, the answer is yes.

We put on our coats and the dog leaped into the air. The nearest mailbox was on the corner of Fifty-fifth Street and Cornell, about three blocks away. The snow was still fresh. No one was out. We had Hyde Park to ourselves.

"Remember Mama talking about the true meaning of Christmas?"

"Which was?" Ludi asked.

"Whatever it was," I said, "I think we're about to violate it. If Daddy had wanted the money he would have sent in the form."

"Maybe he forgot," Ludi suggested.

"Besides, I don't like the idea of making money from Cookie's death. Over thirty million lire apiece; it's like thirty pieces of silver."

Ludi had the letter, though, with VIA AEREA written all over it and some extra postage for good measure. I was holding the dog, who leaped and turned for joy. We saw a few cars on Fifty-fifth

Street, where the traffic lights were blinking. I thought of grabbing the letter and ripping it in half. I imagined the dog grabbing the letter and running away with it. She sometimes did stuff like that, like going through the house and emptying the wastebaskets during the night.

"We didn't make a copy of the letter," I said.

"Too late." Ludi slipped the letter into the mailbox on the corner of Fifty-fifth.

I didn't believe we'd get the money, not from the Italian government. But the money didn't matter. What mattered was that I'd crossed a line, like crossing the border into another country. It was like losing my virginity with Aaron Gridley. Sort of. But not what I expected, because everything was turned around. Instead of guilt, I experienced a kind of joy. I wanted to leap into the air, like the dog. I had declared my independence. Ludi had joined me in Chicago. But I'd joined her in another country.

"Do you remember," I said, "how Cookie used to play the Maria Callas tape on Sunday mornings when Mama and Daddy were in bed? We thought they didn't get it when Cookie imitated them when she was eating her eggs: 'Mmmmm, oh God, mmmm mmmm mmmm, oh God that's good.'"

We remembered that time and other times too, for in this new country memory was not a burden but a gift.

Testimony

On Friday, August 15, 1980—Assumption Day, the middle of the August holidays—a young woman and her boyfriend, dressed as German tourists, placed a bomb in the second-class waiting room in the train station in Bologna. The bomb exploded at 10:25 in the morning, killing eighty-six people. On the next day the two young people, Angela Strappafelci and Niccolò Bosco, went to Rome to procure false papers from a mutual friend, Filippo Forti. Niccolò was arrested two months later and subsequently murdered in prison, along with Pasquale Barbiani, one of the prosecution's key witnesses; but Angela made her way to Argentina, where she lived for several years in a suburb of Buenos Aires with Franco della Chiave, one of the founders of Rivoluzione e Ordine. The bombing was one of a series of bombings intended to destabilize the government and thus pave the way for the emergence of a strong leader who would steer a course between the Scylla of capitalism and the Charybdis of communism. And yet the government itself had done little to further the investigation and much, in fact, to impede it. Witnesses had been intimidated, had even been killed; Pasquale Barbiani had been decapitated in prison; important documents had disappeared; the *magistratura* in Bologna had not been given the financial support that it needed; secret service agents had planted false evidence to mislead investigators; the records of Judge DiBernardi's investigation of neo-fascist groups such as Rivoluzione e Ordine, Avanguardia Nazionale, and Ordine Rivoluzionario Armato, which had originally claimed credit for the bombing but had later denied it, had been, after DeBernardi's brutal murder just a few days *before* the bombing, classified as top secret and could not be subpoenaed.

These things hadn't made sense to Woody when he'd read about them in the bulletins from the Association of the Families of the Victims, which had been lobbying to have this top-secret classification—*Segreto di Stato*—abolished in cases of terrorism, and they didn't make sense to him now, traveling from Milan to Bologna on a train that was so crowded it was impossible for the conductor to move through the narrow corridor to punch the tickets.

He was traveling with a single suitcase, but it was a large one, and heavy; and with his guitar, which was also very heavy. Between the suitcase and the guitar and his briefcase, which was full of books and papers, it had been practically impossible to get on the train, and it was absolutely impossible to move once he was on. It was not even possible to sit down on the suitcase. Woody's colleagues at St. Clair tended to speak of Italy as a kind of paradise, and Woody, who had spent two different sabbatical years in Rome, often talked this way too, even though he knew better. Standing on the train, hardly able to turn around, he felt disoriented. An American woman in her fifties who'd been on the same flight had attached herself to him briefly on the bus from the airport to the train station in Milan. She'd been pulling a large green duffel bag on wheels. She was from California, where she was building a utopian retreat where creative people who shared a love of Italy could come together to share their creativity and their life experiences. Woody would be one of the first to receive an invitation. She was on her way to Florence, she said, and wanted to know if they'd be taking the same train. Woody said he didn't know; nor did he know where to buy tickets or to change money; he'd never been in Milan before, he said; he'd always flown to Rome. Which wasn't quite true, because he and Hannah had flown to Milan after the *strage*. He stayed put till the woman went off, pulling her green duffel bag behind her, like a large lazy dog on a leash. When Woody finally located the *biglietteria*, which was downstairs, the woman, who didn't speak a word of Italian, was already at the ticket window, at the head of a long line. Later he saw her poke her head out of one of the compartments on the train; somehow she'd gotten a seat.

Woody had located an apartment through the Association of the Families of the Victims, but he hadn't been able to reach the *padrona*, the landlady. He'd phoned from the train station in Milan and left a message on her answering machine. In Bologna he lugged his suitcase and his guitar and his briefcase down the stairs of the underpass and up the other side into the station itself. He sat for a minute to catch his breath before calling the *padrona* again. She wasn't there, so he left another message. And then he called again an hour later. He didn't feel comfortable in the station, but he didn't know where else to go. He sat in the second-class waiting room, in front of the *lapide*, a stone inscribed with the names of the eighty-six people who had been killed in the bombing. He let his eye travel down the list of names till he came to Cookie's.

Maria Rivera	27
Carolyn Woodhull	22
Pio Pandolfini	69

Name and age. The names were not in alphabetical order, not in any particular order that he could see, though some families had lost three people and their names had been kept together. A portion of the wall behind the *lapide* had been left untouched when the station was rebuilt. Below the *lapide*, in the bomb crater, someone had left a dozen roses, wrapped in cellophane.

Woody called the *padrona* again and left another message on her machine. He asked a woman sitting next to him to keep an eye on his suitcase and briefcase while he went to the bathroom, but he took the guitar with him. On his way back from the bathroom he bought a newspaper. Iran and Iraq had resumed the tanker war in the Persian Gulf, and a quarrel between Bologna and Modena over the classification and labeling of hams was described as a prosciutto war. Jessica Hahn had bared her breasts for *Playboy*, but the Italian reporter covering the story was not impressed. President Bush was coming to Italy to meet with the president of the senate, and the University of Bologna was going to give honorary degrees to Pietro Barilla, the head of the giant pasta company, and to Mother Teresa. Bob Dylan was giving a concert in Verona. Woody took his guitar out of its case and played for a while. A man in a business suit dropped a thousand-lire note and some change into the open guitar case. Woody laughed for the first time since he'd arrived in Italy. "No no," he said; he wanted to explain, to give the money back—he wasn't a street musician, a beggar—but the man waved him back into his seat and walked away.

He didn't reach the *padrona* till seven o'clock. The apartment she'd been planning to rent to him was not going to be vacant for several weeks. In the meantime, she said, there was another apartment, in Via Solferino, very near the Tribunale, very convenient. She had a slight speech impediment, as if she were speaking Italian with a French accent, and he had trouble understanding her.

"I'm sorry," he said several times; "could you repeat that?"

She might have tried to speak more clearly, or at least more slowly, Woody thought; but she didn't.

"What happened?" he asked. "I thought it was all arranged."

"It *was* all arranged, Signore, but arrangements . . ." She didn't finish the sentence, but she didn't have to; Woody already had a mental image of her shrugging her shoulders.

"What am I supposed to do now? I've been sitting in the station since four o'clock."

"What does my ass have to do with the forty hours?" she said. At least that's what Woody thought she said.

"Pardon?"

"Take a cup of coffee," she said, "or take the number thirty-three bus from in front of the station; get off at Porta San Mammolo and follow Via Savanella to Via Solferino. There's another apartment, very near the Tribunale, very convenient. This will be much better."

"I'll take a taxi," Woody said. "I've got my suitcase, and a guitar."

"You're a musician?"

"Not exactly."

"Then I think a cup of coffee would be best, don't you? About nine o'clock?"

Woody understood that she meant taxi, not cup. "I've been waiting for four hours," he said again.

"Around nine o'clock, then," she said. "I would take you for a walk myself, but I've lost my driver's license."

"That's all right," he said. "I've got nothing to do."

"Ciao."

"Ciao."

Woody wasn't sure why he'd mentioned the guitar. Maybe he wanted to identify himself. He played a few more songs and several people tossed bills into the guitar case.

THE TAXI driver waited for him to ring the bell on Via Solferino. There were no lights in any of the windows, at least in the front of the building, and no one buzzed him in or came to the door. The driver was reluctant to leave him alone, but Woody thanked him and waved him on. He was in a narrow street, a short, dark street with porticoes or arcades on both sides. He couldn't make out the hands of his watch, which were still set on Chicago time. After a while he thought of calling again, but there was no telephone. There was an *osteria* on the ground floor—Osteria Trebbiano—but it was closed.

The *padrona* finally arrived on a Vespa. "I lost my driver's license," she explained a second time as she removed her helmet, which had flattened her curly hair against her scalp. She carried the guitar and led the way up the stairs. Woody followed behind her, carrying the heavy suitcase. He wondered what her ass had to do with the forty hours.

By the time he caught up with her at the top of the stairs she had unlocked all four locks on the door. "There's some chickpea soup," she said, giving the *c*'s a *tz* sound: *tzetzi* rather than *ceci*. "Chickpeas and fish. From the *osteria*. Downstairs." She bent over to remove a large pot from a tiny, under-the-counter refrigerator. "And some cheese, and wine." The wine was on the table, in a Chianti flask with no label. "And I've brought some bread." She took a half loaf of bread out of a plastic sack she had wrapped around her wrist and put it on the table next to the wine.

"You must be tired," she said, lighting the gas with a clicker and putting the pot of soup on to heat.

"It's harder coming this way than going back home," he said. "When you get back home it's time to go to bed; but when you get here, you've got a whole day in front of you that you have to get through."

She nodded. "You have to stir the *tzetzi*," she said, "so they don't burn on the bottom."

300

"May I ask you something?" he said.

"Of course."

"What does your *culo* have to do with the forty hours?"

She laughed. "My mother used to say that," she said, "when she was scolding us and we tried to change the subject. The forty hours, that's the Easter vigil. It just means, What does *x* have to do with *y*?—nothing."

When she had gone Woody used a cup to ladle some of the soup into a bowl. It wasn't really hot yet, but he was too tired and hungry to wait. He unwrapped a piece of cheese and poured a glass of wine, which was young and strong without being too rough. Not Chianti. He wondered what you had to do to lose your driver's license in Italy.

WOODY HAD never spoken to anyone about his own experiences in Bologna in the days immediately after the *strage*. He'd tried to speak to Hannah, of course—she'd been with him, after all—but her memories of Bologna could not be reconciled with his, as if they'd been to two different cities with the same name, or read two different books with the same title. And every discussion had led to an argument over the tombstone. *La sua voluntade è nostra pace.* She wouldn't let it go. He'd think it had been settled, but like one of those trick candles for birthday cakes, it would relight itself every time he blew it out.

"It's what I want," she said one night, just after she'd started teaching in Chicago. "What difference does it make to you? You don't believe anything anyway. What have you come up with that's better? Nothing, Woody. Nothing. Nothing at all." She'd spoken through clenched teeth. They'd been drinking red wine in the kitchen. She'd knocked her glass over and without bothering to wipe it up had poured herself another. The spilled wine puddled in a hollowed-out section of the butcher's table, like rainwater in a low spot in a cornfield. She got it on her sleeve, without noticing, or without caring. He reached over to lift her arm out of the spilled wine, but she jerked away; she didn't want him to touch her.

She'd had to know, at some level, that Cookie had still been alive; that her suffering had been unimaginable; that Woody thought she'd recognized him; that he'd gone back that night to the hospital and then to the morgue, to make sure that it was really Cookie, because Hannah thought it wasn't; and that later that night she—Hannah—had offered herself to strangers on the Via Rizzoli as a prostitute for Christ—she'd thought she was Mary Magdalene—and the *carabinieri* had picked her up and taken her to Policlinico Sant'Orsola, where she'd spent four weeks in the psychiatric ward. Woody had wanted to thrust this knowledge into her, like the blade of a knife, but he'd remained silent. Later on, when she was asleep, he ran some cold water in the sink in the laundry room and put her blouse in to soak; he watched the wine color the water and then he smoked one of her cigarettes on the back porch, inhaling hard, so the smoke made him dizzy, as he tried to understand what had just happened, and whether or not it would have made a difference if he had spoken. He hadn't known at the time about the young person who had followed her, or that God had made his presence known to her like a dog in the house. He hadn't known these things till she'd stopped to see them last Christmas. If he *had* known, would it have made a difference? Would he have given in? What would it have cost him, just to let it go? *La sua voluntade è nostra pace.*

He had not wanted to burden his daughters or his friends with what had happened, which was so painful to him that he had hardly spoken to himself about it, had not really put it into words, that is. They remained a shapeless mass, like a rough draft. Unformed. He'd thought, briefly, that he might speak something like the truth at Cookie's memorial service, but it had been out of the question. But now, here in Bologna, he wished to speak it aloud, to give it shape and form in a place where he would be understood; he wanted to tell his story, and he wanted to hear others tell their stories. He wanted to bring his old life to an end, so that a new life could begin.

THE APARTMENT was small but snug, like a ship's cabin; the bed, tucked under a small window, was like a berth, with drawers underneath and cabinets above. He took a bottle of shampoo out of his dopp kit. The bookshelves on the opposite wall were empty except for a stack of women's magazines—*Cipria* and *Donna*—with articles on men and on clothing, food, the emotions, beauty, fashion.

Woody took a shower and then settled down in the apartment's one comfortable chair, in the kitchen, to read the copy of Goethe's *Italienische Reise* he'd brought with him. Turi had given it to him. He'd started it on the plane. He had to admire Goethe's resolve, his sense of purpose, the sense that like Columbus he had embarked on a great voyage of discovery, confident that he could rise above the darkness in which most men live, rise above it as easily as he could climb the Asinelli Tower, which he did on his first day in Bologna, October 18, 1816.

That afternoon, after eating another bowl of the soup, which was delicious, Woody, like Goethe, climbed the three hundred twenty-seven steps of the Asinelli Tower in Piazza Ravegnana, so that he could see with his own eyes what Goethe had seen: the red roofs of the city, the towers of Modena to the north and west; the foothills of the Apennines in the south, and, almost invisible in the distance, the northern chain of the Alps, covered in the same mist that had prompted Goethe to compare his own homeland to Homer's dark Cimmerian realm.

Goethe had gone rock hunting, and he'd gone to the Pinacoteca Nazionale to see Raphael's *Santa Cecilia*, and the painters of the Bologna school, Carracci, Guido Reni, Domenico Zampieri, but in the late afternoon Woody parted company with Goethe—who, impelled by a force that he couldn't understand himself, had impulsively fled from the city—and struck out on his own. He hadn't written out his speech and he wanted to sharpen his memory by walking around the city. Before the *strage* Bologna had been, to him, a railroad hub, a place where the train stopped on the way to somewhere else. But now it was the place where Cookie had spent her last day. Woody tried without success to imagine this day. He knew she'd found an apartment, but he didn't know where; he knew that she'd met someone, but he didn't know whom. Where had she spent the night? Where had she eaten lunch? Had she checked the bulletin board at the Johns Hopkins library? He walked all the way to the Ospedale Maggiore, where she'd been taken from the station, and then all the way back to the morgue on Via Irnerio. Looking through the bars of the gate he remembered the truck that had been parked in the drive, full of wooden army coffins; more empty coffins had been stacked up against the wall. He resisted an impulse to ring the bell. And then he walked to the station, map in hand, trying to summon up some wisdom, his best wisdom; but his best wisdom eluded him, kept its distance, like a dog that doesn't want to be put on a leash.

He sometimes had trouble picturing Cookie and would have to remind himself by looking at the graduation photo he kept in his billfold; but he could sometimes hear her voice, as if she were whispering to him from a long way away. And in fact he continued to imagine her life as if she were alive in some distant place. As if she were growing older, even old; loving a man, maybe more than one man; having their children. Her children. Singing in some other place, where he could just barely catch the sound of her voice once in a while. And that evening, as he wandered the streets, he thought from time to time that he recognized her: in Piazza Maggiore, drinking wine in an *osteria* on Via Pratello, or walking down Via Garibaldi, riding a bicycle in a skirt so short you could see her underpants. He had to shake himself so that he wouldn't call out her name, or run after her and take her in his arms.

He didn't want to be one of those people who never move on, who keep their dead child's room exactly the way it was when she was alive, as a kind of memorial. And in fact Sara had moved into Cookie's room even before they got back from Italy. But he couldn't help himself; he was drawn back to the station, to the second-class waiting room, just as he'd been drawn to the cemetery in St. Clair. Like a man with a secret vice. Thinking that maybe she was sitting here, or here, or here. No matter how he tried he couldn't make sense of her story. It was, he often thought, as if the pages had been ripped out of the book he'd been reading. There was no sense of an ending. That was why he'd come to Italy. He wanted to finish her story, his story.

THE TRIAL resumed, after the summer recess, the next morning, Tuesday, September twenty-second. The court convened on the second floor of the Tribunale in a room named after Vittorio Bachelet, a judge who had been murdered by the Red Brigades in 1980. All the courtrooms, in fact, were named after judges who had been murdered, if not by the Red Brigades, then by the Mafia or by some neofascist organization. A small plaque on the right side of each door indicated the judge's name and the name of the group that had murdered him. The plaques were furnished by the Lions Club International.

The courtroom was like a theater. Center stage, facing the audience, sat the president of the court, the presiding judge. To his right, the professional judges and alternate judges sat in chairs with backs that were higher than the backs of the other chairs, but not as high as the back of the president's chair. At the far right, another high-backed chair was reserved for the *pubblico ministero*, the public prosecutor. On the president's left hand sat three *giudici popolari*, not exactly jurors, but "citizen judges," and two alternates. Each citizen judge, Woody learned later, had a vote equal to the vote of each professional judge and of the president.

In the front of the court a small table for the clerk was flanked by six large tables for the defense attorneys and for the attorneys for the *parte civile*, that is, the lawyers representing the interests of the relatives of the victims of the *strage*. There was a microphone on each table. The lawyers chatted with each other. Three steps down, on the main floor, were seats for the press and chairs for about two hundred people. In the back were bleachers for the general public. TV cameras recorded the proceedings from a balcony above the bleachers, but Woody hardly noticed these things. What he noticed were the *gabbie*, the cages for the prisoners. The one on the right resembled the two-tiered jury box familiar to all Americans, but extending upward from the handsome wood paneling, almost indistinguishable from it in color, were painted metal bars, bars on all three sides, bars separating the two tiers or levels, and bars overhead. The one on the left was similar, though instead of being divided into two tiers it was divided into two parallel sections.

Cookie was the only American who had been killed—though two other Americans had been injured—and Woody was very conscious of being an American himself. America still enjoyed, at least in Italian eyes, some moral prestige. There was a kind of faith that the U.S. could make things right, make things better. Though there was some bitterness too. The U.S. had delayed the extradition of Roberto Rosselli from California, and the State Department was suspected of being involved in withholding information about an airplane that had been shot down, possibly by a missile, over Sicily.

The radar records for the five crucial minutes had disappeared, like the eighteen and a half minutes on Nixon's Watergate tape. And all the records had been sealed, covered by *Segreto di Stato*. The CIA was also suspected of being involved in the murder—the beheading—of Pasquale Barbiani, a key witness for the prosecution.

When Woody imagined himself standing before the court, he felt slightly nervous, but excited too. As if he were about to play his guitar in front of an audience. He had made a few notes on a single sheet of paper that he had folded in half, but he didn't feel any need to review these notes or to go over his speech in his mind. He knew that when the time came he would stand before the court and speak boldly and clearly, and he knew that his slightly imperfect accent would add to rather than diminish the impact of his words.

At about ten-fifteen the doors in the back of the *gabbie* opened and the prisoners entered. Woody couldn't take his eyes off them. He recognized them all from their photos in *Il Resto del Carlino*. Aldo Trimarchi, the explosives expert charged with building the bomb and delivering it to Angela Strappafelci and her boyfriend at the station; he'd stayed around to see the big bang and had been injured by a piece of falling debris. He was hospitalized and later arrested by the traffic police for reasons that were not clear to Woody. Carlo Campobello, Angela Strappafelci's *rettore*, or thesis director, at the University of Rome. Roberto Rosselli, who had been the liaison between della Chiave's Rivoluzione e Ordine and similar right-wing groups in France and Spain and Germany. Lieutenant Colonel Milazzo and General Palumbo, the secret service agents who had fabricated false evidence that had led investigators to waste valuable time in Austria and France instead of looking for the terrorists at home, almost bringing the investigation to a halt. *Depistare* was the word for the charge against them. It wasn't in Woody's dictionary, but it meant to lay down false trails or red herrings.

By the time the president called the court to order the room was full, overflowing. The clerk introduced the interpreters who would assist the foreigners who were going to testify, Maria Varese (English and German) and Thérèse Brissand (French). The president took note that on the previous morning at nine-thirty Bruno Conti, the Maestro Venerabile of the notorious Fraternità e Lavoro, had turned himself in to the *giudice istruttore* in Geneva. One of the lawyers representing the *parte civile* requested that extradition proceedings begin immediately. Conti, an enormously wealthy financier, had been linked to every major political scandal in Italy over the past twenty years.

One of the defense lawyers embarked on a eulogy for a colleague who had died over the weekend: "We weep for him; we commemorate him; we wish that he were still among us with his voluminous petitions. He exists no more, but I am certain that his memory will remain with us and with all those who knew him." On and on, concluding with a request that the president suspend the hearings for one minute. Another lawyer requested that the eulogy become part of the permanent record of the trial.

The president wanted to get on with the testimony of the *parti lese*, the injured parties—the survivors of the bombing and the families of those who had not survived—but other lawyers had other business to bring up. The dead colleague had left some written requests and a cassette tape, about which the president knew nothing. And the business of Conti wouldn't go away. Conti was wanted in connection with the bankruptcy scandal of the Banco Ambrosiano, and for perjury, and for many other things, including belonging to subversive organizations. On behalf of the *parte civile*, Avvocato Giampaolo Pistrelli wanted to declare Conti in contempt for failing to show up at the trial. A lawyer for the defense countered that Conti was not really a fugitive because he was in jail in Switzerland, though in fact he wasn't really in jail, he was in a clinic in Geneva. Another lawyer argued that if Conti had turned himself over to the Swiss authorities in order to avoid prosecution in Italy, he could still be considered a fugitive.

What Woody understood by the end was that the defense position was this: (a) that Conti's absence was immaterial because the defendants had no connection whatsoever with Conti and his various organizations, and at the same time (b) that without Conti, who was accused of being one of the *mandanti*, one of the "senders," one of the big shots in the background who had ordered the *strage*, there was absolutely no point in proceeding.

THE FIRST witness for the *parti lese* didn't testify till the afternoon session. She had lost her brother but had not been present, nor had she been questioned by the *giudice istruttore*. Was she in a position to furnish the court with any pertinent information? Unfortunately not. The president dismissed her, and called the second witness. The procedure was the same. Even witnesses who had been present had little to say. No one had seen a *fiammata*, a burst of flame, but many had noticed the smell of gunpowder. One of the defense lawyers insisted on asking how they knew it was gunpowder. This led to philosophical questions about how one can recognize or describe a smell, any smell.

No one was in a position to furnish the court with any pertinent information. That was it. Woody had been expecting something more flamboyant, more passionate, more heartfelt—*cris de coeur.* This was Italy, after all.

When his turn came Woody declined the assistance of a translator, but Signora Varese, the translator, instead of resuming her seat, stood next to him, shoulder to shoulder, running her fingers under the lapels of her blue suit as she waited for him to speak. They stood facing the president, their backs to the lawyers and the general public.

"You have constituted yourself," the president said, "a member of the *parte civile* because of the death of your daughter, is that correct?"

"That is correct."

"And how old was your daughter?"

"Twenty-two."

"Were you present at the time of the explosion?"

"No, I was in the United States."

"Are you in a position," the president asked, "to furnish the court with any pertinent information?"

Woody hesitated. No one expected him to say anything more, but he opened his mouth to speak, to explain, looking from left to right and then back to the president, who sat directly in front of him, though on a higher level. But what was there to explain? Everything was perfectly clear. Like a man who has just recognized an optical illusion, he needed to adjust his thoughts. He opened his mouth again, to speak, to explain. Once again he looked from left to right and then back to the president. It occurred to him for the first time that he had made a terrible mistake. That if he'd listened to Sara and

Ludi, and to Mac and even to the dean—to everyone except Turi—he would now be standing in the front of a classroom on the third floor of Clair Hall, introducing his students to Homer, or to the *mi*-verbs, instead of standing before the court of the first instance, in Aula Vittorio Bachelet, with no pertinent information to offer. That at the end of the day he would be going home, to the farm, instead of holing up in someone else's tiny apartment. The dog would run to greet him, would rub against his legs. He would sit down at the kitchen table in the house in which he had raised his family. He had embraced his wife and conceived his youngest daughter in their bed-room upstairs, which he had painted a light blue; he'd painted the trim cream, and he'd built a long, low chest under the windows to hold sheets and pillowcases. And he'd thrown it all away. This real-ization stunned him, like a hammer blow. He opened his mouth to speak, to explain. But what was there to explain? Everything was perfectly clear. He had made a mistake, had overturned his life. He could see finally what everyone else had seen from the beginning. What had looked like a rabbit was clearly a squirrel. What had looked like a young woman was clearly an old hag. He'd been taken in by an optical illusion.

"Do you have any pertinent information?" the president asked again, addressing the translator. Signora Varese repeated the ques-tion in English: "Do you have any pertinent information?"

He'd thought that like Goethe he'd been embarking on a great voyage of discovery, but Goethe had been a young man at the time, in his mid-thirties. Later in life, when he was Woody's age, he'd dug in his heels in Weimar, consolidated his gains instead of squander-ing them; he'd written *Faust*.

"Do you have any pertinent information?" the translator asked again, in English.

Once again Woody opened his mouth to speak, but he had noth-ing to say. He couldn't tell the truth here any more than he'd been able to tell it at the memorial service in Cambridge.

"No," he said.

"The witness may step down."

THE LAST witness of the day was one of the conductors of the Adrian Express, which had been stopped on track number one—the track nearest the station. The train was about to depart. The signal had already been given; the stationmaster had already called for the doors to be closed; the conductor had been closing the last door of the train; his hand had been in the air—he demonstrated—to give the signal to depart, when the explosion occurred. He was thrown against the side of the car. For a moment he was covered by a cloud of gunpowder, and then the platform roof collapsed. He was struck by a piece of concrete that knocked him off his feet and under the car, and then for a moment he didn't feel the pain in his legs. Crawling out from under the car he saw a man whose face had been terribly burned and whose left eye was hanging out of its socket. *"Aiutami,"* the man called. "Help me." People were saying that a boiler had exploded, but there was no odor of gas. The smell was gunpowder, not gas. He went on to describe the scene, the dark cloud of dense soot that had seemed to open up a corridor through the station, and then the confusion, the cries of the victims, the arrival of the firemen and the police, the initial attempt to locate fellow railroad workers.

Finally someone had offered some pertinent information.

IN HIS room that evening Woody lay on his back on the bed. He had taken his shoes off but still wore the chinos and the white shirt he'd worn in the courtroom. He felt a little dizzy, like a man who's had too much to drink, or who's about to be seasick, or who has failed an examination, or done something shameful that has been found out and made public. He tried to read another chapter of the *Italienische Reise*, but the German words seemed as foreign to him as Finnish or Basque.

He dozed off for a while. When he woke it was already starting to get dark, but he wasn't hungry. He took his clothes off and hung them up in a closet, and then he began to page through one of the women's magazines, looking at the pictures and at the ads for cosmetics. There was an article on male nudes. Was the male nude interesting to women? Very few men, according to Alberto Moravia, can allow themselves the luxury of looking good in the nude. You can look at a nude man and decipher with absolute certainty his social class, his disposition, his relationship with his family. Women on the other hand are less fully integrated into society. They stand with one foot outside of society, and therefore are less embarrassed, less encumbered. The male nude, said a woman psychiatrist, with his attributes on display suggests tyranny. The penis is a sword. Women want fantasy, not penises on display. A list followed of prominent men—including John Major and Caspar Weinberger—who had refused to be photographed in the nude, as well as photographs of some men who were less inhibited.

"Men are more concerned about size than women," said a female sociologist at the end of the article. "Men compete. If the male nude isn't exactly right, the effect is comic . . . It's really the advertisers . . . Women's bodies have been commercialized; now it's men's turn."

Would Woody have posed in the nude if he'd been asked? But who would have asked? Could an expert—Alberto Moravia himself—decipher his social condition from the way he stood in the nude? Grasp his disposition, his relationship with his family? Woody stood in front of the mirror on the bathroom door and looked at himself. He stood solidly, facing the mirror, his weight distributed evenly on both feet. He always thought of himself as small and wiry, a second baseman, like Phil Rizzuto or Nellie Fox, and was always surprised by the discrepancy between this image of the inner man, or this inner image of the man, and the long and lanky self, slightly awkward, that mimicked him in mirrors. He tried to see himself as a woman might see him. As Hannah had seen him. Allison. Turi. As a stranger might see him. Would she, the stranger, be able to decipher his social class, his disposition, his relationship with his family? What woman would want to clasp this body to her own, to fit it to her own? He couldn't imagine it. And yet women had. A few women anyway.

He raised his hand, as if to wave good-bye to himself, and as he did so an image of the conductor who had testified that afternoon came unbidden into his imagination, his hand raised, like Woody's, to give the signal for the Adrian Express to depart for Milan. He pictured Cookie in the waiting room, turning the pages of a book—she was always reading—and then the explosion and the dark cloud of soot.

Mr. Jelly Roll Baker

Woody's apartment, in Via Solferino, two minutes from the Tribunale, was located over a noisy *osteria*. The *osteria* was owned by his landlady, Gabriella del Monte, who also owned several other apartments in the same palazzo. The *osteria* was deep and narrow; two rows of long tables were separated by a central aisle. Double doors in the back opened onto a garden that Woody could look down on from his bedroom window. The small kitchen, located in the front, was hardly a separate room, more like a space that had been partitioned off. At eight o'clock the *osteria* was almost empty; at nine o'clock it was almost full; from ten to midnight it was impossible to find a seat; at two o'clock in the morning Woody could still hear, through his bedroom window, the sounds of people eating and drinking and talking. If he listened closely he could make out snatches of conversation between lovers, friends, casual acquaintances, perfect strangers. Some voices became familiar after a while. At least there was no live music, though once in a while a man with a harp showed up and played for half an hour. The sound of the harp was sharp and penetrating, like the sound of a banjo. Woody would never have guessed it was a harp, in fact, if he hadn't seen it out the window. It was about three feet high and maybe eighteen inches deep. Sometimes he sat on the edge of his bed and played his guitar, leaving the window open, as if daring someone—Gabriella, for instance—to complain. But no one seemed to notice.

It wasn't the noise of the *osteria* that kept him awake, however; it was the knowledge that he had made a terrible mistake, a mistake that he would have to drag around behind him, like an anchor. Try as he might, he could not locate within himself even a trace of the original impulse that had led him to throw over his old life, like Abraham, and head out into the wilderness in search of a new one. If instead of listening to whatever voice that had whispered to him in the dark, promising him a new life—more like one of the voices he could hear from the *osteria* beneath his window, he thought now, than a voice addressing him personally—he had listened to the voices of those who knew and loved him, and who had spoken loudly and clearly—Sara and Ludi and Mac—he would be spending his days in the classroom instead of the courtroom. He kept going over the same ground, round and round in a circle. Instead of coming home to this tiny apartment, he'd be coming home to a real house with a porch and a comfortable farm kitchen and an old-fashioned narrow back stairway; a house with books on the shelves and pictures on the walls, and a shower curtain in the bathroom. In Via Solferino there wasn't even a place to hang a shower curtain; the water just poured out of the shower onto the toilet and into the sink and onto the floor; there were no plants, no piano. He cooked his supper in a warped frying pan that couldn't have weighed much more than two or three ounces, and he ate with plastic knives and forks and spoons. His attempts to give the place a little life by lining up bottles of red wine along a mysterious ledge in the living area, which was really no more than an extension of the kitchen, only made it seem more pathetic. Instead of moving forward, he'd gone backwards. He was, in fact, as homesick and insecure now as he'd been as an "occasional scholar" at the University of Esfahan; and Bologna seemed as strange and incomprehensible to him now as Esfahan had seemed then. At least in Esfahan he'd had a host family—Ebrahim Agha and Ashraf Khanom, who had no children of their own—to look after him, to leave a plate of fresh apricots on the little table next to his bed, and a small pitcher of sweetened rosewater. He'd spent two years in Rome, of course, to say nothing of shorter visits, but the Italy he thought he'd known—beautiful, happy, sensual people gesticulating on the streets, haggling over the price of an orange and shouting *"Mamma mia"*—had turned out to be an illusion; though in fact, now that he thought of it, he wasn't sure that in all the time he'd spent in Italy he'd ever heard anyone haggle over the price of an orange or shout *"Mamma mia."*

In the evenings he sometimes went down to join the revelers—he thought of them as revelers—in the *osteria* and to drink a quarter liter of red wine, stretching it out with mineral water. Sometimes he recognized a few faces from the courtroom—one of the lawyers for the *parte civile* who had argued one morning that nothing was *intuibile*, that this was a trial; that if the defense lawyers believed otherwise, they should open *uno studio di precognizione*; two couples who sat with the families of the victims in the courtroom and who often sat together in the *osteria*; and even one of the defense attorneys. He was tempted to introduce himself to the lawyer for the *parte civile*, or to the two couples, but never seemed to find the right moment. He had never thought of himself as a shy person, but somehow he couldn't make the effort, and a quarter liter of wine wasn't enough to get rid of his inhibitions. He was thankful if Gabriella sat with him for a few minutes. She was writing a book about food and seemed to think that he might be able to help her find an American publisher, and he promised to recommend the book to publishers in New York. Sometimes she'd bring him something to eat, even when he didn't ask for it—a sandwich or a piece of baked cheese garnished with deep-fried vegetables, or a plate of *tagliatelle*—because she didn't like to see him drinking wine without eating; but she always charged him, and the food wasn't cheap. At least it cost more than Woody wanted to spend. He had thirty-four thousand dollars left, after the settlement with Hannah, and that would have to last him till his pension, which wouldn't amount to a whole lot, kicked in. In 1993. Six years. Ludi's room and board came to three thousand a year; and he was paying five hundred a month in rent . . .

"A classical education," Woody had written more than once on a blackboard in Clair Hall, "teaches you to despise the wealth it prevents you from earning." It was a joke, and his students always laughed; but Woody had believed it deeply, and he always cited Lucretius when he wanted to illustrate the dative of advantage: *Divitiae grandes homini sunt vivere parce / aequo animo*—It is great wealth for a man to live sparingly with a calm mind. Woody's salary during his last year at St. Clair had been $32,800—at the low end of the AAUP guidelines for full professors. And yet he'd always felt that he was a rich man. But the classical ideal of the simple life was one thing; the Christian ideal of poverty that St. Francis had embraced—and Hannah too, for that matter—was something else. Something to be admired, but from a distance. "Therefore I say unto you, 'Take no thought for your life, what ye shall eat, or what ye shall drink; nor yet for your body, what ye shall put on. Is not the life more than meat, and the body than raiment?'" The fact was, Woody found these words thrilling. They had spoken to him as a child in the Methodist Church in Grand River, and then as a young man at the University of Michigan, and now they spoke to him again in Bologna, but briefly; for he was hungry, and when Gabriella came by to see how he was doing, he asked for a *tomino* with prosciutto and another quarter liter of wine. After all, Hannah had insisted on her half of the estate, and the convent lawyer had made sure she got it. She had taken more thought for the morrow than he had.

EVERY MORNING he drank an espresso in a bar in the piazza in front of the Tribunale and read the accounts by Guido Viscardi and Bruno Calda in *Il Resto del Carlino* of the previous day's hearings, which he didn't always fully understand. When the armored vans that transported the accused from the prison in Ferrara and from the Dozza, the prison just outside Bologna, arrived in the piazza, he'd have a second espresso before entering the Tribunale and climbing the broad Roman stairway, always crowded in the mornings, that led from the courtyard up to Aula Vittorio Bachelet on the second floor. He'd show his passport to one of the guards who sat at a table outside the door to the courtroom, and then take a seat. He was painfully conscious of having made *brutta figura* in front of the court, of having stood before the court with his mouth hanging open, stunned, like an idiot, and for this reason he sat in the back of the courtroom with the general public instead of in front with the families of the victims.

He'd been counting on one or two hundred dollars a week for covering the trial for the *Chicago Tribune*, more if his editor could syndicate the articles; but now he found he could barely follow the proceedings, which were conducted according to the inquisitorial model laid out by the Napoleonic Code rather than the accusatorial model of common-law countries, England and the United States.

The lawyers—and there were over a dozen of them, representing not only the defendants but also the families of the victims—spent a lot of time arguing with each other and with the *pubblico ministero;* the president, instead of being an impartial referee, interrogated witnesses himself, and intervened when the lawyers were asking their questions; the witnesses spoke directly to the president, with their backs to the spectators, so it was hard to hear them; and several of them—and several of the lawyers too, and even the president—seemed to have the same speech impediment that made it difficult for him to understand Gabriella; but this speech impediment turned out to be nothing more than the Bolognese accent. Woody couldn't always be sure what had happened till he read about it in the newspaper the next day.

"It's the language of comedy," Gabriella explained to him. She followed the trial closely; they'd go over the newspaper account together in the evening, before the *osteria* got too busy. "My husband's Florentine friends . . . they think *toscano* is the only true Italian. They thought everything I said was hilarious. I'd say that I'd made *zuppa di tzetzi* and everyone would burst out laughing. I didn't think it was so funny. But maybe they were right. You can't pray in Bolognese, but you can laugh in Bolognese; you can joke around."

AFTER THE afternoon session he read back issues of *Il Resto del Carlino* in the library of the Archiginnasio to get a better sense of the earlier portion of the trial, which had begun in January. Trimarchi, Rosselli, Campobello, and the two secret service agents had made statements in May, but had refused, as was their right under Italian law, to answer questions from the *pubblico ministero* and from the lawyers for the *parte civile.* Della Chiave and Angela Strappafelci had *still* not arrived in Italy, though their extradition from Argentina had been imminent for several months.

But Woody had begun to have doubts, and he had become depressed and anxious. From a distance, political corruption in Italy had always seemed a kind of joke—almost benign, paternalistic, families looking out for themselves, trading favors, a kind of tribalism. Even when he'd been living in Rome the patronage system of the Christian Democrats—perhaps the most corrupt political party in the history of the world—had seemed more a vestige of an older, agricultural society than a political instrument that threatened the social fabric of the entire country, especially in the south, where it had prevented economic and political development. But it was the extent of sympathy towards the right wing that truly astonished him, as it had astonished Judge DiBernardi. The investigations of the various *stragi*, or massacres, six bombings since 1969, had been blocked at every turn—witnesses intimidated, important documents disappearing, the records of DiBernardi's investigation unavailable, *giudici istruttori* transferred at key moments.

Woody's first article for the *Tribune* was a narrative account of the bombing itself; the second was an update on the trial, focusing on General Palumbo and Lieutenant Colonel Milazzo. What had they been trying to cover up? Why? Why had high-ranking members of the secret service intervened to impede the investigation of a bombing that had killed eighty-six innocent people, the worst massacre in Europe since the war? It made no sense. The third article was on Judge DiBernardi, who had been murdered by Angela Strappafelci and her boyfriend, Niccolò Bosco, who had later been killed in prison in Rimini. DiBernardi had repeatedly asked for police protection, but his immediate superior, Judge Giovanni Neri, a member of Fraternità e Lavoro and closely linked to Bruno Conti, had refused and had in fact leaked information about the investigation that almost certainly led to DiBernardi's death. There had been a great public outcry when he was murdered while waiting for a bus. Bosco had been arrested shortly after the bombing; Strappafelci had escaped to Argentina. Neri had been asked to step down as head prosecutor of the Roman judiciary before being promoted to head of the appellate court.

Woody typed these articles onto a primitive fax machine at the office of the Association on Via d'Azeglio. The machine, which was made by Texas Instruments, had a typewriter keyboard built right into it and had to be hooked up to the telephone each time it was used. Once you typed something in, that was it; there was no going back.

He had expected the Association to be a support group, like the support group he and Sara had joined, briefly, in the Quad Cities. He had expected a funereal atmosphere, people in mourning.

"That's what everyone expects," the secretary told him. Her hair was dyed copper red like Gabriella's. "People come on tiptoe"—she

317

demonstrated, taking little mincing steps—"with their handker-chiefs out. There have been plenty of tears, believe me, but we laugh and joke around too. And of course there's always more work to be done."

The office contained books, newspapers, court records, tran-scripts of the trial. The records from various terrorist trials were being computerized so that the testimony of the witnesses and the statements of the accused could be cross-checked. But the principal work of the Association was to put pressure on the government to act. If it hadn't been for the Association, the investigation would have been brought to a halt by the *depistaggi*—the red herrings—of Palumbo and Milazzo, and Rosselli too, who was expected to pro-vide a link between secret services and the neo-fascists.

GABRIELLA KNEW what it was like, she said, to be so far from home.

"How's that?" Woody wanted to know. He was sitting at a table in the *osteria*, near the kitchen.

"I lived in Florence for ten years. When I was married."

Woody looked at her to see if she was joking. It was a Wednes-day night, eight-thirty. The *osteria* was half empty. Or half full. "Florence is only an hour away," he said.

She shrugged her shoulders. "You have the mountains in between," she said. Woody looked at her face again for a trace of irony. But she was serious. She was an attractive woman whose efforts to conceal her age were skillful and even lighthearted, piquant rather than pathetic—mascara but no eyeliner; a touch of powder; lipstick the same shade of red as her fingernails. She wore simple spaghetti-strap dresses, in black or beige, that swished around her legs when she walked down the aisle between the rows of tables. When she bent over to talk to a customer Woody could see the line of her bikini underpants. When she bent over to talk to Woody, he could see the tops of her breasts, nestled in half-cup bras.

Woody came down to the *osteria* more and more frequently, and then every night, and whenever she sat down at his table she'd touch his arm. Sometimes she'd stand next to him, leaning over, with her hand on his shoulder. Her touch was an invitation, and why not? They were, he thought, two adults, two seasoned campaigners in the wars of love. There was no reason they shouldn't come together, shouldn't become lovers. But once again Woody found himself, like someone lost in the woods, circling back towards his adolescence, choosing the comfortable fantasy over the threatening reality of another person, masturbating in his room at night instead of . . . whatever it was adults did to get the ball rolling. In his fantasies things just sort of happened. One minute they were chatting and the next they were locked in a passionate embrace. But sitting across from her, or next to her, at a crowded table, he couldn't imagine speaking the clever things he spoke to her in his fantasies. Everyone at the table would stop talking and turn to look at him. Everyone in the *osteria* would turn to look.

The book she was working on was called *Errori della Tavola, Errors of the Table*. Not a very inviting title, Woody thought.

"What's an 'error of the table'?" he asked.

It was Saturday noon; the fifth week of the fall session of the trial had concluded with the interrogation of the president of the Comitato Parlamentare, who had confirmed the existence of a SUPER-SISMI—a doubly secret secret service agency concealed behind the regular secret service agency. Woody had met Gabriella at the fountain in Piazza Nettuno, presided over by a giant statue of Neptune by Giambologna, and she'd taken him to the Osteria del Sole for lunch. "They have a great lunch," she said, "but you have to bring your own food." The oldest *osteria* in Italy, dating back to the fifteenth century, the Osteria del Sole served nothing but wine. "And if there are too many clients, they throw everyone out and play cards among themselves."

She bought salami, prosciutto, bread, cheese, olives, fruit, and *cicioli* or pork cracklings, which she called *tzitzioli*, in small shops along Via Pescherie Vecchie. Back at the *osteria* she ordered two glasses of a special white wine and they sat down at a table under a small window.

"Doesn't look like we're going to be thrown out," Woody said.

"I've *heard* that's what happens; I haven't witnessed it."

She started to open the packages of food. *"Errore numero uno,"* she said, holding up one finger. "Guess."

Woody had no idea. "Putting your elbow on the table while you're eating?"

She laughed, and then became serious.

"Serving red wine with fish?" he said.

"That's not so serious," she said. "A nice young Rosso del Bosco with fresh tuna? Why not?"

"Then I guess I don't know."

"What's the first thing a newborn baby sees?" she asked.

Woody shrugged his shoulders. She touched one of her breasts with her middle finger. "Mother's breast?" he said.

"Right. Second thing?"

"I don't know."

She patted her cheek with her fingertips.

"Mother's cheek?"

She shook her head and placed her hand on her face.

"Face?"

"Right. Third thing?" She leaned across the table and touched his face with her fingertips.

"Father's face."

"Fourth thing?"

Woody lifted his head up and rolled his eyes back as far as they'd go. "I have no idea."

"Italians dumping Parmesan cheese on everything!"

Woody laughed. "You're joking."

"I never joke about food."

"What's wrong with Parmesan cheese?"

"Nothing's *wrong* with it, Whoody. Parmigiano-Reggiano is the noblest cheese in the world. In the country of cheese, Parmigiano is king. With *tagliatelle alla bolognese,* of course you serve Parmesan cheese. With tortellini, or *cappelletti in brodo.* With *risotto alla milanese.* But Whoody, imagine a risotto prepared with wild mushrooms, porcini or chanterelles. Who is your protagonist, Whoody?"

She waited for him to answer.

"The mushrooms?"

"Of course. You don't want to cover your protagonist. You want to support him. Do you understand?"

Woody said he understood, though secretly he couldn't imagine a risotto without gobs of Parmesan cheese on top.

"Or *spaghetti alla puttanesca,*" she went on, "a southern dish. You don't want to cover the anchovies with cheese, do you? No. So you season it with *peperoncini,* hot pepper flakes, not Parmigiano."

Back in St. Clair he'd been regarded as the ultimate authority on Italian cooking, but now he had nothing to say.

"A piece of Parmesan with a simple salad on the side, and a glass of Lambrusco." She made little kissing noises.

"Well," he said, "I guess I've got a lot to learn."

"Quite a lot, I think," she said, picking up an enormous green olive and putting it in her mouth. "It's very smoky in here."

She opened the window behind them, but a large man in a white apron—a man in his late sixties or early seventies—came over to the table immediately and closed it.

"It's very smoky in here," Gabriella said. "I thought we'd get some air."

"This is a place for smokers," he said. "If you don't like it, you'll have to go somewhere else."

"So," Woody said, "maybe we'll get thrown out after all."

"Eat," she said. "*Mangia tutto.* Eat it all up."

"What's error number two?" he asked.

"I think we'll save that for another day," she said. "One step at a time. *Piano, piano.*"

THE PROCEEDINGS the next morning began with the interrogation of Alberto Solerio, a double agent, though it wasn't clear whether he was a member of the secret service who had infiltrated ORA— Ordine Rivoluzionario Armato—or a member of ORA who had infiltrated the secret service. Solerio's testimony was so evasive and so inconsistent with his earlier statements to the *giudice istruttore* that he was placed under arrest at the end of the day.

Woody, who had become used to the Bolognese accent and to the inquisitorial mode of the proceedings, was able to understand everything. He was still acutely conscious of having made *brutta figura* on the witness stand, but his discomfort there had actually opened a door that admitted him to another Italy, an Italy characterized by serious purpose, by a commitment not to personal revenge but to social justice, by an anger directed not at individual terrorists but at a government that lacked the political will to root out the legacy of fascism. He'd been working with people at the Association, who were glad to have an American presence, and with the lawyers for the *parte civile*, who were never too busy to help him understand the finer legal points of the proceedings. At the beginning of the last week of October he resumed his seat with the families of the victims in the front of the courtroom.

That night, after sending off an article on the involvement of the Italian secret services with neo-fascist groups and with Fraternità e Lavoro, Woody drank his customary quarter liter of red wine and then asked Gabriella if he could play his guitar in exchange for a meal. It was a Monday night, but the *osteria* had filled up early; only a few empty chairs remained at the long tables. Later on it would be even fuller, especially since the garden had been closed down for the winter. A few smaller tables had been tucked in corners. There were no tablecloths on the tables, just paper placemats with word games and riddles printed on them.

A group of young people sat at a table near the door drinking Coca-Cola. Two or three drank beer. At another table a group of men—it was hard to place them: were they poor or rich? Woody couldn't even guess at their occupations—were passing a book around. At another table two young women were arguing about something, a bottle of white wine between them. A bottle of mineral water too, and four glasses. A few old men were tucked in here and there, at the end of a table, or between two groups, and there were a few single women too.

Gabriella had been going over a bill with a customer at Woody's table. The man had changed his mind so many times about his first course that he couldn't remember what he had actually eaten.

"I couldn't afford to let you play for a meal," she said to Woody when the man finally left; "we're too small. But you could play and then ask the clients for money. You've seen Jorge."

"Jorge?"

"The man with the harp."

"*I* couldn't do *that*," Woody said.

"Why not?"

"I just couldn't, that's all."

"You couldn't ask for money? Of course you could. Just play for fifteen minutes, then pass the tray, then play another song and you're done."

Woody's heart was pounding. "I couldn't do it," he said again.

She shrugged her shoulders. "Have you written to New York about the book?"

Woody waved his hand in front of his face. "I want to go over the manuscript first," he said. "I've got to have a better idea. And I'm not sure about the title. 'Errors' doesn't sound very inviting. *Errori della Tavola.*"

"Whoody," she said. "People care about food. They want something authentic. They want to know. You were curious, admit it."

"It's not quite the same in the States," he said; "but yes, I was curious."

"You see."

He ate a plate of prosciutto and fresh figs and then went up to his apartment to get his guitar. "I'm coming back," he said to Gabriella as he paid his bill at the counter near the door.

"You're bringing your guitar?"

He nodded. It was cool, almost chilly. His own door, next to the entrance of the *osteria*, opened into a long corridor that led to a small courtyard with two stairways leading up to the upper floors. His apartment was on the second floor. He sat on the bed for a few minutes, going over a playlist in his head, and then he made sure the guitar was in tune.

It was just the kind of atmosphere Woody liked best. Not too critical. Not totally focused on him. People were occupied with other things so that the music could enter their lives indirectly, could be part of these *other things*, whatever they were, could become part of whatever the two young women were arguing about, for example, so that later, when they remembered . . .

The guitar itself was enough to attract attention. The people at the tables close to Woody stopped talking and looked when he took it out of the case. He sat on a straight-backed chair in the back of the *osteria*, in front of the doors that opened into the garden, and rested his left foot on the bar of a second chair and started to play: "Mr. Jelly Roll Baker, let me be your slave." He knew enough to plunge right in, not to play tentatively, but to play as if he knew what he was doing; to play as if everyone had been waiting just to hear him.

"When Gabriel blows his trumpet, you know I'll rise from my grave, for some of your jelly; some of your sweet jelly roll. You know it's doin' me good, way down deep in my soul." It was the first song he ever learned from a record, an Otis Spann album. It had taken him a month of hard work. He leaned into the music like a man leaning into a strong wind, till there was a kind of equilibrium. Tension. Stasis.

"There was a man in the hospital, all shot full of holes. Nurse let that man die; she had to go get her jelly roll; she loves her jelly, loves her sweet jelly roll. You know it's good for the sick; sho' 'nuff good for the whole."

He climbed up the neck to an E7 chord on the ninth fret like a man who was not quite sure where he was going, like a man who was just trying to keep from being blown away. And then he turned a corner and found himself out of the wind on a quiet street that took him home. He was enjoying himself, relaxing into the present moment, putting the trial out of his mind:

> (You know) I was sent up for murder,
> Murder in the first degree;
> Judge's wife cried out
> You got to let that man go free;
> 'Cause he's a jelly roll baker,
> Bake the best jelly roll in town.
> You know he's the only man around,
> Bake good jelly roll with his damper down.

He could remember Mac of all people explaining that phrase to him: *bake jelly roll with your damper down.* That was the day Mac had taught him how to tie a tie properly.

He sang the first verse again, this time in Italian:

> *Signor Pasticciere,*
> *lasciami essere la tua schiava;*
> *Quando Gabriele suona la tromba*
> *tu sai che mi alzarò dalla tomba,*
> *Per qualche dolce;*
> *per qualche dolce marmellata;*
> *tu sai che mi fa star bene;*
> *Penetra profondo nell' mi'anima.*

The audience was with him now, laughing; someone asked him to sing it again; Gabriella brought him a small glass of wine. She was laughing too.

He played Big Bill Broonzy's "Willie May," and then Mississippi John Hurt's "Candy Man." And then he dropped the low E string down to a D and played Taj Mahal's version of "Sweet Home Chicago." The younger people knew it from the Blues Brothers film and began to sing along on the chorus: "Back to that same old place, Sweet Home Chicago." Taj Mahal sang "Back to that livin' large city," and Robert Johnson, who was weak on geography, sang "Back to the land of California."

He played for an hour instead of fifteen minutes, and then put the guitar away, tired but satisfied, gratified by the applause. He hadn't touched the glass of wine Gabriella had brought him. He drank it down now, put the empty glass on a table, and walked up to the register in the front, where Gabriella was waiting. She handed him a tray, one of the little brown plastic trays the waiters used when they brought the check.

"What's this for?"

"Money. You have to ask for money."

"Money? I couldn't do it. How about something to eat?"

"I already told you; let the *clienti* pay. *Chiedi, chiedi*. Ask. Ask." She waved her hand.

"I couldn't do it. Really."

"Of course you could do it. What are you talking about? *Chiedi, chiedi.*" She put the tray in his hand. Woody was not prepared for this. The guitar was very heavy in his hand. He set it down. It was eleven o'clock. He was hungry. He suddenly wanted another glass of wine. He wanted to fuck one of the girls who'd continued their argument, off and on, all the time he was singing. Either one. They were both young. They wore tights under skirts so short they might as well not be wearing them. They kept their long legs spread wide apart, feet planted, as if ready to leap into the air, over the table at each other. He'd been watching them. Singing to them, in fact.

"*Chiedi*," she said again, "and then I'll give you something to eat. Maybe a nice *tomino*, but you have to pay. This isn't a charity establishment."

The plastic tray was heavier than it looked.

"You just go to each table and say '*Per la musica.*'" She took him to a table in the corner behind the door, leading him by the hand. "*Per la musica,*" she said, taking his elbow and pushing his arm forward. The tray tipped. "Hold it level," she said. "I don't understand you. This is business."

She seemed to think it was perfectly normal to ask for money. To beg. Well, why not? he said to himself. But as he went to the next table, and then the next and the next and the next, he knew that he'd entered a place he'd never been before. He had crossed the border into a new country. *Per la musica, per la musica, per la musica.* The money piled up on the tray. Everyone gave generously. At least a thousand-lire note; often more, two thousand or five thousand; and there were eight or ten people at each table. The two *ragazze*—that's how he thought of them; you couldn't call them "girls," and they didn't look like women to him—were good for two thousand lire apiece, and one of them told him how much she liked the music. Her boyfriend played the guitar, she said, and had taken her to hear John Jacksons last summer. "Jackson," Woody corrected her. He told her that he knew John Jackson, which was true. John Jackson had come to St. Clair. Woody'd arranged gigs for him at the high school and at the prison too, and on Saturday night he'd come to a party at Woody's and Woody'd recorded over thirty songs. (Later he found out that the "John Jacksons" who'd given a concert at the Palasport di Casalecchio di Reno was someone else, a pop singer, not John Jackson from Roanoke, Virginia, but Jon Jacksons from New York City.)

Woody couldn't believe he was doing this, begging for money. He wanted to ask the *ragazze* what they'd been arguing about (if they'd been arguing, or just talking animatedly), but he went on to the next table. *Per la musica.* He collected so much money it kept falling on the floor. He didn't think to fold some of it up and hold it in his hand, or put it in his pocket, till Gabriella, who followed him from table to table, suggested it. He had trouble folding it. Finally he just wadded it up and shoved it in his pocket. He was embarrassed and humiliated, but exhilarated too. As if he'd done something shameful; as if he'd been caught masturbating; but then no one cared; no one else thought it was shameful. It was perfectly all right.

AFTER THAT Woody played almost every night. He even developed a regular following, a few people who asked for the same songs over and over: "Police Dog Blues," "Sittin' on Top of the World," "John Henry," and, of course, "Mr. Jelly Roll Baker." *Signor Pasticciere.* Woody was good at improvising and sang part of every song in Italian, usually just the first verse, but sometimes more than one. Every night after passing the tray he'd sing one last song and then sit with Gabriella till she closed up, about two or three in the morning. He started taking a nap in the late afternoon so he wouldn't be too tired. On the weekends she showed him the city. Every little street had, for her, a special memory, a special meaning, which she tried to impress upon him as if she were stamping an envelope with a rubber stamp. Via Marconi was straight because that's where the American planes had strafed it as they were taking out the German ammunition dump at the end of the street, near the station. Here was a portion of the old medieval wall, the second wall. The two towers. The *portici.* Santo Stefano. One Sunday she took him on a bicycle ride (he rode her niece's bike, which had a very uncomfortable seat) out to the river. There were canals under the city, she said. He didn't believe her. They bicycled down Via Riva di Reno. Woody saw with his own eyes, through an opening in the street that contained a machine to strain out garbage, a canal flowing underneath them. On Via Piella, a little street not far from the center—a perfectly ordinary Bolognese street with bars and an *osteria,* a *cartoleria, portici*—they leaned their bicycles against the wall near an opening covered by a wooden shutter.

"Open it," she said.

Woody opened the shutter. He couldn't believe his eyes. It was as if he'd opened a window onto Venice. Small boats floated in a narrow canal. Washing flapped on lines strung over the water. The surface of the canal reflected the houses and the sky and the shirts on the clotheslines.

Woody closed the window and looked around him. He was back in Bologna. He opened it again, and he was in Venice.

"You mean there are canals all over the place under the city?"

"Not all over the place; but in a few places."

"But you can't see them?"

"Just in a few places. You have to know where to look."

"Why did they cover them up?"

"They needed room for streets."

Woody couldn't get over it. It was like a trick postcard. You look at it one way and you see one thing; you look at it another way and you see something else. A city hidden in the city. Romantic Venice concealed in earthy Bologna. But you had to know where to look. He thought that people were like this too, concealing within themselves wonderful romantic places. You just had to find the window, the shutter on the wall, and open it. He knew that he'd just been propositioned.

Back at his apartment—he had never been to Gabriella's house, though he knew where it was—he was going to fix *spaghetti alla carbonara* for her. He'd fixed it a thousand times and didn't see how anything could go wrong.

She couldn't conceal her skepticism. "An American man? You must be quite something, Whoody, if you can prepare a good *carbonara*. Are there a lot of men like you in America?"

"I love to cook," he said. "I've always done the cooking in our family."

"Tell me how you prepare this *carbonara* in your kitchen."

"There's nothing to it. You beat up two or three eggs and add a little pancetta. We can't get real pancetta in St. Clair, but American bacon works if you parboil it first. Some *peperoncini*."

She wagged her finger at him, from side to side. She was sitting on the little couch she'd bought for the living room of his apartment, not exactly a living room, really, but an extension of the kitchen. "You must not put the pancetta in with the eggs."

"Why not?"

"It keeps them from cooking properly when you add the pasta. But put in a lot of pepper. Black pepper. But the real secret," she went on, "is not to drain the spaghetti too much. You leave a little of the boiling water to cook the eggs fast. Shake it one two three in the colander, no more, and add it immediately to the eggs and mix it together. Then you can add your pancetta and your *peperoncini*. Do you understand me?"

He'd forgotten that sometimes the eggs were runny. At home he served *carbonara* in a Spanish earthenware pot that he could use on top of the stove. He'd put the pot on the stove for a minute or two to cook the eggs, but then they'd be like scrambled eggs. He'd forgotten all these things. But now he understood. He beat the eggs with a fork in a large bowl, and when the spaghetti was done he shook it one two three in the colander and poured it into the eggs before all the water had drained off. She was standing over him watching.

"*Bravo. Perfetto.*"

They ate the *carbonara* and a salad that contained every type of lettuce Woody'd been able to find at the *ortolano* on Via XII Giugno.

"The first time I came to Italy," he said, "I took an intensive language course. This was in Rome, at Scuola Leonardo da Vinci. Eight hours a day. Including lunch. There was an Englishwoman there who ran a hotel in Austria. They had a lot of Italian clients and she wanted to learn more Italian. But she was a tyrant about the salad. You wouldn't believe it. She'd put some oil in this big spoon and add some salt and mix it around with a fork; then she'd put it on the salad and stir everything around. Then she'd add some pepper and stir again. Then the vinegar. The rest of us were glad when she left. We thought now we could do anything we wanted to."

Gabriella looked at him disapprovingly. "Whoody," she said, "she was right. That's the proper way to dress a salad. You coat the leaves of the salad first so the pepper will stick. Then you add the vinegar last. If you add the vinegar first, all the salt and pepper will run to the bottom."

"It's just that she made such a big deal of it."

"It *is* a big deal, Whoody. These little things are important, don't you think?"

"Do you like arugula?" he asked. "You can't get it in the States, you know. But I planted some in my garden."

"I think this whole country has gone crazy over arugula. A little bit, to flavor the salad. *Basta.* A nice green salad," she said, leaning back, "you have a base of nice tender lettuce, and then you season it with a few leaves of arugula, a bit of radicchio for color, a bit of endive. You don't want to be overwhelmed. You don't want to destroy the balance."

When she went to the bathroom he picked through the salad, taking out as much of the arugula and the radicchio as he could, so the salad wouldn't be too explosive. He dressed it the way the Englishwoman had, wondering how many times he'd told the story about her. He'd have to revise it now. It was more complicated.

After supper. After supper they went into the bedroom.

The sheet didn't fit the bed properly, but he'd gotten it tucked in pretty neatly. It was a clean sheet too. He'd just washed it in the terrible washing machine in the bathroom, a German machine with impossible instructions. *Pumpen*. It didn't stop by itself. It shook and shook and jumped all over the bathroom. *Pumpen*.

Nothing else to do but go to bed. Two seasoned campaigners in the wars of love, he told himself for the hundredth time. This moment had been inevitable from the beginning. Two lonely people, thrown together by chance. There was nothing out of the ordinary in the situation. It was a way to pass the time, to satisfy the urge, to hold loneliness at bay for a while.

She was wearing a short skirt with buttons all the way down the front. But the buttons were for looks only. She unsnapped a hidden snap at the back and the skirt fell to the floor. She picked it up, folded it carefully, and put it on the built-in shelf where Woody kept his notes in folders, American folders that weren't quite big enough for standard Italian paper.

He could already foresee complications. She was needy. That was the word. He'd laughed when she told him she'd tried computer dating.

"It didn't work," she said. "I'm too strong; I'm too complicated."

"No, no," he'd said in protest, not knowing exactly what he was protesting. Certainly not that she wasn't strong or complicated.

She took off her blouse and turned her back to him so that he could unsnap her bra. Then she turned towards him. Her breasts were about twice the size of Turi's, and when she lay down on the bed, on her back, they fell to either side. Her pubic hair curled out from under her bikini underpants like wisps of dark flame.

He was beginning to feel less seasoned. He didn't feel very seasoned at all, in fact. He could still count the number of women he'd made love with on the fingers of one hand, Turi being the fifth. He wasn't one of these Italian men who walked around like kings, their jackets wrapped around their shoulders like capes. He was just Woody. Once again, he thought, instead of moving on into his *vita nuova*, his new life, he had circled back to a time in his adolescence, to a time when all he knew about sex he'd learned from a book called *Into Manhood* that had appeared mysteriously on his desk one day when he was about fourteen or fifteen; and all he knew about women's bodies he'd learned from the pictures in *Playboy*.

He asked her to turn over. He pulled the top sheet up over her and began to rub her back. And the back of her neck. He felt safer—less unseasoned—when she was covered. He thought of her ex-husband, who'd come into the *osteria* one evening—an extraordinarily handsome man who had in fact worn his coat over his shoulders. What had gone wrong? She couldn't bear to live in Florence, so far from home. He imagined other lovers she must have had, handsome Italian men who had trodden the path he was about to tread, churning up the muck at the bottom, leaving traces behind them like muddy footprints.

He was standing in front of his mythology class, offering his students a choice between Penelope and Calypso, knowing all along he would choose Calypso, just as he knew he would choose formless immortality over a well-wrought life. And he knew that he'd always known this. But then, he didn't have a choice, did he? Maybe that was the point.

He thought of a line from one of the songs he'd played the night before: *"Who's been digging my potatoes while I'm gone?"* And he thought about the *carbonara*, how the eggs had been cooked perfectly, and about the salad. She had eaten the salad, but she'd picked out most of the arugula and the radicchio and left them on the side of her plate.

He began to rub her lower back and to kiss the back of her neck. He told himself that if it hadn't been her it would have been someone else, maybe the girl who'd told him she liked his music, who'd been to the Jon Jacksons concert. And he thought of Turi. What an odd stroke of fortune. He'd received a letter from her, at the Association, reminding him of their anniversary, October thirty-first. She was doing well, she said; her classes were easier than she'd expected; she was playing the field, staying out of major trouble. Her father wanted to see him, she said in a P.S. that made Woody apprehensive. Her mother too. He should give them a call in Rome. She included the number of her father's private line. Her father, she said, had been very curious about her underpants—what had they been doing on Woody's clothesline?—and the whole story had come out on the trip back to Chicago. Baba Joon and Mama had not been happy. She hadn't mentioned it when she'd called him during the summer because she hadn't wanted to worry him, but now she thought he ought to know. He didn't know exactly what his feelings were, but they were complicated by another letter, from President Hanson at St. Clair, who also wanted Woody to call. ASAP. Alireza Mirsadiqi was holding up the money—the ten million dollars—until a few things had been cleared up, and he, President Hanson, hoped that Woody would consider this year a well-deserved sabbatical and that he would resume teaching in the fall. But the main thing was to talk to Mr. Mirsadiqi and get him to release the money. The president could not emphasize enough how important this was for the college.

Woody pulled the sheet down to Gabriella's waist and continued rubbing. He kept her buttocks covered. He wasn't sure just what he was doing. He wasn't exactly frightened, nor was he exactly excited. When he lowered the sheet farther he saw that her underpants were wedged up a little between her buttocks. He loosened them with his fingertips and smoothed them with his hands. He couldn't really feel anything with the tips of his fingers, which had become hard and smooth as stones from the guitar strings. But when he put his fingers under the edge of her underpants he could feel the skin of her buttocks on the backs of his fingers. Then he spread the palms of his hands out on her underpants. Then he slid them under the smooth silk. It was an extraordinary sensation. Whoever could have imagined such a thing? He couldn't remember anything like it. It was as if he'd never touched a woman before.

She turned over and peeled her underpants down while his hands moved over her body, her breasts, pausing at her nipples, which he rubbed lightly with the palms of his hands. He climbed over her so he could be on her left side. (The fingernails on his right hand were too long to touch her between her legs.) He moistened the tip of his middle finger and began to explore this mysterious terrain, but she pushed his hand away, pulled the sheet back over her; and he knew that she was frightened too. Or at least a little nervous. He was still dressed. He unbuttoned his shirt and took it off. She had her eyes closed, but not all the way. He unbuckled his belt and took

332

his pants off. His erection popped out of his shorts and she reached over, took it in her hand, and then pulled her hand away as if she'd touched a piece of hot metal; but then she took hold of him and pulled him towards her.

He kissed her for the first time, and when she arched her back he put his hand back on her cunt. This time she didn't push him away. She put her hand on top of his, moving back and forth till she was ready. "Why don't you put it in," she said.

Woody went into the bathroom and rummaged in his dopp kit for a rubber; struggled with the wrapper. When he entered her she let out a little cry and wrapped her legs around him, and he felt he'd entered a place as strange and unexpected as the place he'd seen through the little window on Via Piella, Venice tucked into Bologna, a romantic city of canals hidden away inside prosaic Bologna. And it was there all the time, every day. You just had to know where to look for it, and he'd found the place. His body ached with the discovery, ached with gratitude.

"*Attenzione, attenzione,*" he whispered into her ear. He wanted her to be careful, not to make him come right away.

She laughed. "*Attenzione, attenzione,* the king is about to read an important proclamation." But she must have understood him because she slowed down. He moved on top of her in a slow circle. *Piano, piano.* No gymnastics, no fireworks, no hot peppers. More like a plate of pasta with a simple tomato sauce after too many elaborate dinners. After about ten minutes her eyes glazed over. Everywhere he touched her made her moan. She kept her hands on his bottom, digging her fingers in between his buttocks, harder and harder till there was no turning back.

"*Attenzione,*" she cried out. "*Attenzione,* Whoody. *Attenzione, attenzione,* I'm coming."

She came and then he came. She started to laugh and kept murmuring "*Attenzione, attenzione*" in his ear, but after a few minutes she started to cry. She turned away from Woody and cried softly into the pillow, and Woody held her. He didn't ask her why she was crying, and she didn't tell him, but he thought he knew: they were two strangers whose paths had crossed in a wonderful place, a place like Venice, a place they'd both visited long ago and which they would soon be leaving behind.

ABOUT A week later the harp man came into the *osteria* while Woody was playing. Woody was a little worried. He'd been encroaching on the harp man's territory; but the harp man sat down next to him, propped his harp up on a chair, and started to play along—blues scales and riffs, or something like them in a pentatonic scale—over whatever Woody was playing. He was a real professional, from Argentina. The harp, which was Peruvian, was loud, piercing. There was nothing angelic about it. They played for half an hour and would have played longer, but the harp man had to move on to the next *osteria*. Woody deferred to him in the matter of money. "Go ahead," he insisted. "This is how you make your living."

"But Signore," the harp man said, "this is how you make your living too. Isn't that so?"

"I guess it is," Woody said. And while he was passing around the tray, asking for money, he realized that the new life he'd been longing for, his *vita nuova*, had already begun without his even noticing it.

La Vita Nuova

The problem, Giampaolo Pistrelli was explaining to Woody, who was taking notes, "is how to connect the three groups. You've got your executors, Strappafelci and Bosco and Trimarchi; you've got your theorists, the *mandanti*, the senders, Rosselli and Campobello and della Chiave; and you've got your secret service men, Palumbo and Milazzo . . ." Giampaolo, one of the lawyers for the *parte civile* who sometimes sat with them in the evening, had known Gabriella for years; they had gone to the Liceo Marconi together.

Woody's new life was turning out to be much like his old one. He followed the same routine every day, every week: got up at the same time every morning, had an espresso and a *dolce* in the same bar, the Cafe Tribunale, while he waited for the armored cars to bring the defendants from the Dozza and from Ferrara; he sat in the same place in Aula Vittorio Bachelet; he took notes on the proceedings in handsome black and red notebooks, imported from China, that he bought at a *cartoleria* on Via G. Petronio, near the university, in the same palazzo as Gabriella's apartment, and every afternoon he worked at the office of the Association, writing the articles that he faxed to the *Tribune* every Monday during the noon recess. In the evening he slept from seven to ten and then went down to the *osteria* to have something to eat and to play his guitar. Sometimes he went to other *osterie* with Jorge, the harp man; but at the end of the evening he'd find himself sitting with Gabriella while she counted the receipts and filled out the tax forms. The only difference was that

Gabriella sometimes spent the night in his apartment upstairs, though her father, a nuclear physicist, who had recently retired as director of the European Pressurized Reactor Project, disapproved.

"General Palumbo and Lieutenant Colonel Milazzo . . ." The lawyer paused dramatically. Woody put his pen down and took a sip of wine. "Now why are a general and a lieutenant colonel in the secret service trying to cover up a right-wing bombing? That's the key. Who gave the orders? They're both members of FL, right? Conti and the Brothers; it all comes back to that."

And yet everything *was* different. He was no Dante; and Gabriella was no Beatrice. He was fifty-four, and she must have been about the same age; at least she could remember a time when her mother would call to one of the mule carts bringing produce into the city from the *campagna* and ask the driver to take Gabriella to the open-air market near the station so she could spend the day playing with her cousins; then in the evenings her aunt, her mother's sister, would find a mule cart to take her back home. She could remember a time when no one used olive oil in Bologna, or tomato sauce.

Woody found this hard to believe.

"We used butter, not oil."

"No olive oil? In Italy?"

"There aren't any olive trees this side of the Apennines. And tomato sauce. I remember my father coming back from Calabria with canned tomatoes. He liked to cook and made *spaghetti alla puttanesca*, with anchovies and capers. It was like something from another world."

He was moved nonetheless to buy a copy of Dante's *Vita Nuova* at the Feltrinelli Bookstore by the Two Towers. It was a young man's book, and he'd tried to read it as a young man, in a translation by Dante Gabriel Rossetti, back in Ann Arbor when he was in love with Hannah. It hadn't made much sense to him then, in translation, and the original Italian didn't make much sense now—the God of Love himself, a lord of terrible aspect, feeding the poet's flaming heart to the beloved. It wasn't Woody's style; and yet he always kept his eye on Gabriella when he was playing his guitar on the little dais she'd had built for him in the back of the *osteria*, watching for her glance, waiting for her smile, moved by the sight of her jostling her way towards him with a glass of wine in her hand. She was no angel, but he might have said, with Dante, who imagines himself addressing the damned in hell: "I have seen the hope of the blessed." He committed the line to memory because he knew it would please her: *Io vidi la speranza de' beati.*

The lawyer, Giampaolo, had been in love with Gabriella too, he told Woody, when they were at the Liceo Marconi together, but now he had a wife and three children. He carried their pictures in his wallet. Like Woody he was waiting for her to come and sit with them, but the *osteria* was busy and one of the cooks was sick and she had to help out in the kitchen.

"They think that if they can create enough *tensione*," the lawyer went on, "that the people will welcome a strong leader when he steps forward, but who's it going to be? Conti's too old, and sick—"

"I'm going to lay a little blues on this crowd," Woody said, interrupting, "before it gets any later. Thanks for your help."

"I guess I'll be going too," Giampaolo said, touching Woody's arm. The lawyer paid his bill and the two men left the *osteria* together—Giampaolo home to his family; Woody upstairs to get his guitar. If he hadn't said anything to Gabriella about the letters from St. Clair, it was, he thought, because he didn't want to disturb the equilibrium, the delicate balance between possible futures; it was because, instead of looking back, to the past, he'd started to look ahead, to the future, to a future that was beginning to take shape in his imagination, a future beyond the trial, a future that included Gabriella.

He hadn't mentioned the letters to Gabriella; nor had he answered them. He had put pen to paper several times, but he'd never been able to find just the right words, never been able to set just the right tone. He didn't want to gloat, but he wanted to remind the administration at St. Clair that he now had the upper hand, that until he personally intervened with Alireza Mirsadiqi, the ten-million-dollar gift would remain, as it were, in escrow. If Woody returned to his job at St. Clair in the fall—and the trial was expected to be over in March or April, depending on the extradition of Angela Strappafelci and Franco della Chiave—he wouldn't have to worry; he wouldn't have to worry about putting Ludi through vet school; he wouldn't have to worry about Sara; he wouldn't have to worry about what he was going to do with the rest of his life because he'd be able to pursue his vocation as a teacher; and he thought that Gabriella could pursue her vocation too—a small restaurant, simple but authentic, right in St. Clair. He thought she must be tired of living with her father and her aunt. He even had a spot in mind: the old city hall annex on Charter Street, which had been standing empty for two years. Italian food was universally popular, but Woody had never been in an Italian restaurant in the States that served the meal Italian style—a pasta course and *then* a main course and *then* the salad. He could imagine people driving forty or fifty miles—from Moline and Peoria, even Chicago—to eat Gabriella's food. He'd even thought out a scheme for pricing the different courses so that American diners, used to a single price for a dinner, wouldn't balk. He might even be able to buy back the farm, so that Sara and Ludi would have a place to come home to. He wouldn't be at all surprised if those idealistic kids who'd bought the place were tired of the snakes and mice and other small animals that came into the house at this time of year, looking for a place to spend the winter. He wouldn't be surprised if they were tired of fussing with the old converted coal furnace, tired of trying to force slivers of dry ice down the well pipe when the drill point jammed, tired of bringing bottled water from town and of plowing the snow that drifted deep over the long driveway, even when there was only two or three inches on the fields.

So he was pleased when she invited him, at the end of November, to eat Thanksgiving dinner with her family.

"I didn't know Thanksgiving was an Italian holiday," he said, reaching over to touch her. It was two o'clock in the morning; she was sorting out credit card slips and checks and banknotes into separate piles. Woody was drinking the last of a half liter of slightly fizzy red wine. Earlier in the evening he'd gone to three other *osterie* with Jorge and they'd collected over four hundred thousand lire.

She smiled. "Poppi got an American cookbook at the Coop; they're giving them away. He wants to meet you, and he thought it might be nice to fix an American Thanksgiving dinner for you."

"Thanksgiving's on a Thursday," Woody said, "not Sunday."

"Thursday I have to be at the *osteria*. Sunday, Thursday, what's the difference?"

"There isn't any," Woody said. "I thought your father disapproved of me?"

"Not you, Whoody. He doesn't disapprove of you; he just wants to see me once in a while. I haven't eaten dinner at home in three weeks."

ON FRIDAY afternoon Woody typed up a draft of an article on the *primi pentiti*, the first penitents, whose testimony painted a disturbing picture of the political right in Italy—fanatical neo-fascist organizations, such as Rivoluzione e Ordine and Avanguardia Nazionale and Ordine Rivoluzionario Armato, that hoped to create a state of terror that would destabilize the government and pave the way for a strong leader to step in and restore order, just as Giampaolo had explained to Woody the week before. The fact that the Italian people had not risen up to support the abortive coup d'état of Prince Junio Valerio Borghese, a Fascist war hero, in December 1970 had done little to dampen the revolutionary fervor of these extraparliamentary groups, which multiplied and divided like Protestant sects in the American South.

On Saturday he went with Gabriella to the Etruscan cemetery in Marzabotto, about twenty kilometers from Bologna. On Sunday he went to dinner, an American Thanksgiving dinner, at her family apartment. He took his guitar and a bouquet of flowers. He was nervous, but not *too* nervous.

Ever since her divorce Gabriella had been living with her father and her aunt—her mother's sister—in a sixteenth-century palazzo in the university quarter, just a few steps from Piazza Verdi. Woody had walked by several times, just to have a look, but had never been inside. The entire palazzo, which contained several apartments and, on the street level, the small *cartoleria* where Woody bought his notebooks, had belonged to her grandfather, and just inside the front door of the apartment was a framed notice, like the death notices that are still posted in small towns in Italy. But this was a life notice, a notice offering thanks and gratitude to Dottor Giuseppe del Monte for restoring to life a child, Maria Draghetti, who had been in grave danger of death. Maria's father had composed a sonnet in an antique Italian that Woody couldn't understand without help from Gabriella's father, who read the last part of the poem, in which the doctor is hailed as the conqueror of death, aloud:

> *O vero amico al mortal! tu dei felici*
> *Le fiorite non sequi e facil' orme*
> *Com'è costume degli infinti amici;*
>
> *Ma solo accorri ove il dolor t'invita,*
> *E mentre altri tripudia, o poltre, o dorme,*
> *Tu morte vinci e torni in fior la vita.*

"It's too bad," he said to Woody, "that no one was able to intervene in the case of your daughter, to challenge death on the battlefield and disarm him. I'm very sorry."

Woody had expected something else, a different tone, something more standoffish. "Yes," he said, handing the old man—he had to be in his late seventies—the flowers he'd brought; and then he remained silent because he couldn't think of anything else to say. He looked around for Gabriella.

"This is a house for friends," said Gabriella's father, "but we always put our friends to work. On Sundays," he went on, "the men cook, you and I." He raised a finger in the air. "I have never prepared an American dinner before, so I will need your expert counsel. I have turkey, I have sausages, I have pumpkin, *cranberries*"—he said the word in English—"and potatoes. I have beer if you like. Everything, you'll see."

The house was an old one with lots of oddly shaped rooms, and hallways going off in different directions. On the way to the kitchen, Umberto, which is what Gabriella's father wanted Woody to call him, showed Woody into his study, a huge room full of radios—French radios, German radios, Italian radios, American radios, including an old Philco console like the one Woody had listened to as a boy in Grand River.

"All in working order," Umberto said. "I'm in charge of the Marconi Centennial."

Woody tried to think of something to say about Marconi.

"It's a few years off," Umberto said, "but these things take time.

I have a mechanical television in the basement too; I'll show you when we go down for the wine."

The kitchen was long and narrow with two large windows that looked out onto a courtyard.

"The turkey's in the oven, and I've already made the dough for the pumpkin. We just have to roll it out."

Woody assumed he was talking about pumpkin pie, which Woody had never cared for, but he was talking about tortelli. "Gabriella says you got an American cookbook at the Coop."

Umberto waved his hand at a small paperback on the table with a picture of an American Indian, in full regalia, on the cover. "I use it for a starting point," he said, "to generate some suggestions. The only problem is *cranberries*. I didn't even know the word for them in Italian—*bacche del muschio*. Irma's bringing some. We'll see."

Woody picked up the book and glanced through it. It was full of pictures, poorly reproduced, by Andrew Wyeth and N. C. Wyeth and James Wyeth. Woody assumed that James was a member of the same family as Andrew and N. C. There were some familiar recipes: chocolate chip cookies, brownies, clam chowder—and some sur-prises: buffalo stew, grapefruit-avocado soup, Dakota eggs, and, from the Midwest, Heavenly Hash (prepared with eggs, sugar, but-ter, whipped cream, chopped nuts, and vanilla).

Umberto sprinkled some flour on the table and proceeded to roll out the first of two balls of dough with a *matterello*, a thin rolling pin about three feet long.

"Feel the dough," he said; he indicated a second ball of dough that was covered with a dishtowel. "Roll it around. Like this." He motioned with his hand.

Woody lifted the towel and touched the dough with the tip of his finger.

"With your whole hand," Umberto said; "squeeze, but not too hard. It must be very elastic, you see." He looked over his shoulder. Gabriella was standing in the empty doorway.

"Like a woman's breast, right, Poppi?"

"I didn't say that."

"But that's what you were thinking."

"More like a young woman's buttock than a breast." Umberto patted the dough into a flat circle. "That's how you should describe the dough in your cookbook. Smooth and sleek as a nice firm buttock."

Gabriella laughed.

"My friend Vincenzo," Umberto went on, addressing Woody, "says that in the United States you need three eggs to do what one egg does here." He rolled the *matterello* back and forth over the circle of dough, sprinkled the dough with a little more flour, wrapped it around the *matterello* several times, and then rolled it back and forth rapidly under his hands. "You want to stretch the dough," he said; "you don't want to press it. Your hands go out like this, away from the center. Very easy."

He unrolled the dough, turned it, sprinkled it with a little flour, and repeated the procedure. Gabriella stood behind Woody, her hands on his shoulders.

"Let Whoody try it."

"He can do the second ball, the other cheek." Umberto laughed.

Woody washed his hands and rolled up his sleeves. The doorbell rang just as he was starting to pat the dough into a flat circle, the way Umberto had done, and soon the kitchen was full of people. Woody had an audience: Gabriella's two brothers (Marcello and Pietro) and their wives (Carla and Irma) and more children than Woody could count. The brothers busied themselves with a bottle of a homemade aperitif, and the wives—Woody already had the names mixed up—arranged trays of antipasti that they had brought with them, including a bowl of raw cranberries. One of the wives, Irma, spoke English: "My cousin bring cranberries from the American base in Livorno, but I think they too sour." She made a face.

"You have to chop them up with oranges and add a lot of sugar," Woody said, also in English.

She tipped her head back and nodded slightly. "A lot of sugar, a very lot."

Woody nodded. The brothers lit cigarettes; their wives carried dishes and silverware into the dining room.

Woody had, in his time, rolled out plenty of dough for pies and tarts, but the sideways motion you needed to stretch the pasta dough was tricky.

"The first time it's not easy," Umberto observed. He was mixing salt, pepper, and nutmeg into a bowl of cooked pumpkin, using his bare hands, squeezing the pumpkin mixture in his fists till it oozed out through his fingers. "Would you break two eggs into this?" he asked Gabriella. "Maybe three eggs." Gabriella broke the eggs into the bowl and tossed the shells into the garbage under the sink.

"That would be nine American eggs," Woody said.

The dough kept tearing, and every time it tore, everyone reassured Woody that it wasn't easy the first time and that he shouldn't worry. There was a first time for everyone. You just had to go through it. It wasn't easy, and he did worry, but the sheet of pasta wrapped around the *matterello* got thinner and thinner, and finally Umberto pronounced it done and began to cut it into two-inch squares, cutting around the tears.

"I thought tortelli were made like ravioli?"

"Yes, yes." Umberto nodded his head. "Tortelli are stuffed with pumpkin," he said; "but I prefer the tortelloni shape. It's more interesting, don't you think? Like a belly button. You know the story?"

"About the innkeeper?"

"Yes, he caught a glimpse of Venus, naked, when she visited Bologna, saw the divine belly button."

"I thought it was tortellini?"

"Tortellini, tortelloni." Umberto shrugged to suggest that the difference wasn't important. "The shape is the same—the intricate folds . . ." He took a paper napkin from a holder on the table and wadded up a second napkin to serve as the filling.

"And I thought it was in Castelfranco Emilia, not Bologna."

Umberto threw his head back and rolled his eyes. "You're as bad as my daughter. A stickler for details. She doesn't approve at all. Outside they look like tortelloni, but inside . . . they taste like tortelli. It upsets her; she's very strict, you know. She likes to stick to the old ways. I'm more of a free spirit." He folded the square into a triangle and then folded the triangle around his finger.

"Now you try it."

Woody tried. "I always used circles," he protested.

"Don't twist it," Umberto said. "It's like your collar. You see?"

Woody tried again. "*You're* twisting it," he said to Umberto.

"No, no. I'm holding it flat. Look."

It took Woody a while to catch on, but he finally did.

Umberto cut the sheet of dough, the *sfoglia*, into squares, and

Woody and Gabriella's brothers and their wives began to fill them with the pumpkin mixture. Woody was definitely not fond of pumpkin, but he enjoyed filling the tortelloni, scooping a small spoonful of pumpkin onto the little square, folding it into a triangle, sealing the edges by dipping his finger in a bowl of water, wrapping the triangles around his finger. Gabriella, who had disappeared, had not prepared him for this sort of gathering.

Gabriella's brothers washed their hands and lit more cigarettes. Irma, the wife who spoke English, poured little glasses of the aperitif.

Gabriella returned with a camera with a flash attachment. "Hold up one of the tortelloni, Whoody," she said, "or tortelli. I never know what to call them."

Woody held one of the little stuffed pastas in the palm of his hand.

Umberto raised his glass and everyone fell silent.

"To an American Thanksgiving," he said. They raised their glasses; the flash exploded, and they drank. The aperitif was strong and bitter, made from parsley root and various other ingredients for which they had no common language.

The turkey was served on a bed of *tagliatelle*, surrounded by caramelized onions and sausages cooked on a special rack in the fireplace. It had been stuffed with prosciutto and basted with white wine and then Marsala, and Umberto carved it into slices like a Peking Duck, cutting right through the bones. But the tortelloni, or tortelli, were what really surprised Woody. They were fabulous. Really. He could imagine himself serving them: to Sara and Ludi—who were always after him to make pumpkin pie at Thanksgiving and Christmas—and their husbands, and children; he could imagine himself in his own dining room, looking back on this moment, telling the story, how he'd learned to make them, folding a paper napkin around his finger to show his sons-in-law, fastening it like a collar. Don't twist it, he'd say. No, no, like this. Look. He could imagine Gabriella laughing as she showed them the photo she'd taken, like a Benson & Hedges ad—a kitchen full of sophisticated European types, warm, friendly, knowledgeable about food. And then Woody: tall, pale, American-awkward, holding out his hand with a single *tortellone*, or *tortello*.

LATER THAT afternoon Woody and Gabriella took a bus to Porta Saragozza and walked up to the church of San Luca. The weather was crisp rather than cold, not unlike Thanksgiving at home. They'd finished off the meal with fruit and cognac, and, finally, with a tiny spoonful of homemade balsamic vinegar that Woody could still taste, though he'd had only a few drops, a tiny silver spoonful.

"In 1433," Gabriella said, "they carried the madonna down to the city because the rain was ruining all the crops. When they went into the city through the Porta Saragozza the rain stopped. People have been making pilgrimages to give thanks ever since. For passing exams. For love. For having a child. For recovering from an illness."

"Mmm."

It had started to rain, but it didn't matter, because they were walking under the longest portico in the world—almost four kilometers from the Arch of Meloncello up to the church at the top of the hill. Six hundred sixty-six arches, according to Woody's guidebook, but Gabriella said there were only six hundred sixty-five.

"Six hundred sixty-six," she repeated; "the number of the beast." She shook her finger at him, as if he had proposed something indecent. "I counted them myself. Six hundred sixty-five. This is the Bolognese idea of a pilgrimage—not too rough. They built it so it would be easier to carry the madonna down."

"A lot of work anyway," Woody said. The slope was steep and they were walking fairly rapidly. Woody, who was starting to sweat, was ready for a break. They sat down on a bench that faced a private shrine, set into the wall—a fresco so faded you couldn't make out what it was. A saint, Woody supposed, in glory, though there were several shadowy figures.

"One time my brothers vowed to make the pilgrimage if Mama recovered from an illness," she said. "With beans in their shoes."

"Not good," Woody said.

"She got better for a little while, and they made their pilgrimage. By the time they got to the top Marcello was almost crippled, but Pietro was fine."

"Let me guess," Woody said. "Pietro put *cooked* beans in his shoes."

345

She cocked her head at him. "Really, Whoody, you're too clever."

He'd read the story—about two brothers in the eighteenth century—in one of his guidebooks, but didn't say so. He was starting to feel chilly.

"What are *you* thankful for, Whoody?" she asked. "Anything in particular?"

"I'll be thankful if there's a bar near the church," he said, though he knew that she was asking him for something more. "What's error number five?" he said, standing up. "Or are we up to number six?"

"*Numero cinque*," she said, holding up all five fingers of her right hand. "Pouring cream all over everything; that's French, not Italian."

"Cream is good," Woody said. "We had tortellini with cream in a restaurant in Florence once, just across the river from the Uffizi. Butter and cream and little bits of fresh basil. They were wonderful."

She struck her head with the heel of her hand. "I've got my pork loin," she said, putting her arm through his and then removing it again because she needed her hands to talk. "I've got my capon breast; I've got my mortadella; I've got my prosciutto di Parma. I call these my four evangelists. On them I will build my tortellini."

To say that he'd eaten something in Florence was, he knew, hardly a recommendation in her book.

"You cook the meats separately—the capon and the pork—with a bay leaf, and while they're cooling you make the *sfoglia*. Or you can cook them the day before." She put her arm through Woody's, and they kept on walking. "A little Parmigiano, a little nutmeg, a little salt and pepper, and good *brodo*. *Basta*. So delicate, Whoody, it would be a crime to pour cream over them. The French pour cream and butter over everything to cover it, in case it's not so good. Just *brodo*, and really good Parmigiano-Reggiano."

Woody said that he didn't see why Parmigiano-Reggiano would cover the flavor of the anchovies in *spaghetti alla puttanesca* but not the delicate flavors of the different meats in tortellini.

"You have to respect the integrity of the dish," she said, exasperated. "You have to respect its history. They didn't *have* Parmigiano in the south. Maybe a little pecorino. But just a little. But Parmigiano . . . absolutely not."

Every so often a gate in the wall revealed a house and garden, ordinary life going on, but concealed. You couldn't get a good view of the city center, which was directly behind them, but you could see the Certosa, the big cemetery constructed in the 1820s, after Napoleon made it illegal to bury bodies in churchyards in the city.

"My uncle's buried there," she said. "My mother's brother— 'The dark-gray seal with the heart of a lion and arms of steel; he wore the laurel of victory proudly and brought honor to his country.'"

"A seal?" Woody wasn't sure he'd heard her correctly. A seal wearing a laurel wreath?

"He played water polo," Gabriella explained; "he was on the Olympic team that won the gold medal in 1948. The first Olympiad after the war. Italy's first gold medal. There was a big parade in Rome. It was the greatest moment of his life." She seemed out of breath. They walked for a while without talking.

"Bologna è una città di portici," Woody said after a while. "A line from my *Teach Yourself Italian* book."

"Thirty-seven point eight two kilometers of them."

He looked at her, as he often did, to see if she was making a joke, but she wasn't.

Plaques on the wall named the donors who had financed each of the six hundred sixty-six, or six hundred sixty-five, arches. It took them a little over an hour to reach the church of the Madonna of San Luca. One seventeenth-century church looked much like another to Woody's eyes, though the original church in this case actually dated back to 1194. The view of the city revealed factories and skyscrapers (fifteen or twenty stories) that photographers were at pains to conceal when they wanted to emphasize the city's medieval origins, represented by its towers and its wonderful red roofs.

They paid their respects to the Byzantine Madonna, who had been brought to Bologna in 1160 from the Hagia Sophia in Constantinople, and then poked around the gift shop, which featured, in addition to religious items, different kinds of honey prepared by monks and nuns, and various tonics and potions and lotions, including one guaranteed to reduce cellulite. Woody bought a couple of postcards—views of the city—for Sara and Ludi. Ludi'd been studying for an exam the last time he talked to her. Someone else had been in the room. Saul, probably. She sounded happy. Sara'd been at

347

home too. She'd had lunch at the Drake with the wife of her lover. She thought maybe they would become good friends. Woody didn't have any advice for either of them, but he was glad to hear their voices. So far away. He told each of them that he was fine; a little lonely, but who wouldn't be? He could tell that they were worried about him.

Woody and Gabriella stopped to drink at a faucet on the lower level, near the parking lot. Gabriella took off her shoes and stuck her feet under the faucet and then splashed water on her legs. It had stopped raining, but it was chilly. Gabriella didn't seem to mind.

Instead of walking back down, they walked on past the church to a bar where they stopped for a drink while they waited for the bus to take them back down to the city.

"You see," she said to Woody when they had settled themselves at a table, "your wishes have come true. There *is* a bar, and there *is* a bus that comes every half hour. We don't have to walk back. Are you thankful?"

"Yes," he said; "very thankful."

She reached across the table and put her hand on his arm. "Do you know what *I'm* thankful for?"

He shook his head, though he thought he knew.

"I'm thankful that you came to Bologna," she said. "It's been so long since a man propositioned me, I'd forgotten what it was like."

Woody tipped his head forward and made a face to express his disbelief, but he didn't remind her that *she* was the one who had propositioned *him*.

"I'm very thankful too," he said, "that we've had this time together. I'm thankful that this trip has turned out so well, better than I could have anticipated. I've got an active social life in a foreign language, and that's very important to me. I'm never going to be really bilingual, but I do all right; I eat lunch with other family members from the Association, and with some of the lawyers, and I hit it off with some of the young people at the *osteria*—Carlo's going to be a very good guitarist, you know—and I'm actually making money. My articles are being syndicated in Miami, Minneapolis, Cincinnati, Los Angeles, Boston, and San Francisco; I'm actually making a living as a writer. I'm doing all right as a musician too, which is pretty amazing. Jorge and I collected almost four hundred thousand lire at the Cafe Bentivoglio the other night. And it's all tax-free."

"And you're getting laid regularly," Gabriella said.

"I was coming to that."

Gabriella leaned forward, her hands holding on to the seat of the chair, as if to prevent herself from getting up.

"The main thing," he said, "is that I think I've accomplished what I came to do. Without even realizing it. I can hardly remember what Cookie looked like, I have to look at the picture in my billfold, though sometimes I can still hear her voice, in my imagination, as if she's calling to me from time to time from a boat that's drifting farther and farther out to sea. And maybe this is the way it should be. It's time to turn my back, time to walk away from the shore, to walk inland till I come to a place where I can't hear her voice over the pounding of the surf. Do you see what I mean? And the trial; it's like Roman history. I thought it was going to be more exciting, but there's no real cross-examination, it's all arguing over depositions. Do you see what I mean?"

"You were going to tell me about getting laid."

"*Sì, sì,*" he said, "*allora.*" And suddenly the picture he had of himself telling the story of the dinner to Ludi and Sara, and to their husbands and children, came to him more clearly than ever. He could see Gabriella sitting at the opposite end of the table. He could see the table itself, bottles of wine, mineral water, plates of food, candles. Everything seemed possible.

"'Getting laid,'" he said. "It sounds so ugly when you put it that way." He reached across the table and touched her hand. "What I'm saying," he went on, "is that I've been thinking ahead, past the trial. I've got my job back, Gabriella. All I've got to do is make a few phone calls. You could open a little restaurant in St. Clair, do things right. A *primo* and then a *secondo*. People are hungry for something genuine, the real thing. Even in St. Clair. I'd like you to go with me. I'd like you to be my wife. I'd like to keep on making love to you; I'd like to just be with you. I'm fifty-four, you're . . . you must be close to that . . ."

Everything seemed possible. Everything had become clear.

"Shall we have a glass of *prosecco*?" he asked. He knew that yes to the *prosecco* meant yes.

She didn't say no, but she didn't say yes. She was crying a little, and Woody knew that she was crying for the same reason she'd cried after they'd made love for the first time. They'd both been here before, but they couldn't stay long.

"I couldn't do it," she said. "So far away. In another country, another language."

Their stories had intersected, like the train tracks that crossed in New Cameron. They were protagonists in different stories, minor characters in each other's lives, characters who shared the same stage for a while, as if two plays had gotten mixed up, as if Othello had been courting Portia or Rosalind instead of Desdemona.

But then she wiped her eyes and smiled. They each drank another beer.

"I'm sorry," he said.

"Me too. I couldn't bear it, that's all."

"I'd forgotten. Even Florence is too far away."

She nodded. "You could stay here," she said.

Woody laughed. "I've got my job back. They're actually paying me right now, half salary. The dean's not happy about it, but I'm part of a package." The idea of a small liberal arts college was so foreign to Italian life that Woody no longer tried to explain, but he did explain about Alireza's ten-million-dollar gift, and the endowed chair in classics.

"So why don't you call this Alireza?"

"I had an affair with his daughter. I don't think he's too happy about it. I had an affair with his wife too."

"That's quite astonishing, Whoody. The mother and the daughter. I'll have to keep my eye on you."

"It's not what you think."

"What do I think?"

Woody thought a while, but he had no idea what she was thinking.

"How did he find out? This Alireza. About the daughter?"

Woody explained about Turi's underpants, and about Allison too. Everything. He was feeling freed up, enjoying the luxury of confession to a stranger. For Gabriella now seemed like a stranger to him.

"But he's still going to give the money?"

"Yes, but he wants to have a little talk first."

"Ah. A little talk." She smiled. "Men never like to have a little talk."

"We're having a little talk now."

"We've already had our little talk. Now we're just talking."

Later that afternoon, sitting next to her on the bus that took them back down to the city, he thought to himself that he'd known all along that she'd say no, that she'd never leave Bologna, and that he'd asked her to make things easier, to make her feel better about his leaving, about being rejected. Now she could feel that she was saying no to him. And this way was better. Better for her; better for him too.

But later still, as he opened the door to his apartment, he could feel his own tears foaming up inside him like the foam on the beer he'd drunk at the bar near the church. It was eight o'clock, dark out now, but he opened the wooden shutters on his bedroom window. The pilgrimage had taken four hours. The *osteria* was closed. The courtyard was empty. The tables had been moved inside. All he had to do, he reminded himself, was to make a few phone calls and everything would be all right.

A FEW phone calls and everything would be all right . . . But he hadn't called St. Clair, and he hadn't called Alireza in Rome. The letters and telegrams and phone messages that came to the office of the Association were becoming more and more insistent. It was getting to be a joke. Turi and her boyfriend from Harvard would be in Rome. They wanted Woody to come for Christmas. The college couldn't move from the silent phase of the capital campaign to the public phase without Alireza's ten million dollars. He could sense the dean's struggle to be polite in her letters, and the president's struggle to restrain himself, and the chairman of the board's frustration. There was even a letter from Mac that made Woody think of old Phoenix on the embassy to Achilles. Mac reminded Woody that he, Woody, hadn't even known how to tie a necktie properly when he'd come to St. Clair, and that Mac had shown him on the night of his first president's reception. But Woody couldn't bring himself to respond. He didn't understand his own motives. Oh, it was easy enough to dredge up some motives—revenge, perversity, a desire to make them sweat, to make them appreciate him, acknowledge his importance, anxiety about the little talk with Turi's father. But none of these explanations were adequate to his indecision.

Sara and Ludi wanted him to come home for Christmas; Gabriella wanted him to spend Christmas with her family at her brother's in Modena; Allison wanted him to come to Rome for Christmas. In the end he told Sara and Ludi that he was spending Christmas with Gabriella; he told Gabriella that he was going to Rome for Christmas; and he told Allison that he was going back to St. Clair. What he wanted was to spend Christmas alone. Actually, this wasn't what he *wanted*, but it was what he needed to do.

In his early teens his anticipation of Christmas had become so intense that he'd begun to experience post-Christmas letdown in mid-December, even before Christmas had actually arrived. And then when the kids were young, and they had to drive up to his folks in Grand River, or to Hannah's folks in St. Joe—spending Christmas Eve with one family and Christmas Day with the other, driving along I-94 in all sorts of weather, him doing the cooking wherever they went . . . he'd lost his taste for Christmas. But then it came back to him, an unexpected pleasure of adult life. Cookie had gone off to Harvard; Sara had moved into the dorm at St. Clair; Ludi was still at home. For a period of three years everyone came to their house in St. Clair—grandparents, and Hannah's brother and his family. Woody had been at the center, baking bread, starting new traditions, revising old ones. That was the way he'd wanted it to stay. Even after his folks died and Hannah's folks moved to Florida. Now, a middle-aged man, facing Christmas alone, he wanted to discover if he could stay afloat on a sea of nostalgia.

He bought a small tree and a string of lights. He decorated it with candy canes and stuck candles in empty wine bottles, which he'd deployed around the kitchen-living area—an inexpensive Sangiovese di Romagna that Gabriella disapproved of. And then he arranged his presents around the tree. There was something special from Gabriella, a large package from Ludi and Sara that had been sent special delivery at the last minute, after they'd found out he wasn't coming home, and a rug from Allison and Alireza. The rug, which was tightly wrapped in heavy paper and tied up with twine, had been delivered to the office of the Association by a special courier service. And there were the presents he'd bought for himself, at

Ricordi. Half a dozen blues tapes and a small cassette player. There was a better selection of blues than he'd ever seen in the States—Big Bill Broonzy, Lightnin' Hopkins, Son House, Big Joe Williams, and a few contemporary artists, Paul Geremiah and Rory Block and Roy Book Binder. He wrapped the tapes up individually and stuck them under the tree.

For supper on Christmas Eve he fixed some tortellini he'd bought at Atti's on Via Clavature, where the counterman had told him to cook them in broth. No cream. No tomato sauce. *Brodo. Basta.* With a little Parmesan on top. No one ever sold him tortellini without telling him how to cook them. Just broth. No butter, no cream. After he'd eaten the tortellini he pan-fried a small filet and added butter and garlic and balsamic vinegar to the pan juices, and he fixed a salad with lots of arugula. And he drank a whole bottle of expensive wine, a *brunello*.

When he woke up on Christmas morning he discovered that the worst was over, and he lay in bed till nine o'clock. It was a Friday. He'd had trouble getting to sleep, tossing and turning on waves of nostalgia. But now he felt tired and so heavy that his limbs sank into the bed. He lay on his back in the narrow bed, enjoying a morning hard-on. Not moving or touching himself, just feeling the weight of the covers on his prick, which was pointed down towards his feet, straining to lift the heavy blanket.

The sun was shining in his window, and it was cold. But not really cold, not like St. Clair. Gabriella kept insisting that it got *really* cold in Bologna, but Woody was never sure what she meant by "really," since he didn't know how to convert centigrade into Fahrenheit. It didn't seem *really* cold to him, though it was too cold to open the window. He still had a hard-on when he went into the bathroom and he had to lean over the toilet, one hand on the wall, to keep from peeing on the back of the lid. He showered and shaved, put on a new turtleneck and then a white shirt, and then he went out for a long walk, a walk without a plan.

He'd walked everywhere with Gabriella, who knew every inch of the city, and was starting to feel that the story of the city was a part of his own story. This never happened when he saw a place for the first time, only when he'd come back to a place he'd been before. As he walked he could make out the outlines of the medieval city, the late-thirteenth-century city that had been one of the largest and most prosperous cities in Europe. He could see the outlines of this city, and he could enter it in his imagination. He walked to Porta San Mammolo, near his apartment, where there was some traffic but not much—a bus, a handful of cars. He followed the *viale*, which ran along the course of the old medieval wall to Porta Santo Stefano, and then turned in towards the center of town on Via Santo Stefano till he came to the church. The piazza was perhaps the most beautiful in the city—red and yellow ochres, like leaves turning in the fall. Once there were seven churches here; now there were four, one of them built on the original site of a Temple of Isis. Charlemagne had worshiped here in the eighth century, on his way to France, and people were worshiping here now; but Woody didn't join them. He followed Via Santo Stefano to the Two Towers.

In Canto xxxi of the *Inferno* Dante mistakes a row of giants, who are standing around the well at the very bottom of hell itself, for a city of towers, and when the giant Antaeus picks him up, along with Virgil, and lowers him into the well, he compares the experience to the dizzying sensation of looking up at the Garisenda Tower while a cloud passes over it, moving against the incline. Woody read the inscription again, on a plaque on the tower itself, in Piazza Ravegnana. A traveler approaching Bologna in the thirteenth century would have seen a similar city of towers, almost a hundred fifty of them, rising above the plain like the row of giants that Dante saw, or like the scale model of the city—bristling with towers—that Saint Petronius, the patron saint of Bologna, holds in his hands in at least five paintings in the Pinacoteca Nazionale. The two towers that remained—that hadn't been truncated in the Renaissance as municipal governments strove to assert their authority over the individual families or clans that used the towers as fortresses—tilted at such odd angles that Woody was reminded of a couple of drunks staggering home after a toot. He crossed the city to Via Piella, which was empty. He had the Venice window to himself. He opened the wooden shutter and had a look. Clothes hung on a line over the canal; a boat bumped against a wooden dock. Where would you go in the boat? Woody wondered.

The fixed-price menu at La Torre de' Galuzzi was L. 70.000. Fifty dollars. Woody, who hadn't eaten anything, was feeling a little

dizzy. He was tempted: *Cappelletti Ferraresi in Brodo Villa Gaidello.*
Capon basted with sweet Marsala and stuffed with prosciutto, like
the turkey he'd eaten at Gabriella's. Various side dishes: steamed
broccoli, sweet-and-sour onions, sweet fennel *alla Giudia.* Dessert:
chocolate spice cake, or fresh pears with Parmesan and balsamic
vinegar, or strawberries in red wine. But he didn't want to spend the
money.

Back in his apartment he made a sandwich: prosciutto and olive
oil on the day-old bread. Then some leftover salad. It was almost
five o'clock, time to call Ludi and Sara.

He went to the station to call, as he always did on Sundays—a
half-hour walk. Less. There were people on the street now, walking
off their Christmas dinners, or going out to dinner. Restaurants
were open, and there were lines at the ticket windows at the station.
He drank a caffè at a bar in the station and asked for change for the
telephone. He tried to imagine Sara's apartment in Chicago, over
Powell's Bookstore. Ludi would be there, and the dog. He was short
of breath. There were Christmas lights everywhere. He placed the
call from a phone in the second-class waiting room at the station.
From where he was standing he could see the *lapide.* But then he
could see it wherever he was; all he had to do was close his eyes. The
bomb crater was full of flowers wrapped in cellophane, the stems
bound with red ribbons. Letters and cards too had been tossed into
the bomb crater. He hadn't expected this. He put two one-hundred-
lire coins into the phone, waited for the tone, and dialed; but when
it rang, he hung up. He had to get control of himself. He was almost
there. If he could only get through the rest of this day.

A family came into the waiting room bringing more flowers.
The signora began to cry as she reached up to touch a name on the
lapide. Her husband held her as she ran her fingers over the name.
Woody had seen them in the courtroom on the day he testified. He
waited for them to leave, and then he walked to the stone and
touched it himself. Like the woman, he ran his fingers over the letters of Cookie's name, which was near the bottom of the right-hand
column. The marble was hard and cold, the letters sharp under his
fingertips. Sharp grooves. He touched each letter, and then, on the
far right, he touched the numbers of her age, 22, and then he went
back to the phone. He didn't mind the commercialization of Christ-

mas. He liked shopping in crowded stores; he liked wrapping presents and unwrapping them and throwing the crumpled paper into
the fireplace or a wastebasket; he liked the lights everywhere and the
street-corner Santas and the corny music piped through loudspeakers; he liked "Frosty the Snowman" and "Rudolph the Red-Nosed
Reindeer," which you could hear even on the streets of Bologna. It
was the spiritualization of Christmas that troubled him. The hunger
for birth, or rebirth, the fear of letting go of the old, of being made
new. He dialed again. He heard a telephone ringing three thousand
miles away and then Sara's voice: "Hello?" He could hear Ludi in the
background: "Is it Daddy?" Woody hesitated just a moment before
saying "Merry Christmas."

Children of
the Sun

When, after innumerable delays, Franco della Chiave and Angela Strappafelci finally arrived in Italy, in the middle of January, an unauthorized Roman magistrate swooped down in a helicopter on Ciampino, the military airport in Rome, where a special Italian airforce jet had brought the two prisoners. The magistrate issued unauthorized warrants for their arrest and met privately with them without the presence of an attorney, and the next day it was rumored that della Chiave might be tried separately in Rome, that he might be extradited to France or Germany, that he had already been interrogated by the CIA. A commission was appointed to begin an investigation into the incident that would doubtless drag on for months if not years, but in the end the judges from Bologna prevailed. Della Chiave was brought to the Dozza prison, where, in a press conference, he promised to empty the sack. The sack was going to be completely *vuoto*, as the newspaper headlines put it—empty. Everything was going to be out on the table.

His photo was on the front page of every newspaper, along with that of Angela Strappafelci, who was of special interest not simply because she was accused of actually placing the bomb in the station, but because the thesis she had written at the University of Rome promised to provide a link between neo-fascist theory and praxis. The thesis had in fact never been presented to her committee, and no one had given it any thought till an enterprising journalist from

357

Corriere della Sera turned up a copy—the only copy—in the evidence room at the central police station in Rome. The thesis, *Il Terrore e la Politica*, had been in one of the boxes of books and papers that had come from a closet in Campobello's old office at the university.

Large excerpts from *Il Terrore e la Politica* were published in *Il Resto del Carlino*, and a copy of the entire work, which was about one hundred fifty pages, was published hastily by Einaudi in an edition that sold out immediately. Woody bought a copy at the newsstand in front of the Tribunale and read it in one sitting in his apartment.

Strappafelci's philosophical heroes were Nietzsche and Baron Julius Evola, who had been a leader of the Dada movement in Italy in the twenties, and who had met with Hitler after the fall of Mussolini to discuss the possibility of setting up a new government in Italy, one that would adhere uncompromisingly to the principles of fascism. Evola had inspired three generations of fascist youth in Italy, and his disciples, who called themselves the "children of the sun," thought of themselves as a conservative elite, like the Teutonic Knights, prepared to make any sacrifice to destroy the outmoded rationalist values of the bourgeoisie and prepare the way for Evola's proposed *civiltà solare*, or solar civilization.

It wasn't always easy to sort out Strappafelci's own beliefs from those of Nietzsche and Evola. On the one hand, like Nietzsche, she despised the "slave morality" of the bourgeoisie; on the other, like Evola, she looked back to the organic society of the Middle Ages, which she seemed to identify with J. R. R. Tolkien's Middle Earth—a world in which the great chain of being manifested itself in social and religious hierarchies, in monarchy, in myth and ritual and race, values that had been dramatically eroded since the Renaissance.

Sitting in the *gabbia* in Aula Vittorio Bachelet in the Tribunale, her nose in a book, Angela Strappafelci didn't look to Woody like an *Übermensch* or a Teutonic warrior or a child of the sun, or like someone obeying a higher law that justified mass bombings. She looked like a young woman about Cookie's age—the age Cookie would have been—who was farsighted and who probably needed a new pair of glasses. At least, she held her book too close to her face and had to keep pushing up her wire-rimmed glasses, which slipped down her nose as soon as she pushed them up. She wore a man's shirt that needed to be tucked in, and she looked up only when della Chiave was speaking. Woody hated her nonetheless, and he hated her even more when he learned that the book she was reading was *La Compagnia dell'Anello*, the first volume of Tolkien's *Lord of the Rings*. He hadn't noticed this in the courtroom, but a reporter for *Il Resto del Carlino* had noticed, and Woody read about it in the paper the next morning. He was sitting in the *osteria* with Gabriella and Giampaolo, reading an article on the neo-fascist youth movement.

"It doesn't make sense," Woody said. He was reading parts of the article aloud. "It talks about Pino Rauti's Camp Hobbit—that's where they met. A neo-fascist summer camp, sponsored by the Movimento sociale italiano, in the mountains of the Abruzzi. Think of it: thousands of young people putting on Celtic crosses, listening to Wagner, and reading *The Lord of the Rings* while they prepare to defend Europe against the twin evils of communism and capitalism. I've read *The Lord of the Rings* aloud three times. I can't believe this. Terror is the 'hygiene of history,' the bourgeoisie need to be cleansed by 'a purifying rite of violence' . . . She gets this out of *The Lord of the Rings*, and now she's reading it in the *gabbia*? I can't put it together."

Gabriella was working on *Errori della Tavola*, making some notes. Woody rattled the newspaper. His own piece on della Chiave had been translated into Italian and printed on the first page of the Bologna section. He tried to read it, but he couldn't collect his thoughts.

"You have to understand something, Whoody," Gabriella said. "Italians have always been fascinated with northernness. It's a mythological condition. My cousin ran off to fight with the Nazis at Torgau, when the war was practically over. He was fifteen. The Germans were finished. It was a heroic act. Sacrificial. The twilight of the gods. Ragnorak. The last battle."

"What happened to him?"

"He got killed . . . It was a good thing. He couldn't have come back home. My uncle was a partisan, my father too."

"I can't get a handle on it. On her . . ."

"Maybe it's because she's a woman."

Woody'd heard this opinion before, from the dean. "That makes it worse, you're right. It shouldn't, but it does."

"You think that women are better than men, basically good."

Woody nodded. "I suppose so. I can't help it."

"And it's worse because it was your daughter who was killed."

"I suppose that's right too."

"Did you ever wish you'd had a son?"

Woody shook his head. "The father-son routine never appealed to me. Tossing the ball around in the backyard. Cooking was more my line. The girls are all good cooks."

"Do you think it would be different if your son had been killed?"

"'For God so loved the world that he gave his only begotten son.' John 3:16. I had that drilled into my head in Sunday School. 'That whosoever believeth in him . . .' Something like that. 'Should not perish . . .' 'Everlasting life.'"

"Do you think God would have given his only begotten daughter?"

Woody couldn't suppress a smile. "No," he said. "Not even God could have done that."

THE EVIDENCE against della Chiave, which took several days to unravel, was circumstantial, and his own promise to empty the sack came to nothing. Like others before him, he began by blaming the secret service agencies and finished by denying everything. He himself, he told the court, was a victim of terrorism, state terrorism. His young companions had been hunted down. Members of his own organization, Rivoluzione e Ordine, had actually *prevented* a bombing in Padua in March 1980. *They*, not the police, were the *pompieri*, the firemen.

Woody tried to pay attention to the complicated arguments put forward by the *pubblico ministero*, but he found it hard not to stare at Angela Strappafelci; his eyes were drawn to her, just as they would have been drawn to the outbreak of a fight in the street, or to flames shooting out of an open window. He could imagine, could not stop imagining, how easy it would be to—his mind revolted at the fantasies, sexual in their insistence—to hold her head down in a bucket of water for thirty seconds at a time, then maybe a little longer, forty-five seconds, a minute. Talking to her in between, reminding her of what she'd done, and of what he was going to do as she choked on the water in her lungs. To stop himself he would go out onto the balcony overlooking the piazza, where the lawyers sometimes stepped out for a cigarette, and stand in the cold till his face and hands felt numb.

There was another thing, too, that upset Woody. Her father— Angela's father—had been coming into the *osteria*. He sat in a back corner, not far from where Woody played his guitar, near the doors that opened into the courtyard, drinking wine and eating *tagliatelle* or tortellini. He was dark, a southerner, but he had a broad, flat face and straight black hair that he combed sideways over his bald crown. According to Giampaolo he was in his fifties, not much older than Woody, but he dressed like an old man, in a heavy brown wool suit, and he walked with an old man's shuffle. Woody had noticed him in the courtroom too, but hadn't known who he was till Giampaolo identified him one night. Woody hadn't thought of Angela as someone who had a father.

"Strappafelci," he said. "What kind of a name is that?"

"It's an old Roman name," said the lawyer. "*Felci* are weeds. They grow along the highway. In ditches. Local governments used to hire peasants to pull them up. Now they just poison them. *Strappare*. To pluck. Strappafelci. He's an *ortolano*, a greengrocer. He's rented an apartment on Viale XII Giugno, just around the corner. So he can be near his daughter."

"His daughter's been living with della Chiave in Buenos Aires for seven years?" Gabriella asked. It wasn't really a question. She was just giving the conversation a nudge.

"A suburb of Buenos Aires," Giampaolo corrected. "A big Italian community. Plenty of old Nazis too. Nobody asks too many questions."

"So what the hell was going on in Rome?" Woody asked.

Giampaolo, who had been helping Woody with an article on Filippo Forti, leaned back, thrust out his chest, pulled back his shoulders, opened his palms out, and looked up at the ceiling, right through the ceiling to the night sky.

"How am I supposed to put that into words?" Woody asked.

"You could take a photograph." Gabriella put her hand on the lawyer's arm. "If I get my camera, will you do that again?"

They kept talking for a while, their eyes on Signor Strappafelci.

"Don't let him see you staring at him," said Gabriella.

"Right. Did he have anything to eat?"

"He asked Francesco for *spaghetti alla puttanesca* last night. Francesco told him, 'This is Bologna.'"

"Did Francesco"—Francesco was one of the waiters—"know who he was?"

Gabriella nodded. "I should have told him *you'd* fix it for him. That's one of your specialties, Whoody—*spaghetti alla puttanesca*. But please, no Parmigiano!"

Woody laughed, but he was upset; he played his guitar, but only for fifteen minutes, and he skipped the man's table when he was passing the tray *per la musica*. He stayed away, but the man motioned to him, waving a five-thousand-lire note. Woody backed away. It was too much. But the man stood up and started to push his way out of his corner. Woody leaned over and held out the tray, which was full of notes and change. The man placed the banknote on the tray carefully, pushing down on it as if he were sealing an envelope. Woody had to push back to keep the tray from tipping.

When Woody returned to the table Gabriella and Giampaolo were discussing the terms of Bruno Conti's recent extradition—provisional liberty for reasons of health—which had come as a surprise to everyone.

"It's like seeing Hitler's dad in a McDonald's," Woody said, unable to follow the lawyer's explanation of how it was possible that Conti should be at liberty in Italy but not possible for the Italian government to prosecute him for anything other than a minor traffic violation committed in 1982.

"Don't mention McDonald's," Gabriella said. The city council had recently given McDonald's permission to open a restaurant in the very center of town, on the corner of Ugo Bassi and Via Independenza.

"I think you should ask him to go somewhere else," Woody said.

"You're not serious."

"I'm very serious. I can't stand to look at him. It's bad enough I have to look at him in the courtroom, and his daughter."

"Signore," said the lawyer, reaching over and putting his hand on Woody's arm. "The man sitting at that table"—he nodded towards Signor Strappafelci—"did not put the bomb in the station; and besides, I don't think you want to demonize even the terrorists themselves. That's a step in the wrong direction. You hold them accountable, yes; but they are not demons. You don't want to turn them into the *other*. Terrorism is always a symptom of a political problem . . ." The essentially political nature of terrorism was one of the lawyer's favorite themes.

"We used to stage a debate at St. Clair," Woody interrupted. "The college where I used to teach," he added, though he didn't try to explain what a college was. "Between Freud and Marx. For the whole freshman class. That was before the new dean came along. I always played Marx, and Steve Byrd in Philosophy played Freud. None of the psychologists believed in Freud anymore, but the kids loved it: What's the source of evil and suffering? Why are men at odds with each other? How can you explain constant warfare, domestic violence, senseless murders, serial killings? In Davis Recital Hall. We had posters made—Freud and his mother; Marx and his family dressed up like respectable Victorians—and we both dressed up too. Steve had a monocle and a cigar. We both put on fake beards, and then later we both grew real beards! We'd start out by quoting set passages from the texts at each other—*Civilization and Its Discontents, The German Ideology*—but then we'd start ad-libbing, and that worked fine because we both believed what we were arguing. But it always came down to the same nub, the same bone: the problem of evil. Steve would throw one example after another at me, the Holocaust, the gulags, stuff from last night's newspaper, and I'd have to try to explain it away: the economic causes of World War II, and that Soviet communism wasn't true socialism, that under true socialism you wouldn't have these problems because men would be free. And I believed it. I thought that evil could be explained away, explained politically and economically, that it had been demystified. But I don't believe it anymore."

Both Gabriella and the lawyer leaned forward as if they were having trouble hearing him.

"You can see why Freud's *Todesinstinkt* has been conceptualized as the devil," he went on; "an active principle of evil, not just the Augustinian idea of 'an essential nothingness,' or Hannah Arendt's 'banality of evil.' More like the Puritan devil, Satan, a real devil, not an abstraction."

"What are you trying to say, Whoody?" Gabriella asked.

"My wife," he said—he was confused himself—"she wanted to

think of the *strage* as an act of God, like an earthquake or a tornado, something you just have to accept. That's what we quarreled about. Cookie's tombstone. 'God's will is our peace.' That's what she wanted on the tombstone. *'La sua voluntade è nostra pace.'* But I could never agree with that. I couldn't see it that way. It wasn't a religious issue; it was a political problem. With a political solution. But now I'm not so sure. When I see that woman in the *gabbia*, reading *The Lord of the Rings*, and now her father, slurping his wine and eating noodles . . . Look at him; he's disgusting. Political ideology's just a screen, an excuse, a justification; a cover that we paste over the truth. Freud had it right all along, Freud and Plautus and a lot of others: *homo homini lupus.*" Woody was thinking of Angela Strappafelci, but he was also thinking of himself, discovering in his own hatred, in his own impulse to destroy, the secret that had been eluding him.

THE PRINCIPAL witness against Angela Strappafelci was Filippo Forti. Forti had been murdered in the summer of 1983, so the court had to rely on his depositions, taken over a period of two years, and on the testimony of his mother-in-law, his wife, his housekeeper, and Luigi Bosco, the brother of Angela's boyfriend, Niccolò.

On August sixteenth, according to Forti's depositions, which were summarized by the president, Forti's friends Angela Strappafelci and Niccolò Bosco came to his apartment in Rome. They wanted Forti to provide them with false documents so they could leave the country. *"Hai sentito lo scoppio?"* Angela had asked. "Did you hear the big bang?" Forti assumed she was referring to the bomb at the station in Bologna but didn't ask. They were afraid that someone had recognized them in the station in Bologna. They'd been dressed as German tourists, in lederhosen and alpine hats. Angela had dyed her hair blond, so she needed new identification to go with her new blond hair. Forti at first said he couldn't get the false documents, but Angela threatened to kill his four-year-old son, Stefano, threatened to do to Stefano what they'd done to Francesco Bevilacqua, another one of their comrades from Camp Hobbit and ORA. Forti, who ran a small photocopying shop, got the documents. It took two days, and the quality wasn't very good. He'd been afraid for his son, but it was all he could do.

The defense mounted a ferocious attack on Forti's testimony, arguing that Forti could not in fact have been in Rome on August sixteenth, calling for an examination of Strappafelci's hair by experts to determine if it had ever been dyed blond, and claiming that at the time of the bombing Angela and Niccolò had in fact been in Palermo, in Sicily, where Niccolò had murdered Judge Cipriani, who—like Judge DiBernardi—had been investigating links between the Mafia and various right-wing organizations. The next day the court heard additional testimony from Signora Forti and her mother, Forti's mother-in-law. Both women were confused and uneasy, unable or unwilling to explain inconsistencies in their testimony. Caught up in something they didn't understand, they were no longer sure of anything. Niccolò's brother, Luigi, on the other hand, who had testified against his brother at every step of the way, could not be shaken. Forti, he said, had been like a father to him. It was the first place he'd gone when he got out of prison on August fourteenth, the day before the *strage*. He hadn't actually seen Forti, but he'd spoken to the housckeeper, who told him that Forti was *facendo il pendolino*. That was the key phrase—making the pendulum, going back and forth every day between Rome and his vacation cottage.

Woody was uneasy. He couldn't get rid of the sense that things were out of control, that he was entering a new realm, that still another *vita nuova* was about to open up before him. He still had this feeling when Signor Strappafelci approached him that night in the *osteria*.

"Signor Whodull," he said, "excuse an old man for intruding."

Woody didn't say anything. His first thought was that the man wanted to apologize. Hitler's dad, apologizing to a Jew.

"Signor Whodull," he said, "the United States is a great country, the greatest country in the world. It always try to do the right thing. I'm telling myself, you can help me." He spoke with a Roman accent, but uneducated. He was wearing the same heavy brown suit that he wore every night, and the same woolen tie, spotted with wine and pasta sauce.

"Do you know who I am?" Woody asked.

"You're a father like me, and you're a *giornalista americano*."

"What do you want from me?"

"Signor Whodull, I want you to write something about my daughter for your American newspaper."

"Signor Strappafelci," Woody said, "your daughter left a bomb in the station that killed eighty-six people. One of those people was my daughter. Under the circumstances I don't think we have much to say to each other."

Signor Strappafelci shook his head violently. "The thing is impossible."

"It's very possible. My daughter is very dead, Signor Strappafelci. She's been dead for seven years. She was the same age as your daughter, who is alive."

"But Signor Whodull." Signor Strappafelci put his hand on Woody's wrist, as if to prevent him from running away. "Filippo Forti could not have been in Rome when he says. It's not possible."

"You've read the depositions?"

He nodded. "Yes, I read all the depositions; I listen to the witnesses today. Signora Forti and mother-in-law, they both say it's impossible that Forti went away to Rome for a day."

"I listened to the witnesses too, and I've read the depositions, Signor Strappafelci. You know that Signora Forti and her mother both changed their testimony *after* Forti was murdered?"

"In the deposition of November twenty-second, 1983, they say it was possible, yes. But by March twelfth, 1986, they don't remember so clearly."

"It's the other way around," Woody said. "After Forti is murdered they suddenly remember *more* clearly. Because they're afraid. But Bosco's brother talked to Forti's housekeeper on August fourteenth, the day he got out of prison. Forti wasn't there, but the housekeeper said he was *facendo il pendolino* between Rome and Montalto di Castra. Making the pendulum, Signor Strappafelci. Going back and forth every day. Is that clear?"

"May I sit down?" He took Gabriella's chair at the end of the table. The *osteria* was full. "I don't go to the university, Signor Whodull. It's not easy for me to understand these things. My daughter and Nicco, they go to find Forti, but not in August, in April. Signor Forti is not lying, he make a simple mistake."

"But Angela asked him, *'Hai sentito lo scoppio?'* Do you think she was asking about the big bang?"

"I don't understand."

"The 'big bang,' the creation of the universe."

"You'll have to ask God about that," he said. "It was a boiler that explode, in Via San Donato, not a bomb."

"In August? Why would a boiler be on?"

"That's what I say to you. Not in August, in April." He asked the waitress for a liter of red wine. Woody tried to object, but it was too late.

"But why would they need false papers in April?"

"Angela, she get in some trouble. Hard to get out. You got to have papers in Italy or you can't do nothing."

"Signor Strappafelci, your daughter threatened to kill Forti's four-year-old son if Forti didn't provide them with false *documenti*."

"She say she make him cry, yes, but in April, not in August. In August she was in Palermo. In April a boiler explode in Via San Donato. That's what she mean."

"She didn't say 'make him cry'; she said they'd do to him what they did to Bevilacqua. Do you know what they did to Bevilacqua? Do you know?"

"Nicco say he have a personality disorder."

"Did you read that in a deposition too?"

"Yes, I read many depositions."

"Bevilacqua was their friend, Signor Strappafelci. Their *friend*. They met at Camp Hobbit; they were in ORA together. They killed him and cut his legs off so they could stuff him in a trunk."

"He was going to betray them."

"For what, Signor Strappafelci? What had they done that he was going to betray them *for*?"

"Nicco say he have a small personality, he's a little man."

"And Judge DiBernardi? Did he have a personality disorder too? Was he a little man? Did he deserve to die? You read Niccolò's depositions. Your daughter walked up behind and shot him in the head. As if it were nothing. As if he weren't a human being, as if he weren't a man with a family." Woody made his fist into a pistol and pointed it at his own head. "He was standing outside his house waiting for a bus. They killed him because he was doing his job."

"No, he don't deserve it, but you can understand, can't you . . . ? He sentence Nicco to prison for a traffic violation. He was prejudice from the beginning because he know about the radio station."

"Why shouldn't he be prejudiced? They shot seven women. One

367

of them's still in a wheelchair. While the program was on the air, for Christ's sake. Because they didn't like their politics?"

"But that is not part of the official acts for the traffic case. He got no right to do what he do based on something out of the legal record. He break the law just as much as they do."

"Nonsense. They killed him because he was about to empty the sack on ORA and because he had information about the *strage*, Signor Strappafelci, in advance, *in anticipo*; he knew something was about to happen. He tried to warn his superiors. All his records are on tape. Nine years now and no one can listen to them because they're classified top secret. It's ridiculous."

"The point is, Signor Whodull, these killings, whatever you call them, were *mirati*. Just like the Red Brigades. They were *aimed*. Bevilacqua. Judge DiBernardi. There were reasons to kill them. But the *strage*—the *strage*, Signore, is a different thing. Why would Angie put a bomb in the train station? This *strage* is another thing, Signor Whodull."

"I don't see that as a very strong defense, Signore: 'We murder only one person at a time, so why should you think we'd put a bomb in the station?'"

"Signor Whodull, you are in the courtroom today; you hear the mother-in-law say that Forti always go to Montalto di Castra in August. If he is in Montalto di Castra, how can he be in Rome?"

"He could have driven to Rome; it's only two hours. And besides, Luigi, Niccolò's own brother, says he talked to Forti's housekeeper in Rome. We've already been over this."

"Luigi is a traitor; he say anything to make trouble for his brother."

Woody looked up and saw Gabriella standing in the door to the kitchen.

"I want you to write the truth about my daughter for your American newspaper please. I want somebody to tell the truth about her. These Italian *giornalisti*"—he waved his hand—"all they care about . . . They're *stronzi*, turds." He pinched his nose to indicate how bad they smelled.

"The truth about your daughter, Signor Strappafelci—I'm not sure that's something you want to read about in the newspaper."

THE RUG from Alireza and Allison was very old. Woody didn't know very much about rugs, but he could see that it was the work of a master weaver, a Kerman or a Kashan, he thought. He offered it to Gabriella, but she wouldn't take it. "I couldn't take it, Whoody; it's too valuable. You should get it insured. It must be nice to have such rich friends. I hope you sent them a proper thank-you letter."

"Of course," he said. Actually, he had written to Allison thanking her profusely but insisting that he could not possibly accept the rug, but Allison had written back saying that he should know better than to refuse a gift from an Iranian. Hadn't he learned anything in Esfahan? He had the rug mounted on the wall opposite the bed so that he could look at it while he was lying in bed, or while Gabriella was sitting astride him. He hadn't recognized it at first, but it was the rug that Turi had described, Tanteen Minoo's rug.

"What are you looking at?" she'd say if he put his head to one side so he could see around her; "you're supposed to be looking at me!" and she'd cover his eyes with her hands, and then she'd twist around to have a look herself. It was so beautiful: brightly colored birds on a maroon base, and, at the center, next to a turquoise pool, a fawn sucking its mother's teat.

One Sunday morning they drove out—Woody drove Gabriella's Fiat 500—to a place she had in the country, her Horatian retreat, near Dozza—not the prison but a small town famous for its murals and for the Enoteca Provinciale where Gabriella bought the wines for the *osteria*. She'd said that the house was poor and ugly, but Woody thought it was charming. There were three rooms, one on top of the other: the kitchen, with a stone floor, on the bottom; a sort of salon or living room on the second floor; and a bedroom on the top. On a kind of ledge built out over the stairs was a stereo set and lots of records. Gabriella climbed out on the ledge and put on some music, Bellini's *Norma*, with the volume turned up high.

"We need to put some olive pits in the furnace," she said. Woody could hardly hear her. "Can you lift fifty kilos?"

Woody nodded, not so sure.

"We'll do it together," she said.

The furnace was in a shed next to the house. The pulverized

olive pits were in large sacks, like potato sacks, stacked against the far wall.

"I get a truckload from the Abruzzi," she said, "every four or five years. I don't come out here very often. This is for when I retire."

"I never thought of you as someone who might retire."

"I'm tired, Whoody," she said.

Together they lifted one of the heavy sacks and emptied it into a bin. A screw at the base of the bin fed the olive pits into the *bruciatore*.

"This is amazing," Woody said. "You actually heat this place with olive pits? Somebody brought us a little sack of olive pits once, to put on the charcoal grill. Then we started saving the pits, but I always forgot to use them. We had three or four bushels left when I sold the place."

"I'm too far out in the country to get hooked up to the gas. Olive pits are cheaper than propane."

Not in any hurry, they sat in the kitchen for half an hour with their coats on, drinking a glass of *prosecco* and waiting for the pulverized olive pits to warm them.

Following her up the stairs to the bedroom on the third floor, Woody lifted her long skirt and splayed his hand out on her bikini panties. He'd been afraid that his proposal, and her refusal, in the bar behind San Luca would change things between them. And it had, but not in the way he had anticipated. It seemed to him, in fact, that she too was relieved that there was now no future to worry about or guard against. The danger was past, and they could afford to be more open and reckless with each other. Though neither of them said anything explicitly, they became, at the same time, more thoughtful and more physical too, as if the subtle knot linking their bodies and their souls had been drawn tighter, as if nothing they could say or do now would ever be held against them.

THE DEFENSE was successful in suppressing Angela's thesis, on the grounds that it had been obtained improperly—the police officer who originally found the thesis had not had a warrant to search Campobello's office at the university—so no one would be allowed to ask the questions that Woody found most troublesome, questions that went beyond Angela's analysis of the political conditions that had caused terrorism to flourish in the twentieth century, in Algeria, in Ireland, in Palestine, in Italy; questions that he hardly knew how to formulate, or that he didn't wish to formulate. He had no sympathy for the Red Brigades, or for the IRA, or Hamas; but he could understand them, could understand their aims, could understand the use of terror as a weapon against a superior power. But the suggestion that terror was an end in itself—a "good," in Plato's terms—he could understand only in terms of the feelings he experienced for Angela herself, feelings—he didn't want to name them—that like a cancer gnawed at his side and left an unpleasant taste in his mouth, especially when he found himself at the station, or the Ospedale Maggiore, or walking past the morgue on Via Irnerio, places that reminded him of Cookie's last days, hours, minutes; though to the other people in the courtroom, or in the *osteria*, he seemed perfectly healthy, simply another middle-aged, middle-class man—Molière's *homme moyen sensuel*—who was no doubt looking forward to a glass or two or three of wine at supper.

On Monday Angela surprised everyone by taking the stand herself. Under Italian law she was allowed to do so without submitting herself to cross-examination either by the *pubblico ministero* or by the lawyers for the *parte civile*, though she would be questioned by the president of the court.

She stood facing the president and, speaking in a clear voice, described in great detail how she and Niccolò Bosco had gone to Sicily to help a comrade from ORA escape from Granguardia prison in Palermo, how the escape had failed because their Sicilian contact had been arrested for attempting to break into an army munitions depot, and how, with the help of a third man, they had murdered Judge Gianfranco Cipriani, much as they had murdered Judge DiBernardi, walking up to him and shooting him. The role of the third man was unclear.

It was the first time Woody had heard her voice, and he listened more to the sound than to what she was actually saying, as if trying to understand her on a different level, the way aphasics were said to understand Ronald Reagan when he spoke on television. But when she described the shooting itself, he listened carefully.

"He had just gotten out of his car," she said, "in front of the Palazzo di Giustizia, and was waiting for the driver to drive off. I called him by name, his Christian name: 'Gianfranco.' He looked behind him, and then he looked at me. The car pulled away. 'Gianfranco,' I said, 'I want you to meet someone, I want you to meet my friend Niccolò Bosco.' 'I don't understand,' he said, 'do I know you?' 'Now do you understand?' I said. Nicco had the gun in his pocket. He pulled it out and shot him in the chest, and then he put the gun back in his pocket and we walked down the Via dei Candelai and then over to the Corso. Every time we passed a church Nicco wanted to go in and pray, but I told him, 'Just a little while longer, just a little while longer. Everything's going to be OK.'"

The *pubblico ministero* protested that the murder of Judge Cipriani had all the earmarks of a Mafia killing and that there was no evidence to support the claim that Bosco and Strappafelci had been in Sicily. The president of the court—though he was not an impartial referee, like the judge in an American trial, but the chief investigator—scolded the defense lawyer for springing this story on the court without warning and declared the court adjourned for the rest of the day.

Woody was in a state of shock, but in the *osteria* that night Signor Strappafelci was elated. "I told you," he said to Woody. "They were in Palermo, not Bologna; you heard how they kill Judge Cipriani. It's like Judge DiBernardi. *Mirato.* Aimed. Not a bomb in the station."

Woody'd been over the same ground too many times: *We murder only one person at a time; why would you suspect us of leaving a bomb in the railroad station?* "There's no evidence that they ever went to Sicily."

"Of course there's no evidence. The police want them. They have to cover their tracks."

Woody experienced a powerful impulse to strangle Signor Strappafelci. He wanted not just to refute the arguments; he wanted something more: to open his eyes, tear off the blinkers, make him see his daughter as she really was. He was too upset to play his guitar. He ate a *tomino* and drank a half liter of wine and talked to Gabriella, whose niece Flavia was going to be in a dance recital or program of some sort in a nearby town on Sunday night. Woody agreed to go. Later on, when he saw Signor Strappafelci push his chair back and stand up, though the carafe of wine on the table was half full, he lowered his head as if he were studying the handwritten menu. He didn't want Signor Strappafelci, whose suit was too small even though he was a small man, and whose food-stained tie appeared to choke him, whose cheeks were covered with white stubble though his hair, what was left of it, was still black . . . he didn't want to speak to this man again tonight. But Signor Strappafelci stopped at his table anyway.

"You didn't play your guitar tonight."

Woody shook his head, too angry to speak. No, not angry—he didn't know what to say. "You saved five thousand lire," he said finally.

"The money, it's nothing. The music is everything. It makes the evening bearable." Signor Strappafelci stood by the table, shifting his weight back and forth from one foot to the other. "She used to have a bird, Signor Whodull; Angie did. A parrot. Cost a lot of money. Beccone, she called him—Big Beak. She used to bring him in the store, and when the telephone ring Beccone used to say 'Pronto,' and then he'd make like he was talking on the telephone to someone: 'Sì, um-hum, um-hum, sì, no, sì sì.' Sometime he walk real funny, all kind of hunched over, and he say 'I'm sneaking away.' Nobody knows about Beccone. All those turds know about is Forti and Bevilacqua and DiBernardi."

Woody didn't say anything.

"Beccone's dead," Signor Strappafelci went on. "Long time ago. The Communists killed him."

"The Communists killed him?" Woody was curious.

"On the street. Angie was taking him to the doctor, the vet. She had a little traveling cage for him, a little box I make, like a little suitcase. I got a little fruit and vegetable shop in the Vicolo del Piede in the Trastevere. The Communists were moving into the neighborhood, you know. Trying to take over everything. I didn't want her to go alone, but I couldn't leave the store, and she didn't want to wait till my wife come back because Beccone break off a big feather and she was worried about him getting an infection, and it was only two streets away. But the Communists come and the big-shot leader he put his hand in the cage, and Beccone bit him and then he grab Beccone and squeeze him in his fist till he kill him, and then he throw him in the street." Signor Strappafelci held out his fist. "She never get over it."

"Are you suggesting, Signor Strappafelci, that this childhood trauma is at the root of your daughter's sociopathic behavior?"

"I don't know about that," he said; "but we don't have no *giardino* to bury Beccone. I make a little coffin out of a raspberry flat and we wrap up Beccone in my wife's yellow scarf and take him to Ponte Garibaldi and put him in the river, not off the bridge, but down by the edge of the water. Let the river take him out to the sea, out by Ostia Antica."

Woody checked an impulse to sympathize. "When was the last time you talked to your daughter?"

Signor Strappafelci thought for a moment. "She got better things to do than talk to an old man like me."

It was getting late, after midnight. There were empty spaces here and there at the long wooden tables.

"But she's allowed visitors, isn't she? Rosselli's family comes down from Milan every week; Trimarchi's brother and sister are there every week; and Campobello's family, all the way from Rome. When was the last time she looked at you, Signor Strappafelci? Is there something I don't understand? Does she have more important things to look at?"

"She don't want to see no one," he said, pushing his chair back from the table. "She don't want to hear nothing."

"She don't talk to you," Woody said; "she hasn't talked to you in years, has she? She never wrote to you from Argentina, did she? Not a single letter. She didn't write a single letter, did she? Not one. She don't look at you because you don't belong in her *civiltà solare*." Woody was unconsciously imitating Signor Strappafelci's Roman dialect, his bad grammar. "You and me aren't children of the sun like her and Niccolò and Mussolini. You and me are little men, like Bevilacqua and Judge DiBernardi. We got personality disorders; we can't rise to their elevated conception of things."

"I got an uncle who was Rachel Mussolini's private secretary for twenty years, after the war . . . He was blind. He lost his eyes in the war."

"It's hard to get through to you, Signor Strappafelci."

"You think I'm blind too. You think I don't see, but I see you, Signor Whodull. I feel bad for you, for your daughter, but I don't

374

think you see me, and I don't think you see my little girl either. I don't think you want to see us. Maybe I don't blame you."

"Why won't your daughter let you visit, Signor Strappafelci? Why won't she even look at you? What did you do to her?"

"I don't do nothing to her, Signore; I never touch her, I never slap her face, I never raise my fist to her. Nothing."

"When was the last time you talked to her? It's been years since she talked to you."

"You know what I think sometime?" Signor Strappafelci leaned forward, putting his two hands on the table and bringing his face close to Woody's. "Sometime when I see my daughter in the *gabbia* I think of Beccone in his cage. He can't fly no more; he can't get away. What do you think, Signor Whodull, do you wish it was my daughter was dead and your daughter was in the *gabbia*?"

Woody knew that he'd finally struck home, like a hunter who's brought down a buck or a bear or a cloud-flying goose. But his triumph was tinged with remorse, as if he himself had crushed Beccone in his fist, had crushed the life out of the little body the way he'd like to crush the life out of Angela; as if he himself had placed the little body in its coffin and sent it on its way, down the Tiber to Ostia Antica, where Aeneas first set foot on Roman territory, and out into the Tyrrhenian Sea.

"Maybe we can talk again," he said; "maybe I could write something true about your daughter."

"Thank you, Signor Whodull. You're a father too, you can understand these things."

Ergastolo

In February the court heard additional testimony from the secret service agents whose testimony at an earlier trial had led to the arrest of General Palumbo and Lieutenant Colonel Milazzo for *depistaggi*, but it was still impossible to establish exactly what the general and the lieutenant colonel had been covering up. At the end of the month the court heard the testimony of the ballistics experts, who said that the explosive material in the bomb had resembled Parmesan cheese, and additional testimony from a second group of *pentiti*, members of ORA and other neo-fascist organizations who had been induced to testify against their comrades-in-arms. At the beginning of March the *pubblico ministero* spent a week summing up the prosecution's case against the seven defendants. The lawyers for the *parte civile* had their say, and then the lawyers for the defense spent another two weeks with their harangues. On Wednesday, March thirtieth, the president of the court declared the debate closed, and the court withdrew to the Camera di Consiglio. The trial had taken seventeen months. Over two hundred hearings had been held.

Woody sent off an article every week to the *Tribune*—eighteen articles in eighteen weeks. He received one hundred fifty dollars a week from the *Trib*, and a hundred dollars a week from each of eight other papers in different parts of the country which ran the articles the day after they appeared in the *Trib*. His editor at the *Trib* had been approached by an American publisher, and he was planning to turn the articles into a book. He had written about all the major players in the trial, including several who had not in fact appeared in the courtroom. But he hadn't yet written anything about Angela Strappafelci, whose alibi had not, at least in Woody's opinion, stood up very well under questioning by the president of the court. There were no plans to press charges against her for the murder of Judge Gianfranco Cipriani in Palermo.

Now that there was no chance to see his daughter in the *gabbia*, Signor Strappafelci had returned to Rome. Before he left Bologna he reminded Woody of his promise to write something true about Angela, but Woody kept putting it off. He was becoming more and more involved with the work of the Association, which was in the process of computerizing the records of *all* the *stragi*—Piazza Fontana, Piazza della Loggia, Brescia, Italicus, Ustica—so that the testimony given by defendants at different trials could be cross-checked; and he made several trips to Rome with Signor Monte-fiore, the president of the Association, to meet with Senator Cavallini, from Turin, who had from the very beginning champi-oned the attempt to abolish *Segreto di Stato* in cases of terrorism.

"Putting it off" was not quite accurate, however. Woody was not a procrastinator. When he sat down to write, he wrote. But every time he sat down to write about Angela Strappafelci, he was driven or carried backwards, like a man trying to swim against a current that is too strong for him. He would fill up two or three pages with random notes; he would set down "facts" in chronological order; he would list the reporter's questions—who? what? when? where? why?—at the top of a blank page. But at a certain point he would pic-ture her pushing her glasses up on her nose, or turning a page of *The Lord of the Rings*—she was halfway through the third volume when the trial came to an end—and his feelings would overwhelm him and he would fill page after page with obscenities, pressing down so hard that he ruined the nib of his good fountain pen, a present from Han-nah, and had to write with a ballpoint. When he was done he would tear the pages up into tiny pieces—he didn't want Gabriella to see them—and put them in the plastic garbage sack under the sink. If he thought that Gabriella might be spending the night, he'd carry the sack out to one of the dumpsters stationed at intervals along the street.

THE JURY'S announcement that it had completed its work took everyone by surprise. It had not been expected till the end of June. The *pubblico ministero* was on vacation in Sicily; attorneys for the defense and for the *parte civile* were scattered all over the country. Woody and Gabriella canceled a trip to Trentino, where Gabriella's cousin had a cabin in the mountains. Woody had written three more articles—on the Italian judicial system, on Fraternità e Lavoro, on the movement to abolish *Segreto di Stato*—but nothing on Angela Strappafelci.

On the night before the verdict was to be announced, Woody and Gabriella walked by the Hotel Roma in Strada Maggiore, where the jury had been sequestered for slightly over three weeks. Woody had been trying to look into the future, but he couldn't see past this moment, the moment in which the president of the court would pronounce the word *ergastolo*. Life imprisonment. The death penalty had been abolished in Italy, but *ergastolo* would do for Angela, though some of the other defendants were expected to receive lighter sentences. He tried to look past this moment, not to see what his future life would be, but to see how he would feel once the trial was over, the guilty punished, justice done.

Woody had no doubt that justice would be served in this case. Mysterious and powerful forces in the government had placed many obstacles in the path of the prosecution since the beginning of the investigation in 1980—judges had been transferred unexpectedly, or had not been provided with secretarial help; information had been withheld or lost; one of the lawyers for the *parte civile* turned out to be a member of FL and had been reporting directly to Bruno Conti in Switzerland—but the *magistratura* in Bologna had prevailed. If there was anything to worry about, it was the apparent levity of the jury. One of the citizen judges had broken a finger playing soccer in the courtyard of the hotel and had been taken to the hospital. A lawyer for the defense was already talking about a mistrial, since jury members were not supposed to communicate with any outsiders.

Standing in front of the hotel, Woody listened. For what? Sounds of another soccer game? One of the guards who had been stationed around the hotel eyed him suspiciously, keeping a finger on the trigger of a submachine gun, as if Woody were a suspected terrorist. Gabriella tugged at his sleeve.

Woody did not go down to the *osteria* that night because he didn't want to risk meeting Signor Strappafelci, who had doubtless come back from Rome. Woody sat down at a typewriter he had borrowed from Gabriella, a small Olivetti with an Italian keyboard. He kept typing *w* for *q* and vice versa. He used up a whole matchbook of whiteout paper.

He drank one beer and opened another and began to type whatever came into his head. After fifteen minutes he realized that he was writing *to* Angela instead of *about* her. But she was a moving target, or an invisible target. A zero, a cipher. A mystery. He didn't know how to wound her, didn't know where to aim:

It's been seven years since you left the bomb in the 2nd-class waiting room at the station, a bomb that killed 86 people, including my daughter, Carolyn. Cookie. Since that time I have not spent a quiet night. I've lost my wife. I've given up my vocation as a teacher. I often hear my daughter's voice, but I can't make out what she's saying.

While you were living in Argentina, with Franco della Chiave, I have lived out my life. I've loved my other daughters. I've cooked for them, and held them in my arms. My wife left, and since then I've loved another woman, two other women, in my fashion.

Since the day of your arrest last October—a year ago last October—I've never stopped thinking about you. Not a hurricane, not a tornado or a forest fire or a tidal wave or an avalanche or an airplane crash. Someone decided. Gratuitous. You. You took it upon yourself, with your own hands, dressed like a German tourist, a bomb in your rucksack. Did you know that the explosive material looked like Parmesan cheese? Did you look around you? The waiting room was crowded. Did you think about the people in the crowded room? Did you ask yourself about their lives? How they would be affected?

We got to Bologna on a Tuesday. I'd been through

379

Bologna on the train, but always on the way to somewhere else, on the way from Rome to Venice, or Venice to Rome, but I'd never gotten off the train, except to buy a newspaper, or to wait for another train. Tracks one and two had been severely damaged, but trains were running, and the station had been rearranged. There's a chain-link fence around the disaster area. On the fence people have put up poems, messages scrawled on pieces of paper, cards, letters, even music. I can still see them. Later on I will put up a letter myself. (A letter to you, though I don't know who you are at the time, and I still don't.)

It's very hot and I'm wearing jeans and a white shirt, with the sleeves rolled up, which is what I always wear, my academic uniform; and my wife is wearing one of her summer dresses, though I can't remember which one. I can barely see her now in my imagination, but I can see the police and soldiers everywhere, and the streets lined with posters—some professionally printed, some handmade—protesting the *strage*. Black flags fly from the government buildings in Piazza Maggiore.

My wife and I hold on to each other. We haven't given up hope yet. On the flight to Milan we've told each other things we'd never told each other before, though I no longer remember what they were. We haven't slept, but we're not tired. The uncertainty is too terrible for sleep.

Allison Mirsadiqi—Cookie had been staying with an old friend in Rome—has driven up from Rome to meet us. She's already arranged for a hotel room. The city itself—the best-organized city in Italy—is providing free accommodations for the families of the victims and tickets for free meals at the CAMST restaurants.

There is an office at the Palazzo d'Accursio where we can go for help. There are telephones and translators. I'm proud of my Italian, but I let Allison help me. She telephones the morgue, the hospitals.

My wife is having some trouble. She can't stop talking. She seems almost exhilarated. Allison takes her to the hotel while I wait for information. But I don't wait very long. Instead I ask directions and then walk to the morgue—through the center of town and out one of the spokes of the wheel to the Institute for Legal Medicine in Via Irnerio. Did you know that Irnerius was one of the founders of the university in the Middle Ages? Maybe you don't know. Bologna's not your city. Your only quarrel with Bologna is that it's run by the Communists . . .

Most of the bodies have been claimed, but a group of volunteers is still there to help the families through the ordeal. Coffins are stacked up in the back of an army truck, and against the wall of the institute, wooden boxes, rectangular. Some people are sitting on a bench. It's still very hot.

I'm worried about my wife, but I have to know. I sit on the bench with one of the volunteers, waiting my turn. About two dozen bodies are left, and I move slowly from one to another, looking, hoping not to find. I'm not good at finding things. "Just keep looking till you find it," my wife always says. "Why would I keep looking after I found it?" I always answer.

I keep looking, making a second pass, and my heart lifts a little as I begin to hope.

I can picture Cookie standing in the station, holding her suitcase in her hand. She didn't want a new one, she wanted my old duffel bag. She said she didn't want to spend money on a new suitcase when the attic was full of old ones. Old canvas and old leather. But in fact it was just her style. Something between a backpack and a suitcase.

Where did she spend the night in Bologna? Where was she going to live? I wonder. What kind of a place had she found? Could she be there now, maybe sleeping, maybe in bed with a lover, oblivious of the tragedy?

My heart beats with hope. She's sleeping, she's with a lover; or she's been injured and is in one of the hospitals.

I take a cab back to the Palazzo d'Accursio. The cab drivers provide free rides for families of the victims. I like to walk, but I'm in too much of a hurry now.

At the city hall I learn that there's a young woman at the Ospedale Maggiore who hasn't been identified yet, a young woman who might be Cookie. Unidentified. In the cab—

Woody was having trouble breathing. He tore the last page out of the typewriter. Then he tore the whole letter into pieces, and then he tore the pieces into smaller pieces; but he couldn't tear up his feelings.

IN THE morning Woody got up very early and went to the station, like a man going to mass before facing a difficult day. It was a Monday, and Via d'Azeglio, which was closed to traffic, was still empty, though Woody could hear in the distance the familiar sound of a beggar, a terrible moaning sound, like a bassoon: *Aiutami, aiutami.* Help me, help me. Woody encountered him everywhere, Via Garibaldi, Via d'Azeglio, Via Independenza. The voice never stopped. It cut through the sounds of the city like a foghorn. Woody always gave him something. But not this morning.

In the station he sat in the second-class waiting room with his sleeves rolled up. The trains ran all night and day; there were always plenty of people.

Woody was convinced, now more than ever, that the dead communicate, that Cookie still spoke to him. Not in a voice, as she had from time to time in the cemetery, but because she was so much a part of him, sprung from his seed. Something of her remained in him, carved as firmly in his body as her name on the *lapide*.

Today was the first day of still another new life, another *vita nuova*, for which he had been long preparing, and which he fully expected to begin with the reading of the verdict, *Ergastolo*. Life imprisonment without possibility of parole or pardon. From a Greek word meaning a workhouse for slaves. Woody didn't think the word occurred in Homer, but Demosthenes used it as a metaphor for hell. And God promised to deliver the Jews from the *ergastolo* of the Egyptians. What God would deliver Angela Strappafelci? It was unthinkable.

Woody pictured the moment: President Turone in his black robe, his white beard rippling as he pronounced the word: *ergastolo*. What will Woody *do* after that? Who will he *be*? Someone opened a door and the sound of a train on track one filled the room—a *rapido*, according to the voice on the loudspeaker, on its way from Milan to Rome.

Woody and Gabriella hadn't made love for several weeks, not since the jury had been sequestered. He'd been too tense. She was going to meet him at noon, after the verdict had been read, at the Fountain of Neptune. He was listening, always thinking that he might hear Cookie's voice again. If not here, where? A child ran across the crowded station and jumped into her mother's arms. Woody did not regard this as a sign, but it pleased him nonetheless. He still hadn't written the article on Angela Strappafelci, but he thought that once she was safely in prison, without hope of pardon or parole, he would know what to do.

THE PIAZZA in front of the Palazzo di Giustizia was full of people and police—*carabinieri* in their sharp blue uniforms with red piping, traffic police, military police with submachine guns. Traffic had been blocked off, but the traffic police were letting the city buses through. Woody drank an espresso at the Cafe Tribunale. He was surrounded by faces that seemed familiar; they looked excited, expectant. He paid for his coffee and walked across the piazza to the Palazzo di Giustizia. He showed his passport to the guard at the door at the top of the wide Roman staircase. It was only nine o'clock, but the courtroom, like the piazza, was already packed. He took a seat in the section reserved for families of the victims. The prisoners had not been brought into the *gabbie* yet, but Signor Strappafelci was in his usual chair, as close as he could possibly be to the left-front *gabbia* where his daughter would sit without looking at him.

There was a long wait—over an hour—with nothing to do, though there was some excitement when the guards started bringing the prisoners into the *gabbie* at nine-thirty. Trimarchi. Palumbo and Milazzo. Campobello. Rosselli. Della Chiave. All assembled. Angela Strappafelci shared her cage with Campobello.

At ten o'clock there was a cry from the gates. "They're coming."

On the portable transmitters carried by the police and the *carabinieri* Woody could hear agitated voices and static and then (through the open windows) the sound of motorcycles coming into the courtyard, sirens, squealing tires. Then the police cars with the magistrates and citizen judges. The crunch of tires on gravel. Car doors slamming. The motorcycle police, who entered the room first, wore bulletproof vests and carried submachine guns.

The judges and the alternate judges took their places. When they were all seated President Leonardo Turone, without any pre-amble, began to read the names of the dead and injured. Woody braced himself for Cookie's name, Carolyn Woodhull, and could see other families doing the same, like students waiting to be called on in a classroom while the teacher strikes now here, now there. "Car-olyn Woodhull." Like most Italians President Turone couldn't pro-nounce *w*'s and *h*'s. "Carolyn Voodall," he said. But it was close enough. Sharp tears rose to Woody's eyes and then quickly subsided. The president read the names of all the lawyers, and Woody won-dered if they too waited expectantly to hear their names. A list of the charges followed, taking up almost half an hour. And finally the sen-tences, the moment everyone had been waiting for.

There were few surprises. Della Chiave was absolved for lack of evidence, but the principal defendants were sentenced to life in prison, some, including Angela, without hope of pardon or parole. *Ergastolo*. Bruno Conti was sentenced in absentia to ten years in prison. Woody experienced a sense of relief rather than of triumph, the way he felt after a Cubs victory. No matter how big the lead, you never quite believed the Cubs were really going to win till it was over.

The prisoners did not seem surprised. They were defiant rather than abject.

President Turone said that they had taken a step forward but still hadn't gotten to the bottom. The legal system had identified and condemned the assassins on the one hand, and those who, on behalf of powerful and mysterious forces within the government itself, had laid down false trails to impede the investigations. But they hadn't established the link between the two. In his closing remarks he said they were literally exhausted and needed to be carried to the sea for a vacation. Woody was exhausted too.

The mayor spoke briefly, expressing his hope that now the dead could rest in peace.

The lawyers for the *parte civile* were moderately satisfied, but

Signor Montefiore, the president of the Association, was not. Woody saw him speaking to reporters.

The *pubblico ministero* announced in a loud voice that he hoped the government would appeal the absolution of della Chiave.

The president was still standing at the podium from which he had read the sentence. Guards were coming through the doors in the back of the *gabbie* to take the prisoners down to the holding cells. Someone joked about the *giudice popolare* who had broken a finger playing soccer in the courtyard of the hotel.

Woody was standing directly in front of the podium.

"Scapegoats," Trimarchi cried out as he was being led out by a guard.

Della Chiave too was indignant. He should have been cleared entirely, he shouted at a reporter, not just for lack of evidence. "Now for the burning at the stake in the piazza that everyone's been waiting for," he said loudly as he left the courtroom.

Woody moved closer to Angela's *gabbia*. He wanted a look, wanted to see her face up close. Her father was standing directly in front of her. Campobello had already been led away, and a female guard had entered the *gabbia* to take her down to one of the holding cells. The door at the back of the *gabbia* was standing open, but Angela was holding on to the bars at the front. Woody could see her face clearly, but it was blank. He couldn't read it. He felt a thrill of hatred, or anger, or contempt . . . There wasn't any word precise enough for what he felt. There was something numinous about her, as there is about a dead body, or someone who's suffered some terrible tragedy that puts him or her outside the limits of normal human experience, someone who's spent time in a convent, or a concentration camp. You don't know what to say to them unless you're a journalist, willing to shove stupid questions in their faces.

A second female guard had now appeared, from the door at the back of the *gabbia*, and two *carabinieri* approached from the front to pull Signor Strappafelci away. The two women were trying to take Angela by the arms, but she held tight to the bars of the *gabbia*, her hands crossed on the outside, her fingers wrapped around the bars. They tugged at her arms but couldn't loosen her grip.

Woody looked around at the president, who was still talking, and then back at Angela. He imagined calling out her name: *Angela,* but he couldn't imagine what he would say, other than that he was glad that she'd spend the rest of her life in prison. But he was reluctant to plunge into this feeling.

The other prisoners were gone; the two guards had given up trying to loosen Angela's arms and were waiting for reinforcements. The courtroom was crowded and full of commotion. A young woman who had become a symbol of the *strage*—because of a photo of her taken as she was being carried out of the station on a stretcher—shouted at a reporter, "I don't want to say anything; don't ask me anything. I'll say it again. Nothing. Just one thing: eighty-six dead. Is the sentence just? Who can say? I don't know."

Two *carabinieri* were restraining Signor Strappafelci; a third approached Angela's *gabbia*, fiddling with one of the buttons on his magnificent uniform. He listened while one of the female guards explained the situation, and then without a moment's hesitation smashed the butt of his submachine gun down on Angela's fingers. It was a glancing blow; the gun butt smashed into the bars. The bars rang dully. Angela gasped but didn't let go. Blood ran down her broken fingers and dripped on the floor. Woody looked around him. The president had left the courtroom and others were following. The *carabiniere* drew his submachine gun back to strike again. Angela's father struggled to break free and then he closed his eyes, waiting for the blow to fall. Angela looked at Woody momentarily. The *carabiniere* planted his feet firmly. He was about average height, but powerfully built. He took careful aim this time. Woody moved forward, pushed through the cordon of police. The *carabiniere* brought the heavy submachine gun back to strike again. Woody reached forward, took hold of the gun barrel just as it started to move forward, and spun the *carabiniere* around. The *carabiniere* had to struggle not to lose his balance. Someone laughed. Back on both feet again he swung the gun sideways, hitting Woody on the side of the head with the barrel. Woody didn't feel the blow, but he felt a force push him backwards. He sank to his knees, his head spinning. He could see Signor Strappafelci kissing his daughter's bloody hands as the guards pried her loose from the bars. Her broken fingers had no strength to hold on. There was nothing left. Her father followed along beside her, his hands darting in and out through the bars of the *gabbia*, like the legs of a football player running the grid, till he came to the wall and could go no farther. Angela disappeared through the door, leaving a trail of blood.

"He grabbed me from behind," the *carabiniere* said; "he shouldn't have grabbed me from behind; he grabbed my gun."

For just a minute, looking up from the floor, Woody thought he saw things more clearly, and then he saw a flash of light, and then he couldn't see anything at all.

A Dark
Cimmerian
Land

When Allison Mirsadiqi learned that Woody had booked a room at the Hotel Sant'Anselmo, on the Aventine Hill, she called the hotel herself and canceled the reservation. "It's out of the question," she told Woody on the phone; "what were you thinking of? We've got plenty of room. Besides, we have to have a talk." And in fact their home, their house, their palazzo, also on the Aventine Hill—on Via di Santa Sabina, not far from the Pyramid of Caius Cestius and the Protestant Cemetery, where Keats was buried, and Shelley, or at least Shelley's heart—was almost as big as the hotel itself. From his bedroom window Woody could see the Tiber and the square belltower of Santa Maria in Trastevere and the red roof of the Villa Lante at the top of the Gianicolo. Woody did not want to have a "talk" about his relationship with Turi; nor did he wish to avoid it at all costs. He supposed, in fact, that a "talk" was necessary, but he didn't give it much thought because he had more pressing matters on his mind.

It was the last day of the third week in June. Woody had left his guitar, and the rug, and his clothes—he'd cleaned out his apartment so Gabriella could rent it to someone else—at Gabriella's. Gabriella had come with him in the taxi to the station to see him off. Woody had kissed her on the station platform, wrapping his arms around her and kissing her on the mouth.

"You're getting to be just like an Italian," she said, pushing him away. "Or at least what you think is an Italian. You're going to miss your train if you don't hurry."

Woody had booked a room at a hotel for two reasons. Partly he was apprehensive about meeting Alireza again after the business with Turi's underpants; and partly he wanted to be alone to think about his impending visit to Angela Strappafelci in Regina Coeli prison. He had prepared a list of questions, mostly about Angela's thesis, but these political questions had seemed incidental to a more personal issue that had begun to trouble him in the hospital in Bologna, Ospedale Maggiore, where he'd spent several days recovering from the blow from the *carabiniere*'s gun. *Love your enemies, do good to them which hate you.* What if these words—despite Freud's ridicule—were not an impossible commandment but a practical necessity? What if you forgave people not to demonstrate (to yourself, or to others, or to a higher power) the extent of your charity, but out of necessity, so you could get on with your life, so you wouldn't carry around the burden of hatred? What if you thought of it as a practical matter, not a theological one? Not even a moral one?

He'd had several unexpected visitors in the hospital, including the mayor and the *pubblico ministero* and the editor of *Il Resto del Carlino*. It was clear that none of these men realized exactly what had happened in the courtroom, only that a distinguished American journalist, the father of the only American killed in the *strage*, had accidentally been struck down by a *carabiniere*. The *carabiniere* had been stripped of his rank and transferred from Bologna to Bolzano. Signor Strappafelci had visited too, but Signor Strappafelci *did* understand what had happened and wanted to thank Woody.

"I couldn't go back home without saying something," he said.

Woody, who was wearing patches over his eyes, was startled when Signor Strappafelci touched his hand.

Signor Strappafelci had talked to Angela's lawyer, he said. Angela was going to be in a special *braccio*, or wing, for political prisoners at Carcere Regina Coeli in Rome, at least until the appeal, which was expected to take over a year. There were only a dozen women, he said. Eleven Red Brigades and Angela. It was a minor triumph. Signor Strappafelci'd been afraid she'd be sent to the new electronic prison in Turin, where everything was remote-controlled—the guards had no contact with the prisoners. Or to Rebibbia, which was on the other side of town. But Regina Coeli was not far from the Trastevere, where Signor Strappafelci had his shop. She had in fact already been sent to Rome. Signor Strappafelci had been waiting in Bologna till he could see Woody.

"Very convenient," Woody said.

"It's enough to be close," Signor Strappafelci said. "It's something anyway; you have a daughter, you know what I mean."

Woody had often walked past Regina Coeli, which was at the bottom of the Gianicolo, near the Villa Farnesina and the Galleria Nazionale d'Arte Antica, but without giving it much thought. It was a large palazzo, like other large palazzi. Like most Italian prisons, it had once been a convent. Two separate convents, actually, that had been joined together in the eighteenth century.

"I'm sorry I haven't written about her," Woody said.

"She saw what you done for her," he said. "She give you a good story."

In his dark world Woody could see the *carabiniere* bring the butt of his submachine gun down on Angela's fingers. He could see, in his imagination, the fear in her face, the incomprehension. That this was happening to her, that her life had come to this point. She had dropped her guard for a moment, opened herself up to the truth. He could see the look of surprise on her face, and on the face of the *carabiniere* as he looked down at Woody. And he could see her father, his arms darting in and out of the bars of the *gabbia*, trying to touch his daughter. In that moment, which lasted hardly two seconds, Woody had seen her as his own daughter, as Cookie.

It was Signor Strappafelci who had begun negotiations for the visit by appealing to the *pubblico ministero*. "Out of the question," Woody said when Signor Strappafelci told him what he'd done. And it *was* out of the question *then*. But a week later, sitting in Gabriella's darkened living room, his guitar on his lap, he'd begun to toy with the idea, the way a man will toy with a sexual fantasy while he's occupied with other things, waiting for the light to change at a busy intersection, or sitting at his desk with a half hard-on.

He had not been in a lot of pain, but the doctors had diagnosed a subdural hematoma—blood oozing from his cortical veins—and his vision had been affected. Sitting in the dark, patches over both eyes, he thought of Blind Lemon Jefferson being led around the streets of Dallas by Huddie Leadbelly, and Blind Willie McTell, with his big twelve-string Stella, and Blind Connie Johnson, from Philadelphia, who played "Key to the Highway" in G instead of E. And Homer too, Demodocus, cherished by the Muse, who gave him both good and evil, gave him the gift of sweet song, but took away his sight:

τὸν πέρι Μοῦσ' ἐφίλησε, δίδου δ' ἀγαθόν τε κακόν τε·
ὀφθαλμῶν μὲν ἄμερσε, δίδου δ' ἡδεῖαν ἀοιδήν.

The *pubblico ministero* had made the necessary arrangements with the Ministry of Grace and Justice in Rome. Officially Woody was going to visit Angela Strappafelci in his capacity as an American journalist. Unofficially it was assumed that he was going to forgive her.

WOODY ARRIVED in Rome on Saturday. On Sunday evening the Mir-sadiqis gave a small dinner party. "We've invited some Americans," Allison told him, and Woody assumed that he was the guest of honor. He'd worn the leather sports coat Gabriella had given him for Christmas, which was a little too warm but which made him feel snug and secure; but he hadn't brought a tie and wouldn't believe Allison when she told him he wouldn't need one. Actually he wanted an excuse to get out. He followed a narrow path down the hill to Piazza Bocca della Verità, crossed the Tiber on the Ponte Palatino and bought a cheap necktie at an open-air market in front of Santa Maria in Trastevere, and then he walked down Vicolo del Piede, where waiters were starting to set up outdoor tables at the restaurants that lined the narrow street, to Signor Strappafelci's little fruit and vegetable shop. There were several customers in the shop, and Signor Strappafelci didn't notice Woody at first. When he did he called to his wife, who appeared through a narrow door in the back of the store. She smiled shyly at Woody when her husband intro-duced her, and then the two men went down the street to a bar, to drink a cup of coffee and discuss their plans, their stratagems: how, where, when, and why. But what choices did they have other than to meet at the little bar on Via delle Mantellate, across from the visi-tors' entrance? Signor Strappafelci drew a little sketch on a napkin so that Woody could find his way. He slipped the map into the inside pocket of Woody's leather jacket.

Hors d'oeuvres were served that night in the rooftop garden, where dates and figs grew alongside lemons and oranges, and bougainvillea covered the walls and plunged over the railing of the balcony. Woody assumed that everyone would speak Italian, but the Iranian businessmen preferred to speak Persian, which their American wives spoke fluently. Woody's assumption that he was the guest of honor gave way to the feeling that he was an extra, if not actually in the way. But he couldn't be absolutely sure. The men were traditionally courteous. They addressed him as Jenab-e Agha-ye-Professor Voody and spoke slowly and clearly so he could understand them, and they listened carefully to him. The two American women, however, spoke rapidly and exchanged glances whenever Woody couldn't understand, or when he spoke in Persian. After a few minutes they made a point of ignoring him.

The conversation was mostly about the war with Iraq, about the tentative agreement to begin cease-fire negotiations. Woody could follow along all right, and when he was asked about his own feelings about Khomeini, he simply said what he'd said ever since he came back from his year in Esfahan, that the United States should never have interfered to prevent Mossadeq from nationalizing British Petroleum in 1953, that Mossadeq had represented the interests of the common people of Iran in their struggle against imperialism and against the Shah, and against the ayatollahs too, who had aligned themselves with Qavam because they feared social reforms— women's suffrage, in particular, and land reforms; that the overthrow of Mossadeq had paved the way for political despotism on the one hand and for an answering religious fanaticism on the other.

This view had never been popular in the United States, and Woody didn't imagine it would be very popular with these businessmen, these great *bazaaris*. Woody could tell that this was certainly not the answer they had expected, but he couldn't interpret their expressions. Did their polite smiles express amusement or did they conceal anger? He couldn't even tell, in fact, if these couples were old friends of the Mirsadiqis, or of each other, or if they were perfect strangers who had been invited solely because the two men happened to be married to Americans. And where were Allison and Alireza?

Allison, he learned from a servant who kept filling his glass with pomegranate juice, was preparing the meal herself in the absence of the cook, whose daughter was visiting from Tabriz. And Alireza . . . Earlier in the day he had encountered Alireza without a trace of awkwardness, but Alireza had been preoccupied. A ship containing almost two thousand rugs had been damaged by an Iraqi mine in the Gulf of Oman, and the captain, instead of putting in for repairs at Aden, had decided to push on to Civitavecchia. The ship, which had taken on a lot of water, was now tied up to a floating dock in Port Said, at the mouth of the Suez Canal, for temporary repairs. If the water had entered the containers holding the rugs, the rugs would expand and take on weight, which would make them difficult to unload, and arrangements would have to be made to dry them, which was no small matter. "You don't put a silk Kashan in your electric drying machine," Alireza said to Woody, putting an arm around his shoulder. Alireza had spent the afternoon on the telephone, and he was called to the phone several times during the meal, which they ate in the traditional Persian fashion.

One of the men, Nader Kasravi, a lawyer—not a businessman, as Woody had assumed—who was writing a book about the Tobacco Revolt in the nineteenth century, told a story about a man whose tailor turned out to be the devil. Nader himself was beautifully dressed, in an Italian silk suit: splendid, glowing, radiant. He spoke slowly so that Woody, who was sitting across from him at the table, could follow. But the story was long and complicated and eventually Woody lost the thread. When it was over he wanted to say, in Persian, "Agha-ye-Vakil, and who is *your* tailor?" But he thought that if he said that, everyone would stop talking and stare at him.

After supper, sitting in the living room, Woody drifted in and out of the conversation, thinking about his impending visit to Regina Coeli. The appointment had been fixed, but there were still forms to be filled out in several different offices.

Nader told another story, about one of the great merchants in the Qai Sarieh Bazaar in Esfahan, and this prompted Woody to tell the story of finding the letter from Hannah lying in the street in Esfahan. The story provoked the usual reaction from the American women: disbelief, skepticism, it was impossible.

But it was true. He hardly remembered what was in the letter, just the shock of finding it. Lying there in the street. He'd been homesick, but not wanting to give in to the homesickness, or even to admit it. The university had been totally disorganized. He'd had no idea what was expected of him. He was having trouble understanding and making himself understood in Persian . . .

He let the protests go on before beginning to explain: the area they lived in, behind the old market, had been surrounded by a wall. You had to pass through this particular street—Kheyabun-è Bisoton—to get to their apartment. Perhaps the mailman hadn't been able to make out the number of the address and had left it in the street, knowing that whoever it was addressed to would pass that way. Maybe he'd just dropped it by accident.

But no amount of explaining could take away the wonder of it.

Everyone looked at Woody as if he were some kind of wonder himself, a magician or a wandering dervish, like the one Woody'd seen sitting in a tree when he'd gone with Ebrahim Agha and Ashraf Khanom to the mountains outside Shahr-è-Kord; or as if he'd described a miracle, a rent in the predetermined web of universal stuff.

"Nothing happens by accident," said Nader.

"Or else," Alireza said, "*every*thing happens by accident." He smiled and put his glass of tea down on a small table.

"That's what my daughters used to say," said Woody; "'It broke *by accident.*' All sorts of things happened by accident in our house."

"It comes down to the same thing, doesn't it?" said Nader.

"How's that?" Woody asked. "I don't see what you mean."

"Alireza's ship hitting the mine. Was that an accident?"

"Of course it was an accident," Woody insisted. "That's not the same thing as finding the letter. Think of it. In a foreign country you find a letter on the street and it's addressed to you."

"And here in Rome? Have you found any letters in Via Santa Sabina?"

"No." Woody laughed. He was starting to enjoy himself. "No," he said, "not in Italy." But he was remembering the letter. He'd been on his way to the university when he found it, just before he got to the bazaar, and then he'd turned back. Ashraf Khanom had just gotten out of bed and was making tea and stirring yogurt into a bowl of fruit. She turned the letter over and over in her hand. She was the only person who believed him immediately, without questioning him; but then, she believed that the Sufi who begged outside the

Madrase-ye Chahar Bagh, where Pasolini's *Arabian Nights* had been filmed, could converse with the pigeons that pecked for bits of bread outside Amir's bakery, where she purchased two loaves of Barbari bread every morning, and that a woman who stared too long at the moon would give birth to a mouse. It had happened to her cousin.

Ebrahim Agha had believed him too, and so had his friends at the university, though they'd asked a lot of questions first. It was only at home, back in the States, that he had trouble convincing people. He was never sure that anyone really believed him one hundred percent. But it was true. It had happened to him. He could still see the letter lying facedown in the dirt of the narrow street that you had to go through to get from the Jolfa quarter to the Chahar Bagh, a letter from someone he loved; someone who loved him, who was thinking about him when he was so far from home.

THE PALAZZO di Grazia e Giustizia was a huge building on the other side of the Tiber, across the Ponte Umberto I, just east of the Castel Sant'Angelo. Woody walked along the river—Allison had dropped him off in the center—because he wanted to have a look at the prison, Regina Coeli, which he could see from the Lungotevere Farnesina. Regina Coeli itself was on a lower lever, on Via della Lungara. The two streets merge near the Ponte Mazzini. The guard at the front entrance pointed Woody to the visitors' entrance but wouldn't answer any questions. "I can't stand here chatting with you," he said.

Woody ordered a *caffè* at a bar, opposite the visitors' entrance. It was Wednesday morning, three days after the dinner party at the Mirsadiqis'. The little alley between the bar and the prison was crowded with people carrying big plastic bags full of food and clothes. There were still more forms to be filled out at the ministry, but he sat in the bar for an hour, just to watch.

All the forms had to be stamped at a *tabaccheria* and then taken to different offices. Everything happened without incident, however. Woody was expecting at least a week to prepare himself, but his visit was scheduled for the next afternoon. He was to present himself at the main entrance to the prison at five o'clock, long after regular visiting hours were over. He called Signor Strappafelci to let him know.

The next morning he wanted to be alone, but Allison persuaded him to take a group of Iranian students to the Capitoline Hill. He didn't want to do it, but she was in a bind; the teacher who was scheduled to take the students on the tour was sick and she needed someone to fill in. He didn't want to make *brutta figura* by refusing.

"You could do it with your eyes closed, Woody," she said. "It'll be good for you, take your mind off this afternoon. Then when it's all over—I mean after you've seen la Strappafelci—we'll have a good talk, OK? I know that Alireza wants to speak to you. There are some things to be settled, but don't be afraid, he's a good man."

Woody nodded. They were in Allison's Porsche, driving through central Rome to the language school, which was located on Via del Pellegrino, behind the Cancelleria.

"Where do you park?" Woody asked.

"I rent a space, you'll see. It's not a problem."

The morning lessons were divided into two sessions, grammar and then conversation, or vice versa, with a twenty-minute break at 10:50. Woody sat in Allison's office drinking coffee from a machine that ground the beans on the spot and then turned out an espresso or a cappuccino or a *caffè macchiato*, whatever you wanted. The school served an international clientele, but because of Allison's Iranian connection there were a lot of Iranian students. Allison's window offered a view of the back of the Cancelleria, but from the bathroom window Woody could see the Castel Sant'Angelo and the dome of St. Peter's. Allison had become a real professional, keeping up with the latest developments in language instruction, going to international conferences on language teaching, delivering papers. She herself spoke Persian, Italian, French, Spanish, German, and a little Arabic, and she had a staff of attractive and energetic young teachers, who popped in and out of the office all morning.

"I need to think about what I'm going to say," Woody said.

"Are you going to forgive her?"

"Where does everyone get that idea?"

"You're not going to forgive her?"

Woody didn't want to reveal his inner feelings. "I don't know."

"What are you trying to accomplish? What do you want to happen?"

"I've *got* to write *some*thing about her. I suppose I want to understand."

"Understand what?"

"I want it to make sense."

"What could she tell you that you don't already know?"

"I don't know," Woody said. "She was a girl, she was Cookie's age. What was going through her mind? The others, what can you say?—a bad lot, a bunch of thugs. But she thought about what she was doing." Woody felt he was getting off course. He felt that perhaps he really did want to forgive her, but at the same time he felt that there was something shameful or embarrassing about this impulse.

THEY COULD have walked from the school to the Capitoline Hill in half an hour, but they took a bus instead. The students—all Iranians—had their own tickets or passes. Allison handed Woody two tickets before they left, and gave him directions to the bus stop.

The bus was so crowded that Woody couldn't be sure that all the students had gotten off at their stop, in Piazza Venezia, but what did it matter? The students plopped themselves down on the edge of the fountain. They thought that *this* was what they'd come to see—the Monument to Vittorio Emmanuale II, Italy's hideous monument to its own unity, or perhaps its own vanity—and didn't want to walk up the hill to the Capitol. Woody looked in Allison's *Blue Guide*. Everything symbolized something. The students bought ice cream.

"Do you want just to remove your presence from this scene?" Woody shouted in Persian. "Do you wish to set out by yourselves along the road that leads back to the school, or do you wish to return to your houses of residence?"

The students started to laugh. "Distinguished Professor," someone said, "we did not divine the great honor that has been bestowed on us." He bowed to Woody.

"All right," Woody said, switching back to Italian and speaking slowly and clearly. "Now that I've got your attention . . . Signora Mirsadiqi warned me that you were lazy and that I shouldn't speak to you in Persian. I gave her my word. Now, let's go up to the Capitol."

The students seemed happy now to follow him up Michelangelo's famous staircase, past the steps leading up to the medieval church of the Aracoeli, to the Campidoglio, where a balustrade defined the open end of the piazza with colossal figures of Castor and Pollux. Woody attempted to explain in basic Italian: Michelangelo had completely redesigned the piazza so that it opened onto the expanding city . . .

He was supposed to take the students to the Capitoline Museum to see the *She-Wolf Nursing Romulus and Remus* and the Capitoline Venus and the *Dying Gaul*—Allison had given him a list, but she'd mixed up things from two different museums—but instead they wandered around behind the Senate, where they could have a good view of the Forum. The narrow street was crowded with tourists who were too cheap to buy tickets to get into the Forum itself. It wasn't a bad idea, though. You got a better sense of it from up here, and you could buy a *gelato* or a sandwich, and there was even an Iranian—the students spotted him immediately—selling little wind-up toys, winding them up and letting them go all over the place. The toys were fantastic: little animals with moving legs, like spiders or crabs; soldiers that marched; tanks and trucks that zoomed in one direction and then suddenly turned around and zoomed in another. The Iranian himself zoomed around, as if he too had been wound up, changing directions abruptly, righting toys that had tipped over on the rough pavement, retrieving ones that had stopped and needed to be wound up again. His big smile revealed gleaming white teeth under a thin mustache.

At the beginning of *Civilization and Its Discontents* Freud chooses Rome to symbolize the human mind. His knowledge of the different layers of the city, which had been superimposed on each other, was extraordinary, and Woody always wondered if he'd written the passage from his own knowledge or if he'd had a guidebook open in front of him. The students didn't know who Freud was and didn't care, but Woody, always the teacher, tried to rise to the occasion. His first rule of teaching was that if *you* (the teacher) weren't interested in the material, then you couldn't expect your students to be interested. But what did *he* care about?

From where he was standing he could see the city that he had studied first in his high school Latin class, and then as a young man at the University of Michigan—a city that had become familiar to him over years of teaching. At his feet he could see the Forum, where Mark Anthony made his famous speech, and the Arch of Septimus Severus and the Mamertine Prison, where St. Peter had been imprisoned, and the Basilica Julia. And beyond: the Colosseum and, on the other side of the Palatine, the Baths of Caracalla. Rome itself is difficult to grasp. But the *idea* of Rome is simple. Rome is a palimpsest. Layers upon layers, as Freud pointed out, like the layers of the human mind: pre-Roman, early Roman, republican, imperial, medieval, papal, the Rome of Garibaldi, and later, of course, of Mussolini. Every great city is, in its own way, a palimpsest; but in Rome all the layers are so clearly visible.

"There are two stories I want to tell you," he said in Italian, keeping it simple. "You can see them coming together from this spot, just as if you were looking down at train tracks and seeing two trains coming together.

"When Aeneas landed in Italy, history turned a corner. Things would never be the same again. For the first time history had a direction, a meaning, a purpose. That's the difference between the Romans and the Greeks. It's like the difference between Firdousi and the Ghoran. In the *Shah-nameh* the fall of a city changes nothing; it's all in a day's work. For the Greeks the fall of Troy meant nothing, really. Homer doesn't even show the fall of Troy in the *Iliad*. But for the Romans it was the beginning of a story that gave meaning to human history. This story is one of the frames of reference that made life intelligible for almost two thousand years. The other is Christianity."

A few students were listening politely, but most of them were more interested in the Iranian's wind-up toys, which were zooming around at their feet, and Woody, projecting himself into the future, realized that what they would remember when they looked back on this moment—if in fact they ever looked back on it—would be their countryman selling wind-up toys. And that's what he would remember too.

At half past four Woody met Signor Strappafelci at the bar across from the visitors' entrance. Although he had thought this visit through a hundred times, he still had a sense of entering unfamiliar territory, of being lost in the woods, not sure where he was, or where he was going, or how to find his way, or what he was going to do when he got wherever he was going.

A couple of reporters were sitting at a small table with Signor

Strappafelci, and a priest too. There was a fruit basket on the table. The visitors' entrance was closed, and the bar was almost empty. The weather was hot, but not hot enough to sustain conversation.

One of the reporters, from *Corriere della Sera*, had covered the pope's visit to forgive the Turk who shot him in St. Peter's Square in 1981, and Aldo Moro's widow's visit to Adriana Faranda the year before. Both Mehmet Ali Agca, the Turk, and Adriana Farandi had been in Rebibbia.

"Did you get to talk to the pope?" the priest asked.

"No, it was a real *casino. Carabinieri* everywhere. Swiss guards."

"That was big news."

"And this is small potatoes?" Woody asked.

"Piccole patate?" The reporter didn't understand the phrase. Woody explained.

"Usually it doesn't happen so soon."

"What's that?"

"The urge to forgive. The pope was an exception, but the pope has his own agenda. It was a good move politically. With Moro's widow it was two, three years. Then they became friends, those two women. You think something like that's going to happen with you and . . ." He nodded in the direction of the prison.

Woody was annoyed that what seemed to him to be something extraordinary taking place inside him should be understood by this reporter as a matter of course. He didn't think anyone could understand such a profound mystery. It was as if the reporter were mocking a man who was about to get married, or a woman who was about to give birth to her first child.

"But for you—hasn't even been a month. But of course I suppose you had a few years to think about it."

Woody supposed that it, whatever *it* was, was like sexual intercourse. Before you've ever done it, it's an overwhelming mystery. And yet all around you are people who've done it dozens of times. Hundreds. Thousands of times. But for you it's still an overwhelming mystery. You can't know what *it* will be like.

But *it, this,* was different too. The reporter hadn't forgiven someone who'd killed his daughter. Of the four men sitting at the table with him—the two reporters, the priest, and Signor Strappafelci—only the last seemed to realize that something important was about to happen.

The reporter was oblivious. "You been in to see her yet?" he asked Signor Strappafelci, taking an apple from the fruit basket.

"Not yet." Signor Strappafelci took the apple from the reporter's hand and put it back in the basket. "Excuse me," he said, "that's not for you."

"I heard she doesn't want to see you."

"She's got better things to do than *chiacchierare* with an old man like me."

"Can't fit you into her busy schedule, eh?" Looking at Woody, he tipped back in his chair. Woody was tempted to push him over.

At five o'clock Woody presented himself at the main entrance to the prison. His heart was knocking, and his left hand, when he held it out in front of him, was trembling. He found himself in a long, shallow room with a long counter that ran the entire length of the room, like the ticket counter at an airport. In his right hand he held Signor Strappafelci's fruit basket. The guard he'd talked to the day before—who'd said "I can't stand here chatting with you"—was watching TV. Three men in different uniforms stood behind the counter talking. Woody had his papers and his passport ready. He saw that what looked like a TV was really some kind of monitor.

No one paid him the slightest attention till a fourth person entered the room through a door behind the counter, a door so close to the wall on the right that there wasn't even room for the jamb.

Woody had been in the minimum-security prison in St. Clair once, when John Jackson had given a concert at the college. The warden had called him at his office to see if he'd bring Jackson out to the prison for a short program. They'd been searched, and Jackson had not been allowed to take in the handle of an old kitchen knife that he used for a slide. Woody was searched this time too, perfunctorily, before being led up to the office of the *direttore*, the warden, which was in the front of the building. He had to leave Signor Strappafelci's fruit basket in the entrance room. Signor Strappafelci would have to bring it to the regular visitors' entrance in the morning. Two windows opened onto Via della Lungara. Woody could see the spot where he'd stood, yesterday, looking in the windows and wondering what was inside. It was just an office, filled with a row of filing cabinets and two metal desks. A secretary sat at one desk; the director sat at the other, a florid man who had loosened his tie and unbuttoned the top button of his white shirt.

Looking out the window, past the warden, Woody could see some trees, and through the trees a glimpse of the palazzi on the other side of the river.

Woody had been expecting a self-important bureaucrat, but the man seemed pleasant enough. In fact, once they started talking, he seemed genuinely interested in Woody's thoughts and feelings. Like the official at the Ministry of Grace and Justice he had spoken to the day before, and like Allison, and like the unpleasant reporter, the warden assumed that Woody's real intention was to forgive Angela, and that the official intention—the interview for an American newspaper—was secondary.

"I wanted to see you . . . ," the warden said, "I've always been fascinated by this sort of thing . . . So seldom rises to the level of . . ."

Woody was aware that the secretary was taking a special interest in him too. Or maybe he just felt that she would take a special interest in him if she could see what was taking place inside him.

"When I learned of your request, in fact, I intervened in your behalf . . ."

"I'm very grateful."

"You know that Signorina Strappafelci has refused to see her family?"

"Yes. I know her father. We've become . . . we're on friendly terms."

A pause.

"Here," the warden said, waving his arm, "you enter into the concrete reality of the State. The State is an abstraction, you think, but here you enter into the *penetrali*, the *sancta sanctorum*."

Woody thought for a moment that he had said *genitali*.

"Here the abstract becomes concrete," the warden went on. "You can lay your hands on it, touch it. Sovereignty. Here you enter a dark Cimmerian land—"

The warden looked at Woody to see if he'd caught the reference. Woody nodded.

"—secret places, hidden, subtracted from view. Places you know exist, but prefer not to know, like the land of the Cimmerians . . ."

"Humani nihil a me alienum puto," Woody responded, not wanting to be bullied by classical references. "Nothing human is alien to me."

"But we make a distinction," the warden went on; "we try to separate out the *reprobi*, so as not to *inquinare* the healthy part of society." He paused, trying to assess Woody's response. "We are not like the police. No glory for us. Not much excitement. The police seek the truth. They enjoy the excitement of the chase, the intellectual and physical challenge. But ours is a task *poco ambìto*, circumscribed, poorly paid, fatiguing, squalid, deprived of charm. There are no heroes among our ranks. We are treated like morticians. And the analogy is perhaps not unjustified. We live the life of the dead, the same life as the prisoners, can you understand? Prisons are enormous and complex worlds. The responsibility for governing them is dispersed. Magistrates and judges who should oversee our work prefer not to visit us; they prefer to examine dossiers in their well-appointed offices. And yet we are not indifferent."

"No," Woody said.

"After your thieves and murderers and rapists and drug dealers, one turns with relief to the terrorists; the level of interest increases. They are all operating on strong ideals. They have made an effort to acquire some culture, some political interests. They are more intelligent than the others, more intriguing to talk to. Also more dangerous. They react to prison with discipline, with self-control. They study their classics. They are better informed. They share a certain *disprezzo* for the other prisoners, and yet they get along better with prison personnel. Why? Because for them the enemy is not these individuals but the State itself, *lo Stato stesso*. But they try to manipulate us, to use us as a political vehicle for their ideas, their justification. They can lead you astray. You can't take stock in what they say. You have to be careful."

"And you think I'm in danger of being led astray?"

"I wouldn't put it exactly like that, not at all." The warden paused. "And yet anything is possible, Signore. It might be why she's agreed to speak to you. An American journalist . . . If she can enlist your support . . . ? You have to be on guard. Don't let your sentiments interfere. Don't get caught up . . ."

"You mean she must have an agenda?"

"Exactly. Something she wants to say to the world that she hasn't had a chance to say, a message she hasn't had a chance to deliver. It will be very interesting to see. And then afterwards there will be some reporters here when you come out. It can't be helped."

"There were two reporters in the bar," Woody said, "across from the visitors' entrance."

"Already? We try to keep these things quiet, you see, but there are always . . ." The warden spread out his fingers and tapped them lightly on the desk, as if he were testing the action of a piano. "I don't ask you to lie to them. I don't ask you to conceal anything from them. I ask only this: Be careful. Do not say things that you haven't thought through. Don't worry about making a good impression. Think think think think think, that's all. *Before* you speak."

"That's what I tell my students," Woody said.

"Then I'm sure you're a very good teacher."

THE DOOR that communicated to the different wings of the prison—to the cell blocks—was on the third floor. After another search, more thorough this time, Woody was led by a *secondino*—a young man doing prison work instead of military service—down a dimly lit corridor that bore little resemblance to Woody's image of prisons, which came from American films and from his single visit with John Jackson to the minimum-security prison in St. Clair. The prisoners were lodged not in brightly lit barred cages, like the cages in a zoo, but in narrow cells that for over three hundred years had heard only the whispered prayers of nuns. Woody was reminded that even now his wife was living in a convent, had chosen this life over their life together. *Nuns fret not in the convent's narrow cell.* Keats, he thought, or Wordsworth.

"Smells like someone's cooking something," he said. He could smell olive oil and oregano and garlic.

"The prisoners do their own cooking," the *secondino* explained.

"That's amazing. What do they cook on?"

"Camping stoves. Little ones."

"Where do they get their food? Do they go shopping?"

"They order it, two days in advance. On Monday you order for Wednesday. And the families bring food too. Most of these cells have been joined together. In this wing there're either eight men or four in a cell. They usually cook together."

"How do they pay?"

"They each have their own account book. As long as someone puts money in the account, they can order whatever they want."

"Whatever they want?"

"More or less. If you want something special you can make a request to the *capo* of the wing."

Woody, not usually claustrophobic, felt shut in, short of breath. He thought he could feel the eyes of the prisoners on him at the little windows in the cell doors. He was thinking about what the warden had said and was resolved not to be manipulated.

Another set of locked doors opened into the women's section of the political wing. Three guards, women, stood at an open counter, like a nursing station, examining a chart.

Woody thought he might ask the *secondino* to take him back, out, away, but after all the trouble people had gone to to arrange this visit, he didn't want to make *brutta figura*. What had seemed not only possible but simple at one point now seemed impossibly complex. He clutched his notes, the list of questions he'd written out when he was still pretending to himself to be a journalist. He felt now what he had felt for a brief moment in the courtroom, that Angela was a person on the far side of human experience, someone who had traveled to a far country of the mind, someone whose experience of suffering, loneliness, degradation, had given her a kind of authority—like a nun, or a leper, a survivor of a concentration camp, or one of the torturers.

The *secondino* led him to the end of another corridor, knocked sharply on a heavy wooden door, and peeked in the little window, as if he were paying a social call. "Anybody home?" he called, winking at the female guard, who tried several keys on a large ring before finding one that unlocked the door.

Woody, who had to stoop to enter the cell, stared about him, looking at everything except the figure lying on the narrow bed—at the toilet bucket, which gave off an unpleasant smell; at the stack of books on a wooden table; at the metal grate—a system of slats—that covered the window.

"I'll be right outside," the guard said. Woody could hear her closing the door behind her, and then he could hear her saying something to the *secondino*, and then he could hear them both laughing.

Angela was lying on her side so that her small breasts sagged to one side under her thin T-shirt. Her back was to the wall, and a book was propped up on the bed beside her. The fingers on her right hand were bound up on splints. She looked at him without curiosity and turned back to her book. Woody waited till she came to a stopping place—the end of a chapter, or the end of a story—and let the book fall closed on the bed.

"I've been reading your thesis," he said, falling back on his prepared text. His legs were trembling; he didn't know how long he could stand. "Do you mind if I ask you a few questions?"

She said nothing.

"Do you mind if I ask you some questions?"

She lay on her side looking at him. Her face registered no emotion. "What do you want?"

"I'm an American journalist," he said. "They told you I was coming. They told me it was all arranged."

"I have so many visitors," she said, "it's hard to keep them straight."

Woody thought she must be speaking ironically, but there was no irony in her voice. "May I sit down?"

"Sit down," she said; "and if you have something to say, say it."

Woody pulled the chair out from under the table, which was bolted to the wall, and sat down. Angela sank back on the pillow.

"You're an admirer of Jack Kerouac and Allen Ginsberg," he said, "and the early Norman Mailer."

"The beat generation, yes," she said, pronouncing "beat generation" in English, only she said "bit generation." "They were reacting to an immoral bourgeois culture. It was a natural reaction, but pathetic. They had no plan, no coherent philosophy, no serious alternative to the status quo. All they could do was make some noise, to set themselves off. It was pitiful really. Existential despair is always pitiful."

"Because it abandons traditional values?"

"What other values are there? When you're cut off from your

moral bearings, what's left? When you mock honor and truth and justice, when you say that they're just the product of this or that socioeconomic or psychological force, then what do you expect? You need a philosophy that goes beyond these things, and beyond existentialism. Existentialism is a stopgap measure."

"And who's cut us off from our moral bearings?"

"Your Jewish professors, Freud and Marx." She raised herself up on one elbow.

"And you have an alternative philosophy?"

"I thought you'd read my thesis?"

"A return to traditional values?"

"What's the alternative?"

"That's what I had trouble understanding, this alternative, this notion of traditional values."

The smell from the toilet bucket was pervasive. Whatever thoughts he might have had about forgiving her gave way to a persistent fantasy, only this time he imagined shoving her head down into a bucket of her own excrement.

"Hitler went too far," she said, "but he offered men something that Freud and Marx had taken away; he gave men back their dignity. Men aren't just the puppets of vast impersonal forces, unless they think they are. A man should be like lightning out of a dark cloud."

"Evola?"

"Nietzsche: 'I want to teach men the sense of their existence, which is the Superman, the lightning-out-of-the-dark-cloud man.'"

"And that's what you want to do, teach men the sense of their existence?" He'd been keeping his feet flat on the floor, but now his legs started to bounce involuntarily on the balls of his feet, the way he'd sometimes bounced them deliberately when he was a schoolboy to make the windows in the classroom rattle.

She suddenly sat up on the edge of the bed and began to stare at him, as if he had finally caught her attention.

"You're not a journalist," she said sharply. "You sat with the *parenti*, in the courtroom."

"Not always. I'm a journalist too. Sometimes I sat with the *giornalisti*."

"What did you come here for?"

Woody didn't know what to say.

"Did you come to forgive me?"

"I . . . I . . . Yes," he said, though in fact at the moment forgiveness was the last thing on his mind.

"I can't believe this, I really can't. They told me you were an American journalist, but you're somebody's relative and you've come to forgive me. And you're not even an Italian. Don't you even know you're supposed to wait awhile, a couple of years, till the system has beaten me down? This is an outrage."

"My daughter was killed in the station."

"So you want to make a noble gesture. So you'll feel better. You want to be healed. You want to put an end to your pain. You can't do it, can't bring your daughter back. The door is closed. But if you forgive me, then that will release some of the pressure. Are you going to see the others too? Aldo? Carlo? Roberto?"

Like the reporter, she had perhaps grasped his purpose more clearly than he himself. As if he were not the last to know, but the last to fully understand. He had not been able to conceal his innermost secret from anyone, not even from his daughter's killer. He recognized a three-volume set of *Il Signore degli Anelli* in the stack of books on the table.

"I've read your thesis," he said again, without thinking. "Would it be all right if I asked you some questions. I'd like to ask you about *The Lord of the Rings* too. I read that aloud to my daughters. Three times. I'd be curious—"

"It's a little early, isn't it?" she said, interrupting him. "The trial's hardly over."

"My daughter was still alive," he said, "when I got to Bologna, my wife and I. I looked through all the bodies at the morgue on Via Irnerio and she wasn't there, she was in the Ospedale Maggiore, in the intensive care unit. A young woman who hadn't been identified, they said at the Palazzo d'Accursio."

"You should have waited a decent interval."

"I conjugated the *mi*-verbs in the cab, I teach Greek. The doctor tried to prepare me, it took a while in the hospital, I had to put on a hospital gown and little plastic booties over my shoes."

"Stop it," Angela said. "Just stop it."

"Why do you think I've come here?" Woody asked. "Do you really think I came to forgive you?"

She looked at him again and let out a startled cry, but Woody was on top of her. "If you scream I'll kill you," he whispered. He had his hands around her throat, pressing gently but not too gently. He listened for the guard, half expecting her to push the door open, but there was no sound.

"I could hardly breathe," he said, "I couldn't afford to cry, but little crying sounds kept coming out of my mouth anyway, little animal sounds, I couldn't hold them back. 'Cookie. Aaaaah, aaaaah, aaaaah.' I couldn't stop." In Angela's ear he repeated the little animal cries that had come out of his mouth in the intensive care unit: *Aaaaah, aaaaah, aaaaah, aaaaah, aaaaah. Aaaaah, aaaaah. Aaaaah, aaaaah, aaaaah.* In his fantasies he had often closed his hands around her throat, just as he had often fucked this woman or that; but the reality was different from the fantasies, just as the reality of Allison and Hannah and Turi and Gabriella had been different from the sweet tang of fantasy, humbling him and yet filling him with joy at their touch. He could feel the pulse in her throat, a small bird trembling in his hands.

"The doctor put an arm around me," he whispered. "I wanted to embrace her, but the doctor pulled me back, she'd been too badly burned, on her upper body, I had to be careful not to disturb the bandages. I touched her legs and her stomach and then I touched her between her legs through the sheet, I could feel her pubic hair, it was sharp and wiry like a pot scraper.

"'Cookie, it's me, Pop.'" He repeated the words in Angela's ear, his lips touching her. "'Cookie, it's me, Pop.' And I thought, She can hear my voice, she's moving a little under my hand. 'Your mom and I are here. Mom's at the hotel with Allison. I want you to hang on, I can't tell you . . . I can't tell you . . . I can't tell you . . . Christ, I don't know what I'm saying.' Just like now, Angela. Angela Strappafelci. I was thinking she used to weigh a hundred twenty-five pounds, five feet six inches, she played volleyball at Harvard, and she played the guitar a little, and the piano since she was five years old. I was already thinking about prostheses. One arm was gone from the shoulder; but the other was only half gone. There was even a kind of joy in these thoughts. Her first words were 'Piggies run in houses.'"

Angela twisted suddenly, broke free and tried to cry out, but only a small, thin sound came out of her mouth.

Woody pushed her head down into the hard prison mattress, choking her. "You have to listen to me," he said; "you're the only one I can tell this to."

He waited for her to stop struggling, and then he lay down on the bed beside her, keeping his hand clamped around her throat.

"It was a small room just like this one, and Cookie had her own nurse. There were other people in other rooms, but I couldn't think about anybody but Cookie. I could see her in her lumberjack shirt, black leather hands, or hooks, sticking out the sleeves. I didn't know what was available, what was the latest in prosthetic arms. I started to ask the doctor but I couldn't think right in Italian. Do you know what a lumberjack is? *Un taglialegna. Taglialegna.* The doctor took me by the arm, out of the room, into a corridor. There were elevators, the lobby was crowded but air-conditioned. It was too far to walk *to* the hospital, but not too far to walk *back*. At the hotel my wife was trying to rest, but she got out of bed every five minutes to smoke a cigarette. The room was full of smoke, even though the windows were open. Allison, our friend, had her own room but she stayed with us. I drank some mineral water and then we got something to eat, which we paid for with tickets from the Comune. Allison paid cash for hers. Then we went back to the hospital in a taxi, but when we got to the intensive care unit Cookie wasn't there. Out the window I could see the river. I didn't know its name then, but now I know it's the Reno. I'm looking out the window while the doctor— the same doctor who talked to me earlier—tells us that Cookie's dead. Someone had been trying to call us at the hotel. I was stunned, but my wife—she hadn't stopped talking, she talked right through the doctor's explanation—she didn't believe the doctor. She wanted to see Cookie. I didn't think it was a good idea, but I didn't know how to stop her. The doctor found someone to take us down to the hospital morgue—her body was still on a gurney. My wife took one look and started to laugh. 'That's not Cookie,' she kept saying, and laughing. 'That's not Cookie, that's not my daughter.' Allison helped me get her back to the hotel. She wanted to go to a bar in the piazza to get a beer. She wanted to sit outside. She wasn't hungry, but she drank some beer and smoked, and afterwards she fell asleep in her clothes on the bed in the hotel. Later on I went back to the hospital. I knew Hannah was mistaken, I knew there wasn't any hope, I knew it was foolish, that I couldn't have mistaken my own daughter, but I had to know for sure. Maybe the woman in the hospital all blown up wasn't Cookie, but the body'd already been taken to the morgue on Via Irnerio for an official autopsy. The taxi took twenty minutes to get to the morgue. There were only two volunteers left, but I was glad to see them, to have someone walk with me down the wide corridor to the chapel. There was dried blood on the tile floor where the bodies had been laid out, and there were coffins stacked up all along the corridor with numbers chalked on the sides; I could see bodies on the tables in the autopsy rooms. The morgue was air-conditioned, but the smell of the bodies was strong, bodies and carbolic and camphor. Cookie was in a wooden coffin in the chapel. I could see blood on the sheet that was pulled up over her. There were only a couple of unclaimed bodies, but bodies were coming from different hospitals for autopsies. What I was looking for was a V-shaped scar on Cookie's bottom where she fell on a piece of broken glass at the pool in St. Clair when she was six years old. I've only seen it two or three times since she was a little girl, but I can see it in my mind. The attendant helped me lift her out of the wooden coffin onto a gurney. We turned her over, and there, on her left buttock, the scar spread its wings, like a bird in a child's drawing. When we turned her back over I pulled her tight against me, I didn't need to worry about her burns now, or her bandages. Without her arms she seemed skinny, like a little girl. The sheet fell off and she was naked. I ran my hands through her hair and I kissed her neck and another attendant came and we got her back into the coffin. No one tried to stop me from kissing her, they just waited till I was done, and I remember thinking, This is Italy."

He stood up, releasing his grip on Angela. He thought that if she started shouting he would have to kill her, but she remained quiet. He waited until the silence became unbearable, and then he said, "I'm sorry."

She rubbed her throat. "Who the fuck do you think you are?" Her voice was hoarse.

"I'm sorry," he said again. "It's been so long, I didn't think . . . It wasn't what I meant . . ."

"You're only sorry you lost your nerve," she said. She had lost all fear. "Pathetic," she said. "You're like my father. You and my father: nobodies; little men; cowards; afraid of everything. Middle-class comfort, that's what you want. Middle-aged, middle-class men, functionaries, flunkies, afraid to get involved in politics, afraid to commit yourself to a noble cause, *les hommes moyens sensuels*—oh yes, I learned some French too—afraid to fuck, afraid you'll lose your pension, afraid of what people will think, afraid of being alone, afraid of dying, afraid to kill—*una mezzatacca*, that's my father, afraid to play bridge for ten lire a point. Once he bought a leather jacket for three hundred thousand lire. Then it wasn't the color he thought it was in the store window. It looked different in the light and he was upset, but he was afraid to take it back. He already had a leather jacket. My mother was furious, so she bought a leather jacket too."

"And in your *civiltà solare* people wouldn't play bridge or have affairs, or be afraid of dying? They wouldn't have little dinner parties, or spend too much money on clothes?"

"Individualism is the problem, the whole problem. When you think of yourself as a discrete atom, you experience all these fears. When you think of yourself as part of a greater whole, then you don't have to cling to your own little individuality, your own paltry little achievements. You start to think about your responsibilities to the community rather than your precious individual freedoms to do whatever you want. Which means playing bridge and buying things and having little dinner parties."

"And you, you've chosen the heroic life?"

"Yes," she said without hesitating.

"You were Frodo Baggins carrying the ring up Mount Doom, only you carried a bomb to the station, to blow up the corrupt bourgeois civilization."

"Fuck you."

"You and Niccolò Bosco. Which one of you was Frodo and which was Sam? Disguised like German tourists. Jesus Christ. I think you got it backwards; I think you got your signals crossed. Do you know I've read *The Lord of the Rings* aloud three times, to my daughters? I have three daughters."

"Like a king in a fairy tale," she said. "A big-fucking-deal king."

"Your father would like to see you," he said. "He's waiting in the little bar across from the visitors' entrance. You never wrote to him from Argentina, did you."

She shrugged her shoulders.

"Do you know how much it would mean to him? So what if he's a little man? I'm a little man too; you let me come."

"I didn't know who you were."

"You want to teach men their true existence, like Nietzsche?"

She said nothing.

"You've taught me," he said. "In a way. Not the way I would have chosen."

"I think you'd better go," she said.

"Did your father abuse you? Did he beat you? Did he . . . touch you, frighten you?"

She laughed dismissively, blowing her lips out: "Phuh. You're like Dottor Freud," she said; "you want a psychological explanation for everything."

"I'd prefer a Marxist explanation, but I can't find one. I think your political agenda's all smoke; I think you're just making noise with your bombs, like the beats. You think you're the company of the ring, a small heroic band, but all you can do is mock. *Épater le bourgeois.* Anybody can play. But the truth is nobody wants another *duce*; you don't have a plan, you've got a fantasy."

"Get out."

"Will you let your father come to see you?"

"No."

"Do you remember Beccone?"

For the first time he saw an opening, a chink in the armor, a small crack in the wall that indicated a secret doorway.

"How do you know about Beccone?"

"From your father. He asked me to write something true about you, and that's the only true thing I've been able to find. You must have loved your father then, when you took Beccone down to the river and let him go in his little coffin. Wasn't that something true?"

"My father was afraid. He should have killed him, he should have killed that bastard Scarpisi, Vincenzo Scarpisi, that was his name, that cocksucking Communist; he was just a kid, but he thought he was a big shot; Babbo should have gone to the MSI section leader if he was afraid to kill him himself—someone there would have done the job, the Communists were trying to take over the neighborhood—but he was afraid, afraid, a coward."

"Is this the way you felt at the time?"

"I didn't understand at the time. All I knew was that Beccone was dead, and he killed him, Vincenzo the big shot. Later I understood."

"Later you joined the youth section of Msi and then ORA?"

"Yes."

"And this is your *civiltà solare*?"

She said nothing.

"When I saw you holding on to the bars," Woody said, "I imagined for a moment that you were my daughter. It was only two seconds, but that was enough. I loved my daughter so much." As he reimagined this moment the possibility of forgiveness, which had vanished so completely, now returned with renewed force, as if the earlier possibility had been a fantasy and now he was confronting the reality, the *Ding an sich*. "At that moment," he went on, "I knew I could love you too. I didn't think it all out then. I could still love you. You were right at the beginning. You understood what I wanted better than I did myself. I thought that's what I wanted, and then it wasn't, but then on another level it really was. I *have* to love you, because hating you is too hard. I can't bear it."

Woody suddenly felt that in spite of everything great forces were being concentrated in him, like rays of sunlight in a magnifying glass, concentrated on a piece of paper. Rays of love. Not coming out of him but through him, concentrated on Angela Strappafelci, the source of all his anguish. He knew his intentions fully and clearly now, not through a glass darkly but face to face. He watched for the first trace of smoke, and then the orange glow, and then the yellow flame. He thought that if he could hold her in his arms, let the tears flow, let his tears mingle with hers, then the source of his greatest anguish might be transformed into a source of great joy. "Your father built a little coffin for Beccone," he said. "You took Beccone down to the river so he could drift out to sea. You must have loved him at that moment. Your father. That's what has to be true. Hold on to the reality, not the theory."

He took a step towards her, but she started back, as if he had raised a hand to strike her, or to make an unwelcome advance.

"I'm sorry," he said.

"Get out," she said for the third time.

"Will you let your father visit?"

She shook her head.

"What shall I tell him?"

"Don't tell him anything, *niente, nulla*. Do you understand? You shouldn't have come here."

Woody stood, transfixed, trying to think of what he might say, but she turned away from him, like the shade of Telamonian Ajax turning away from Odysseus in the land of the Cimmerians; and like Odysseus, Woody wondered if in that darkness she might still have spoken to him, might have conquered her indignation and her pride; he wondered what he might have answered; wondered what else he might have said; wondered if they might still have embraced each other, like Achilles and Priam. He stood, looking at her back, at her sharp shoulder blades and her dark hair, cropped close, till the silence became too terrible to bear and he began to pound on the door to summon the guard.

THE WARDEN'S office was full of reporters.

"*Nulla, niente,*" Woody repeated. "I have nothing to say. Please."

"Did you forgive her?" they wanted to know, asking over and over. "What did she say?"

"It's not a question of forgiveness," Woody said, and then he sat in silence, refusing to say a word, till finally the warden sent them away.

"You were right," the warden said, "not to say anything."

"What do you mean?"

"Sometimes the truth is too hard. It could destroy everything."

"You were listening?"

"Of course."

"You heard every word?"

"Not every word—you were speaking softly—but enough. It was not what I expected; the guard should have intervened. If something had happened to her . . . But don't worry. I shall see that the tape is destroyed."

Woody was disgusted.

"You're upset. Of course," the warden said.

"Yes. Of course."

•   •   •

SIGNOR STRAPPAFELCI was waiting for him in the bar. Woody set the fruit basket down on the table. Signor Strappafelci looked at it, a man recognizing an ill omen. He was wearing the same wool suit and tie he'd worn in Bologna, though he'd had it cleaned. Woody ordered an espresso. He didn't allow his face to give any hope to Signor Strappafelci. It was hotter than it had been earlier, but the sun was starting to go down and soon it would cool off. The bar was about to close. Woody paid for his coffee. "Let's go for a walk," he said.

They walked along the river, past the Palazzo Salviati, now an international hostel for pilgrims, to Piazza delle Rovere and then turned left, up the Gianicolo, which rises steeply from the Tiber. They climbed the hill in silence, and when they got to the top they sat on a bench.

"Orange?" Signor Strappafelci took a small knife out of his pants pocket. "So, how is she?"

The fruit basket was on the bench between them. Woody picked up an orange. "She's all right. Very strong." He took the knife from Signor Strappafelci and started to peel the orange.

"She don't want no fruit?"

"No," Woody said. "You'll have to drop off the fruit in the morning at the visitors' entrance. They can't accept fruit at the main entrance. Someone has to go through everything."

"But she'll take it? You asked her?"

"No, I didn't ask her about the fruit."

From the inside pocket of his jacket Signor Strappafelci pulled out a large white handkerchief and handed it to Woody to wipe his hands.

They walked along the top of the hill—unable to see down into the city because of the trees—till they came to Piazza del Faro, where there was an ice cream truck. Kids were leaning against the truck, eating ice cream. From here they had a good view of the prison below them. Regina Coeli. Queen of Heaven. You could see the shape from up here. The two convents, which had been joined in the eighteenth century, extended towards them like a huge cross, the top pointing towards them, wings shooting off to the left and to the right, angling towards the Gianicolo. Three more wings farther back, on the left, intersected the main trunk of the cross at right angles. On the right the wings were asymmetrical. Probably where the two convents had been joined, Woody thought.

"That's the wing for politicals." Signor Strappafelci indicated one of the arms of the cross. "Where you were. You can see her window. There aren't many women, just her and a few Red Brigades."

Woody could see the black iron slats, on a frame, that covered the windows—*bocche di lupo*, wolf mouths, they were called. The slats were at an angle, like Venetian blinds, to allow some light and some air, but they prevented the prisoners from communicating with anyone outside, or from shouting to each other out the window. There had been lots of protests.

"In the old days," Signor Strappafelci said, "there were women who stood on the hill, right where we are now, to shout messages to the prisoners. News from the family, you know. If somebody had a baby. They had great big voices so you could hear them a long ways off. The prisoners would come to the windows. You had to pay them, the women, but now . . ." He shrugged.

Woody looked out at the city, the reverse image of what he'd seen that morning from the Campidoglio. The Palatine Hill was now to his right, Santa Maria Maggiore to the left. The great stories into which we fit our lives. He hadn't conveyed this to the students this morning.

"You see Santa Maria Maggiore?" he asked Signor Strappafelci, pointing.

Signor Strappafelci nodded.

"You know it snowed in A.D. 358, on August fifth, my birthday. The Virgin Mary appeared to the pope and told him to build a church on the spot where it snowed. In August. It was hot, but it snowed."

Signor Strappafelci nodded. "They do it every year," he said, "but with rose petals coming down out of the ceiling, except now they use something else, gardenias. I guess the rose petals got too expensive."

"We went to see it when we lived in Rome," Woody said. "The girls got a big kick out of it."

They sat in silence for a while.

"How about visitors?" Signor Strappafelci asked. "Did you ask her?"

Woody looked at the white stubble, like snow, on Signor Strappafelci's face. It was getting dark.

"Look!" Signor Strappafelci said, as if he'd seen a shooting star. "She's turned her light on." Lights were coming on here and there in the prison. Woody could see thin strips of light outlining the *bocca di lupo* on Angela's window. He was thinking about Marlow's lie to the beloved at the end of *Heart of Darkness*. He too would tell a lie, if he could, if he thought he could get away with it. He'd tell Signor Strappafelci that his daughter's last words were that she loved him. But he'd be found out the next day, or the day after, and it would only cause more pain.

He was also thinking about the end of the *Aeneid*—Aeneas killing Turnus, undermining the whole big story. At least that's the way it seemed to him at this moment. The death of Turnus—not the founding of Rome—was the moment of truth. And he thought farther back in the story, to Achilles and Hector and Odysseus. Especially Odysseus, who was closest to Woody's heart because he saw things more clearly than the others. It's not the great stories that give meaning to the little ones; it's the other way around. He'd had it backwards this morning.

He turned away. "No," he said. "No, she doesn't want to see you. I'm sorry." He was tempted to add "Not yet, anyway," but he didn't. It wasn't a time for fudging.

For the first time Signor Strappafelci lost his grip and gave way to tears. He was seeing clearly too. As he wiped his face with his handkerchief he knocked over the fruit basket, which he'd set down on the top of the low wall where they were standing. Apples and oranges and kiwis and avocados rolled over the wall and down the hill, into the trees. Some fell into the dirt at their feet.

"What am I going to tell my wife?"

There's nothing to tell her, Woody thought. They were up against a mystery that couldn't be explained, or explained away, couldn't be deconstructed.

"Tell her . . . ," he said. But the truth was too hard. It was like a rock in the river, or an island, that couldn't be worn away. The river would wash around it forever, the way the Tiber washed around the Isola Tiberina.

"Tell her . . . ," he said again. But he had no wisdom adequate for this occasion.

They backed away from the wall and sat down on a bench. Stars were shining overhead now, as numerous as the fires in the Trojan camp. Indifferent, though. Indifferent? But why? Why project indifference onto the universe when in fact our deepest experiences are full of meaning and purpose, and love? What experiences should we take as clues to the true nature of things, *rerum natura*?

If it had been in his power, Woody would have placed Signor Strappafelci on the wall with Hector and Andromache; in the tent with Achilles and Priam; in Hades with Odysseus, trying in vain to embrace the shade of someone he loved, or waiting for a word from an old comrade.

"Tell her . . . ," he said a third time. He knew that love too is a mystery that can't be explained away. Harder than the rock; deeper than the river. More mysterious than the darkness that was gathering around them. He knew this in his heart, but he didn't know if he'd be able to explain it to the old man sitting next to him on a park bench on the Gianicolo, overlooking the eternal city.

My
Love
Is
Carpet

Woody did not return to the Mirsadiqis' that night. Instead he wandered around the city for several hours, describing a rough circle from St. Peter's Square to the Pantheon to the Colosseum to Santa Maria Maggiore, then northwest to Piazza Barbarini and the Spanish Steps and Piazza del Popolo, where he took his shoes off and sat with his feet in the big central fountain, the way the girls used to do when they'd lived around the corner on Via Savoia—one of the happiest years of his life. He didn't walk past their old apartment; he just sat and looked at the Egyptian obelisk and Valadier's nineteenth-century lions, and then he put his shoes and socks back on without drying off his feet and walked all the way down the Corso to the Monument to Victor Emmanuel. Too tired to walk any farther, he took a cab to Piazza Ostiense, near the Protestant Cemetery. At three o'clock in the morning he peeked through a little hole in the wall at Keats's grave: "Here lies one whose name was writ in water." And then he went to the nearby Hotel Sant'Anselmo, in Piazza Sant'Anselmo, which was where he'd originally planned to stay while in Rome.

The night clerk was asleep at the front desk. There were no rooms, he said, when Woody woke him up.

Woody folded a fifty-thousand-lire note between two fingers and held it out to the man. "I have to have a room," he said.

"I'm sorry."

Woody sat down on a thinly padded sofa. "Then I'll sleep here," he said, and began to untie his shoes.

A chambermaid was called; a room was found, a tiny *cabina* on the roof. Woody paid with his credit card and handed over his passport and the fifty-thousand-lire note, which the night clerk slipped into his pants pocket. The chambermaid showed him the elevator and told him to wait for her on the top floor. When she appeared with her arms full of sheets he followed her out onto a balcony and then up an outside flight of stairs.

"It will be very hot," she said. "When American writers come here, they all want to stay in this room—ever since someone famous wrote about it for a big airline magazine, the kind that people read right on the plane. He comes here once a year and always stays in that room. It's very romantic, but in summer it's too hot. The sun beats down all day. You can leave the door open, though. Nobody comes here now. I'll lock the balcony door."

"Could you bring me some *acqua minerale*," Woody asked.

"And some white wine?"

"Please."

The room was unbearably hot, but by the time she brought the water and the wine he was asleep in the narrow bed. He dreamed not of Angela Strappafelci but of Cookie. She must have been twelve or thirteen because she was wearing her first pair of glasses and looking up at the sky. It was dark and she was standing out on the back-porch steps, where he had stood with Turi when he released the bat; where he'd been sitting with Allison when the owl landed on the grape arbor. "I can see them perfectly, Pop," she cried; "I can see the stars." And he knew that she had finally come to say good-bye. She ran towards him, and in his eagerness to embrace her he started forward, but she slipped through his arms, like ether, like air, like a dream.

He woke with a start. It was raining and the room had cooled off. The chambermaid had left a bottle of *acqua minerale* and a bottle of Frascati on the table next to his bed. The wine had been opened and the cork stuck halfway back in the mouth. Woody poured himself a glass and sipped it, looking out the open door at the rain. When he'd drunk half the bottle of wine he filled his glass with sparkling water.

He showered, and then he lay on the bed, naked, listening to the rain drumming on the roof of his *cabina*, and then he slept again. The next evening the chambermaid brought another bottle of wine and another bottle of *acqua minerale* and some bread and cheese. Woody heard her footsteps on the gravel of the roof and covered himself with the sheet.

"Are *you* a writer?" she asked, looking down at him.

Woody shook his head.

"If you need anything else," she said, "you can call on the phone. I'll be here all night."

On the evening of the third day he heard footsteps on the gravel and covered himself with the sheet, but it wasn't the chambermaid, it was Allison Mirsadiqi. She sat on the edge of the bed and put her hand on his forehead.

"You're running a fever," she said. "I guess you can stay home from school. If you promise to rest."

"I can't make any promises."

"Woody, what happened?"

"A dark Cimmerian land," he said: "ἔνθα δὲ Κιμμερίων ἀνδρῶν δῆμός τε πόλις τε." He took her hand. "'By night we sailed on to the edge of Ocean, to the land of the Cimmerians, hidden in mist and cloud. The eye of Helios never lights on those men, at morning, when he climbs the starry sky.'"

"Did you see her?"

"Yes. She came to me in a dream."

"Who came, Woody?"

"Cookie. She was standing on the back steps and then she was running towards me and I opened my arms to hold her. Like Odysseus and his mother, Anticleia. τρὶς δέ μοι ἐκ χειρῶν σκιῇ εἴκελον ἢ καὶ ὀνείρῳ / ἔπτατ'. 'Three times she went sifting through my hands, like a shadow, or a dream.' But it was only once, Allie," he said, using his old nickname for her. "Not three times. She was wearing her new glasses."

"Woody, I'm so sorry."

"Yes," he said; "she came to say good-bye."

"Did she *say* anything? Like Anticleia?"

He nodded his head. "She was wearing her new glasses," he said; "she could see the stars."

At six o'clock the chambermaid brought more water and wine, a half loaf of bread, and a chunk of Gorgonzola. He broke off a piece of bread for Allison and then one for himself. "Do you want some wine? There's another glass in the bathroom."

She shook her head. "I'll pour some for you." She filled the glass on the small table by the bed. "What about la Strappafelci?"

Woody picked up the glass and swallowed some wine. "Angela? Yes. I saw her too. I did hold *her* in my arms. I almost killed her. I *could* have killed her. I was *that* close." He held up thumb and fore-finger, almost touching.

"But you didn't?"

He shook his head again.

"They left you alone with her?"

He nodded.

"Only in Italy," she said.

"Only in Italy."

"Did you forgive her?"

"I'm not sure. It wasn't yes or no, either/or. It wasn't like that at all."

"Will you come back with me now?" She shut his eyes with her fingers.

"Yes," he said.

"About Turi . . ."

"I'm not going to say I'm sorry," he said, "so if—" but she covered his mouth with her hand.

"You don't have to explain anything," she said. "Not now, not ever. At least not to me. Though I have to say . . . I hardly know *what* to say. For a while some pretty choice words kept bubbling out of my mouth; I'll bet I dialed your number fifty times. But I never let it ring more than once. I always hung up at the last minute. I didn't want to say something I didn't really want to say. If it hadn't been for her underpants . . . on your clothesline . . . But I suppose if it hadn't been that it would have been something else. But how could such a thing happen, Woody? You amaze me."

"Allie," he said, "you saved my life once. In Bologna. And Turi saved my life too. In St. Clair. I was dying. My life was over. I didn't realize it at the time; I didn't realize it till just now, but it's true. It's that simple. My life and my soul."

She smiled. "Don't you think your idea of salvation is a bit unconventional?"

"For a Christian, perhaps, but not for a practicing Muslim."

"Do you think you could explain that to her father?"

"I suppose I owe him that much."

"Don't be afraid, Woody; he's a good man."

"I'm not afraid," he said. "I'm not afraid of anything."

DURING THE long, hot days Woody sat in the rooftop garden amidst the bougainvillea and the fruit trees—palms, oranges, lemons, dates. He'd browse through a copy of the *Odyssey* that Allison bought for him or pick up Babak's guitar, a National Steel, like his own, but with a large single-cone resonator instead of a tricone. Less sustain, but more punch. He tuned it to an open D so Babak could play simple chords up and down the neck with just one finger. Alireza flew to Port Said to see about the ship, and then to Dubai on other business. When he returned two weeks later he and Woody drove to Civitavecchia in a vintage Alfa Romeo, a stunning coral-colored four-seater with wide whitewalls and wire-rimmed hubcaps with coral-colored spokes—one of the models that had made America fall in love with Italian cars after the war. "I've had this car completely rebuilt," Alireza told him as they turned onto the *autostrada* that circles the city. "A new Giulia engine, but exactly the same as the original. Mechanically this car is perfect." He paused. "And you're looking good too. Maybe not perfect, but better."

The top was down and the wind felt good in their faces, but it was hard to hear. Alireza was saying something about a horse with a blindfold. "My grandfather took me," he shouted, turning towards Woody, "to see the Portuguese Castle on the island of Hormoz." Near the castle, Woody gathered, there was some kind of mill. "The horse went round and round," Alireza shouted. "I asked my grandfather about the blindfold. He said that without the blindfold the horse would get dizzy, always going in a circle." There was something else that Woody couldn't catch. "I think you're like that horse," Alireza went on.

"Blindfolded?"

"Yes, going round and round."

"And if I take the blindfold off?"

"Exactly. I think you've already taken it off."

"And now I'll be too dizzy to walk straight?"

"Not if we take off your yoke and give you some nice oats to eat. Then you'll be able to walk a perfectly straight line." Alireza put his hand on Woody's knee. "I was thinking of your daughter. Cookie." Alireza shouted something else into the wind that Woody couldn't catch. "You gave us quite a scare, you know. We waited for you till three o'clock in the morning and then Allison Joon called the metropolitan police. But she's told you all that."

"It wasn't what I expected," Woody said. "I think I was in a state of shock."

"It seldom is," Alireza said, "when you go to a place like that."

They drove in silence for a few minutes.

"I remember her very well," Alireza said, picking up the thread of their earlier conversation. "She took Turi to Piazza del Popolo. Shapur was chasing all over the city after them. Turi's bodyguard. And then they went to see my aunt, who lived over one of my rug shops. Tanteen Minoo, everyone called her, because she was so proud of her French; but she never learned Italian."

They passed a sign for Cerveteri. "There's an Etruscan cemetery here," Woody said. "My wife and I and the girls came down here one day when we were living in Rome."

"That's where we're going to dry the rugs," Alireza said.

"In the cemetery?"

"Near the cemetery. A large wheat field. Two fields. Summer wheat. It was harvested three days ago. The little ears were not quite ripe, but I . . ." He took both hands off the steering wheel and trilled octaves on an imaginary piano.

"The Greek vase that Thomas Hoving bought under the counter for the Metropolitan Museum was stolen from here. Hard to believe he got away with it. I'd like to see it again, the cemetery."

When Alireza finally brought up the subject of Allison, and Turi, he switched from Italian to Persian. Woody pretended not to understand. This was what he'd been afraid of all along. But now the wind, which had been his enemy, had become his ally. He kept shaking his head and throwing up his hands to indicate that he couldn't hear well enough to understand, and they drove without speaking, past the Furbara exit on the *autostrada*, and before Alireza could say something more, Woody said, in Italian, "How often do you go back to Iran?"

Alireza leaned back in his seat, and Woody knew that he had won a reprieve.

"Twice a year, usually. I have many contacts I like to keep fresh: with officials, *bazaaris*, tax people, relatives. I like to get a sense of what's going on."

"Do you always go to the same place?"

"No, no, I go to many places. Each city has its bazaar. You learn everything. I have a factor in the big bazaar in Tehran who really knows what's what. I don't buy anything without his say-so. He knows everything, the quality of rugs, the market conditions, everything. I don't go anywhere without him."

"What happens to the rugs?"

"The rugs are sent to be washed. If there are any problems with the fringes, these are put right. Then the rugs come back to the factor, who wraps them up—three or four rugs in a burlap sack, depending on the size of the rugs, of course. Then the sacks are bound together into bales and sealed in plastic. When everything is ready, the factor contacts a shipping company and makes all the arrangements, except in this case. I had a ship coming empty . . ." He raised his palms up before his face.

"What usually happens?"

"They take the rugs to Italy in a truck. That is what's usual. Or sometimes by air. Not usually by ship. If there are one or two thousand rugs, then maybe I ship them in a boat. If they are going to Rome they go to Civitavecchia. The trucks used to go through Yugoslavia. It's no longer possible, so they have to go to Turkey and take the ferry from Izmir to Brindisi. It takes twelve days."

"And the rug you sent me," Woody went on; "I don't know how to thank you."

Alireza was silent for a moment. "It belonged to my aunt, you know, Tanteen Minoo. She brought it with her from Tehran before the revolution."

"Is it a Kerman?" Woody asked.

"A Kerman? No, no. A Nain. It has a very different weave pattern. If you look closely you'll see that the lines of the weft are bowed; you can't see them along a complete traverse. The threads, you see; they use threads of different thickness so the weft widens and narrows. Some of the rugs from Esfahan look similar, but the weave pattern— the weave pattern you can see at once is very different."

Woody kept asking questions about the rug and the rug business, and about the fort designed by Michelangelo, and about a film that Alireza had mentioned—filmed in Civitavecchia—and about Stendhal, who had been the French consul in Civitavecchia at the time of his death, till they were safely in the port.

"No ships over ten thousand tons," Alireza said, looking around impatiently. "Mostly ferries to Sardinia."

A crew of dockworkers was already unloading the ship, but the weight of the wet rugs was so great that a cable on a crane had broken and they'd had to wait while the ship was moved to another berth.

A big crowd had assembled—Iranians and Italians; it was hard to tell them apart—to watch the containers being lowered onto the dock, which was lined with small vehicles: trucks, vans, even a couple of pickup trucks. Alireza knew many of the men personally, but he greeted strangers too, welcomed them, touched them, shook their hands as if they were old friends. He introduced Woody as he went along, to the customs inspector, to the insurance agent, to the two independent experts, one Iranian and one Italian, who would estimate the damage to each rug.

The first of the several containers holding the rugs was already on the dock. Two men standing on top of it were threading the hook of a second, smaller crane through the ropes binding the bales, which were too heavy for a man to lift. The bales at the top were unloaded quickly, but the wetter ones towards the bottom had expanded so that it was impossible to get the hook of the crane through the ropes. New ropes had to be worked around the bales, which were then lowered onto the dock, where they were cut open with hooked utility knives and spread out on an area of the pavement that had been swept clean.

"What do you look for?" Woody asked one of the experts, just to make conversation.

"The main thing is the colors," he said. "Have the colors been ruined?—that's the main question. Plain water itself won't hurt the rugs, but salt water can do damage, and dirty water from the hold. Who knows? You have to see."

Some of the rugs needed immediate attention. Certain colors were bleeding into others; the bleeding could be stopped only by the application of a certain acid, but if the acid touched another part of the rug, a part that was not bleeding, then that part would be ruined. "You drop a little tablet," the expert explained, "like an aspirin, into hot water, so you have a little broth. Very difficult. Very time-consuming."

The rugs were unfolded one at a time; the experts looked them over, conferred with the insurance agent, made some notes. They spent about two minutes per rug. Alireza, who recognized each rug, would announce its provenance and the price he'd paid for it, and then would help the insurance man locate it on the bill of lading, which must have been sixty or seventy pages long.

When the experts were done each rug was rolled up and loaded on a small truck, to be taken immediately to the wheat fields near the Etruscan cemetery. Woody was glad to lend a hand without being asked, glad to do something physical. The wet rugs, which weighed up to one hundred kilograms, buckled in the center and were hard to manage. They smelled like damp dogs. The Iranians, who were used to handling rugs, showed the Italians how to roll them loosely and double them over, cradling them in their arms. One of Alireza's men, who was organizing the small trucks, barked orders in Italian and then in Persian, keeping track of everything. Woody counted a dozen trucks.

They worked like that all morning. When they broke for lunch Woody did some calculations in his head. They were processing a rug every two minutes. A thousand rugs at two minutes per rug would come to two thousand minutes. Two thousand divided by sixty . . . about thirty-three hours. The rugs were all shapes and sizes, but if you figured the average was about six feet by eight feet . . . 6 x 8 x 1,000 would be 48,000 square feet. Divided by three, 16,000 square yards. No, you'd have to divide by nine, 48,000 divided by nine. Equals 5,333 square yards. A football field was, what, 100 yards by about 53 yards: 100 x 53 would be 5,300. So, a thousand rugs—and there were more than that—would cover an area the size of a football field, more if you allowed for space between the rugs.

In the afternoon Woody rode in one of the trucks out to the cemetery, which was about fifteen kilometers back towards Rome and in a little way from the coast. Alireza was totally absorbed with his work, and Woody had been absorbed too, not thinking about anything, especially not thinking about Angela Strappafelci; just cradling the wet rugs in his arms, hoisting them onto the trucks. But now he needed a break.

The truck drove slowly. Woody sat in the back on the damp rugs. The driver turned in from the coast on a narrow road that went through the modern city of Cerveteri, then on to Banditaccia, which was lined with cypress trees and pines and oleander with white and purple flowers. On the right were vineyards.

The driver dropped Woody off at the entrance to the cemetery, where he bought a ticket and picked up a map showing the principal tombs. Cookie had been sixteen when they visited in 1974. Sara had been ten, and Ludi five or six. Woody remembered the guide with the acetylene lamp who had led their group, about ten tourists, down into the major tombs. Woody'd had to carry Sara, and Hannah had carried Ludi.

He and Hannah had been reading D. H. Lawrence's *Etruscan Places*, which begins in Cerveteri, and though they were both skeptical of Lawrence's conclusions about phallic consciousness, they'd both been excited by the beautifully carved stone penises at the entrances and by a wall painting of a couple about to engage in anal intercourse, the tip of the man's long penis nudging the cleft of the woman's upraised buttocks. Woody asked the guide to hold his acetylene lamp up so they could get a better look. The rest of the group tittered, but everyone wanted to see. And then silence. And then on to the next wall painting.

They'd stopped in Cerveteri for an early supper before driving back to Rome, and Hannah went into a pharmacy on the edge of town and bought a tube of Vaseline. That night she knelt on the bed, her head down, like the woman in the wall painting, as if she were about to turn a somersault. Woody rubbed the Vaseline on his prick and entered her. "Oy oy oy," she cried when he finally got it all the way in. "Oy oy oy." And Woody thought that maybe Lawrence was right after all, and all those couples in the tombs were smiling because, like Woody and Hannah, they had a secret.

Woody wanted to see the image again. The kneeling woman. The man. He wanted them to speak to him again, though he wasn't sure what he wanted them to say.

You have to love the Etruscans, he imagined himself saying to Alireza that evening. *Their conception of the afterlife . . . There's no fear. No ingenious tortures in hell; no incredible boredom in heaven; just more fucking . . .* But then he thought that this wouldn't be the thing to say. *It must reflect a sense of well-being*, he imagined himself saying instead, *of being at home in the world.*

Since their visit in 1974 the major tombs had been equipped with electric lights, like chapels in a cathedral. You put two hundred-lire coins in the slot and the lights went on for two minutes. In the Tomb of the Reliefs Woody saw a dog and a goose carved in the wall of a funeral bedchamber. There were pillows on the bed, and even a pair of slippers. In other tombs couples reclined together, relaxed, captured in moments of affectionate intimacy by a camera that preserved their images in stone; or actually embracing under thin sheets of stone, their eyes locked together forever and ever; or handing each other eggs symbolizing immortality. (According to the experts. Maybe they just had a taste for hard-boiled eggs. There were big eggs *on* the tombs too.)

The anal-intercourse couple was in the Tomb of the Three Amphori. Woody waited for a group of German tourists, accompanied by a German guide, all carrying German cameras and German guidebooks, to move on, but they took their time. The guide kept putting more coins in the machine as he lectured.

Woody wanted the lovers to speak to him again, to reveal their secret. Was it that they had left behind an ennobling conception of death, had refused to let the prospect of death poison their lives? Was it that they had joined together the highest and the lowest? Gabriella had told him that the tastiest, most delicate part of the cow was the anus but that very few butchers knew how to prepare it properly. Most just threw it away. He wondered now if she'd been hinting at something. The idea gave him goosebumps.

But what about the eggs. Were the eggs an indication that the

Etruscans had wanted more? That this, whatever *this* was, wasn't enough? Woody wanted more too, not immortality, but the metaphor, the image, the melody that would make things right.

It was almost six o'clock by the time he left the cemetery. He walked down the road towards the wheat fields. A truck passed him from behind, full of rugs. He kept on walking. Another truck, empty, approached. He flagged it down and rode back to Civitavecchia.

All four containers had now been unloaded, and trestle tables had been set up in front of two of the restaurants that faced the wharf. Alireza had reserved rooms at a nearby hotel. Woody wanted to lie down for a while before supper, but waiters from the two restaurants were already setting bottles on the tables, red wine for the Italians, Coca-Cola for the Iranians, *acqua minerale* for everybody. The waiters soon returned with baskets of bread.

Inside the door of one of the restaurants was a picture, from *Paris Match*, of an Etruscan statue—a large man reclining. The top of his head was bald, but the long hair on the sides of his head was combed back carefully. A medallion on a chain around his neck rested on his fat belly. Below this was another photo, of an Italian man, also reclining, also bald, his hair swept back too, a gold chain around his neck, a medallion resting on his fat belly. He might have been the model for the Etruscan statue. That was the point of the article. Woody was too tired to read the entire article in French, but he picked out the general idea: that the blood of the Etruscans ran in the veins of modern Italians, not only in Tuscany but in Latium as well. Later he realized that the owner of the restaurant, who was walking up and down the rows of tables, was the man in the picture.

The dinner was very good—several kinds of pasta, served family style, were followed by platters of grilled meat and fish. Alireza, who seemed preoccupied, ate with the customs man and the insurance agent and the two experts. But he called down the table in Italian: "So, Voody Khan, you went to the tombs? Did you discover the famous secret of the Etruscans?"

"I think so," Woody said. "I think I discovered the secret."

Alireza looked surprised. "You'll have to tell me," he said, "but later, not now."

•　　•　　•

431

WORK BEGAN again early the next morning. Waiters from the various bars in the piazza brought coffee on trays, paper napkins twisted over the tops of the little demitasse cups, and plates of croissants and brioche, and a local Iranian restaurant provided Barbari bread and butter for the Iranians, and hard-boiled eggs and quince preserves.

Over half the rugs were already in the field, and Woody couldn't see the men in the bottom of the container that was being unloaded. A small crane dipped its hook, lifting out one bale at a time. Woody helped spread out the rugs, each one unfolding like a beautiful flower, which were then rolled back up and either loaded on one of the trucks or taken to another area of the parking lot to be treated with acid. The insurance agent smoked, dropping ashes on whatever rug he happened to be looking at.

Just before noon Woody rode out to the field itself to see the rugs, which, under the direction of Alireza's agent, had been and were being spread out systematically—not just flopped down—in rows, the good side up, the edges straight, worked into a pattern, like flagstones on a patio, so that no space was wasted.

The last load of rugs was sent off about three o'clock. Alireza conferred with the experts and the insurance man and the customs agent. One of Alireza's men sat at a table distributing money to the workmen, writing down their names.

Woody was ready to go home—back to Rome, that is. He was glad that he'd seen the cemetery again. He thought that the Etruscans had in fact spoken to him, not in a loud voice, as they had spoken to Lawrence, but softly, *sotto voce*, offering a kind of quiet revelation. No clouds parting, no bolt of lightning, just the sense that death need not poison life. He would remember the dog and the goose, and the stone slippers in the bedroom, and the couple engaged in anal intercourse, and Hannah crying "Oy oy oy" when he entered her *buco di culo*. No small comfort.

ALIREZA WAS tireless. He'd been working when Woody went to bed the night before, and he'd been at work before Woody got out of bed in the morning.

"Now we're going to take some pictures," he said.

They drove to a photography studio in Civitavecchia in a borrowed truck, and then out to the military airport with a professional photographer who had a very important-looking camera. The photographer himself was not an especially large man, but he refused to put his equipment in the back of the truck, so they were very crowded in the cab.

It was his studio camera, he said; a Mamiya RZ67 with a ninety-millimeter lens. "With anything longer your corners won't come into focus." He seemed quite excited about this assignment, and Woody guessed that Alireza had made it worth his while; but when he saw the military helicopter that Alireza had arranged to borrow, he started shaking his head.

"No no no."

"What's the matter?"

"You didn't say anything about a helicopter. You said an airplane."

"What's the difference?"

"You can't take the window out."

"They're taking the door off."

The photographer rolled his eyes.

"We'll do what we can," Alireza said.

The rotor on the helicopter was already whirling around, almost invisibly, and as they approached the helicopter it became harder and harder to hear what the photographer was saying.

"We'll just do what we can," Alireza shouted again; "it's too late to go back. It's almost four o'clock . . . the light . . ."

The photographer shrugged.

Two men in military uniforms were removing the door of the helicopter. There was no point in talking now. Too much noise. The pilot, smoking a cigarette, shook hands with Alireza. They talked in a kind of sign language, gesturing and nodding.

When the soldiers got the door unbolted they still had to pry it off its hinges with a pry bar. It—the whole enterprise—looked dangerous to Woody. A kind of harness had been attached inside to the roof and sides. Like . . . it wasn't like anything Woody had ever seen. Maybe a kind of sling. The photographer saw it too and started to look around him.

Woody indicated that he had to go to the bathroom.

"Hurry." Alireza mouthed the word, first in Persian, then in Italian.

He went into the hangar. When he came back Alireza and the photographer were arguing with their arms and hands. They were shouting too, but Woody didn't think they could possibly hear each other. The photographer was pointing and shaking his head. The pilot motioned them to get inside, pointing to headsets. They'd be able to hear each other through the headsets. But the photographer wouldn't get into the helicopter. Alireza and the pilot tried to take him by the arms, but the photographer shook himself loose.

A second pilot, the copilot, arrived and joined in the nonverbal argument.

Finally Alireza and the photographer went into the hangar where Woody had used the bathroom. In about five minutes Alireza came out with the big camera. There was no sign of the photographer.

Woody was anxious to get going. He was physically tired and wanted to sleep. He wanted to be alone, to reflect. But there was no time.

The inside of the helicopter was about the size of a car, with seats for six facing each other, three and three. It took Woody a while to realize that *he* had been elected to take the pictures. The pilot was already strapping him into the harness. When the pilot snapped the last hook and tightened the last strap, Alireza hung the camera over Woody's neck, and then the pilot put on the helmet with goggles and a headset.

In a few minutes Alireza's voice came over the headset. From a distance. Woody couldn't tell at first if he was speaking Persian or Italian: "Do you read me, Voody Khan? Over and out."

Woody tried to turn to see him, but the harness made it impossible to turn far enough.

"Don't try to turn, Voody Khan."

"This is what it must be like to be swaddled," Woody said.

"Can you hear me all right?"

"Yes, I can hear you."

"Good. Then we can talk better now. In the car . . . too much noise."

Woody's heart sank.

"This is a special kind of camera," Alireza went on. "It's very complicated, but very simple at the same time, if you know what I mean. You have to control only the light, like I showed you. You see? It is already set for a sunny day. You don't touch it unless the sun goes behind a cloud. Allah forbid."

The helicopter shuddered. Woody could see the tarmac moving through the opening where the door should have been. The tarmac remained still for a few seconds and then began to move again, first to the right and then doing a quarter turn beneath him as the helicopter shot up into the air. There was nothing to hang on to. The helicopter tilted to the left, and Woody could see the little airport beneath them. And the *autostrada*, running along the coast, the old Via Aurelia.

"You know, Voody Khan, I was very interested to meet you at last. In St. Clair." Alireza's voice again, coming through the headset. "I had heard so much about you, of course. My wife told me everything. It was no secret."

"I see."

"Everything, you understand."

"I'm not sure this is the time to talk about it."

"So I was very interested to meet you, to encounter this man who knew so much about my wife. And to see how I would react myself. Yes, I had my own agenda. You see, in my country it is not customary for a man of my position to choose a wife who has—how shall I put it?—danced with other men, the old dance of love, if you know what I mean. We have a special word for such women, and a special place for them. I know that it is different for you, and I know that you were not the only one. But for me it seemed at first to be a thing out of the question. A cultural imperative would militate against it. And then to learn that you two have fucked each other in Bologna . . . Did you know, Voody Khan, that I went to Bologna myself and stayed in the very same hotel, in the very same room, on the Via d'Azeglio, Via Massimo d'Azeglio? So I was not prepared to like you when we met in St. Clair, in the office of your president. But to . . . how shall I say?—to test my own strength, as an enlightened man . . . it has given me great pleasure. I experienced my own strength, my own generosity—ten million dollars, that's almost a billion rials, not a small sum, even for a man like me. But I *did* like you, Voody Khan. I sensed immediately that you were a kindred spirit, and I signed the papers in the office of your president, gave my pledge, my bond. And gave it gladly. I made special provisions for you. And then, Voody Khan, to discover that my daughter . . ."

He had evidently gone over this speech in his mind, perhaps had practiced it in front of the Venetian mirror that Woody had glimpsed through an open bedroom door. Through the door of the helicopter Woody could see nothing but the Tyrrhenian Sea.

"Just as I was congratulating myself on being such a noble spirit, and was wishing to congratulate you too, we drive to your beautiful villa, but no one is there, and my daughter retrieves her *tomoon* from your clothesline, and I realize . . . you have gone where I cannot follow you. Now my cultural imperative was different. It was not my obligation to kill you—we are not barbarians—but to take measures, steps. I no longer felt bound by my promise. But I resisted, and I have overcome the hot anger that boiled up inside me. And once again I started to congratulate myself. And then, once more, to learn that you are leaving your position at the college, a position that I have created to honor you. This is still another blow from you, Voody Khan. A shower of blows I have received from you in return for my kindness and generosity. I was already thinking about the money. I had given my word, but under false pretenses. But this too I have overcome. And now here we are like two pals, having an adventure."

The helicopter veered to the left. Woody could see the coastline again.

"My emotional life, you see," he went on, "had been expanded at the expense of my humanity. That is what I had to learn. But all the while I had my beak in salt water. I thought I was seeing clearly, but I had my beak in salt water."

"I don't know what you're talking about," Woody said.

"It's simple, really. I had forgotten what every Sufi knows, what every child knows. I had been thinking that the material things were the reality. 'The bird that doesn't know sweet water has his beak in salt water all year.'"

Woody was not sure what to make of this. He didn't know if Alireza was trying to tell him something important or if he was deliberately trying to confuse him.

"I was mistaking my emotions for spiritual insight. And I knew what I was doing, but I couldn't stop myself. That's what was so disturbing. And then I remembered the words of Abu-Yaqub al-Susi:

the Sufi is 'one who doesn't care when something is taken away from him, but who continues to search for what he does not have.' Do you see, Voody? *'One who continues to search for what he does not have.'*"

The helicopter banked harder, and Woody was no longer standing; he was falling forward towards the open door. But at the same time he was suspended by the harness, suspended over the little town, and then over the Etruscan cemetery, the Banditaccia.

"Can you see all right, Voody Khan?"

It would have been a wonderful view of the vast cemetery, but Woody was too frightened to take it in. His hands were trembling, a sort of counter-trembling that was out of sync with the vibrations of the helicopter. Like a guitar string that's not in tune. They passed over the Tombs of the Five Chairs and the Triclinium and the Sarcophagi, over the Tomb of the Tarquins . . . colossal tombs. But Woody had no time to process the information. In a second they were passing over the field of rugs. He wanted to *see* Alireza. He was half expecting Alireza to loosen the hooks of the harness and send him plunging to his death. He tried again to look behind him but without success. He tried to imagine the fall. How long would he be in the air before hitting the ground? Would he be conscious or would he pass out? Would he be able to breathe or would he be falling too fast to suck in air? What would he think about as he fell? Would he spin round or would his body move stilly and slowly, like a stone falling in water? What would his last thoughts be? He couldn't imagine them. Maybe that was the way it was. You couldn't think your last thoughts because you were always thinking ahead, wondering what your last thoughts would be; of course, then *these* would be your last thoughts. But in the meantime he braced himself, thinking he could hit Alireza with his elbows, or smash the camera into his head.

"The camera, Voody Khan; the camera. Shoot, shoot."

Woody's hands trembled. He raised the camera to his eye, but before he could find the viewfinder . . . It was too late. The helicopter slid down the steep aerial embankment it had climbed, and Woody was on his feet again. Alireza was cursing in Persian, a tiny voice in Woody's ears. "Your mother is a whore, son of a whore. May your father burn in hell . . . The pilot will make another pass," Alireza's voice said. "You have to be ready this time."

437

The pilot made three more passes, following the same route, banking high over the cemetery and the field of rugs, like a motorcycle rider banking on a steep curve. On each pass the ground tilted up at Woody—the coastline appearing first, then tiny cars on the *autostrada*, and then the small city of Cerveteri, where the vestal virgins had taken refuge when the Gauls invaded Rome in 390 B.C.—till he was suspended in his harness directly over the open door, the cemetery rushing by underneath him and then the field of rugs, till the helicopter slid back down the side of the sky and Woody could stand up again. On the second pass he got a shot of the cemetery, which is what *he* really wanted, but he had trouble advancing the film and missed the field of carpets. He was tempted to drop the camera into the Tyrrhenian Sea, but it was fastened around his neck.

"How do you advance the film?"

"May Allah who helps the poor and those in need cure your stupidity. The lever at the side," he said, "the lever at the side, just like I showed you, at the side . . . The lever is at the side. May Allah help the blind see and the deaf hear." Woody realized that Alireza was not cursing but praying. On the third and fourth passes Woody got two shots. His goggles had begun to steam up. Alireza was talking non-stop. The helicopter was heading back to Civitavecchia. Woody was looking inland this time instead of at the sea.

"Look," Alireza said, his voice calmer now. "That's Lake Bracciano. When Napoleon was crowned emperor in Paris the French launched a huge fire balloon, from right in front of Notre-Dame. It came down in Lake Bracciano. Some people thought it was the end of the world."

It wasn't till that evening—Alireza had the negatives developed at once and enlarged, too, to poster size—that Woody actually saw what he had seen. The photo of the cemetery turned out pretty well. He could make out the large circular tumuli, crowded together. And the smaller rectangular chambers, even the Tomb of the Painted Animals and the vineyards next to the cemetery. Neat rows, as if the earth had been strung like a guitar, or a giant lute. He could see the cypresses and oleanders that bordered the cemetery.

What he wasn't prepared for was the beauty of the rugs. Only one of the shots turned out, but it was spectacular. Even the corners were in sharp focus. He'd forgotten how powerful beauty could be.

And this was the most beautiful thing he'd ever seen. The beauty struck him in the chest like the blow of a hammer, leaving him short of breath.

Alireza too was excited. He was laughing and kept touching Woody, putting his hand flat on Woody's back, between his shoulder blades, as they stood around the dining room table looking at the enlarged photo. Allison touched him too, and touched her husband, who pointed first at one rug and then at another. He knew each rug and its story. He knew where he bought it—Tabriz, Esfahan, Shiraz, Mashhad, Kashan—and he knew the people who had made it. "There is much suffering," he said, "that goes into these rugs."

Suddenly everything became clear, or clearer. Woody couldn't believe he had actually seen the field of rugs with his own eyes. He *had* seen it, of course, but he hadn't *seen* it. He tried to remember. He could remember the pull of the harness, the weight of the camera around his neck, the rushing of the wind through the open door, the cold knob of the lever that advanced the film, the pressure of his finger on the shutter release. But the thing itself—the *Ding an sich*—had eluded him.

The rugs were still there. They would be there for two or three days before Alireza's men started rolling up the ones that were completely dry. He could ask Alireza if they could go up in the helicopter again. So he could see again. The thing itself. Not a photo, not an icon, but the reality.

"My love is carpet," Alireza said suddenly, in a loud voice, in English. "Signor Voody, *my love is carpet*." It was quite a strain for him to pronounce the words in English. Woody was surprised, as if a bird had spoken. "Do you understand me?" Alireza said in Italian. "How can I explain?"

Things were turning around, like the ground turning beneath him when the helicopter was taking off.

"It is not so easy to make money with *carpet*," Alireza went on in Italian, but using the English word "carpet" instead of *tappeto* or *ghali*. "I have twenty ships that go back and forth across the Persian Gulf every week, from Bandar Abbas to Muscat and Dubai, from Bushehr to Kuwait and Qatar. Not carpet, but oil and steel and copper and dates and sugar beets, machines, phosphates, and sulfur. Rials and dinars and dirhams, and rupees, lire and dollars and francs and marks. There is so much money in the world, Voody Khan, and so much suffering too, so much evil and death. Evil and death, Voody Khan. So many wise men have wrestled with evil and death. How to explain them so they don't destroy everything else? But the truly wise man, the Sufi, wrestles with beauty. That is the true mystery that cannot be denied; you cannot explain it away no matter how you try; and now, Voody Khan, you are like the Sufi who hears about the fire; and then he comes close to the fire and feels its warmth; and then he thrusts his hand in the fire, and he is burned. You have thrust your hand in the fire, Voody Khan. You have been burned."

Alireza had posters printed that were sold in bookstores and tourist shops everywhere. Large advertisements appeared in newspapers, not just in Rome but in Milan and Florence and Bologna and even Naples. Four-color ads featuring Woody's photo were commissioned for glossy magazines—*Amica* and *Gioia* and *Casa Viva*—but by the time the glossy magazines went to press the rugs had all been sold. Everyone wanted one. Alireza collected the insurance money, *and* the money for the damaged rugs, which sold for more than they would have normally. He made a lot of money from the posters too. "But it's not the money," he explained to Woody. "The money is nothing. *My love is carpet.* Do you understand now what I am telling to you?"

"Yes," Woody said; "I understand."

In
Another
Country

Cookie's death was like a cable, binding us to the past. Sometimes
we'd think we'd slipped the cable and were running free, but then
we'd be brought up short, like a dog that forgets it's on a chain. At
least that's the way it seemed to me. I thought I'd slipped free when
Ludi and I put the letter to the Italian government in the mailbox on
Christmas morning. And then again when Daddy called to say the
trial was over and that Angela Strappafelci had been sentenced to life
in prison; and then again when I fell in love with Daniel Alexander,
a friend of Richard and Sally's, another physicist; and when I got
promoted to full-fledged exhibit developer at MSI; and then when I
got a check for L. 100.000.000, about $65,000, from the Italian gov-
ernment; and again when I found out I was pregnant.

   That was in the summer of 1989, a year and a half after Ludi and
I had mailed the letter on Christmas morning. Mama had taken her
final vows and was now a fully cloistered nun. Ludi had finished her
junior year at Grinnell and was already looking ahead to vet school.
And I was in charge of my own exhibit, on bats, at MSI. Four thousand square feet of exhibit space, all my own. The exhibit was moving toward its final phase. We had persuaded our colony of big brown
bats *(Eptesicus fuscus)* to demonstrate their sonar skills by negotiating
an obstacle course that included a large electric fan, but we hadn't
managed to trick them into doing it during the day instead of at
night, so now we were trying to alter their diurnal schedule by
manipulating the lighting in small increments—fifteen minutes every

twenty-four hours—till it coincided with ours, so that the bats would be active during the museum hours. Sonia, my assistant exhibit developer, thought we were being cruel to the bats and that if people wanted to watch them they should come at night.

"The museum's closed at night," I told her.

"Whatever," she said.

And Daddy. Daddy was still in Bologna. I hadn't seen him in almost two years. He'd been planning to come home after the trial, but he'd been struck on the head by a *carabiniere*, right in the courtroom, and had been hospitalized; he'd been planning to come home for Christmas, but then he'd been elected vice-president of the Association of the Families of the Victims and didn't feel he could leave. It was an honor, he said on the phone, and I could tell he took it seriously. Then in the winter the father of the woman he was living with died; and in the spring he and Signor Montefiore, the president of the Association, were arrested in Rome, in front of the Senate, for leading a mass demonstration. They were trying to present the new Italian prime minister with a petition—with over seventy thousand signatures—to abolish *Segreto di Stato* in cases of terrorism; they wanted some tapes released; they wanted the results of some investigation to be made public. Their anger was directed less at the terrorists than at the state itself. For failing to act upon what it knew. For its persistent sympathy towards right-wing terrorism at the highest levels. There was even a picture of Daddy in the *New York Times*, shouting into an electronic megaphone. I put it up on the bulletin board in my office cubicle at MSI. And then in June 1989 the appellate court in Bologna overturned the convictions of the terrorists. Angela Strappafelci was still serving several life sentences for a series of murders, including the murder of a judge—the judge with the tapes—and of one of her own friends, but the *mandanti*, the planners, had been released. The verdict had been sent to the Italian supreme court, which would probably order a new trial.

By this time I didn't care. I thought it was time to let go. And for Daddy to let go too. I think that this was the hardest thing, actually: living with the hope that somehow we could go back in time, that Daddy would go back to his job at St. Clair, maybe even buy back the farm with the money from the Italian government. It wasn't out of the question. There was still a position for him at St. Clair, though he had never mentioned it on the phone, or in his letters. We'd learned about it from Turi, who flew to Chicago to spend Christmas with Ludi and me in 1988. That was one of the conditions of her father's gift to the college—that the position remain open for Daddy. That's what Alireza Mirsadiqi wanted, and whatever Alireza Mirsadiqi wanted, St. Clair wanted. So I couldn't get rid of the notion that it could still happen, that it wasn't too late. And maybe that's why Ludi and I flew to Bologna on the tenth of August for the ninth anniversary of the bombing. I'd told Daddy about Daniel; but I hadn't told him about the L. 100.000.000; and I hadn't told him I was two months pregnant and that he *had* to come home because Daniel and I were going to get married at the end of September, right after the opening of the bat exhibit. I wanted to tell him in person.

We left the dog with Daniel, who had moved into my apartment, and flew to New York and then to Milan. My Italian, which had once been pretty fluent, got us on the bus to the station—a depressing ride through ugly urban sprawl—and then onto a train to Bologna. We were met at the station by Gabriella del Monte, a small, dark woman in a flimsy spaghetti-strap dress, with lots of curly black hair tied back with a red ribbon.

"I recognized you by your pictures," she said.

At first I thought she had a slight speech impediment, but later I realized that everyone in Bologna had a slight speech impediment—the Bolognese accent.

"Where's Daddy?" I asked. I knew Daddy'd been living with Gabriella, but he'd been rather vague about the nature of their relationship, and I hadn't given her much thought. But now I realized I'd overlooked something. I began to wonder, in fact, if *she* was the real reason he hadn't come home, the psychosexual substructure, so to speak, underlying his conscious agenda. Perhaps the blow on the head, the election to the vice-presidency of the Association, the arrest in Rome, even the overturning of the convictions, were simply elements of the superstructure, excuses. I couldn't fit her into any obvious categories: housewife, *femme fatale*, nurturing mother, clinging vine, husband hunter, witch. She was just a woman. But maybe that was enough. She seemed to have a lot of energy—she carried our suitcases to the taxi stand outside the station—and I knew right away that she was in love with Daddy, whom she called Whoody.

"Whoody had to go to a big meeting," she explained. "The prime minister has been accused of *rapporti* with Bruno Conti and all the political parties have rallied around him to deny it, except for Pci." She must have seen that I didn't understand: "Partita communista italiana," she explained. "Msi wants the word *fascista* removed from the *lapide*, the stone with the names of all the dead. With Cookie's name."

"MSI?" I wondered aloud. To me MSI meant only one thing: the Museum of Science and Industry.

"Movimento sociale italiano, the neo-fascist party. And a group of left-wing intellectuals has issued a manifesto declaring that the *strage* has been covered with straw as if it were a *lapide* of an epitaph from *Spoon River*. They wanted to express their solidarity with the Association."

"*Spoon River*?" I asked.

"Yes, the *Spoon River Antologia*; it is very well known here. Someone wrote a *Spoon River Antologia* for the victims of the bombing. Each person is identified only by the number that was written on the coffin in chalk."

Ludi had fallen asleep on my shoulder in the back of the cab. I twisted around to get comfortable. "I'm pregnant, you know," I said, out of the blue. I waited for the full effect to sink in. I could see she was at a loss.

"Should I congratulate you," she asked, "or should I sympathize?"

"I'm getting married at the end of September."

"Then I guess it's congratulations."

"Yes. We're very happy."

"Have you told Whoody yet?"

"Not yet. That's why we came. I didn't want to tell him on the phone. And we got a check for one hundred million lire. From the Italian government."

It took her a minute to process this information. "Good," she said; "I think your father will be very happy. He worries that he hasn't enough money for you and your sister. This will take a worry off his mind."

444

"He doesn't have to worry about us," I said. "We're the ones who have to worry about him."

"What do you mean?"

I didn't want to explain—I didn't think I needed to—and I didn't try, because the taxi was pulling up to Via G. Petronio 32, where we'd been sending letters to Daddy. It wasn't the way I'd pictured it. Just a door, next to a small *cartoleria*, in an ochre-colored wall.

"You'll each have your own room," she said, taking her keys out of her purse as the taxi driver unloaded the suitcases from the trunk. "Whoody should be back before seven. We'll eat at the *osteria*. But you'll want to sleep now; you must be tired. You can explain later, when you've had some rest."

"Yes, later," I said. But drifting off to sleep I couldn't explain what I meant, even to myself.

THE DEMONSTRATION was a much bigger affair than I had imagined. Twenty thousand people from all over Europe assembled to watch the parade from the main piazza to the station, and there must have been five thousand of us in the parade itself. It was a national event. Daddy had been spending all his time at the office of the Association, making last-minute hotel arrangements for people—families of the victims—coming from out of town, and greeting people, and dealing with local officials and with the press.

We were stuck with Gabriella, who was friendly enough, though I think she knew in her heart of hearts that we'd come to take Daddy home. She wanted to know about our life in Illinois. She couldn't imagine St. Clair, she said, though *Whoody* had told her all about it, and all about us. Sometimes I pretended not to understand, but the piazza, in the center of town, was full of people, many of whom held banners and flags, and I was glad that we weren't on our own. Ludi and I followed Gabriella to a room on the second floor of the medieval city hall for a press conference. The prime minister himself was there—the same man, I think, who'd come to visit the Warren Farms in St. Clair, though he hadn't been prime minister at the time—and the mayor and various officials. The mayor made a speech, which I couldn't understand, and then he made the same speech in another room, and I could understand it a little better this time; at least I could tell that it wasn't a pleasant speech, and the prime minister didn't like it very much, though he put a good face on it.

Survivors of the bombing marched at the front of the procession along with the families of the victims—about two hundred people in twenty or twenty-five rows. They were followed by the flag bearers of the Comune, the Province, the Region, the University, and of various political parties, labor organizations, and other political entities. Ludi and I wound up in the very first row, along with Daddy and Gabriella, Signor Montefiore (the president of the Association) and his wife, the mayor, and another man whom I didn't recognize. We started at the city hall at nine-fifteen. In Piazza Nettuno, actually, which is right next to the big piazza. I pushed in between Gabriella and Daddy. "He's *my* father," I said in a low voice, so Daddy, who was talking to a photographer, wouldn't hear; "it was *my* sister who was killed."

"Yes, of course," she said, and stepped to one side.

I felt a little thrill of triumph, but I was also embarrassed as we linked arms, stiffly, like two people who don't want to be dancing with each other.

After the inevitable delays—two trade unionists had to be rescued from a group of anarchists, and a group of Czech tourists got out of a Pullman from Florence and was trying to get into the crowded piazza; the police were trying to figure out how the Pullman had gotten past the barricade at the end of the main street—the army jeep leading the parade started to roll forward. The parade was under way.

Several photographers walked backwards right in front of us, taking pictures every few seconds and asking questions. The questions were directed at Signor Montefiore and at Daddy. I was afraid they were going to ask me something. I was trying to figure out what to say in Italian: my sister had been killed, she had come to Bologna to study international law. That was probably enough. They were also interested in a woman marching in the row behind us. I recognized her from a photograph that had been taken of her being carried out of the station. It was on posters everywhere. She was angry. "You keep at me," she said; "you keep pushing and pushing and pushing; you want to make me cry so you can get a good photo, but I won't cry. See, look at my eyes. Look. They're dry as stones."

446

A little girl ran out from the crowd lining the street and took her hand. She bent over and kissed the little girl, who ran back to her parents. At every step of the way the crowd would begin to applaud just as we came abreast. As if we'd done something important. It seemed odd at first, then moving, so many people.

I was too overwhelmed to know what I was feeling, except that I was feeling a certain amount of anxiety about what I'd said to Gabriella. I'd gone too far. But I felt a sense of victory too.

At the station the survivors and the families of the victims stood under large umbrellas, to protect us from the sun, on a special plat-form. It took a long time for three thousand marchers to reach the piazza in front of the station. More and more people kept pouring out of Via Independenza. But they got there before the minute of silence at ten twenty-five. Of course the station clock, I learned later, is always at ten twenty-five.

After the minute of silence the prime minister spoke. I got the idea that everything had been done that should have been done, and that everything would be done that should be done. But then Signor Montefiore spoke. He had lost his wife, and his son had lost an eye. He was very angry, bitter, not about to let the prime minister off the hook. He attacked the prime minister; he attacked the government. There was nothing polite about his speech. He was from Rome, and it was easier for me to understand him because Rome was where I'd learned Italian in the first place.

Daddy spoke too, very briefly; but it was pretty astonishing to hear him haranguing the crowd in Italian. He was angry too. And then two young people spoke, a Palestinian Arab and an Israeli, who had been invited as guests of the mayor. The Palestinian spoke in Arabic and the Israeli in Hebrew. Translators translated, and then someone from the Ministry of Grace and Justice spoke, a *partigiano*, and then someone spoke on behalf of the taxi drivers' union.

Afterwards taxis took all the families and survivors for free to La Torre di Galuzzo, a very elegant restaurant where pitchers of orange juice and grapefruit juice and bottles of mineral water and bowls of fruit had been set out on a marble-topped table.

There was a business meeting for the families at which Daddy sat up front, next to Signor Montefiore, who gave an account of all the things the Association had done that year: publications, press

447

conferences, posters, and most important, the campaign to abolish *Segreto di Stato*. He and Daddy had presented the government with a petition with over seventy thousand signatures on it. He told about leading the demonstration in Rome where he and Daddy had been arrested. The treasurer gave his report, and then Daddy placed a call on a special speakerphone to a man in England whose daughter had been killed. Like Cookie. She'd been traveling with her boyfriend. They'd both been killed. This was the first year he hadn't come to the demonstration. He didn't know Italian—Daddy translated—but everyone seemed to know him and to listen to him as an old friend. He'd stayed home because his mother was ill, he said, and there was a round of enthusiastic applause. He'd done what any good Italian boy would have done. But he'd gone to the cemetery in Leeds at ten twenty-five for a minute of silence.

And then we ate a terrific dinner, perhaps the best I've ever eaten. I kept a copy of the menu:

Bresaola con carciofi
Risotto con funghi porcini
Tortelli di zucca
Filetto all'aceto balsamico
Gelato con macedonia di frutta calda
Caffè
Cognac

And of course there was lots of *vino, rosso* and *bianco*.

I still hadn't told Daddy that I was getting married, or that I was already pregnant, and I didn't think Gabriella had told him either. I thought this might be a good time, but he was sitting across the table from me, between the representatives from two other *stragi*, too far away.

From Gabriella's kitchen window you could see a section of the old city wall that had been uncovered during a renovation of one of the university buildings. The kitchen was at the end of a long corridor that angled off the living room. The shape of the apartment was not at all clear. Obviously it wasn't a rectangle divided into other rectangles. There was an upstairs, where Daddy slept with Gabriella.

The upstairs wasn't exactly off limits, but I was reluctant to go up there, especially when there were other people around, which there were. It was not clear, in fact, just how many people lived there. There was an aunt, though she seemed to have a separate apartment; and Gabriella's cousin, who'd been staying with them, but who was spending the summer in England. Ludi was sleeping in the cousin's room. In the center of the main floor was a huge study with book-cases on all four walls, and in the middle a huge double desk, like two post office desks joined together at the back. The study was full of radios, and the double desk was piled high with books and papers— the manuscript of Daddy's book on the *strage* and the trial, a copy of Gabriella's cookbook, *Errori della Tavola*, which Daddy was translat-ing into English. The floor of the big living room was marble—an intricate pattern of different colors, dark green, red, white.

"A house for friends," Daddy called it. And Daddy seemed to have a lot of friends. He was especially pleased with the fireplace, which had vents in the hearth so you could control the heat when you were cooking something. And there were various contraptions for grilling meat and cooking sausages. But it was too hot to use the fireplace. The wine cellar, which was actually a part of one of the old walls that had circled the city in the Middle Ages, contained an old mechanical television. Daddy tried to explain how it worked, and I took some notes because I thought it might make a good exhibit at MSI.

It was a relief to have the public festivities over, to retire, so to speak, to private life, to spend some time with Daddy, who wanted to show us everything: the office of the Association, the Tribunale, his book manuscript, the church up at San Luca, the sundial in San Petronio, the Osteria del Sole, where you had to bring your own lunch, the *presepio* or crèche in the Martyrium—one of the churches of Santo Stefano—where Charlemagne had worshiped on his way to France in the eighth century. "If you'd been a student in the thirteenth century," he said, more than once, "you'd have come to Bologna. Or Paris. These are the progenitors of the modern university system. Nothing like them in classical antiquity." We walked under miles of arcades. Every once in a while Daddy would quote Petrarch, who'd spent some time at the university. (And so had Dante and Boccaccio, if you believed the guidebooks.) *Inde Bononiam perreximus, qua nil puto iucundius nilque liberius toto esset orbe terrarum—We arrived at Bologna; there is no place more pleasant and free in the whole world.* Daddy was full of energy, never tired. Wherever we stopped for coffee, he always knew someone in the bar.

Evenings we spent at Gabriella's *osteria*, Osteria Trebbiano, which was getting ready to close down for a month. It was here, sitting at Gabriella's private table just inside the front door, that Daddy and Ludi and I negotiated our family's future. It was here that I laid my cards on the table, told Daddy that I was pregnant, and that Daniel and I were going to get married at the end of September. It was here that I told him about the L. 100.000.000, enough to buy back the farm *and* to send Ludi to vet school. Well, it would get her through her first two years anyway. I didn't want any of the money for myself. Daniel and I both had good jobs, I said, speaking faster and faster, trying to keep up with myself. MSI had just put a maternity-leave policy in place . . .

Gabriella, who didn't understand English, stood up and started to clear the table. We'd already eaten a huge plate of antipasti and a *tris*, three kinds of pasta. I think she wanted to empty out the kitchen before the *osteria* closed for the month.

"*Mangia tutto*," she said, pointing to a few *tagliatelle* that I'd pushed to the side of my plate. "*Mangia tutto*." But I didn't see how I could eat any more.

"You're not my mother," I said, and I could see I'd struck home. And I could see that things were not settled between them.

She bit her lip. She added my plate, with its little pile of *tagliatelle*, to the stack she was carrying, and walked off to the kitchen.

"That was uncalled for," Daddy said. I could see that he was angry.

"It's *all* uncalled for," I said, not knowing what I was going to say till I started to speak. "If you and Mama hadn't been so stubborn this wouldn't have happened. We wouldn't be sitting here three thousand miles away from home. '*La sua voluntade è nostra pace.*' What was such a big deal that you couldn't give in?" I'd always blamed my mother for the divorce, but now I wasn't so sure. "It's just a tombstone."

"Maybe I made a mistake," he said. "I don't know; but I know it wasn't just a tombstone. Your mother had to be true to something inside her, and I did too. You know I didn't want her to leave. And I don't think she wanted to leave either."

I was looking at his face, a broad, pale American face that looked out of place, even though he'd let his hair grow long. "Don't you think it's time you let go?"

"Let go? Of what?"

"Of the past, of Cookie. You care more about her than you care about us, about Ludi and me." I looked to Ludi for support. She was slowly peeling the label off the bottle of red wine we'd drunk with the *tris*. But I could see I was asking her for something she couldn't give. She'd been too young . . . I was on my own.

"How can you say that?" Daddy asked.

"Look where we are. Look what you're doing with your life."

"Do you think I wouldn't have done this for you? Do you think I would have let *you* go?"

"It's easier to love someone when they're dead. They don't make any demands on you."

"You're probably right about that," he said. "*Nil nisi bonum.* But that's not something we can choose, sweetheart. Do you think this is the way I would have chosen to love Cookie? When *you* have children—"

"I *am* having children," I said, interrupting. I'd wanted Daddy to be at a loss. I'd wanted to comfort him, to tell him it was all right. But he wasn't at a loss. *I* was at a loss.

"I'm glad you've got the money," he said.

"What money?"

"The hundred million lire. That's over sixty thousand dollars."

"That's *your* money," I said. "We thought you could use it to buy back the farm."

"I want you and Ludi to split it," he said. "That'll be your wedding present, and Ludi's graduation present. I don't need it anymore." He leaned forward. "I think *you're* the one who needs to let go of the past."

Gabriella returned to the table with more food.

"Is that donkey?" I asked. I'd seen donkey on the menu. At least that's what I thought it was: *somarello*.

"Try it," she said; "you'll like it."

"I'm sorry," I said to her. "I'm not a very good loser."

"I'm not your mother," she said, "but I'm not your enemy. You don't know how much your father loves you." She nodded towards Daddy. "He thinks about you all the time. 'I wonder what Sara's doing now; I wonder what Ludi's doing now.' He carries you around with him in his heart. You're part of him, just like Cookie. But he's got plenty of room in his heart; for me too. You need to move over, make a little space."

I slid my chair over so she could sit down next to me. She leaned over and whispered in my ear, so Ludi wouldn't hear: "It's horse," she said; "we're all out of *somarello*."

It was horse, but it was good.

WHEN DADDY got up to play, after we'd finished the horse and the salad and almost a third of a rich chocolate torte, he announced to everyone in the *osteria* that I was pregnant and was getting married. The *clienti* applauded. And then he announced that Ludi was going to vet school, and there was more applause. He sang *"Bella Ciao"* in Italian, using a flamenco strum that I'd never heard before, and then he sang "Sittin' on Top of the World" and "Mississippi River Blues" and then an instrumental, Leo Kottke's "Last Steam Engine Train," and then he wanted Ludi and me to sing "Simple Gifts" with him, which we did, reluctantly. It was a song he used to sing when he sang us to sleep at night. I was too self-conscious, but Ludi got up and sang enthusiastically:

> 'Tis the gift to be simple
> 'Tis the gift to be free,
> 'Tis the gift to come down,
> Where we ought to be,
> And when we find ourselves
> In the place just right,
> 'Twill be in the valley
> Of love and delight.

Daddy handed me a tray and told me to carry it around asking for money. I couldn't do it, but Ludi did. I kept my head down as I walked back to my seat, the way I did when I was embarrassed. Then something nudged my shoulder and I suddenly felt that everyone was looking at me, that I was making a fool of myself. But it was only Ludi.

"*Per la musica*," she said, laughing.

I had a ten-thousand-lire note in my pocket. I put it on top of the pile of money on the tray. Daddy was singing "Trouble in Mind."

> Trouble in mind, I'm blue,
> But I won't be blue always;
> 'Cause that sun gonna shine,
> In my back door some day.

What I realized at that moment was that Daddy was happy. I don't think he knew himself how happy he was, but it was suddenly clear to me, and all of a sudden I started to experience sharp stabbing pains in anticipation of parting, even though we weren't leaving for two more days. I knew that lost years cannot be recovered, and that damage that has been done cannot always be put right. I'd known this for a long time. It was true, but there was another truth that I could feel and breathe in like the cigarette smoke in the *osteria*, like the smoke of my mother's cigarettes. There was this other truth, but you couldn't get to it by thinking. You couldn't locate it on a map and figure out what highway to take to get there, the way you'd plan a trip to St. Louis or Chicago. *Fahren ohne Plan*, Daddy used to say. *Guidare senza meta*. You could only drive without a plan, the way we used to do when we went for a ride in the evening, turning this way and that on country roads, following the Burlington tracks out past the hump tower and then turning off into the countryside. One night we came upon a herd of buffalo. Huge buffalo, in a field right next to the road. There were about a dozen of them, big dark shapes against the horizon. Silhouettes. "Bison," Ludi said, and Daddy started singing "Home on the Range." We couldn't wait to take some of our friends to see them, and when we did we made a big secret of it, playing Twenty Questions. No one ever guessed, and maybe it was just as well, because we never found the buffalo again. Daddy got a big map of Harrison County, and then maps of the adjacent counties, and we searched systematically, ranging farther and farther afield, quadrant by quadrant. We never found them, so we had to *tell* our friends, and we weren't sure that they ever really believed us.

That's what the truer truth was like, and I was afraid to leave the place where I was, my place at the table in the *osteria*, because I was afraid I'd never be able to find it again, never be able to come back. There was an even truer truth, too, that I didn't fully grasp till I saw it in the photo that Gabriella sent to me in Chicago, a photo of all four of us, taken at the station while we were waiting for the train to take us back to Milan, a photo taken by a stranger. Our suitcases were lined up in front of us; behind us was the *lapide*, with Cookie's name on it, and the bomb crater, full of flowers and notes and letters too, that people had left after the demonstration. It was a shock to see Cookie's name in a place so far from home, and it was a shock to see our smiling faces, to see my own face smiling, and to realize that I was happy too.

DANIEL AND I were married at the end of September, in Chicago, out at the Point that juts out into the lake just south of Hyde Park. Daddy came home and stayed at the Windermere Hotel, where we'd reserved a block of rooms for guests. The sun shone and the lake was blue, and Ludi stood up with me, and the street musicians that Daniel had met in the subway on Canal Street didn't show up—just as I'd predicted—but it didn't matter, because Daddy played the guitar he'd bought for Daniel as a wedding present. He played "Simple Gifts" before we ate, and everyone sang the words, and afterwards my uncle Roy, Mama's brother, who'd come all the way from California, played the piano, and Daddy's cousin from Ann Arbor played the harmonica, and his wife played the violin, and the minister's wife sang "Amazing Grace."

The only bad thing was that Mama wasn't allowed to come. She could go to funerals, but weddings were off-limits. Maybe they—whoever "they" were—were afraid of having the nuns see people too happy, people who were about to fuck for the first time. At least in theory. But she came to the memorial service, if that's the right name, that we held for Cookie two days later. It was the only time we could all get together, and I was pretty sure it would be the last time. Mama and Daddy had negotiated a settlement: Cookie got a belated Roman Catholic send-off, and Daddy got to choose the inscription for the tombstone. He spent all day—the day after the wedding—at the Steckley Monument Company while they carved the new inscription. He had to pay overtime, too, for two men, but the stone was in place when we got to the cemetery on Friday afternoon. We stood looking at it, not saying anything, while we waited for Mama to arrive from the convent.

From where we were standing, by Cookie's grave, you could look down and see our old house. You could see that the garden was a mess, and that one of the barn doors had come off its upper hinge and was tilted at a crazy angle. Daniel and I had talked about getting married in that barn, where Cookie and I had once taken turns standing up for each other in make-believe weddings, with Ludi serving as our flower girl, and with various pets as friends and relatives, looking on, mystified, like Laska now, watching us from the back of Ludi's truck. Ludi had spent the summer in northern Wisconsin studying red-winged blackbirds. After the service she'd be going back to Grinnell for her senior year.

In the original plan for the service everyone was going to say something about Cookie, tell stories, the way they'd done at Harvard. The priest from the convent had nixed that plan, but while we were waiting for Mama I was thinking about what I would have said.

I'd learned to jitterbug in the barn. Cookie and I got our own record player one Christmas, and we played it so loud in the house that Mama and Daddy made us take it out to the barn. Cookie, I thought, you were always planning things, and Ludi and I drove you crazy, begging to let us come to the dances and parties you had in the barn. There was hay then, bales like big bricks—not the big round bales you have today. We could build with them, tunnels and secret hideouts. Ludi and I got into our big hideout once before your class dance. For almost two hours before the dance. Ludi wasn't supposed to go into it because of her asthma, but she brought her inhaler. We fell asleep before the dance was over, and when we got out, there were couples lying on blankets all over the place, necking.

You read to us. *The Hobbit*. Daddy'd already read it aloud three times, but we wanted to hear it again, and when you got to the death of Thorin Oakenshield, I started to cry, just the way I did when

455

Daddy read it to me the first time, and then Ludi started to cry too, even though she was too young to understand. You were my teacher, Cookie. You taught me to jitterbug and to do the backstroke, and to read music, and to make an omelet. I remember when I went out to see you before you came home from Harvard the first time. Daddy went out to see you himself, and then later he sent me. He took me out of school and I stayed in your room for a week and we ate at the Tasty instead of the dining hall. That was the first time *you* ever needed *me*. And I was so happy. It was the first time I'd flown alone. You met me at the airport in Boston, and we called Daddy from a pay phone. Daddy'd given me money so we could go out to dinner on the North End, but we spent it on artichokes for everyone in your suite, just like you and Daddy did. It made you feel better. Shopping for artichokes in the North End market. And trying to find green peppercorns. Asking in Italian, but no one understood. *Pepe verde.* The Italians didn't understand their own language. They thought you wanted green peppers. You got mad because the Italians couldn't understand their own language. *Pepe verde*, you kept saying; you were so disgusted.

You were always so far ahead of me, Cookie, but for a minute I caught up with you. And then you pulled ahead again, and now I'll never be able to catch up.

It was hard to cook in the dorm. We borrowed some pots from the master—I think that's what he was called—and we called Daddy to get the recipe for *pasta alla puttanesca* because we couldn't find any green peppercorns, which you needed for *farfalle* with prosciutto and cream. You were always calling him for recipes.

The night before you left for Italy you packed too much stuff. You couldn't get it all in Daddy's duffel bag; you couldn't take it all with you, and we had to repack everything. Mama was sewing stuff the way she always did when someone was leaving or we were going on vacation. And you told me that you were in love with Ben, your last year at Harvard, and that I shouldn't tell Mama and Daddy because you wanted to call them from Italy and tell them that you were officially engaged. Ben was coming to Italy at Christmas. I've never told. I guess I wanted it to be our secret.

You should see Laska, Cookie. She just jumped out of the truck and landed on her head. Do you remember how Daddy cried when Argos died? I guess you were gone already. We took him to the vet. Daddy'd had a hernia operation and Mama had to carry him downstairs. He couldn't stand up anymore, his hips hurt so bad. All of us went and we all held him while Dr. Mitchell gave him the shot. Mama and Daddy were both crying. It was embarrassing, walking out past all the people in the waiting room.

Mama and Daddy cried after you left for Harvard, too, and after you left for Italy. But you know the funny thing? Daddy never cried after you . . . were gone. Really gone. Dead. Blown up. I never saw him cry at all. I never understood it, but I think I'm beginning to understand now.

When they came home, I'd already moved into your room. I hope you don't mind. I should have asked. I fucked Aaron in your bed. That was the first time for me. I went crazy. I'm sorry.

Afterwards they brought you home on the Alitalia plane. To O'Hare. We watched the forklift lift the big heavy coffin down. They could hardly fit it in Mr. Gridley's hearse. All lead. A vault. Sealed. I guess the Italians don't go in for embalming, so there won't be much left of you now.

I can see the limousine coming down Kruger Road. In just a few minutes Mama will be here. Oh, Cookie, I've been down to see her a couple of times at the convent—you sit in a little room like the office in a funeral home—but we don't have much to say to each other. They wouldn't let her come to the wedding. Maybe they're afraid of too much happiness. Afraid she'd run away. But she's here now, and another nun, and the priest. Getting out of the car. Black and white, like penguins. How can she stand it? She was always one for comfortable clothes. I want to run to her now and put my arms around her, but I guess I'll hold back. There was a big argument over the tombstone, but they finally got it worked out. A trade-off. You get a Catholic send-off, priest and all. Not a regular mass, but last rites. And Daddy gets what he wants on the stone. You should see it. Mama wanted a line from Dante—*La sua voluntade è nostra pace*—but Daddy wouldn't go for it. And now I'm glad. He wanted something that tells the truth. And I think he's got it. We went out to Steckley's, out on Route 30. I didn't know it, but they still had the

457

stone that Mama had ordered, and Daddy paid a fortune to have it sanded down. Now it says:

CAROLYN CLIFFORD WOODHULL
JUNE 14, 1958–AUGUST 18, 1980

Contra vim Veneris
herbam non inveneris;
contra vim mortis
non crescit herba in hortis.

Against the strength of love, you will find no herb; against the strength of death, no herb grows in the garden.

DANIEL AND I are back at the motel now. The Ramada Inn, on the square. It's only five o'clock, not too late to drive back to Chicago. We're not leaving for San Francisco till Wednesday, so Daniel and I decided to spend the night in St. Clair, but now I wish we were on the road. It's too strange to be staying in a motel in my hometown. Daniel wants to mess around a little, but I don't think I'm up to it.

The service went off without a hitch. We stood around the grave and the priest said some stuff in Latin, and we followed along on a sheet he'd Xeroxed: *ad postulandam gratiam bene moriendi.* Even I could understand that—I mean I could understand the Latin—and afterwards Mama whispered something to me that I couldn't understand at first: "There *is* an herb against death, if only your father would understand." But then I realized she was talking about the tombstone.

Oh, Cookie, I wish that four trains had come along, the way they did the day you died, or the day that we learned about the bombing. I wish Mama had ripped off her wimple and thrown her arms around Daddy; I wish Daddy had used the money from the Italian government to buy back the farm, so that we'd have a center, a place to go back to. But none of those things happened. What happened was that the California Zephyr came in about six hours late, and a freight train pulled out of the hump yard and started to pick up speed while we were standing around after the ceremony, not knowing what to say.

Daniel's rubbing my back, and the backs of my legs, and my butt, and I'm just letting some quiet tears soak into the pillow. It's as if I'm still up at the cemetery and can see everything, everyone. I can see the farm, and I can see Mama sitting in the backseat of the convent limousine, with Sister Judy driving—that's the other nun who came along—and Father Westergrin riding shotgun; and I can practically see Daddy and Ludi having a cup of coffee in the airport at Moline, and Laska lying down in the back of the pickup. I'm here, in St. Clair, in the center; and they're all moving away.

"How about a quickie?" I say to Daniel. I spit into the palm of my hand and rub the saliva between my legs.

"Are you sure?"

"Yes, I'm sure."

I've always thought that they'd failed; that we had failed as a family. But it's not true, Cookie. I see that now. Mama and Daddy didn't just let things happen; they didn't just drift with the current; they rowed upstream; they gave their lives a shape; they chose more intense lives, Cookie; they looked your death in the face. I'm the one who hasn't faced things. So who am I to say they failed? They moved on. I'm the one who's been stuck. I'm the one who's stayed behind. But think of it, Cookie; think what it was like for them, seeing us go off. I understand, now. We have to let *them* go, as if they were *our* children, as if they were going off to college, or going off to Italy, going off to faraway places, because that's just the way it is, the way things are. Old centers disappear; new ones are born. It's the law of mathematics. As long as you've got three points there's always a center, but the points move around.

"Do you want me just to come?" Daniel asks.

I start to say yes, but then I say no, keep moving. I don't want Daniel to leave me behind too. I love his beard, his patience, his cock. Inside me, like a sharp spear poking into my stomach, prodding the new life that's already there, stirring it up. I'm getting excited too. I spread the cheeks of his rear end so I can work the tip of my middle finger about an inch into his *buco di culo.* I've never done this before, and I don't know what prompts me to do it now, but my fingertip burns, a circuit has been completed, the current flows up through my arm into my head and then down into my cunt. I've got to let go now, Cookie; I've got to say good-bye. Against the strength of love, you will find no herb; against the strength of death, no herb grows in the garden. I think that's as close to the truth as you can get, except it might be just a little closer if you turned it around. Against the strength of death, you will find no herb; against the strength of love, no herb grows in the garden.

Permissions Acknowledgments